GW01607596

Otto Hietsch

From "anbandeln" to "Zwetschkenknödel" An Austrian Lexical and Cultural Guide

From "anbandeln" to "Zwetschkenknödel"

An Austrian Lexical and Cultural Guide

by

Otto Hietsch

Dr. phil., Dott. in Lett., M. Litt.
Professor Emeritus of English Philology
in the University of Regensburg

Tyrolia-Verlag · Innsbruck-Wien

Die Deutsche Bibliothek – CIP-Einheitsaufnahme

Ein Datensatz für diese Publikation ist bei
der Deutschen Bibliothek erhältlich.

2000

Umschlaggestaltung: Elke Staller,
unter Verwendung einer Karikatur von Helmut Kasper
Satz und digitale Gestaltung: Satzstudio Walter Schöpf, Oberperfuss
Lithografie: Laserpoint, Innsbruck
Druck: Alcione, Trient
ISBN 3-7022-2351-7

Contents

Preface 7

The Austrian Anthem 11

Symbols and Chief Abbreviations 12

The Glossary 17

Glimpses of Austria 233

Austrian Songs … now also sung in English

In die Berg bin i gern 244

Tirol is lei oans 245

Andreas-Hofer-Lied 246

Därf i 's Dirndl liabn? 248

Es wird scho glei dumpa 250

Da streiten sich die Leut' herum ('The Song of the Plane') 252

Fein sein, beinander bleibn 254

The Many Lives of the Austrian Chatter Ditty 255

Suggestions for Further Readings 261

Acknowledgments of Illustrations Supplied 263

About the Author

Otto Hietsch, a native of Vienna born in 1924, is a man of many professional incarnations. In his upbringing, from early on, pragmatic and scholarly elements have been happily mixed. A graduate translator and interpreter at twenty-one, and a certificated teacher cum Dr. phil. at twenty-four, he went into tertiary education work in Austria, England, and Italy. For odd stretches of academic freewheeling, the young lecturer and lexicographer sallied forth to study elsewhere, at such cultural centres and dictionary offices as Edinburgh, Ann Arbor, and Sydney.

In 1952, Dr. Hietsch was appointed Professor of German and English at Padua's venerable Bò; and eleven years later accepted a call to the first chair of English Philology at Braunschweig Technical University, the oldest one of its kind in Germany. In 1967, the newly established *alma mater Ratisbonensis* invited him to return to the banks of the Danube.

There, closeness to the Alps and to his beloved Austria inspired him to write a number of comparative studies on regional German and English. Even before, he had edited two sizeable volumes on *Österreich und die angelsächsische Welt: Kulturbegegnungen und Vergleiche,* of which the present sequel should easily prove a linguistic and cultural student's lively source of information (not found welling forth anywhere else). Moreover, the reader will doubtless also go into lightsome chuckles and laughs in between, delighting in the witty sparks of poetry and rousing folk songs, all bridging the gap from homey Austria to the wide and wonderful Anglo-Saxon World beyond.

"In the comparison between native and foreign language lies the key to foreign language learning."

Robert Lado

"La nuance, c'est tout."

Paul Verlaine

Preface

… Officers, without a word of German, were billeted on families, and the town swarmed with G. I. s. Lucia, whose English was always considered so good, had great difficulty in understanding what they said. She had a bewildering feeling of not being able – in the language sense – to 'hear' the phrases used. 'It beats the crap outa me', she heard one say. She could not find the key-word in her English-German dictionary. Nor many other words they used.

Ethel Mannin, *Bavarian Story* (London: Arrow Books, 1964), pp. 143f. [abridged].

Lucia's plight in 1945, and that of untold other non-native speakers before and after, is a common one. In the five decades and a half since then, some very good bilingual dictionaries in the pocket-size, desk and encyclopaedic ranges have been published. Yet, in spite of the praises that have been sung about such publications, most of them have miserably failed to do justice both to the richness of the spoken language on either side, and to the many ways and means by which that richness can, and therefore should, be matched level for level. Such a discovery is as inevitable as it is disconcerting. These general dictionaries, both in what they offer and what they withhold, are, all in all, a sadly distorted reflection of living speech: far too frequently they remain silent, and far too frequently their renderings merely approximate to the usage of native speakers. They may quite tolerably be on target as far as denotation goes, but in the infinitely more subtle sphere of connotation they belie the original: the "equivalents" listed often do not deserve the name, as they incline either towards excessive coarseness or exaggerated gentility, vacillate between verbosity and taciturnity, make unwarranted changes such as the deletion, attenuation or superimposition of metaphorical colouring, and reveal a number of other infidelities besides.

Let the reader beware. But let not the linguists who are qualified to know better gloat over the gaucheries of those preceding them. Here are a few guidelines along which the improvement of present lexical shortcomings might be attempted in our particular field:

Any bilingual lexicographer, after having taken his bearings, is well advised, as a first step, to do some long and thorough stocktaking of conversational speech; he is encouraged to gather evidence from the sundriest of sources – from plays and stories, magazine articles and popular newspapers, but above all from his neighbour next door and the speaker in the street, and from observing how he talks himself. Joe Orton's warning in 1964, "I think you should use the language of your age, and use every bit of it, not just a little bit", though addressed to fellow-playwrights, is worthy of attention by potential editors of dictionaries as well. It seems quite preposterous in this connection (going by a no doubt genuine incident related by Dr. R. W. Chapman in his slim volume on *Lexicography* [Oxford University Press, 1948, p. 12]) that some people in authority make a distinction between dictionary words and non-dictionary words. Clearly, formidable Mrs. Grundy is still active, and is responsible for the enduring banishment, or at best high-handedly grudging admission, of four-letter words. On the other hand, if their teeming vitality in everyday collocations were given unbridled freedom, such words would spread over columns and indeed pages of any larger general dictionary. As it is, present-day Lucias will continue to find little or no evidence of them, and will hence continue to be baffled …

The collecting done, and an *ad hoc* card-index for both languages organized by word field, these riches should be brought into bilingual linear confrontation. The editor and his associates, by thus unearthing and marshalling the hidden resources of the two languages, will have done much to avoid the pitfall of desultory and therefore unrepresentative selection – one of the chronic weaknesses in lexicography. But what is more, rejecting editorial haphazardry will reward them with a host of words and sayings that can be neatly paired, be it in the areas of folk wisdom, weather lore or common everyday speech where the simple man's fondness for colourful metaphors and similes, for emphatic and irreverent witticisms, becomes evident on all hands:

eine blinde Henne findet auch ein Korn even a blind pig finds an acorn some time

ist dein Vater ein Glaserer? (a jeering note to one obstructing the view) your father wasn't a glazier.

Null Komma Josef, gebrochen durch nichts (a humorous and drastic way of expressing total ignorance, lack of funds, etc.) smaller than the little end of nothing whittled down to a fine point

das passt wie die Faust aufs Auge that fits like a saddle on a sow

der Teufel haut sein Weib (a word symbolism to describe the meteorological phenomenon of rain and sunshine at the same time) the devil is beating his wife

der Petrus tut kegelscheiben (a popular interpretation of rumbling peals of thunder) Hendrick Hudson and his crew are at their game of ninepins (New England)

One of the rigorously exclusive and therefore unadulterated types of colloquial speech is dialect; speakers, even when airing their views on human character and things metaphysical, are wont to express themselves not in abstract and learned terms, but in pictures drawn from the everyday world around them. One does not have to go far for graphic illustration. For instance, it is well worth taking a brief look at two old national entities, at our dear Austria and at Scotland, whose communities, still largely rural – in spite of noticeable differences in political, economic, and ecclesiastical spheres – lead simple lives "at the grass roots", which makes them both see eye to eye on many matters. The accumulated knowledge of generations has long been distilled and preserved in proverbial lore and descriptive sayings. Looking at this essence of seasoned experience, one cannot help being amazed at the fact that, again and again, two peoples should have arrived at the self-same conclusions although their lives were divided by land and sea, and although, until after the Second World War, they knew little of and had little or nothing to do with each other:

auf oam Weg, wo vui gfahrn wird, wachst koa Gras (implying that it does not pay to get into a rut) ower sair [sorely] bett [beaten] a roadie niver grows corn

an anbrennts Scheitl brennt besser als an anders (used of a renewed quarrel or love affair) an aal fire's seen kennelt [kindled] *wann da Bettlmann aufs Ross kommt, kann er 's nimma dareitn* (a comment on the haughtiness of many upstarts) set a beggar on horseback and he'll ride a gallop

wo d'Henna kraht und net da Hahn, da is die Wirtschaft übel dran; or *Deandln, de pfeifn, und Henna, de krahn, sollt ma oj zwoa an Hals umdrahn* (a reference to unnatural phenomena) fustlin' maidens an' craain' hens is nae lucky aboot ony man's place

d' Schuastaweiba und d' Schmiedsross gehn barfuß (a caustic comment on the common human tendency to skimp in the face of plenty) the shaymakkar's weif and the smith's meer 's aye warst shoad

's letzte Gwand hat koane Taschn (earthly riches cannot be transferred to the hereafter) shrouds haven't any pockets

nix wia naus, was koa Hauszins zahlt (a warning to get rid of something that does more harm than good) better a teem [= empty] hoose nor an ill tenant

liaba an Augnblick feig als a Lebm lang dout better a livin' cooard nor a deid hero

ojs hat oa End, nur die Wurscht hat zwoa ilka thing has ane end, bit a pudden [= sausage] (*or,* a staff) has twa

a Gsicht, dass d' Muich saua wird (said of one who looks discontented) a face that wid [would] soor milk

These instances of parallelism, so fascinating in content and form, are only random helpings from a huge repository, into which scholarly comparatists, translators, and students of the language at large are invited to dip. Interestingly and yet sadly enough, dictionary makers' eyes – up to the present – have been closed to such riches.

Occasionally, however, one's delight at discovering and recording an exact parallel for dictionary use must be bridled. This caution applies both to lexemes and syntagmas that occur rarely or are limited in scope, and to those containing slang, dialect or vulgarisms known to the insider only. A dictionary, after all, cannot function as a "stretch-as-stretch-can", and a line must be drawn somewhere. The principles of selection my vary somewhat from case to case but, given consistency, ought to be self-evident, preference of course going to those items that are (a) widespread, (b) in current use, and (c) immediately comprehensible without further glossing.

The following compilation, then, tries to remedy the situation with specific regard to Austria. It hopes, as far as space permits, to blend her national characteristics, her language and history (from *Ötzi* to *Auspuff Europas,* as it were, by way of bizarre juxtaposition), her ancient civilization and day-to-day activities with the background of English and the English-speaking world. Whenever the need is felt, entries offer a quick look at the etymology of the headword and its possible relationship with the English word stock; meanings are elucidated and embedding sample phrases added in order to dispel any doubts about the proper uses. In order to show the practical interconnectedness of spoken Austrian and English on a wider scale, this little book also includes some non-lexical pieces of prose and poetry and song, ones that nearly everybody in this country knows, or even loves to give tongue to in the original on the spur of the moment. May they often be heard in bilingual company and in rousing good-fellowship!

Otto Hietsch

Österreichische Bundeshymne

Words by Paula Preradovic, 1947
Music by Wolfgang Amadeus Mozart, 1791
Arranged by Viktor Keldorfer

Feierlich, doch nicht zu langsam

1. Land der Ber - ge, Land am Stro - me, Land der Äk - ker, Land der
2. Heiß um - feh - det, wild um - strit - ten, liegst dem Erd - teil du in -
3. Mu - tig in die neu - en Zei - ten, frei und gläu - big sieh uns -

1. Do - me, Land der Häm - mer, zu - kunfts - reich! Hei - mat bist du
2. mit - ten, ei - nem star - ken Her - zen gleich. Hast seit frü - hen
3. schrei - ten, ar - beits - froh und hoff - nungs - reich. Ei - nig laß in

1. gro - ßer Söh - ne, Volk, be - gna - det für das Schö - ne, viel - ge -
2. Ah - nen - ta - gen ho - her Sen - dung Last ge - tra - gen, viel - ge -
3. Brü - der - chö - ren, Va - ter - land, dir Treu - e schwö - ren, viel - ge -

1. rühm - tes Ö - ster - reich, viel - ge - rühm - tes Ö - ster - reich!
2. prüf - tes Ö - ster - reich, viel - ge - prüf - tes Ö - ster - reich!
3. lieb - tes Ö - ster - reich, viel - ge - lieb - tes Ö - ster - reich!

The Austrian Anthem

1. Land of mountains, purling waters,
   Fields and forests, sainted quarters,
   Folks with zeal their work pursue.
   Great sons duly have filled annals' pages,
   Grace and beauty proved boons in all ages –
   |: Austria, fame and glory are your due! :|

2. Oft embroiled, with feuds invested,
   Europe's midst now, unmolested,
   Like a sturdy heart, and true.
   Holding high your forebears' banner,
   Shouldering burdens in wonted brave manner,
   |: Austria, tests untold you have gone through. :|

3. See us firmly and stoutly striding
   Towards the future, faith abiding,
   Bent o'er work we old trusts renew.
   Sworn to brotherly fealty forever,
   Home, sweet home, we never shall sever –
   |: Austria dear, our love is aye for you! :|

Symbols and Chief Abbreviations

~ *The* ***swung dash*** *stands for the headword; when its initial letter changes from a capital to a small letter, or vice versa, an* ^{x} *is supperimposed.* $\overset{x}{\sim}$

Die **Tilde** vertritt das Stichwort. Groß- und Kleinschreibung kann sich freilich ändern, und dann mahnt ein über die Tilde gesetztes ^{x} zum „orthographischen“ Umdenken.

* *The* ***asterisk*** *(1) serves as a warning, before whole sentences, that in the absence of a close equivalent in English the wording offered must be happy to be a more or less literal translation; and (2) marks a deduced, and therefore undocumented, word form.*

Das **Sternchen** macht (1.) darauf aufmerksam, dass hier im Englischen eine genaue Entsprechung fehlt und so eine mehr oder weniger wörtliche Übersetzung als Brücke zum Verständnis dienen mag; und es steht (2.) vor einer nicht belegten – und daher lediglich erschlossenen – Wortform.

[ ] ***square brackets*** *(1) contain etymological information; (2) vary, and thus stand within, round brackets; and (3) indicate free variations in model sentences, e.g. boys [girls].*

Eckige Klammern bieten (1.) Einzelheiten zur jeweiligen Wortgeschichte, variieren (2.) das Gesagte in runden Klammern und weisen (3.) auf naheliegende Alternativen in Mustersätzen hin – etwa Burschen [Mädeln].

: *the* ***colon,*** *after due definitory preliminaries, is the curtain raiser for the exact and concise equivalent of the headword; in non-standard, the headword here finds its match on the proper non-standard level (colloquial, slang, vulgar, etc.).*

Der **Doppelpunkt** markiert nach den allgemeinen begrifflichen Erklärungen den Absprung hinüber in den fremdsprachlichen Bereich, und zwar auf die genau analoge und bedeutungsgleiche Ebene der Ausgangssprache, ob nun das Stichwort oder eine bestimmte Wendung der Hochsprache oder einer anderen Ebene darunter (Umgangssprache, Jargon; vulgäre Ausdrucksweise) angehört.

<> ***angle brackets*** *enclose individual letters (or graphemes); in other cases, immediately after the headword, they list the basic, concrete meaning which had given rise to the figurative one here discussed.*

Winkelklammern schließen einzelne Buchstaben (oder Grapheme) ein; in anderen Fällen, unmittelbar hinter dem Stichwort stehend, halten sie die ursprüngliche, konkrete Bedeutung fest, von der die hier besprochene bildhafte Verwendung abstammt.

./_	*subscript: short/long stressed vowel or diphthong*	untersetzt: kurz/lang betonter Vokal oder Diphthong
→	*(1) see; (2) the sense develops to*	(1) siehe; (2) Bedeutungsentwicklung zu
=	*exact equivalent*	entspricht genau
≃	*approximate equivalent*	entspricht ungefähr
<	*is derived from*	abgeleitet von
>	*develops into*	wird zu
↑↓	*see above/below*	siehe oben/unten

♪	*agriculture,* Landwirtschaft	☼	*meteorology,* Wetterkunde
✿	*botany,* Pflanzenkunde	⊡	*motoring,* Kraftfahrwesen
†	*commercial term,* Handelswesen	⩕	*mountaineering,* Alpinismus
◆	*ichthyology,* Fischkunde	♪	*musical term,* Musik

📖 *scientific term,* wissenschaftlicher Fachausdruck

a.	*also,* auch
abbr.	*abbreviation,* Abkürzung
adj	*adjective,* Eigenschaftswort
admin.	*administration,* Verwaltung
adv	*adverb,* Umstandswort
AmE	*American English,* amerikanisches Englisch
anim. husb.	*animal husbandry,* Viehzucht
apprec.	*appreciative,* wohlwollend positiv
archit.	*architecture,* Baukunst
attrib.	*attributive(ly),* beifügend
AustralE	*Australian English,* australisches Englisch
bak.	*baking,* Bäckerei
baln.	*balneology,* Bäderkunde
BavG	*Bavarian German,* Sprache des Bayern
BermE	*Bermuda English,* Sprache der Bermudainseln
bev.	*beverage,* Getränk
BrE	*British English,* britisches Englisch
CanE	*Canadian English,* kanadisches Englisch
Chr. n.	*Christian name,* Vorname
civ.	*civilization,* Kultur
colloq.	*colloquial,* umgangssprachlich
comb.	*combination,* Wortverbindung
comest.	*comestible,* Nahrungsmittel
concr.	*concrete(ly),* gegenständlich
contp.	*contemptuous,* verächtlich
cost.	*costume,* Tracht
cp.	*compare,* vergleiche
cpd.	*compound,* zusammengesetztes (Haupt-, Eigenschafts- oder Zeit-) Wort, Kompositum
cul.	*culinary art,* Kochkunst
Cz	*Czech,* Tschechisch
dial.	*dialect, dialectal,* Mundart, mundartlich
dim.	*diminutive,* Verkleinerungsform
dom. ec.	*domestic economy,* Hauswirtschaft(skunde)
E	*English,* Englisch
EastAus	*Eastern Austria,* Ostösterreich
eccl.	*ecclesiastical,* kirchlich, geistlich
econ.	*economics,* Wirtschaft
educ.	*education,* Erziehungs- und Bildungswesen
e.g.	*exempli gratia* (L, for instance), zum Beispiel
el.	*element,* Glied einer (Wort-) Zusammensetzung
e-m	einem
emot.	*emotional,* gefühlsbetont
e-n	einen
entom.	*entomology,* Insektenkunde
e-r	einer
e-s	eines
esp.	*especially,* vor allem
euphem.	*euphemistic(ally),* beschönigend
F	*French,* Französisch
f	*feminine,* weiblich
fig.	*figurative(ly),* übertragen, bildlich
ftb.	*football,* Fußball

G	*German,* Deutsch
garm.	*garment,* Kleidung
gastr.	*gastronomy,* feine Kochkunst
gen.	*(1) general(ly),* allgemein *(2) genitive,* zweiter Fall
geog.	*geography,* Erdkunde
geol.	*geology,* Geologie
ger.	*gerund,* hauptwörtlich gebrauchte Zeitwortform auf *-ing,* Gerundium
Ger.	*German,* typisch für den deutschsprachigen Kulturbereich
Germ.	*Germanic,* germanisch
Gr	*Greek,* griechisch
hist.	*historic(al),* geschichtlich
hort.	*horticulture,* Gartenbau
hum.	*humorous(ly),* scherzhaft
Hung.	*Hungarian,* Ungarisch
hunt.	*hunting,* Jagdwesen
husb.	*husbandry,* Landwirtschaft
IE	*Indo-European,* Indogermanisch
i.e.	*id est* (L, that is), d. h. (das heißt)
imit.	*imitative,* nachahmend
inf.	*infinitive,* Nennform, Infinitiv
interj	*interjection,* Ausrufewort, Interjektion
IrE	*Irish English,* irisches Englisch
iron.	*ironic,* (leicht) spöttelnd, ironisch
It	*Italian,* Italienisch
j-d	jemand
j-m	jemandem
j-n	jemanden
joc.	*jocular,* witzig, lustig
journ.	*journalese,* Zeitungssprache
jur.	*jurisdiction,* Rechtswesen
L	*Latin,* Latein
Lad	*Ladin,* Ladinisch
ling.	*linguistics,* Sprachwissenschaft
lit.	(1) *literally,* wörtlich (2) *literature,* Literatur
m	*masculine,* männlich
math.	*mathematics,* Mathematik
ME	*Middle English,* Mittelenglisch
med.	*medicine,* Medizin, Heilkunde
MedL	*Medieval Latin,* Mittellatein
MHG	*Middle High German,* Mittelhochdeutsch
mil.	*military terminology,* Wehrwesen
min.	*mining,* Bergbau
ModE	*Modern English,* heutiges Englisch
ModG	*Modern German,* heutiges Deutsch
mus.	*music,* Musik, Tonkunst
myth.	mythology, Mythologie
n	*neuter,* sächlich
nav.	*navigation,* Schifffahrt
NHG	*New High German,* Neuhochdeutsch
NorBrE	*Northern British English,* Nordenglisch
numis.	*numismatics,* Münzkunde
nurs.	*nursery talk,* Kleinkindersprache
NZE	*New Zealand English,* neuseeländisches Englisch
obs.	*obsolete,* veraltet
OE	*Old English,* Altenglisch
OF	*Old French,* Altfranzösisch
OHG	*Old High German,* Althochdeutsch
OIcel	*Old Icelandic,* Altisländisch
opp.	*opposite,* im Gegensatz zu
orig.	*originally,* ursprünglich
orn.	*ornithology,* Vogelkunde
P	*person,* Person, menschliches Wesen
pej.	*pejorative,* abwertend
phr.	*phrase(s),* Wendung(en)
pl.	*plural,* Mehrzahl
poet.	*poetical,* dichterisch
polit.	*politics,* Politik
p.p.	*past participle,* Mittelwort der Vergangenheit, Partizip Perfekt

pred. *predicative,* im Aussageteil eines einfachen Satzes stehend
pr. n. *proper name,* Eigenname
pron. *pronounced,* Aussprache
prov. *proverb(s),* Sprichwort (-wörter)
pr.t. *present tense,* Gegenwart (Präsens)

R. C. *Roman Catholic,* römisch-katholisch
relig. *religion,* Religion

sarc. *sarcastic,* ätzend-spöttisch, sarkastisch
sb. *somebody,* jemand
ScotE *Scottish English,* schottisches Englisch
sg. *singular,* Einzahl
sl. *slang,* Sonder-, Berufssprache
slav. *slavic,* Slawisch
slov. *slovene,* Slowenisch
s. o. *someone,* jemand
sobr. *sobriquet,* Beiname, Spitzname
SouAmE *Southern American English,* Englisch der Südstaaten der USA
s-r seiner
Sp *Spanish,* Spanisch
stand. *standard,* üblich
StG *Standard German,* Hochdeutsch
s. th. *something,* etwas
SwG *Swiss German,* Schweizerdeutsch
soc. *social,* gesellschaftlich
syn. *synonym,* bedeutungsgleiches Wort

tech. *technology,* Technik
tex. *textiles,* Bekleidung
theat. *theatre,* Theater

univ. *university,* Hochschulwesen
usu. *usually,* gewöhnlich

v *verb,* Zeitwort
vet. *veterinary,* Tierheilkunde
vinic. *viniculture,* Weinbau
v/i *intransitive verb,* intransitives, auf kein Akkusativobjekt gerichtetes Zeitwort
v/refl *reflexive verb,* rückbezügliches Zeitwort
vt/refl *verb used both transitively and reflexively,* Zeitwort mit Ausrichtung auf ein Akkusativobjekt – in anderen Wendungen aber auch rückbezüglich
v/t *transitive verb,* transitives, auf ein Akkusativobjekt gerichtetes Zeitwort
vt/i *transitive and intransitive verb,* Zeitwort mit Ausrichtung – in anderen Verwendungen aber auch ohne Ausrichtung – auf ein Akkusativobjekt
vulg. *vulgar,* grob-unfein, vulgär
VulgL *Vulgar Latin,* Vulgärlatein

WestIndE *West Indian English,* Sprache der Westindischen Inseln

Yid. *Yiddish,* Jiddisch

zo. *zoology,* Tierkunde, Zoologie

A

abafalln ['ɔ:bəfaln] *v/i dial.* [first el. < *abher* 'down (to earth)'] *(herunterfallen)* to fall down, to drop ‖ a rhymed piece of folk wisdom lackadaisically explaining why life on earth tarries east of Eden: *es gibt halt immer was, / des was den Himmel halt, / dass er net abafallt* *something will always be / so Heaven stays away / and Bliss is held at bay.

abblattln *v/i colloq. (abbröckeln)* of the plaster on old houses, of wall paint, etc.: to peel, to come off; *die Farbe blattelt von den Wänden ab* the paint is peeling off the walls.

abbusseln *vt/refl* [< *Buss(e)l n* 'kiss'] *colloq.* to shower (sb., each other) with kisses: to smother with kisses; *ich war so froh, meinen Freund nach fünf Jahren wiederzusehen, dass ich ihn richtig abgebusselt hab* I was so happy to see my boyfriend after five years that I smothered him with kisses.

abdürsten *v/i hum. colloq.* to quench one's thirst (with alcohol): to wet one's whistle, *AmE a.* to knock back a couple; *nachdem wir jetzt stundenlang geschwitzt haben, ist es Zeit zum* ≚ after sweating (*or* slaving) away for hours, it's now time to wet our whistles.

Abendmaturakurs *m* -es/-e *educ. (Abendkurs, in dem auf e-e Reifeprüfung ausserhalb e-r höheren Schule vorbereitet wird) BrE* evening classes preparing for A-levels, *AmE* evening high school, night school.

abfieseln *v/t colloq.* with reference to a bone of cooked meat *(abnagen)*: to gnaw bare; *ich tu(e) leidenschaftlich gern Knochen* ~ I really enjoy chewing on the bones, I love picking bones clean.

abfretten *v/refl colloq.* to take a lot of trouble (but with little success), to wear oneself out (*sich abmühen*): to knock oneself out (doing s. th.), *BrE a.* to toil and moil; *sie muss sich beim Heizen immer mit diesem alten Ofen* ~ she has quite a job (*or,* she has a terrible time) keeping that old stove going.

Abgänger *m* -s/-, **~in** *f* -/-nen *educ. (Schulentlassene[r]) BrE* school-leaver, *AmE* one who leaves the school; *die heurigen* ~ those leaving school (at the end of) this year.

Note: In Austria, compulsory schooling extends from the age of 6 to 14; in Great Britain, attendance is required from 5 to 16, and in the United States from 6 to 16 and above.

Abgebrochene *f* -n (*Hose* to be supplied) [a rather *hum.* reference as though a full-length pair of trousers had literally been broken off; similarly, American English has *cut-offs,* for an old pair of jeans that have been shortened at mid-thigh length] *colloq. (Lederhose)*(pair of) leather shorts, often with elaborate braces (*AmE* suspenders) showing alpine motifs; *der Frühling ist da, wo ist [sind] meine ~[n]?* Spring is here, where are my leather shorts?; *der Lederhosenträger wird erst richtig stolz, wenn seine ~ vor Dreck steht* somebody who wears leather shorts (*AmE a.* lederhosen) will be truly proud of them only when they stand up by themselves with dirt.

Ablage Papierkorb *office phr.* a humorous piece of advice or command not to file but to dispose of paperwork that has just come to hand: *BrE* file it in the (rubbish) bin!, *AmE* put it in the circular file!, put it in File X [eks] (*or,* File 13)!

Ableser *m* -s/- *colloq.* a man who by vocation records the consumption of electricity, water, and/or gas, and reports to the utility companies: meter man, meter reader; *ist der ~ schon da gewesen?* has the meter man been (*AmE* here)?

abpaschen *v/i colloq.* to leave suddenly without attracting attention *(heimlich, plötzlich verschwinden)*: to make off, *BrE sl.* to do a bunk, *AmE sl.* to sneak out (the backdoor).

abputzen *v/refl* **1.** *(Schmutz von s-r Kleidung [mit der Hand, e-m Taschentuch, e-r Bürste] entfernen)* to brush the dust *etc.* off one's clothes. – **2.** *colloq. (j-d anderem die Schuld geben)* to shift the blame or responsibility: to shove the blame, to put the blame on s.o. else's shoulders, *AmE a.* to pass the buck, to slip the jacket; *die putzen sich ab und ich bin der Petschierte* they wash their hands of it, and I'm left holding the bag.

Abraham ['a:-] *pr.n.* [according to John viii.37, Abraham was the progenitor of the Jewish people, and to lie in his bosom is the synonym for eternal bliss (Luke xvi.22ff.)] in *phr.* **1.** *in ~s Schoß eingehen* to be called to Abraham's bosom, i.e. to die in bliss. – **2.** *colloq.*: *in ~s Wurstkessel* (or, dialectally, *Wurschtkessel*) 'in Abraham's sausage pot', i.e. in the life beyond, (a) *a. in ~s (Schnapp-) Sack* 'in Abraham's kitbag', i.e. dead, but temporarily in limbo, the stage of purification before being admitted to eternal bliss; *mil. sl. in ~s Wurstkessel* [or *Schnappsack*] *kommen* to be killed in action: to bite the dust, to become a landowner in [Vietnam, Iraq, Croatia, etc.]; (b) yet unborn; *zu der Zeit* (or *1990* [etc.]) *warst du noch in ~s Wurstkessel* at that time (*or* in 1990 [etc.]) you were not even a gleam in your father's eye, … you were still coated with fuller's earth, … you were still living in a cabbage patch. – **3.** *~ grüßen* Styrian *dial.* to be more than fifty years old (and, therefore, at risk of dying and being called to Abraham's bosom): to prepare oneself to meet one's Maker, *AmE a.* to get ready to buy the farm.

abschaffen *v/t law hist., colloq.* to declare sb. persona non grata *(j-n des Ortes verweisen)*: to exile, to ban; *Breitensee, heute Teil des vierzehnten Wiener Gemeindebezirks, doch weit ins vorige Jahrhundert dünn besiedelt, galt lang als bevorzugter Ort der aus der Kaiserstadt Abgeschafften* (the then village of) Breitensee, part of today's fourteenth district of Vienna, though thinly populated until well into the last century, was long a preferred place of exile for those deported from the Imperial city.

Abschiedssymphonie *f* – ♪ a masterpiece by Joseph Haydn, written to convey

"In festive garb, before the table of Our Lord, His Light all shining on their heads": Young Austrian lasses prior to Abspeisengehen *– here devoutly kneeling in their pews, about to receive the Sacrament of the Holy Communion for the first time in their lives*

to Prince Nicholas Esterházy his orchestra's anguished hopes of being allowed to return to their families, after a prolonged sojourn at Esterház: as the finale drew to its close, one musician after another, following the score, snuffed his candle and tiptoed out, with only two violins remaining to continue and conclude the soft, songlike Adagio: Farewell Symphony, No. 45, in F sharp minor (1772).

ạbschmalzen *v/t cul.* said of pasta or dumplings: to fry in lard and mix with browned onions and roasted breadcrumbs; to quick-fry.

Ạbschneider *m -s/- colloq. (Abkürzung[sweg])* (short[-])cut, *AmE* cutoff; *e-n ~ machen* to take a short-cut, to cut a corner; *wir haben einen ~ über die Wiesen gemacht – und uns prompt verirrt* we cut across the meadows, and promptly got lost; *durch die Durchhäuser der Wiener Innenstadt lässt sich so mancher ~ machen* quite often short-cuts may be taken through passages and courtyards of houses in central Vienna.

ạbspeisen gehen *v/i R.C.* in rural use: *(zur Kommunion gehen), das heilige Abendmahl empfangen)* to go to, *or* to receive Holy Communion, to take the sacrament.

ạbstrudeln *v/refl* [cp. *Strudel* ↓] *colloq.* *(sich sehr anstrengen)* to try very hard: to wear oneself into the ground, to bend over backwards; *sich nach et.* ~ to beat one's brains out (*or,* to work one's head off) trying to get s.th.; *im Beruf habe ich mich immer fürchterlich abgestrudelt* I really knocked (*AmE* wore) myself out (*or,* beat my head against the wall) at my job.

Ạbwasch *f* -/-en **1.** *(Spülbecken)* kitchen sink. – **2.** *(Spülküche)* scullery. – **~schaff** *n* -(e)s/-e, **~schaffel** *n* -s/-n *BrE* washing-up bowl, *AmE* washbowl. – **~wasser** *n* -s dishwater, *AmE a.* washwater; *contp. der Kaffee (die Suppe) schmeckt wie* ~ this coffee (soup) tastes like dishwater, … is mere wash, … tastes as if (*AmE* like) it's made from old socks, … tastes like nothing on earth.

Ạchsel *f* -/-n shoulder ‖ *colloq. phr.* **1.** said of s.o. unwilling to take sides: *auf beiden ~n Wasser tragen* to straddle the fence. – **2.** *iron.,* said of a religious zealot: *das ist ein Heiliger über die ~n hinaus* he's holier (*or,* more sanctified) than a saint, he is a Bible-beater (*or,* a Jesus freak, a holier-than-thou, a Holy Roller).

Ạcker *m* -s/Äcker **1.** ↓ field; *zu ~ gehen* (or *fahren) (im Frühjahr zu pflügen beginnen)* to start the Spring ploughing; *die Äcker stehen herrlich schön (die Ernte verspricht gut zu werden)* the fields look good this year. – **2.** *fig.: das ist mein ~ (das geht dich nichts an)* that is my territory; *geh aus meinem ~! (lass das!)* get off my property!, don't tread on me!; *jetzt blüht endlich mein ~ (nun kommt für mich eine gute Zeit)* at long last everything's coming up roses, my ship's finally coming in.

A̲dabei *m* -s/-s [first el. < East Austrian *dial. a < auch* 'also'; the word became widely known through *Herr Adabei,* the title of a popular 1908 folk play by Vinzenz Chiavacci, 1847–1916] *colloq.* news-hunting individual, with an insatiable urge to be "in on it too": meddler, busybody.

A̲del *m* -s nobility; in Imperial Austria, it was made up of two classes of society, → *Hochadel* (or *Aristokratie*), and → *Briefadel* (or *Dienstadel*).

Advẹnt [-w-] *m* -s/-e [< L *adventus* 'arrival (i.e. birth) of Jesus Christ on December 25'] Advent season, the period of the four weeks before Christmas, richly devoted in Roman Catholic folk custom to the coming of Our Lord Jesus Christ (see the following, and the entries *Barbarazweigerl* and *Marientragen*); *im ~* in Advent.

Advẹnt …: ~blasen *n* -s *folklore* Advent Bugling, a small group of wind-instrument players performing in public places before Christmas. – **~kranz** *m* -es/…kränze *folklore* a pre-Christmas symbol in evidence only after the First World War: Advent Wreath, made of fir branches, adorned with four candles, red ribbons, and suspended from the ceiling of the main room; each Sunday an additional candle is lit, to the accompaniment of Christmas carols and stories. – **~singen** *n* -s *folklore* carol singing, with small choirs performing in public; in English-speaking countries, the singing of children, who go carolling from house to house the week before Christmas. – **~sonntag** *m* -s/-e Advent Sunday (one of the four, usu. numbered accordingly, e.g. *der dritte ~*). – **~zeit** *f* -/-en Advent.

A E I O U · 1446

A.E.I.O.U. *hist.* a cryptic vowel fivesome, also found chiselled on stone, going back to Frederick III, the first Austrian ruler to be crowned Holy Roman Emperor (1452); it is variously interpreted, indeed plurilingually, as "**A**ustria **E**rit **I**n **O**rbi **U**ltima", "**A**lles **E**rdreich **I**st **O**esterreich **U**ntertan", and "**A**ustria **E**minent **I**n **O**rdered **U**nity", and reflects (if nothing else) that monarch's personality – one imbued with a sure knowledge of his own dignity and majesty.

Agrasel, Agrassel [ˈɔ:grazl] *f* -/-n [< It *agrasso,* in the same sense] *dial.* the small round green sharp-tasting berry of a shrub of the genus *Ribes,* often made into jam, tarts, etc. *(Stachelbeere)*: gooseberry, *colloq.* goosegog, *AmE a.* groser, groset [ˈ-əʊz-].

Ahnlsonntag *m* -s/-e *folklore* in Eastern Austria: "Grandparents' Sunday", the Sunday after Easter, when children visit their grandparents to spend time together and receive presents.

Ajourarbeit [aˈʒʊə-] *f* -/-en [first el., < F *à jour* 'up to the day', here in the sense of 'as far as the window, or open space'] *tex.* a pattern that has spaces in between pieces of thread – a decorative arrangement of stitches brought about by drawing out several parallel threads and catching together the cross threads in uniform groups (*Hohlsaum, Lochsaum*): à jour *or* ajouré work, openwork embroidery, hemstitch. – **ajourieren** [aʒuˈri:ən] *v/i* to do à jour (*or* ajouré) work, to hemstitch.

allein *adj & adv* **1.** alone; *phr.* a witticism by Alfred Polgar, 1875–1955, a Viennese satirical writer and critic: *ein Kaffeehaus ist der rechte Ort für Leute, die ~ sein wollen, aber dazu Gesellschaft brauchen* a café is the proper place for those who need the company of others in order to be alone. – **2.** *(ohne Unterstützung)* by oneself, single-handed(ly); *phr.* (1) a rhymed encomium of personal independence and self-sufficiency: *~ ist ein goldener Stein,* in Viennese dial., *allan is a goldena Stan* more value than a precious stone / the art of going it alone. (2) in a cheery, if somewhat brash reply to the courteous question whether one may help a person into his (*or* her) coat: *nein, danke, es geht ~ schon schwer genug!* no, thank you, it's hard enough to do it myself.

Alleluja *n* -s/-s [actually, a song of praise to God] *colloq.* **1.** jubilation, cheer; *der hat sich nimmer halten können vor lauter ~* he couldn't hold back any longer and exploded with joy; a dire prediction: *er wird das ~ bald ausgesungen haben*

Busy life among the chalets of the Aussergschlöss Alp, East Tyrol, but a mile or so away from the glacier tongue of majestic Mt. Grossvenediger (3660 m [12008 ft.]). The engraving goes back to a painting by Adolf Obermüllner done in the 1870s, a celebrated Austrian landscape artist (1833–1898)

he'll soon have sung his last (song). – **2.** *sarc.* (by inversion, cheer turning to) jeer; *dem habe ich aber das ~ gesungen!* I told him what's what.

Ạlm *f* -/-en [< MHG *alben,* the inflected form of *albe* 'alp'] **1.** ↙ & *econ.,* also *Alpe* (Vorarlberg) and *Schwaige* (Styria, Upper Austria): alpine *or* mountain pasture, situated well above the line of grain fields; *bis zum Zweiten Weltkrieg herrschte auf den ~en um Sennerinnen und Senner ein urwüchsiges Leben und Treiben; es ist heute leider oft verblasst oder gar erloschen, und einsam liegt das Galtvieh auf enger Weide vor der offenen Stalltür* until the Second World War, the dairymaids and lads led a simple and wholesome life, watching over their herds; sadly, this has dwindled or even disappeared, and the young calves lie penned in, alone, before the open stable door; *eine sonnige, blumenübersäte ~, und in der Ferne träumerisches Geläut von Kuhglocken* a sunny, flower-strewn meadow, and in the distance the dreamy sounds of cowbells; an often-quoted line from an alpine song, sometimes with a prurient innuendo about 'love among the haystacks': *auf der ~, da gibt's koa Sünd* in the hills there is no sin, there's no sin in pastures high. – **2.** *tourist trade* often as part of a proper name, chosen to conjure up a cowbell and-dairy-hut rusticity whereas the place actually embodies citified comfort and luxury: (fashionable) mountain lodge. – **3.** only sg. *colloq.* top floor of a multi-storey building, e.g. in the annexe of Vienna's former Technologisches Gewerbemuseum, at 59 Währingerstrasse: *auf der ~* all the way up; *die Abteilung Betriebstechnik lag auf der ~, da musstest du fünf Stockwerke hochklettern* the Department of Business Engineering was right on the top floor, it took a five-storey climb to get there.

Je höher de Alm,	*The higher the dairy,
umso größa da Wind;	The fiercer the win';
je scheena des Deandl,	The fairer the lassie,
umso kloana de Sünd.	The lighter the sin.

Ạlm ...: ~abfahrt *f* -/-en, **~abtrieb** *m* -(e)s/-e in Western Austria, towards the end of Summer – descent, or driving down the cattle, from the mountain pasture; this is a festive procession with yodelling, jangling of bells, and cows decorated with ribbons, paper bows, and a tower of alpine wildflowers on their horns. – **~auffahrt** *f* -/-en, **~auftrieb** *m* -(e)s/-e in Western Austria in late Spring: ascent, or driving up the cattle, to the mountain pasture.

Ạlpen ...: ~dollar *m* -s/-(s) *colloq.,* usu. *hum. (Austrian shilling)* "dollar of the Alps", so called because it is supposed to enjoy about the same respectability as the United States dollar; *die schönsten Versprechen an die Währung sind ohne Stabilität nur noch einen hohlen ~ wert* the finest promises about currency are not worth twopence (*AmE* ... a dime) without stability. – **~festung** *f* - *mil. hist.* the mountainous area of Western Austria and Southern Bavaria, in early 1945, intended by Adolf Hitler to be quickly entrenched and serve as a last battleground, to wrench victory from the Allied Forces in the final stages of World War Two – a modern Armageddon (in the desperado's fevered imagination) to be fought between Good

Driving down the cattle from a Styrian alp

and Evil: (Hitler's) Alpine Redoubt. – **~glühen** *n* -s/pl. rare: - ☼ alpenglow *or* Alpine glow, suffusing the faces of mountain rocks, otherwise ashy-grey, with a bright, rosy gleam when the sun goes down. – **~ostrand** *m* -(e)s *geog.* & ☼ eastern border of the Alps, a term frequently used in weather reports. – **~republik** *f* - *sobr.* an at times *hum.*, but much more often some journalist's glibly mechanical "filler" to avoid repeating the word *Österreich* too often – the national territory, political entity, etc. of Austria: Alpine Republic. – **~rose** *f* -/-n ✿ Alpine rhododendron. – **~trottel** *m* -s/- low *colloq.* a virulent slur by Joseph Roth, an aggressive journalist and novelist (1894–1939), on the Austrian: "mountain moron".

alterieren *v/refl colloq. (sich [unnötig] aufregen)* to be annoyed (at trifles): to make a fuss (about nothing), to get bent out of shape, *AmE* to get one's panties in a wad; *was alterierst (du) dich denn wegen nichts und wieder nichts?* why on earth do you keep getting upset over nothing?

Alzerl *n* -s [< OHG *atzel* 'morsel'] **1.** wee *or* tiny bit, smidgin, *or* smidgen; A: *Noch Käse gefällig?* B: *Grad' ein ~, bitt' schön. A:* Some more cheese? *B:* Just a smidgin, please. – **2.** a small amount that can be picked up between the thumb and a finger, e.g. salt or snuff: pinch. – **3.** *fig.* a small amount, esp. of a good quality such as truth, respect, etc.: modicum; *hätt' er nur ein ~ Verstand, dann würd' er so was nicht machen* if he had a modicum of sense, he wouldn't do such a thing.

Amen *n* -s/ *pl.* rare: – *colloq. phr.* an assertion of an absolute certainty: *so sicher wie das ~ im Gebet* (Ger. … *wie das ~ in der Kirche)* as sure as the pope is Catholic, … as the stars in the sky, … as the sun shall rise, … as you're sitting [standing, *etc.*] there (right now), … as my name is [supply name], *and, as a sarcasm,* … as the sun goes round the earth.

Amtskappel *n* -s/-(n) [second el. < dim. of *Kappe* 'cap'] *colloq. (Dienstmütze)* uniform cap (with a peak, *AmE a.* with a visor); *das ~ aufsetzen* to become coldly officious *(dienstlich werden)*: to put on the braids (*or,* the brass). – **~ton** *m* -(e)s/ … töne brusque officiousness; *man erinnert sich besonders an seinen überheblichen, rechthaberischen, von jeder demokratischen Haltung ganz und gar unberührten ~* what especially comes to mind is his overweening, self-righteous and petty officiousness, bare of even the slightest trace of democratic sentiment.

anbampfen *v/refl colloq.* to eat an excess of starchy food: to stuff (*or,* cram, gorge) oneself, to fill up; *ich möchte mich nicht gleich am Morgen so ~, zwei bis drei Semmeln langen doch zum Frühstück* I don't want to stuff myself so early in (*or,* at this hour of) the morning, two or three rolls will be plenty for breakfast; cp. *bampfen, anschlempern.*

anbandeln *v/t* [second el., < *Bandl n* '(short) ribbon' (with which s.th. may be tied to s.th. else)] *colloq., fig.* **mit j-m ~ 1.** to try and start a conversation with a stranger, just for talking's sake *(mit j-m ins Gespräch zu kommen suchen)*: to go and speak to, just for a friendly chat. – **2.** to talk to, esp. s. o. of the opposite sex, in a friendly way, possibly with amorous intentions *(anhauen)*: to chat up; *in der*

Fremdenverkehrssaison bandeln die einheimischen Burschen gern mit jungen Ausländerinnen an local boys, in the tourist season, are out to chat up foreign girls. – **3.** to cast flirtatious glances at *(mit j-m Blickkontakt suchen)*: to ogle, to give the glad eye, to make goo-goo *or* googly eyes at; *schau, wie der alte Kracher die Augen verdreht … will der mit dem jungen Ding am End ~?* look at the old dodo (*or* gobbler) making goo-goo eyes … well, I like that! having a go at that young thing, is he? – **4.** to become friendly with s.o. after a short meeting, usu. with sexual intentions *(sich heranschmeißen)*: to pick s.o. up; *der war mir zuwider, der hat mit mir ja bloß ~ wollen!* I didn't like him, all he was out for was trying to pick me up. – **5.** to challenge s.o. in an aggressive mood *(sich mit j-m anlegen wollen)*: to try and pick up a quarrel with s.o.

anbauen *v/t* [actually, 'to cultivate', 'to plant'] *colloq.*, mostly in annoyance: *([einen Gebrauchsgegenstand] verlieren)* to lose, forget, or possibly only to misplace; very often restricted to preterite use: to salt away; *ich muss den Schirm heute früh in der Elektrischen angebaut haben BrE* I must have left my brolly behind in the tram (*AmE* … my umbrella on the streetcar) this morning.

anbrennen *v/i* of wood, etc. = *ansengen* ↓.

anbrunzen *v/t* [→ *brunzen*] *vulg.* **1.** to urinate on (*bepissen*): to piss ‖ on *phr.* a quotation from Abraham a Santa Clara (d. 1709), a witty Capuchin divine and Imperial counsellor, fulminating in one of his sermons against the loose morals shown by some female members of the highest circles: *bei Hof gibt es Damen,*

Andreas Hofer
A painting by Oskar Wiedenhofer

die nicht wert sind, dass sie ein Hund anbrunzt there are some ladies at court unworthy even of being pissed upon by a dog. – **2.** *fig.* to reprimand severely (*grob beschimpfen*): to chew s.o.'s balls off.

Andreas-Hofer … *comb.* [< Andreas Hofer, 1767–1810, a South Tyrolean peasant leader and regional deputy, who in *Anno Neun* ↓, skilfully organized his country's resistance against Napoleon's troops]: **~-Bund** *m* -(e)s *polit.* in South Tyrol, during the Second World War: "Andreas Hofer League", an underground organization, with links to North Tyrol and Switzerland, actively working for the overthrow of Fascism and National Socialism. – **~-Heirat** or **~-Hochzeit** *f* -/-en [in jocular allusion to the timely warning, in broad Tyrolese, *„Mander, 's ischt Zeit!"* ('Men, the time has come!'), with which in the Spring of 1809 Andreas Hofer rallied his coun-

"In a month's time, Prince Metternich will be down and out. Long live constitutional Austria!" This inflammatory prophecy, posted on February 29, 1848, makes a small crowd of 'anxiety-hatted' Viennese agonizingly aware of, and furiously excited about, the uncanny events to come

trymen to rise against Napoleon] *hum.* or *sarc.* marriage under the pressure of pregnancy: last-minute wedding, esp. *AmE* shotgun wedding (where, literally or figuratively, the bride's father prods the young man with his shooting-piece to make him do what is necessary).

Ạngabe *f* -/rare: -n *econ. (Anzahlung [als Sicherheitsleistung]*) deposit; *wünschen [brauchen] Sie eine ~ oder geht es auch so?* would you like [do you need] a deposit, or is it all right without? – **ạngeben** *v/t econ. (eine Anzahlung leisten)* to make (*or* put down) a deposit; *soll ich was ~ oder glauben Sie mir, dass ich die Ware abholen komme?* should I make a deposit, or do you trust me to pick up the goods?

Ạngströhre *f* -/-n [a partial loan translation from E *anxiety hat,* for the type of headgear created by John Hetherington, a London mercer, in 1797; the coinage was revived by those Viennese who, in the revolutionary month of October 1848, witnessed the local university students slinking about in top hats (thus showing their fear and lack of commitment), while daring young insurgents, in broad-brimmed slouch-hats, took up arms against the repressive regime of Metternich] *(Zylinder[hut])* **1.** *hist.* anxiety hat; *später nährte sich der Spitzname ~ von dem Umstand, dass der Zylinder häufig bei aufregenden Anlässen, etwa bei Amtsantritten, ja schon bei wichtigen Hochschulprüfungen unerlässlich war* later on, the nickname "Angströhre" (or English, "anxiety hat") kept its popularity through the fact that top hats were often de rigueur on stressful occasions, such as assuming office or even when taking important college examinations. – **2.** *colloq.* top hat, silk hat: topper, high hat, chimney-pot or stovepipe hat.

Ạnimo *n,* and occasionally *m* -s [< It *animo* 'inclination', 'desire'] *colloq.* **1.** *(Lust)* desire; *~ haben* to have the urge (*or,* the craving) for s.th., to have a mind to *inf.,* to feel like *ger.; ~ auf* (or *für*) ein *Schalerl Kaffee haben* to feel like (having) a quick (*ScotE a.* a wee) cup of coffee; *heut hätt ich ~ für einen Heurigen* I wouldn't mind going to a new-wine tavern today. – **2.** *(Schwung)* impetus, drive; *es ist ewig schad, dass er kein(en) ~ hat* it's a thousand pities (*or,* a dreadful [an awful] pity) that he's got no get-up-and-go.

A̲nis ['a:nɪs] *cul.* anise, aniseed. – **~bogen** *m* -s/usu. *pl.* ... bögen, **~scharte** *f* -/usu. *pl.*-n a fine crescent-shaped pastry, with anise sprinkled on top: *BrE* aniseed biscuit, *AmE* aniseed cookie.

A recent Austrian stamp, after a wood carving showing St Anne with Mary and the baby Jesus

ạnklopfen *v/i* to knock *or* rap (at a door, etc.) a rhymed warning, in some underground wine cellars of Eastern Austria, laughingly used vis-à-vis passing visitors who feel tempted (rather mechanically) to probe the level of barrelled wealth with their knuckles:

> *Ich frag dich nicht, mein lieber Gast,*
> *wieviel du in dem Börsl hast;*
> *drum klopf auch du als kluger Mann*
> *nicht mehr an meine Fässer an!*

> * I ask you not, my honoured guest,
> How well your purse with money's blessed;
> So, being wise, please do refrain
> From tapping on my casks again.

Ạnna Sẹlbdritt *f* - - *name* [the adjunct is now a hapax legomenon; lit., 'ranking third (in a group of three)'] *R.C.* & *arts* the devotion to the Madonna, which is considerable in this country, also comes to the fore in numerous representations of St Anne, the Virgin's mother, as part of a trinity spanning three generations: the saint sometimes indeed carries her daughter on one arm, and the infant Jesus on the other: St Anne with Mary and the child, The Holy Family.

Ạnno Neun *n* [actually, the ablative case of a Latin-German hybrid, "(in) the year (180)9", on the analogy of *Anno Domini*] *hist.* The Year 1809, memorable to the Tyrolese for their ancestors' stout resistance against Napoleon, when Andreas Hofer and his peasant army outmanoeuvred and outfought Napoleon's Saxon and Bavarian allies, before finally being crushed by fifty-thousand troops sent out from Italy.

ạnpatzen *v* [< *Patzen m* 'blotch', 'splodge'] *colloq.* **1.** *v/t* to stain someone's or one's own article of clothing, a book, etc. (*schmutzig machen*): to dirty, to make a mess on; *ich habe mir die Krawatte angepatzt* I've made a mess on (*or,* I've messed up) my tie. – **2.** *v/refl* (1) to soil one's clothes (*sich schmutzig machen*): to get one's clothes grubby; *ui je! jetzt hab ich mich angepatzt!* aw, gee, I've dropped something down my front; *das Kind hat sich mit dem Spinat ganz angepatzt* spinach was all over the baby's clothes. – (2) to splatter oneself with a liquid; *du Patscherl* [ˈpɔ:–], *jetzt hast du dich mit dem Hollersaft aber schön angepatzt!* you clumsy clot, now you've gone and spilled that elderberry juice all over yourself.

ạnschauen *vt/refl colloq.* to look at (something amazing, or in amazement): **1.** in a verbal threat: *der kann sich was ~ !* I'll make him pay for that! – **2.** expressing predicament: *wir hätten uns schön angeschaut, wenn wir weniger Zwetschkenknödel gemacht hätten, die Gäste waren ja mordshungrig* we'd have been in a sorry state (*or* in a bad way, *AmE a.* in a pickle, in a mess, up the creek) if we had made fewer plum dumplings, because our guests turned out to be ravenous.

ạnschieben; and somewhat less frequently also, **ạntauchen** *v/i colloq. (protegieren)* to use one's high position in a bureaucracy in order to favour an applicant: to push; *dein Gesuch um Pragmatisierung liegt ja schon endslang im Ministerium; hast du niemanden, der da ein bissl ~ könnte?* your application for a permanency (*or,* for tenure) has been at the Ministry for ages; haven't you got anyone who could pull a few strings?, *AmE* don't you have anyone who could put a little pressure (*or,* steam) behind it? – **Ạnschieber,** less frequently also, **Ạntaucher** *m -s/- colloq.* an influential person in a ministry or other administrative centre, who intervenes in favour of an applicant *(Protektor):* connection, helping hand; *ohne ~ kommt man zu nichts* you don't get anywhere without pull (*or,* connections); *AmE a.* it's not what you know, it's who you know.

ạnschlempern *v/refl* low *colloq.,* often slightly *contp. (übermäßig Flüssigkeit zu sich nehmen)* to drink an excess of liquid: to swill one's innards (*more coarsely,* ... one's belly full) with water, etc.; *die [ihre] löbliche Sitte, sich einen halben Morgen wie Nachmittag mit Tee anzuschlempern* the[ir] good old ritual of bloating themselves with (*or,* of swill-

Cross-country horse-riding can also be part of religious ceremonies: here, at Kirchberg in the Tyrol, the Antlassritt *has been a solemn feature of Corpus Christi Day for fully 350 years*

ing) tea for half the morning and afternoon; cp. *anbampfen* ↑.

Ạnschluss *m* -schlusses/*pl.* rare: -schlüsse *polit. hist.* the incorporation of a relatively small territory or state into a much larger, ethnically related, body: annexation, union, *Anschluss*; dass sich alle deutschen Länder vereinen sollten, wobei auch an den ~ Deutsch-Österreichs gedacht war, geisterte bestimmt schon 1848 durch die Köpfe liberaler Scharfmacher* the idea of all German lands banding together, including the *Anschluss* of German-Austria, was already definite in the minds of liberal agitators as early as 1848; *bereits 1932 waren Teile der Mittel- und Oberschicht für den ~ Österreichs an Deutschland* as early as 1932 some sections of the middle and upper classes favoured the union of Austria with Germany.

* In English, the linguistic takeover of *Anschluss* (usu. capitalized and italicized), for the Austrian upheaval of Spring 1938, was as rapid as the event itself; furthermore, the word is sometimes used with partial reversal of the elements in the above definition, e.g. in: the *Anschluss* of Germany with Austria.

ạnsengen *vt/i* [second el., *sengen v/t* 'to singe' [–dʒ–], actually a causative verb derived from the past tense form of *sin-*

gen, ‘to cause to sing’ (because of the excruciating pain of being burnt)] of a log of wood, a piece of clothing, etc.: to discolour due to excessive heat, to char slightly ‖ *prov.* a vulgarly erotic allusion to the claim that intimacy is more satisfactory with a woman of wide sexual experience: *ein angesengtes Scheit* (or *Holz*) *brennt besser* (a) with apodictic generality: a hot piece burns better, *AmE a.* a damaged piece is easier to light; (b) with direct reference to the person concerned: she’s been round the block a few times, and it’s more fun if she knows the way.

Ạnsitz *m* -es/-e *archit.* in Western Austria, esp. in the Tyrol – a large and stately country residence, usu. one that belongs to a well-to-do landowner in the district ([*großer, repräsentativer*] *Wohnsitz*): manor-house, *BrE a.* hall; *die Grafenfamilie hat einen ~ in den Bergen* the countly family has a manor-house in the mountains.

Ạntlassritt *m* -(e)s/-e [OHG and MHG *ant-* ‘away’ > NHG *ent-*, as in *entlassen* ‘to free from sin’; the modern word, with a different prefix, is *Ablass m* ‘indulgence’, ‘remission of sins’] *folklore* in the Brixen Valley of North Tyrol, on the feast of Corpus Christi (originally on Maundy Thursday): “Ride of Indulgence”, a festive horseback procession from church to church, headed by the Dean of Brixen, who carries the monstrance with the Host; the fact that the horses are decorated with sprigs of larch and peonies indicates that this cavalcade is actually an old fertility cult which has been Christianized (orginally it was a procession through the fields at the beginning of the growing season to ensure a good harvest).

“Wakey wakey, Springtime …
We help to drive out Winter!“

ạntrenzen *v/refl colloq.* to dirty one’s clothes by drinking hastily or carelessly, or by being unexpectedly interfered with in the act: to spill things on one’s clothes; *trink langsamer, sonst trenzt du dich noch an!* drink slower, on you’ll spill it all over yourself!; *der Kleine hat sich mit dem Apfelsaft von oben bis unten angetrenzt* the baby has spilled apple juice all over himself; *wie der vorsintflutliche Zug da über die Schienen holpert, ist es eine Kunst, sich nicht anzutrenzen* the way this antediluvian train rattles over the rails, it is a fine art (*or,* it requires great finesse) not to spill your drink on yourself.

a̲per *adj* [< L *aperire* ‘to open’, ‘to make (the ground) visible’] of meadows, etc. in early spring: *(schneefrei)* free from snow, clear of snow, thawed-out ‖ on a sign near Inzing, Tyrol: *Holzstreifen auf ~em Weg*

Laurels, crown, orb, and sceptre are some of the regalia due to His Apostolic Majesty

verboten! No trailing of tree-trunks unless on snowy ground. – **apern** *v/i* of snow *(schmelzen)* to melt, to thaw; *es apert* the snow is melting, it is thawing; *die Sonne bringt den Schnee in ein paar Tagen zum ~* the sun will melt (*or* strip) the snow in a matter of days; cp. *ausapern* ↓.

Aperschnalzen *n* -s *folklore* on Alpine fields, in late February or March: springtime whip-cracking, done by a single farmer or groups of young men, whirling twelve-foot rope lashes round their heads in a rhythmic motion to finish in the same pattern and with a simultaneous resounding crack; the ritual was designed to drive away evil spirits and encourage the deities of Spring to burst forth from the hard earth.

Ạpfel… *cul.:* **~schmarrn,** less often **~schmarren** *m* -s/pl. rare: – "apple scramble cake", featuring two or three mellow apples, peeled and cubed, in the mix, with everything poured into the pan, scrambled and baked. – **~strudel** *m* -s/- apple strudel, a flaky, light pastry filled with sliced apples.

Apostolisch *adj* [actually, 'endowed with the qualities and powers derived from the Apostles of Jesus Christ'; in particular, from St Stephen, who had led the Hungarians into the Catholic faith in the year 1000] *hist.* an adjective prominently implanted in the sequence of hereditary titles borne by Emperor Francis Joseph from 1867 (cp. *Ausgleich* ↓): Apostolic; *bei öffentlichen Auftritten ließ sich der Kaiser als „Seine ~e Majestät, unser allergnädigster Kaiser und Herr", anreden* at public functions the Emperor insisted on being addressed as "His Apostolic Majesty, our most gracious Emperor and Lord".

Appọrtl *n* -s/-(n) *colloq. (Gegenstand, der geworfen wird, damit ihn der Hund wieder zurückbringt)* object thrown for a dog to retrieve; command to a dog: *such's ~!* go fetch!, fetch it!, (go) get it!

Ạrbeitsstrich *m* -(e)s/-e *econ.* [a *hum.* elaboration of *Strich,* in the sense of 'a prostitute's beat', and *auf den Strich gehen* 'to work the streets'] a stretch of road outside a refugee camp, e.g. that of Traiskirchen, Lower Austria, south of Vienna, where some of the inmates wait for potential employers to take them to illegal jobs: work-pickup, *AmE* pickup strip.

Aristokratie *f* -/-n = *Hochadel* ↓.

Ạrmenbibel *f* -/-n *R. C. & arts* to be seen

in situ on open porches or along the ceilings of monastic cloisters, e.g. at Gurk and Brixen: Poor Man's Bible, L Biblia Pauperum, a medieval fresco providing dramatic episodes from the Old and New Testaments for the illiterate members of society.

Ạrmitschkerl and **Ạrmutschkerl** *n* -s/-(n), the variants showing the well-known phenomenon of the extreme vowels [ɪ] and [ʊ] changing places in the body of the word, *dial.*, either spoken with slight contempt or with pity – **1.** a person deprived, at least temporarily, of financial means, brains, and other indispensable attributes constituting normal life in a modern community (*armseliger Kerl*): poor wretch, *BrE a.* poor sod *or* bugger, *emot.* poor little worm; *die arme Hansi, das ~, so jung und unschuldig, und ganz allein mit dem verrückten Vater zusammengesperrt!* poor Joanie, sad little worm, so young and innocent, and shut up all alone with her mad father!; *was machst du denn da, du geistiges ~, du brichst das ja!* what are you doing, dimwit (*or* dope; *AmE a.,* dumb dodo, lamebrain), you'll break it!; *an Wissen bist du ihm gegenüber ja ein (geistiges)* ~ mind, he's forgotten more than you'll ever know (*or* learn). – **2.** *contp.* an establishment, esp. a business, shop, or type of school, much smaller and less endowed than most of the rest: *ein ~ von einer Musikschule* an itsy-bitsy *or* itty-bitty (*AmE a.,* half-portion *or* peanut) type of music school.

Ạrscherl *n* -s/-n [dim. of *Arsch m* 'arse'] *colloq.* **1.** *euphem. & joc.* for the vicious monosyllable rudely denoting the human posterior (*Gesäß*): sit-me-down, sit-upon, *hum. a.* sit-me-down-upon ‖ *prov.* a seemingly health-orientated distich, rather often met with engraved on a slab of bark-wood (and previously offered at stalls of rural fairs and markets), decorating the "smallest room" of a house in the country –

> *Wenn 's Arscherl brummt,*
> *is 's Herzerl gsund.*
>
> The deadliest farts
> Shan't harm sound hearts.

2. *apprec.,* a baby's or, less often, a svelte woman's buttocks: botty; *schau dir nur das ~ an, so süß und rund!* just look at that botty, so sweet and round. – **3.** *joc.* a familiar form of address to a person who is about to be the butt of a gentle form of reproach, say, for having failed to turn up in time, to buy a certain article, etc: silly-billy, so-and-so; *du ~, was habe ich feststellen müssen?* … you (little) silly-billy (*or,* … so-and-so), what did I have to find out? …

Ạsdagstampfer [first el. < ASDAG, the abbreviated name of a well-known Austrian road construction firm, *A*sphaltierungs-, *S*traßenbau- und *Da*chdeckungsgesellschaft], **Asphạltstampfer** *m* only *pl. sl. contp.* a woman's unshapely fat legs: stumps, stumpy battering rams, *AmE* thunder thighs, saddle-bags.

A̱sien *n* -s *geog., hist. & civ.* the largest of the world's continents, nearly one third of its total land mass, and bordering Europe (part of the same land mass) along the Ural Mountains and across the Caspian Sea: Asia [ˈeɪʃə, –ʒə] the presence, however, ethnically, of millions of people of Eastern Indo-European descent, now resident or once having surged

"Das letzte Aufgebot" – *grimly resolved to fight and die in the face of Napoleon's troops*

around for hundreds of miles further west, makes the described border a purely orographic one – hence, from the standpoint of race and civilization, such a dividing line, it is claimed, should much rather, say, be drawn north-south along the eastern border of Austria (as is implied in two well-known bons mots – **1.** Prince Metternich's ~ *beginnt an der Landstraße* 'Asia begins at the Landstrasse' (which, at the time of its origin, during the Congress of Vienna, 1814–15, was a south-eastern suburb of Vienna [and is now its third district, only separated from the city centre by the width of a single street]); and **2.** Konrad Lorenz's dictum, some 150 years later, *Österreich liegt auf der Schneise zwischen Europa und* ~ 'Austria is perched on the firebreak dividing Europe and Asia' – the truth of both quotations, by greatly distinguished Austrians, one a statesman and the other a behavioural scientist and Nobel Prize winner, can be amply verified in history, from Vienna, once the big outpost of the Roman Empire, by the *Ostmark* 'Eastern March' proving a bulwark in the times of Charlemagne, 800–14, down to the heroic defence of Vienna against the Turkish invaders in 1529 and 1683; and there, too, persist **3.** many open or veiled digs at primitive mismanagement in Asia-like South-East Europe, e.g. *Zustände sind das (, also) wie am Balkan* 'what a muddle this is as though we lived on the Balkans' – spluttered out thoughtlessly most of the time, with no intent really to slur any nation specifically: such prejudice is long-lived, and thrives on human traits … an East European – and an East Austrian, for that matter –, when even minor day-to-day situations are being pilloried, still has to bear up under the taunt, hurled at him with a good-natured laugh or a gentle sneer, that he is a "Balkanized" specimen, a living hotchpotch of heinous laissez-faire and inglorious inefficiency.

Aufgebot *n* -(e)s/-e **1.** *eccl. (öffentliche Bekanntmachung der beabsichtigten Eheschließung)* banns of marriage; *die Brautleute haben das ~ bestellt* the bridal pair have asked for (*or* put up) the banns; *wie lange hängt das ~ schon aus?* how long is it since the banns have been published?; *das da ist erst das erste ~* this is only the first time of asking. – **2.** *arts* in the picture gallery of the Ferdinandeum, Innsbruck: *Das letzte ~* 'The Last Draft', a painting by Franz von Defregger, 1835–1921, with a graphic scene from the waning *Anno Neun* ↑ , the grizzled remnant with scythes, pikes, and sickles determined to defend hearth and home against Napoleon's invading army.

aufgelegt *adj contp. (offensichtlich)* absolute, complete, utter; *das ist ein ~er Blödsinn!* that's complete (*or,* utter) nonsense, *BrE a.* that's utter rubbish!

aufpudeln *v/refl colloq.* [< poodles were used for retrieving game birds from the cold water, and the fur was left long on their chests as insulation] **1.** to put on airs *(sich wichtig machen)*: to throw (*or* chuck) one's weight about, *AmE a.* to put on frills, to strut one's stuff; *pudel dich nicht (so) auf!* get (down) off your high horse! – **2.** to get excited because of a minor matter, while emphasizing one's own importance *(sich künstlich aufregen)*: to puff oneself up with anger; *pudel dich (nicht,* or *vielleicht) auf!* don't kick up such a fuss!, *ScotE* dinna fash yersel'!; *so ein aufgestellter Hühnerdreck* (mostly dialectal, *Heandreck*), *wie sich der aufpudelt!* who the hell does he think he is, that stuck-up (*AmE a.* stuck-uppity) piece of chicken shit!

aufreiben *v/i* **1.** *(scheuern)* to scrub the floor. – **2.** *colloq.* as a threatening gesture: *([mit der Hand] ausholen)* to prepare to lash out at s.o. with the back of one's hand; *was, willst du am End ~?* what! you're not going to give me a backhanded one (, are you)? – **Aufreibfetzen** *m* -s/- *(Scheuertuch)* floorcloth.

aufzwicken *v/t colloq.* in an erotic sense, with reference to a desirable man or girl – to conquer *(für sich gewinnen)*: to pick up, to make; *ich zwicke mir jetzt den ersten Mann auf, der mir in den Weg kommt* I'm going to grab me the first man I run into, I'm going to get hold of the first man who comes my way.

Augen…: ~auswischerei *f -/pl.* rare: -en *colloq.* something said or done to deceive a person into thinking that what he sees is good: eyewash, *AmE a.* snowjob; *das ist (eine) reine ~* that's mere eyewash, *AmE a.* … a mere snowjob. –

~bad *n* (e)s/ …bäder [actually, *med.* 'bathing of the eye(s)'] often *univ. sl.* a token appearance at a lecture in order to be seen: showing up just for the record; *er geht in die Vorlesung, bloß um ein ~ zu nehmen* he only goes to the lecture to show his face (*or,* to make his face known). – **~blick** *m* -(e)s/-e moment: jiffy; *einen ~!* just a moment! ‖ *phr.* a pithy warning against pregnancy: *es gibt im Menschenleben ~e, wo es im ~e Menschenleben gibt* there are seconds in human life when there is human life in a second. – **~braue** *f* -/-n eyebrow ‖ *archit. Haus ohne ~n colloq.* (or *Loos-Haus*) in Vienna's Michaelerplatz: "House without Eyebrows", the first functional business and apartment house without any ornament, architrave or window frame, built by the architect Adolf Loos (1870–1933) in 1910; this novelty, being situated next to the Hofburg Palace, aroused much controversy at the time.

Augerln *n pl., emot.* human eyes (irrespective of actual colour): baby blues.

Augi *n* -(s)/- [dim. of *Auge n*] *emot.* little eye; coaxingly, in familiar speech: *dreh dich schön um, ja, mach die ~ zu, vielleicht kannst du ein bissl schlafen* come on, love, just turn over and close your eyes; perhaps you can doze off for a bit.

Augustin *pr. n.* **Lieber ~ 1.** *hist.* a legendary bagpiper roaming the streets of Old Vienna, whose cheerfulness made him immune to the plague striking the city at that time. – **2.** *arts* a statuette of Augustin awarded by the Vienna Carnival Society to a prominent person known for his sense of humour; comparable to the German "Order Opposing Deadly Seriousness" given by the Aachen Carnival Society.

"Death-defying Augustin ne'er cares a pin"

ausapern [second el. < *aper(n)* ↑] *v/i* **1.** to emerge from glacial snow. – **2.** to reappear after the winter snows; ✿ *in der Schneetälchenflora apert im Frühjahr eine dunkle Erde aus, welche vom mineralischen Staub und organischen Detritus herrührt, der sich auf dem Schnee gesammelt hat* in the flora of the "snow valleys", a blackish earth is left in Spring, deriving from the mineral dust and organic detritus [dɪˈtraɪtəs] which have collected on the snow.

ausfratscheln *v/t colloq. (aushorchen)* to elicit information from s.o.: to pump s.o., to put the screws on s.o., *AmE a.* to give s.o. the third degree.

ausgehen *v/refl ([hin]reichen)* to be sufficient (*or* enough); *ob es sich zeitlich ausgeht, in den paar Stunden so viel zu besichtigen?* will there be enough time to see so much in a few hours?; *gehen sich die Marillen aus, wenn jeder sechs Knödel schnabulieren will?* will there be enough apricots to go round if each person has six dumplings to dispose of?; to one wishing to pass when the space, say, between one's chair and the wall or between two cars, is very narrow: *geht sich's aus?* can you manage?, can you make it?, *AmE a.* can you fit (through)?

ausgemugelt *p.p. & adj colloq., skiing* said of a slope which, through excessive use, has become very uneven: bumpy (through repeated traffic of skiers making several sharp turns, thus forming mounds known as *Mugel*); *der Hang ist ~* the slope has become bumpy.

Ausgleich *m* -(e)s *polit. hist.* Compromise, a bilateral settlement between Austria and Hungary in 1867, which established the latter as a kingdom with internal autonomy, leaving the Hapsburg lands as a loose federation nominally governed by a Parliament in Vienna; outwardly, regarding foreign affairs, defence, and finances, the now renamed Austro-Hungarian Monarchy remained a unity, but internally was split in two.

ausgschamt, less often **ausgeschamt** *adj* [for *ausgeschämt,* the p.p. of an unauthenticated *ausschämen* 'to have lost, or to be void of, all feeling of shame'] *dial.* insolent *(unverschämt)*: brazen-faced, (damn) cheeky; *so ein ~s Weibsbild!* the shameless hussy; *die Bande, die ~e, die hätt' wohl all's von der Erbschaft eingsacklt!* that brazen-faced gang, what a cheek! they'd (just) as soon have grabbed all the inheritance.

Ausg'steckt is [ˈauskʃtekt ɪs] *dial. phr.* a friendly invitation, extended verbally or in writing (on printed postcards sent by tavern-keepers or announced by local newspapers in Eastern Austria), to come and enjoy the pleasures of wine-drinking: "The Bush *has been Stuck Up*", i. e., for a period of two or three weeks, a wreath of evergreens or a branch of fir hangs outside the tavern or private cellar of the local wine-grower as a token that his last year's vintage may now be drunk.

ausheben *vt/i* **1.** *([Briefkasten] leeren)* to empty, to clear; *dieser Briefkasten wird dreimal am Tag ausgehoben* this letterbox is cleared (*or,* the mail in [*or,* from] this letterbox is collected) three times daily. – **2.** *([Buch aus einer Bibliothek] entlehnen)* to borrow, to take out (a book from a library). – **Aushebung** *f* -/-en *(Leerung [e-s Briefkastens])* (postal) collection; *nächste ~ 17 Uhr* next collection (at) 5 p.m.

auskochen *v/i* of small inns and taverns: to serve (*colloq.,* to do) hot meals, as opposed to light refreshments and drinks; *kochen Sie aus?* do you serve (*colloq.,* do) hot meals?; on a notice: *wegen Personalmangels können wir leider nicht mehr ~* we regret that owing to shortage of staff we no longer serve hot meals.

Auslage *f* -/-n *(Schaufenster)* shop-window, display window, *AmE* show window, store window; *in der ~ zeigen* to display in the window: *die ~n anschauen gehen* to go window-shopping ‖ *colloq. in das Büro kann ja jeder reinschauen, da sitzt man (wie) in der ~* everyone can see into this office, it's like sitting in a shop-window.

Auspuff Europas *m* -(e)s - a sobriquet coined to draw attention to a major traffic problem: "Exhaust-Pipe of Europe", the heavily-travelled motorway along the Inn Valley which funnels the traffic through the Brenner Pass; some ninety per cent of the lorries using this route are in transit only.

ausräumen *v/t* [actually, 'to empty a house, a room, a chest of drawers, etc. of chiefly old and valueless contents'] *med. vulg.* to perform an abortion: to clear *a woman* out, *AmE a.* to pick *a woman's* lock; a witty if callous parody of a famous song passage of the 1930s, *was eine Frau im Frühling träumt, / das wird im Herbst dann ausgeräumt* (for the original: *... das ist gar dumm und ungereimt*) *what women dream as springtime hums / is soon cleared out when autumn comes (for: ... / is plain absurd (just ask their mums!)

ausrichten *v/t colloq.,* with reference to persons only – to carp at s.o. behind his back *(bekritteln)*: to pull s.o. to pieces, to drag s.o. through the mud; *die Leute ~* to gossip with malicious enjoyment: to tittle-tattle, *AmE a.* to dish out the dirt; *wenn die beiden alten Tratschen zusammenkommen, richten sie immer einen jeden ihrer Bekannten aus* whenever those two old gossips meet they tear all their friends to shreds.

äußerln *v/i colloq.* said of a dog in a town – to urinate: to pee; *der Hund äußerlt* the dog pees; *den Hund ~ führen* to walk the dog: to take the dog out for a pee.

Außireißer *m* -s/- [first el. < *aushin* 'out'] *dial.* a person, thing, or special circumstance that helps to remedy an awkward situation: godsend, life-saver, just what the doctor ordered.

Austria ['au–] **1.** *n* -s/ *pl.* rare: -s [documented as early as 1147, < *terra auster, austria, austrasia* 'land in the East', Franconian-Langobardic variants for the eastern part of the German Empire (formed on the analogy of *terra oriens, terra orientalis,* an older, less specific collocation for 'land in the East'); in historical Latin documents, Austria proper appears as *terra austrialis* since the sixteenth century] a neo-Latin coinage for the regional entity: Austria ['ɔ–] (> MHG *Ostarrîchi,* [since 996] > NHG *Österreich*); *Mark ~ hist.* the Eastern March (1156). – **2.** *f* -/ *pl.* rare: -s one of several metaphorical uses for private organizations (e.g. the *Bank ~,* or football clubs in Vienna and Carinthia) and national products (e.g. a brand of cigarette brought out by the Austria-Tabakwerke-AG, an Austrian state monopoly).

Austriazismus [au–] *m* -(ses)/ ... smen *ling.* sometimes used with a slightly *contp.* tinge: Austriacism ['ɔ–], a speech peculiarity considered standard in Austria (and sanctified by the use of eminent writers such as Grillparzer, Hofmannsthal, Wildgans, Weinheber, Doderer, and Torberg), but foreign to the rest of the German-speaking countries.

auswinden *v/t* of wet cloth or clothing *(auswringen)*: to wring out; *wir waren* *so nass, man hätte den Hubertusmantel beinahe ~ müssen* we were so (*colloq. a.,* that) soaked we almost needed to wring our raincoats out; of persons: *zum ≗ nass sein* to be dripping (*or,* soaking, wringing) wet, to be wet through, to be soaked to the skin; *beim Empfang war es so heiss, dass alle zum ≗ nass waren vor Schweiss* it was so hot at the reception that everyone was wringing wet with perspiration || *vulg. hum.,* of a man passing water: *den (Familien-)Strumpf ~* to urinate: to shake the dew off the lily, to shake hands with an old friend, *AustralE & NZE* to unbutton the mutton, *BermE* to flop the lizard.

Autodrom *n* -s/-e **1.** *(Fahrbahn für elektrische Kleinautos auf Vergnügungsstätten)* a riotous amusement at fairs, where electrically-powered cars are driven on an enclosed metal floor: dodgems. – **2.** *(Auto-Skooter)* dodgem car, *AmE* bumper car; *wir gehen in den Prater und fahren mit dem ~* we are going to the Prater (amusement park) to have a go on the dodgems.

Auto...: ~reifen *m* -s/- *hum.* or *sarc.* an extra layer of fat that encircles the waist, esp. on a man *(Rettungsring):* spare tyre (*AmE* tire). – **~spengler** *m* -s/- ⊞ *(Autoschlosser)* car mechanic, *AmE a.* auto(mobile) mechanic. – **~spenglerei** *f* -/-en ⊞ *(Karosseriewerkstatt)* garage (for repairs), *AmE* (auto) body shop.

Autrichelieu *m* - [a blend of *Autriche* F 'Austria' and *Richelieu,* the name of the great political cardinal who ruled the French Empire all but single-handedly between 1624 and 1642] *polit. hist.* "Austria's Richelieu", an appreciative sobriquet for Monsignore Ignaz Seipel, 1876–1932, "a man born out of time and place" (Gedye), who in the Austrian cabinet, and especially as Federal Chancellor, 1922–24 and 1926–29, combined rigid personal asceticism with a sure touch for the right propaganda and a single-minded devotion to the political interests of the Church. But what is more, thanks to his almost superhuman stabilization efforts, Austria's post-war economic fever had been stilled, and she again had her place at the international table.

Mgr. Ignaz Seipel, a great clerical Chancellor

B

Baaz *m* -es [< sound symbolism] *colloq.,* sometimes with a playfully pleasant undertone – **1.** mud, or any other slushy mass *(weiche, klebrige Masse)*: goo, *AmE a.* gumbo, glob; *Kinder und Wildschweine spielen für ihr Leben gern im ~* children and wild boars just love to wallow in the mud. – **2.** any other sticky substance the speaker has, often inadvertently, come upon: goo, *BrE a.* gunge, AmE a. gunk; *was ist denn das für ein ~ da unten in der Tasche?... da muss die Schokolade zergangen sein!* what's all that goo at the bottom of this bag? ... the chocolate must have melted. – **baazig** *adj colloq.* said of, or resembling, a sticky substance: gooey, *BrE a.* gungy.

baba **1.** *pred. adj, baby talk* no longer present, or hidden from view: gone; *die Muhkuli(s) und die Hottorossi (sind) ~ BrE* the moo-cows and the gee-gees [ˈdʒi:dʒi:z] (have) gone tatas [ˈtætɑ:z], *AmE* ... and the horsies (have) gone bye-bye. – **2.** *interj.* a farewell greeting to, and from, a young child, but also among family members and good friends (one respondent, as a rule, having to be a female): bye-bye [ˈbaɪbaɪ], *BrE* ta-ta [tæˈtɑ:].

bạcherlwarm *adj & adv* [first el., an endearing dim., with the suffix *-erl* added to the stem form of *bachen,* the dial. variant of *backen* 'to bake'] *colloq.,* always *apprec.* pleasantly warm (and fresh, crisp, etc.): nice and warm [hot]; *wenn's an einem eiskalten Winterabend ~ vom Ofen herweht, dann ist es in der Bauernstubm gwiß am gemütlichsten* on an icy-cold winter evening, with the stove oozing cosy warmth, the farmhouse room's most snug and safe, I'm sure; *die Baunzerl werden ~ aufgetragen* the fritters are served oven-fresh.

Bạckerbse *f* -/ usu. *pl.* -n *cul.* a pea-shaped globule of fried dough *(kleines Mehlteigkügelchen als Suppeneinlage)*: fried batter (paste) drop. – **~nsuppe** *f* -/-n *cul.* clear soup with fried batter drops.

Bạ̈ckerschupfen *n* -s *law hist.* "bakers' ducking", an old punishment for bakers who had produced low-quality bread or mislabelled the weight; the culprits were repeatedly submerged in muddy water in a basket tied to the end of a plank (last occurrence, Vienna 1773).

Bạckhendel, Bạckhendl *n* -s/-(n) *cul.* *(Backhuhn)* **1.** chicken for frying, *AmE* fryer, frier. – **2.** fried chicken in breadcrumbs, breaded fried chicken, i.e. coated with breadcrumbs, then fried in oil ‖ *fig. colloq. Anno ~* in the good old times long ago, *AmE a.* in the horse-and-buggy days. – **~friedhof** *m* -(e)s/ ...höfe *hum.* or *iron.* large rounded stomach, esp. a man's: *(Kartoffelbauch)*: potbelly, *BrE* bay window, *AmE* beer belly, *NZE* beer goitre.

Bahn... railway: **~fahrer** *m* -s/- pupil travelling by rail to and from school every day *(Fahrschüler)*: *BrE* commuting schoolboy, train pupil, *AmE* commuting student. – **~übersetzung** *f* -/-en *(Bahnübergang) BrE* level crossing, *AmE* grade crossing.

Bahöl [baˈhøː] *m* -s [? < Hung. *páholni* 'to flog'] *colloq.* a great deal of noise *(großer Lärm, Geschrei)*: hullabaloo, racket, *AmE a.* ruckus; *die Gäste beim Heurigen haben einen solchen ~ gemacht, dass wir erst lang nach Mitternacht haben einschlafen können* the people at the new-wine tavern made such a racket that it was long past midnight when we finally got to sleep.

Bakschisch... [< *baksheesh* or *backsheesh,* but orig. Persian – '(in parts of the Middle East, Far East, and the Indian subcontinent) a small sum of money given as alms, a gratuity, or a bribe']: **~geist** *m* -(e)s, **~mentalität** *f* - often *contp.* an acquired greed among men and women in a certain number of occupations of calculating on some specific extra material benefit, more or less secretively given, for a "favour" rendered – one that in fact is actually part and parcel of those office-bearers' routine duties: morbid expectancy of tips, kickback mentality; *vom Bakschischgeist befallen sein* to have the gimmies.

Balkan *m* -s [< *geog.* the Balkan Peninsula or the Balkan Mountains] *colloq.,* often slightly *iron.* or *contp.* a vaguely circumscribed territory in South-Eastern Europe where, in the eyes of many Aus-

Prince Metternich, "The Coachman of Europe"

trians, love of order is not necessarily considered a cardinal virtue: the higgledy-piggledy Balkans ‖ *hist.* a winged word – or, rather, one of several variants widely current (cp. under *Asien* ↑) – due to Prinz von Metternich (1773–1859), the famous Austrian statesman, says: *Wien gehört zu Europa, doch gleich hinter Erdberg beginnt der ~* Vienna is part of Europe all right, but the moment Erdberg [= until 1850 a suburb of Vienna, and since then part of its third municipal district] is passed, the inefficiencies of Balkan misrule are beginning to assert themselves.

Ballesterer *m* -s/- [an agent noun in *-er,* blending ModG > NHG *Ball* and L *ballista* 'catapult, i.e. an ancient military contrivance for hurling stones, etc.'] *hum.* or slightly *contp.* football player *(Fußballspieler)*: leather-kicker, *BrE* ball-basher, *AmE* soccerist, soccerite; *da diese ~ nach Ablauf der regulären Spielzeit ja doch nur ein Unentschieden zusammengebracht hatten, war eine Verlängerung notwendig* as those knockabouts had only managed a draw at full time, the game had to go into extra time. – **ballẹstern** *v/i colloq.* to play football (not necessarily in a regular match, but just for fun): to kick the ball about; *geht's woandershin bittschön, vor dem Haus da wird nicht ballestert!* go somewhere else please, no footballing in front of my house!

Bạmpf *m* -(e)s *colloq.* **1.** *cul.* any food that tastes soft and thick and heavy *(dicker Brei)*: mush; *ich mag keinen Erdäpfelschmarren, das ist mir zuviel ~* I don't care for mashed potatoes, they're too mushy; cp. *anbampfen* ↑. – **2.** something crumpled into a ball *(Knäuel)*: wad. – **bạmpfen** *vt/i. colloq. (mampfen)* **1.** *v/i* slightly *colloq.* to eat in big mouthfuls, esp. food that tastes soft and thick and heavy (and that, as a consequence, distends the eater's cheeks): to pig out, to be stuffing the nest. – **2.** *v/t* to eat at a stoically sustained pace: to munch; *vor dem Fernseher sitzen und sinnlos Soletti ~ ist einfach Spitze* sitting in front of the TV and pigging out on pretzel sticks is simply the best.

bạmstig *adj colloq.* **1.** said of a radish or a cucumber that is old, or has been harvested late *(saftlos, schwammig)*: juiceless, spongy. – **2.** said of parts of the human body *(taub, hohl)*: benumbed, numb; *ich habe so ein ~es Gefühl im Finger* my finger feels kind of (*AmE* kinda) numb, as if swollen.

Bạndl *n* -s/-(n) [dim. of *Band n* 'ribbon'] *colloq.* ribbon: string, piece of twine; *fig. phr. j-n am ~ haben* to keep someone under control: to have someone on a short leash cp. *anbandeln* ↑. – **~tanz** *m* -es/ … tänze *folklore* an old folk custom deriving from a dance around the maypole; as the dancers circle, they all progressively plait the red and white ribbons about the pole: ribbon dance.

barabern *v/i colloq.* to do heavy manual work *(schwer arbeiten)*: to slog away; *in den Ferien hat er am Bau barabert, um Geld zu verdienen* in the holidays he slogged away on a building site to earn some money.

Bạrbara *Chr. n.* one of the fourteen auxiliary saints, whose day is December 4: **~zweig** *m* -(e)s, usu. *pl.* -e; more commonly, **~zweigerl** *n* -s, usu. *pl.* -(n) *folklore* "St Barbara twigs", slim branches of a cherry tree broken off on the saint's name day, and put into water (daily renewed) as private oracles – the ones that are in flower by Christmas spell good luck, the barren ones bring tears.

Barbaropa *n* -s [a blend coined by Albert Ehrenstein, 1886–1950, a Vienna-born cultural philosopher, expressionist poet, and novelist] *civ. & lit.* "Barbarian Europe", claimed to be infested with a hollow civilization (witness the sham elegance, and lack of grief, at a good many Austrian funerals; → *Leich 2)* that the cultured might well be tempted to take spiritual flight from.

Bärendreck *m* -s [a drastic metaphorical swing, on the strength of shape and colour, from animal faeces to human food] *comest., colloq.* (*Lakritze*[*nstange* or -*schnur*]) "bear's dung", a confectionery made from liquorice, a black substance produced from the sweet-tasting dried root of Glycyrrhiza glabra, a leguminous plant.

bärig *adj colloq.* excellent: super, *BrE a.* jolly good, not half bad; *ich danke recht schön für den ~en Empfang* thank you very much for the great reception; *die Brettln sind bei der Abfahrt heute ~ gelaufen* my [our] boards raced just divinely down the slopes today.

Barnabịt *m* -en/-en *R. C. relig.* Barnabite, a member of the Clerics Regular of St Paul, or Barnabites, so named after the ancient church of Barnabas in Milan acquired by them in 1538; the order was active in the Austrian Counter-Reformation and promoted the cult of the Virgin Mary (hence the name of the Viennese district, *Mariahilf,* after the order's principal church there, built in 1689).

Bạrtwisch *m* -(e)s/-e *(Handbesen)* hand-brush; *bring mir die Mistschaufel und den ~* get me the dustpan and brush.

Bassena *f* -/-s [< It *bacino* 'basin'] *archit. & soc. hist. (gemeinsame Wasserstelle am Gang e-s alten Wiener Zinshauses)* cast-iron bowl-cum-watertap fixture, one on each floor of old Viennese tenement houses; *an* (or, *bei) der ~ trifft die eine Hausfrau alle paar Stunden die andere, da wird natürlich getratscht und weitergetratscht, aber da entzündet sich auch kleinlicher Streit* every few hours, housewives meet at the tap outside (their flats), which readily becomes a clearing-house for gossip, and also a focal point for petty squabbles. – **~tratsch** *m* -es *(Klatsch niedrigen Niveaus)* cheap gossip(-mongering). – **~wohnung** *f* -/-en *(kleine, billige Gangwohnung)* old and small tenement flat, with no indoor plumbing; *eine ~ steht natürlich unter Mieterschutz, man zahlt dafür nur vier Schilling pro Quadratmeter* of course, old tenement flats are rent-controlled, the charge being only four Austrian shillings per square metre.

Bauch ...: ~fleck *m* -(e)s/-e *colloq., sports* a badly-judged dive in which one's stomach hits the water first *(Bauchklatscher)*: belly flop (*or* dive), belly-flopper, belly-flapper, belly-smacker, belly-whopper, *AmE & AustralE* belly-buster, *BrE a.* (belly-)gutser; *einen ~ machen (*or *fabrizieren)* to (do a) belly-flop, *BrE a.* to gutter. – **~fleisch** *n* -(e)s *cul. (Schweinebauch)* belly of pork.

Bauchi *n* -s/- *baby talk,* and *joc.* in adult speech – stomach: tummy, *AmE a.* tum-tum; *deck dich zu, damit dein ~ nicht kalt bekommt!* cover yourself up so your tummy won't get cold. ‖ → *Bussi.* – **~wehweh** *n* -s/-(s) stomach trouble: tummy-ache; *Mammi, ich hab ~* Mummy (*AmE* Mommy), my tummy hurts.

Bauch ...: ~plätschen *f* -/- = *Bauchfleck.* – **~wehblume** *f* -/-n Salzburg *dial. (Edelweiss)* ⚘ "tummy-ache flower", a popular name for the edelweiss, or "white jewel", because of its medicinal properties. – **~zwicken** *n* -s *med.* stomach cramps.

Bauer *m* -n/-n **1.** farmer; *hist.,* and if referring to a smallholder, peasant ‖ in *colloq.* phrases: (1) a proverbial wisdom bred in the conservative and the cautious: *was der ~ nicht kennt, frisst er nicht* if it's different it is wrong. – (2) a jocular question-and-answer spiel, teas-

A peasant threesome from the Innsbruck area – come alive for us through an old copper engraving by W. Alexander, Picturesque Representations of the Dress and Manners of the Austrians *(1813)*

Peter Anich, "The Peasant Cartographer"

ingly offered by the host (who falls into heavy dialect as he volunteers the solution) at one point when entertaining a tableful of happy eaters: *wann freut sich der ~ am meisten? ... wann's Viech frisst!* *when is the farmer happiest? ... when the cattle are feeding! – **2.** *card playing* in the game of *Bauernschnapsen* ↓: the highest card of the pack (*AmE* deck), exceeding an ace – no mean reflection on the status of dignity inherent in the name *Bauer.*

Bauern ...: ~bub *m* -en/-en young peasant boy. – **~bühne** *f* -/-n peasant theatre. – **~bursch** *m* -en/-en country lad. – **~butter** *f* - *cul. BrE* farmhouse butter, *AmE* home-made butter. – **~funk** *m* -s agricultural radio programme (*AmE* ... program), "The Farmer's Hour", *AmE* "The Farm Report". **~heilige** *m* -n, **~herrgott** *m* -s, *relig. folklore* "saint of peasants", St Leonhard, the patron saint of all farm animals who is therefore given a special status by the faithful in the country. – **~jagd** *f* -/-en *hunt.* integrated hunting area, actually belonging to several farmers, but temporarily leased as a whole. – **~kartograph** *m* -en *geog.* "Peasant Cartographer", an honorary epithet for Peter Anich, 1723–66, a brilliant mathematician as well as designer of globes and mountain maps; his, and Blasius Hueber's, *Atlas Tyrolensis* is a mine of information on his native country before the great changes of the next decades set in. – **~kaviar** *m* -s *cul. hum.* = *Zellersalat.* – **~krapfen** *m* -s/- *cul.* plate-sized hefty yeast doughnut, *AmE* funnel cake. – **~markt** *m* -(e)s/ ... märkte & farmers' market, held in villages or small towns at regular intervals (once a year, every fortnight, etc.); the occasion presents a lively scene where eggs, bacon, pellets of pollen, honey, home-baked goods, liqueurs and brandy are offered for sale from the entrances of private homes or from wooden stalls in the market square. – **~regel** *f* -/-n a piece of rustic weather wisdom (*or* weather lore): weather saw. – **~rennen** *n* -s/- *skiing* country boys' competition; *diese Abfahrtsstrecke ist ja für ein ~ und nicht für Olympiaprofis präpariert* this downhill run has been prepared for a bunch of amateurs and not for Olympic professionals. – **~schmaus** *m* -es *cul.* "Farmer's Delight", sauerkraut, garnished with a slice of roast pork and smoked ham, one frankfurter, potatoes and one bread dumpling.

Note: In Northern Germany, a ~ consists of one fried egg [*Spiegelei*], ham, and fried potatoes.

~schnapsen *n* -s *card-playing* a regional card game: "peasants' brandy dip", a complicated version of *Schnapsen* ↓ in which four people take part; the one who wins all the tricks is the *Bauer.* – **~schnapser** *m* -s/- round (*or* game) of the above card game; *spielen* (or *machen*) *wir noch einen ~!* let's have another round of "peasants' brandy dip", let's get another game of "peasants' brandy dip" going. – **~speck** *m* -s *cul.* home-cured bacon. – **~stüberl** *n* -s/-(n) "rustic snug", a small, cosy room, with plain country-style furniture and, most often, panelled *[getäfelt]* on all sides. – **~theater** *n* -s/- = *Bauernbühne.* – **~trampel** *m* -s/-(n) *contp.* a derisive term for a woman of unrefined manners, often quickly ostracized by city dwellers because she is of rural descent: country bumpkin, *AmE a.* hayseed, hick, hillbilly. – **~viertelstund** *f* -/-n *dial. hum.* in Styria: "peasant's quarter of an hour", i.e. longer than fifteen minutes (cp. *E* baker's dozen 'thirteen'). – **~wiese** *f* -/-n field grass, natural lawn; *um unser Landhaus haben wir eine ~, keinen gepflegten Rasen* there is no proper lawn round our country house, just field grass.

Baum *m* -(e)s/Bäume [actually, 'tree'; in the following phrase used either generally, in the sense of an obstacle planted in the way, or specifically, as a shortening of *Schlagbaum* 'toll bar' or '(customs) barrier'] *AusG colloq.* **einen ~ aufstellen** to raise objections often felt by the angry speaker to be symptomatic of some puny obstructionist policy: to kick up a fuss; *die Anrainer haben überhaupt keinen Grund, gegen die Pläne für den kleinen neuen Flugplatz einen ~ aufzustellen* the local residents have no reason whatever to fuss and kick against the plans for the new airfield.

Baunzerl *n* -s/-(n) [< It *pancino* < L *panicillus* 'small roll'] *bak.* a thin piece of fruit (apple, pear, etc.) sugared and dipped in wine, covered with a mixture of egg and flour and cooked in hot fat *(Beignet)*: fritter.

Baze or **Bazi** *m* -/Bazen *or* Bazi [?< Lum*pazi*vagabundus, a conglomerate word creation by Johann Nestroy for his dialect comedy on the wandering life of a happy-go-lucky Biedermeier threesome (1833)] *colloq.*, often in *dial.* context – either an angry or an indulgently, sometimes even fully, appreciative epithet for a male: **1.** said with bitterness about a dishonest person (*Gauner*): crook, rogue, scoundrel; *das war der größte ~, der je auf Gottes Erdboden herumgelaufen ist!* he was the biggest crook that ever was graced to walk on God's earth, *NorBrE a.* … the biggest rogue unhung. – **2.** *hum.* or in slight annoyance – a person, esp. a child, who plays tricks but is regarded with fondness (*Schelm*): rascal, *BrE a.* scallywag, *AmE a.* scalawag; *wo hat denn der ~ meine Schlüssel versteckt?* where has that rascal hidden my keys? – **3.** *hum.* or *euphem.* in mock abuse, often from the buyer to the seller, after a business has been concluded among partners of many years' standing, and a formal act of hospitality is then asked for to wind up the deal (*Schlawiner*): old rogue *or* villain, (blasted) so-and-so; *jetzt spendierst aber glei' a Trumm Gselchts, du ~, du (ganz) schlechter!* well, it's high time now you dish out a big chunk of smoked meat, you old rogue! – **4.** *apprec.* one who achieved something against heavy odds, or one who did so barely "on the brink of legality" (*Tausendsas*[*s*]*a*): cunning devil, sly customer; *pfüat di Gott, des is' dir ein ~!* jee whizz, there's a cunning devil for you!

bedạkeln = *betakeln.*

Bein…: ~fleisch *n* -(e)s/pl. rare: -(e) *cul.* boiled (bones of) beef – a rhyming couplet, after a humorous dialect poem by Josef Weinheber, describing a self-indulgent Phaeacian, a rather choosy epicure:

> *… ein saft'ges Beinfleisch, doch nicht fett,*
> *sonst kriegt man mit 'm Bauch sein Gfrett*
>
> … some juicy beef, a meaty bone,
> not fat, or else your bowels groan.

~hart *adj & adv* (as) hard as bone – (1) said of a person who is very tough, or completely callous and unfeeling: (as) hard as nails. – (2) said of a piece of ground, a ski-run, a cake, etc.: rock-hard; *der Erdboden war ~ gefroren* the soil was frozen solid. – **~richter** *m* -s/- *med. hist.* the occupational name for a person, usu. not formally qualified, who set broken or dislocated bones (*Knocheneinrichter*): bone-setter. – **~schinken** *m* -s/- *cul.* (hot) ham of pork.

Beinlvieh, Beindlvieh *n* -s [dim.; first el. < *Bein* 'horn'] Alpine *dial.* *(Hornvieh)* horned cattle; *das ~ ist im Stall* the (horned) cattle are in the shed.

Beiried *n* -(e)s; or *f* - *cul.* the choicer part of a loin of beef (*hinteres Lendenstück*): sirloin.

Beisel, Beisl *n* -s/-n *colloq.,* often *contp.* disreputable inn *(schäbiges, kleines Gasthaus)*: grubby little pub.

Beißer *m* -s/- Viennese *sl.* (street) tough, ruffian, rowdy, bully, *ScotE a.* keelie; *ein echter ~ aus Glasgow* a real Glasgow (['glæzgɪ]) keelie. – **~pferd** *n* -(e)s/-e Viennese *sl.* = *Schlurfrakete.*

Beißwurm *m* -s/ … würmer [second el., *orig.* 'anything that creeps'] *dial.* **1.** *(Schlange)* snake. – **2.** *myth.* = *Tatzelwurm* ↓.

Bẹlla gerạnt aliị; tụ, felix Austria, nụbe! Nạm quae Mạrs aliis, dạt tibi rẹgna Venụs! *hist.* a famous distich dating from the fifteenth century (but actually based on a passage in Ovid's *Heroides,* 13, 84); the witticism serves as a confirmation of the policy, adopted by some Hapsburg rulers towards the end of the Middle Ages, to seek dynastic aggrandizement through judicious marital alliances rather than through military conquest (an instance being the marriages, at Vienna in 1515, of Emperor Maximilian I.'s grandchildren, by which Bohemia, Moravia, and Hungary fell to the crown of Austria):

> Let wars be waged by others; you, happy Austria,
> marry! Venus presents you with realms,
> where others must get them through Mars.

Here we can see the process at work, and also how frequently Mars deprived the Hapsburgs of the gifts of Venus.

Bẹrg…: ~feuer, or **Herz-Jesu-Feuer** *n* -s/- [though probably originating in a pagan festival to celebrate the summer solstice, the present custom commemorates the French invasion of Southern Tyrol in 1796, when the Province was spiritually entrusted to the Most Sacred Heart of Jesus Christ] *R. C. & folklore* an impressive occasion on Midsummer Night, but esp. on the second Friday after Corpus

Natives reverently stand around religious bonfires being lit on mountainsides in early summer

Christi Day (or on the Sunday after): mountain bonfire, lit on many crags and slopes; *bei einbrechender Nacht des Herz-Jesu-Festes leuchten rundum auf den Höhen, zumeist in Form eines großen Herzens, ~ auf* by nightfall, during the Feast of the Sacred Heart of Jesus, bonfires flare up all around on high, usually taking the shape of a huge heart. – **~fex** *m* -en/-en *(leidenschaftlicher Bergsteiger)* mountain fan (*or* enthusiast), *colloq.* mountain-climbing freak; *er ist ein ~* he's mountain-crazy; *zünftiges ~enleben* = → *Hüttenzauber.* – **~lauf** *m* -(e)s/ … läufe *sports* a popular physical pastime in the mountain areas of Austria and South Tyrol, but also an event in European championships – (1) as a type of sport: uphill running *or* racing. – (2) as a specific fixture in time and venue: uphill run *or* race. – **~putzer** *m* -s/- in the City of Salzburg: "mountain-cleaner", one of a team that clears the Mönchsberg rock-face of loose stones in Spring, to prevent damage to the houses and streets below. – **~wecken** *n* -s *folklore* in West Tyrol, at Mauls near Sterzing, and elsewhere, one night in late Spring: "mountain reveille" [rɪˈvælɪ], the boisterous herding together, by village youths with whips and rattles, of the local cattle before their making the ascent to the Alpine summer pastures (→ *Almauftrieb*); starting in the wee hours ensures that the mountain snow is still hard enough so that the cattle can safely cross over.

Bẹrschtln *pl. folklore* "Cleansing Demons" (related to the → *Perchten)* and a witch who visit farmhouses in the Lower Inn Valley of the Tyrol on St Nicholas' Day (December 6) or its eve; the demons, decked out in corn husks, jump around wildly in the "best parlours" to spur on the fertility spirits, while the witch officiously sweeps the floor to drive away evil.

beschụmmeln *v/t* [cp. *schummeln*] = *betakeln.*

Beschwịchtigungs …: ~hofrat *m* -(e)s/ … räte [*Hofrat* ↓ here stands for the prototype of 'aulic councillor' at once dignified, mature, mild, and worldly-wise through long years spent in the Austrian Civil Service] *colloq.* (sometimes *sarc.,* if dissatisfied with his role) elderly person who tries to relieve tension between conflicting parties: bona fide mediator (*or*, appeaser), *sarc.* pussyfooting peacemaker, mealy-mouthed go-between. – **~politik** *f* - *polit.* policy of appeasement, that pursued by the Austrian government vis-à-vis Hitler's menace, during the mid-1930s, to bring about the → *Anschluss.*

Beserl *n* -s/-(n) [dim. of *Besen* 'broom', 'besom'] *colloq.* **1.** little broom (e.g., one children use to play house with). – **2.** small broom without a handle: whisk. – **3.** *cul.* basting brush. – **4.** (also, *Tisch~)* crumb brush; *nimm das Schauferl und das ~ und wisch die Brösel vom Tisch* take the crumb brush and tray, and sweep the crumbs from the table.

betạkeln *v/t* [< Yiddish *daggel* 'to cheat'] *colloq. (betrügen)* to cheat: to do, to have; *lass dich nicht ~!* don't allow yourself to be done (in the eye)!, *AmE & CanE sl.* don't take any wooden nickels! – **Betakelei** *f* -/-en *colloq. (Betrug)* cheating; *das ist (eine) glatte ~!* that's a barefaced swindle!

Austrian Roadside Greetings … … of Welcome and Farewell
Such picturesque signboards on the outskirts of many villages have delighted both visitors and passing wayfarers for a long time. Native speakers of English, moreover, for instance Tasmanians, here no doubt find a ready incentive to compare them, and to pair them, with such cheerful messages as "Hello, Strangers" … "Good-bye, Friends" – very similar tokens of goodwill the world over.

Beugel *n* -s/- [< dial. *Baug* 'buckle', 'ring', related to *biegen v/t* 'to bend'] *bak.* a kind of filled bun made of short-crust pastry (*Mürbteig*) shaped like two tiny funnels 'welded' together at an acute angle, its surface having a shiny coating (*Gebäck in Form eines geknickten Hörnchens*): filled cornet, bun; *Mohn~* poppy-seed bun; *Nuss~* nut bun; *Pressburger ~* "Pressburg Crescent", a pastry rather like a coffee-cake, and richly filled with ground walnuts.

Beuschel *n* -s [< MHG *beischerl, beischl* 'edible lung of animals', dim. of *Bausch m* 'bulge', 'roll'] **1.** *cul. (Lungenhaschee)* hashed lung meat, often served with a dumpling. – **2.** low *colloq. phr.* used by one breathless from physical exhaustion, esp. after running very fast: *mir hängt jetzt das ~ raus BrE* I'm bloody winded now, *AmE* (I feel like) I'm dragging a lung behind me, I think I lost a lung back there.

b'hüat di', pfiat di', pfiati (variant spellings, from the near-etymological to the near-phonetic, bat always pronounced [ˈpfɪətɪ], for the unabridged greeting, in standard German, *Gott behüte dich!* God preserve you!) *dial.* **1.** a devout, yet warm farewell among relatives, close friends, and associates on the *du* ('thou' [ðaʊ]) basis, (1) with the speaker rather aware of the religious origin of the phrase, and expanding it into a ~ ~ *Gott!:* God bless (you)!, the Lord bless (you)!, bless you! (2) with the speaker rather detached from, or entirely unaware of, the sacred origin of the phrase: bye-bye!, bye! [often pronounced: ˈbaɪ–aɪ], *BrE* bye-di-bye!, *AmE* take care!, *AustralE* ciao [tʃaʊ]. – **2.** *interj.* an outcry of gentle dismay, simulated or real; often expanded into a *na ~ ~ Gott!* oh good Lord!, oh my God!, oh my goodness!, more *colloq. AmE* lordy(-lordy)!, Southern *AmE* lawsy!; said to one who suddenly appears, say, in a woefully bedraggled state: *na ~ ~ Gott* (or, *~ ~ Gott, Stasi), du schaust (aber) aus!* holy Godfrey (*or,* holy Christopher), you (do) look a sight (*or* a fright)! – **3.** *interj.* (1) jocularly said in farewell to the last drop of wine, beer, etc. before imbibing it: *~ ~ (Gott), Lackerl!* down the hatch, mate! (In English, there is a similar banter, in which the addressee is not the drink but the stomach of the imbiber: "Over cheeks, over gums, / Look out, belly, here it comes!") (2) no longer thinking of sense 3 (1), and solely with the emotive connotation of gentle dismay as mentioned under **2**: *na ~ ~ Gott, Lackerl! BrE* o ye gods and little fishes!, *AmE* by jiminy!, jeepers creepers!

Bịldstock *m* -(e)s/ … stöcke *R. C. (gemauerte oder steinerne Denksäule [mit figuralem Schmuck]* wayside shrine; *der Bauer bekreuzigte sich, als er an dem ~ vorüberging* the farmer crossed himself as he passed the wayside shrine.

A picturesque wayside shrine in the Austrian Alps inviting passers-by to say a silent prayer

Billet<u>eu</u>r [bɪjɛˈtøːə] *m* -s/-e someone who shows people to their seats at a theatre, cinema, or circus *(Platzanweiser)*: usher.

Billẹtt [bɪˈjeː & bɪˈlɛt] *n* -(e)s/-s & -s *(Glückwunschbriefchen)* letter-card of congratulations.

Bịndenschild *m* -(e)s *heraldry* banded shield, red-white-red escutcheon, the central part of the Austrian coat-of-arms, which can be dated back to a seal of Duke Frederick II in 1230.

Bi<u>o</u>tik *f* - *philosophy* a late-Biedermeier system of social ethics, evolved by Adolf Stöhr, 1855–1921, emphasizing the phenomenon of suffering: biotics;

die ~ verfolgt zwei Ziele, ein positives wie ein negatives – jedem Menschen beizubringen, wie er das Leid zu mindern (Ethik) und wie die Freude zu mehren (Kultur) vermag biotics has two goals – its negative task is to teach each individual to diminish suffering (ethics), while its positive function is to promote enjoyment (culture).

bịs *conj. colloq. (sobald, wenn)* as soon as, when; *er soll mich bitte anrufen, ~ er wieder da ist* I'd be happy to get a ring (*AmE* call) from him as soon as he's back.

Biskọtte *f* -/-n, *dial.* **Bischkotten** [bɪʃ-ˈkoːdn] *f* -/- [< It *biscotto* < MedL *biscoctus* 'twice-baked (scilicet *panis* bread)'] *cul.* a small cake shaped like a finger – light and sweet, made from eggs, sugar, and flour but usually not fat (*Löffelbiskuit*): sponge finger, *BrE* lady's finger, *AmE* ladyfinger; *at children's party a.* nursery finger. – **-ntorte** *f* cake made of alternate layers of sponge fingers and cream, *Am.* lady finger cake, refrigerator cake.

Biskuịtfisch [bɪsˈkwɪt–] *m* -es/-e *cul. & folklore* spongefish, a New Year's Day breakfast dainty which for good luck has to be eaten tail first.

bịssi [dim. of *Bissen* 'bite', used affectionately] *colloq.* **ein ~** a (little) bit: *BrE* a wee bit, *AmE* a little teeny bit: **1.** *adv* in *phr. geh leg dich doch hin und schau, ob du ein ~ schlafen kannst!* why don't you lie down and try and get a leetle bit of sleep (*or* some sleep, honey)?; *streng dich nur ein ~ an* (you don't know until you try,) just give it a shot. – **2.** *adj gib mir ein ~ Geld!* can I borrow a tiny bit of money?

Bịtten *n* -s in *phr.* used in slight disappointment or annoyance when an offer of food, material assistance, and so forth is turned down: *~ und Geben ist zuviel* I offered and they *(etc.)* refused my gesture – so much for them *(etc.)*!

bitte sehr, bitte gleich! *phr.* a familiar quotation by Karl Blasel, 1831–1922, a Viennese comedian; once the standard patter of long-serving waiters in venerable cafés, it is nowadays broadly used to give a positive reply a humorously obsequious ring: yes, sir, right away, sir!

blạnk *adv colloq. (ohne Überrock)* without an overcoat; *nach dem heurigen strengen Winter kann man heute endlich zum ersten Mal (wieder) ~ gehen* today is the first time after this year's severe winter that you can go outside without a coat on, after this year's severe winter you need not take an overcoat (*or,* people may walk without overcoats) for the first time today.

Blasiussegen *m* -s *R. C. relig.* on St Blaise's Day, February 3: "Blessing of the Throat", a ceremony in which two long candles are blessed and lighted, and tied together with ribbons in the form of a St Andrew's Cross; sufferers with throat ailments, or those afraid of being afflicted, kneel while the priest lays the ribboned cross under their chins and blesses them.

Blaukraut *n* -(e)s ♣ a short-stemmed plant with a mass of bluish-red leaves, forming a dense head (*Rotkohl*): red cabbage, 🕮 Brassica oleracea var. capitata f. rubra.

Blẹchtrottel *m* -s/- *hum.* or slightly *contp.* personal or other computer (esp. when viewing its blindly obedient, and there-

E. HARRISON
COMPTON

fore often faulty, productions): electronic moron.

Bleigießen *n* -s *folklore* on New Year's Eve: lead-melting, the holiday custom of putting a small figure of lead into a spoon, holding it over the fire, and pouring the molten lump into a bucket of cold water; this congeals into a bizarre shape which is supposed to tell what the next year will bring – a boat means travel, a ring marriage or engagement, small droplets are money.

Blöhu [blø:ˈhu:] *abbr.* slightly euphemistic for *blö*der *Hu*nd 'silly ass': S.O.B. [ˈesəʊˈbi:] (< *s*on *o*f a *b*itch); *so ein ~, hat der schon wieder auf mein Buch vergessen!* what a berk (*BrE; AmE* dork), did he forget (to bring) my book again!

Blọndel *m* -s, or more fully, **der Sänger ~** *folklore* a legendary figure, known through an old French ballad: Blondel, Richard the Lion-heart's minstrel, who in 1193 discovered his captive King's whereabouts at Dürnstein, in the Wachau, after he had wandered down the Danube from castle to castle singing his lost master's favourite songs and listening for a response from behind the walls.

Blumenkorso *m* -s/-s *hist.* floral parade, carnival of flowers; this was initiated in Vienna by Princess Pauline Metternich, 1836–1921, as an annual competition to highlight the traditional May Day parade of celebrities at the Prater.

Blụnze *f* -/-n *gastr.,* rare, a stilted standard form for next, 1 & 2. – **Blụnzen** *f* -/- **1.** *gastr.* a sausage made from pig's blood, often containing small cubes of bacon: *BrE* black pudding, *AmE* blood sausage, blutwurst, *IrE* drisheen ‖ placing an order at an inn: *zwei ~ mit Sauerkraut BrE* one plate of black pudding and pickled cabbage, *AmE* two blood sausages with sauerkraut. – **2.** P *contp.* a fat unshapely person, often an elderly female: *BrE* jelly-belly, jelly-wobble, lump of lard, rubber-guts, fat slag, *AmE* blubberpot, five by five; *das ist (dir) eine ~! BrE* (look,) she [he] 's a right pudding, *AmE* ... a tub of lard. – **3.** *fig.* an expression of crude indifference: *das ist mir ~!* it doesn't make the slightest difference, *BrE a.* I couldn't care less, as if I cared, *AmE a.* I don't care (*or* give) a brass button, I don't give a continental.

Richard I of England at Dürnstein Castle, and Blondel*'s search for him, must have duly inspired the artist E. Harrison Compton*

Boarfak *m* -s/-(en) Tyrolean *dial.* [first el. vowel, <oa> < <ei>, as in *Stoan, Roan* < *Stein, Rain;* second el., < *Ferkel* 'pig' (-a- < -er-; similarly in ModE *star* < ME *sterre, far* < *ferre, farm* < *ferme*)] *hist.* between 1805 and 1815: "Bavarian swine", an abusive term for a Bavarian, or the Bavarian troops collectively, who occupied the Tyrol after it was ceded to the Kingdom of Bavaria, an ally of Napoleon, under the Peace of Pressburg.

Böhmak, Bọmak [ˈbø:–ˈbema:k (imitative of a native's pronunciation)] *m* -s/-en [< *Böhm* + Cz masc. suffix *-ák*] *colloq.,* slightly *contp. (Böhme, Tscheche)* native of Bohemia, Czechia, or Slovakia: Bohemian, Czech, or Slovak: Bohunk, bohunk. – **böhmakeln, bọmakeln** *v/i colloq.* **1.** to speak with a strong Czech accent or intonation (cp. *zusammenböhmakeln* ↓). → **2.** to speak broken German *(radebrechen)*: to fumble around in

German, to speak pidgin German; → **3.** *(unverständlich sprechen)* to talk gibberish; *ich war so müde, ich habe nur mehr ~ können* I was so tired I could only talk double Dutch. – **Bö̱hmen** *n* -s *geogr. & polit.* Bohemia, one of the Crown Countries of the Austro-Hungarian Monarchy, now part of Czechia or Slovakia ‖ *hum.* or *sarc.,* in a phr. directed against s.o.'s slowness in action: *bis du mit der Arbeit fertig bist, vergeht in ~ ein Jahr* (or, *geht in ~ ein Viertel ein)!* Spring will be round again before you have finished that job!, you'll never finish that job at the rate you're going!, *AmE a.* at that job you're as slow as molasses (in wintertime)!

Bo̱snickel, *dial.* **Bo̱snigl** *m* -s/-(n) [second el., < *Nikolaus* 'Nicholas', a once popular Christian name in Austria and Southern Germany – in English corresponding to *Nichol* and *Nick*] *colloq.* an irascible and spiteful person (*boshafter Mensch*): irritable old cuss, nasty thing, *AmE a.* (old) meanie.

Brạmburi usu. *pl.* only [< Czech *brambory* 'potatoes', an adaptation of *Brandenburger,* indicating the original place of cultivation] nearly always *hum. (Kartoffeln)* potatoes: spuds, taters, taties, *IrE* murphies, *AmE a.* kartoffels.

Brạnd …: ~leger *m,* **~legerin** *f (Brandstifter[in f] m)* incendiary, *jur.* arsonist, *AmE colloq.* firebug. – **~legung** *f (Brandstiftung)* arson. – **~statt** *f (Brandstätte)* scene of fire.

brạndeln *vt/i* **1.** *v/i colloq.* (1) to have a burnt smell *(nach Verbranntem riechen)*: to smell burnt; *was brandelt denn da so, habt ihr etwas angezündet?* what's that burning, have you lit a fire? (2) *fig.* said of an impending crisis, a political upheaval, etc. *(kriseln): es brandelt* it is touch and go (with the present set-up, etc.). (3) *fig.* a comment, or a piece of encouraging advice, in the game of hide-and-seek: *es brandelt!* *you may well get a whiff of the fire, you're getting warm (i.e., you are already very close [to the object hidden])! – **2.** *v/t* low *colloq. ([übermäßig viel] zahlen)* to pay an exorbitant sum of money, and/or to pay against one's will: to pay through the nose; *ihn hat die Polizei betrunken beim Autofahren erwischt, er hat ganz schön ~ müssen* the police caught him drunk driving, and that cost him a tidy sum (*or AmE,* an arm and a leg).

Brạndl *n* -s/-(n) *colloq.* [dim. of *Brand* 'fire'] **1.** rarely: little, harmless fire. – **2.** *fig. (kleine Eigenheit)* slight oddity; esp. in the *prov.* often quoted by women when asserting a superior sense of mental balance in the female: *jedes Mandl hat sein ~* every man is a bit touched.

Brạnntweiner *m* -s/- **1.** keeper of a brandy tavern. – **2.** *contp.* one addicted to drinking brandy and other liquor to excess: brandy face, rumpot, *AmE* brandy hound, rum soak. – **~nase** *f* -/-n a fiery red nose claimed to be due to an excessive consumption of heavy alcohol: brandy nose; *der mit seiner ~ will mir weismachen, dass er täglich nur ein Achterl konsumiert!* this character with his brandy nose wants me to believe that he only drinks a jigger (*AmE a.* a snifter) per day.

Brạnntweinschank *f* -/-en *(Branntweinschenke)* brandy tavern.

Brẹnner *m* -s [< "the broones (or Breuni),

subdued among other Northern barbarians by Drusus after his crossing in 15 B. C." *(Chambers Encyclopædia);* or 'the burnt area', i.e. the one cleared of forest trees] **1.** *geog.* also, **~sattel** *m* -s Brenner (Pass), a watershed between the Adriatic and the Black Sea, the lowest place of transit from north to south in the Eastern Alps (1372 metres [4,501 ft]); the col was used even before Roman times and now serves as part of what is derisively dubbed the → *Auspuff Europas.* – **2.** *lit. hist. Brenner,* a distinguished Catholic journal of art and civilization, 1910–1954; orchestrated by Ludwig Ficker, an Innsbruck scholar, it served as a mouthpiece for early expressionist writers and poets.

brẹnn ...: ~heiß *adj & adv, colloq.* usu. in attributive use with reference to soup, an electric iron, etc. – very hot: hot as hell, scorching ‖ *es ist mir eben ~ eingefallen, dass ich ja heute noch Brot einkaufen muss* it just hit me like a brick that I still have to buy some bread today. – **~suppe** *f* -/-n, *dial.* **~supp(e)n** *f* -/- **1.** *cul. (Suppe aus Mehlschwitze)* brown soup, flavoured with onions and wine. – **2.** *colloq. phr.* a claim to be not gullible, but shrewder than given credit for: *ich bin auch nicht auf der ~ dahergeschwommen* I wasn't born yesterday, *BrE a.* I didn't come here on a banana boat, *NZE & AustralE a.* I didn't come down in the last shower.

Brẹttl, much less often **Brẹttel** *n* -s/-(n) [< *Brett n* 'board' + dim. *-(e)l* I. *colloq.* **1.** (a) a thin narrow flat piece of wood (*Brettchen*): slat. – (b) a small thin piece of building material, esp. wood, laid in rows to cover a roof (*Dachschindel*): shingle ‖ *phr.* (a) slurs on an uncurvaceous female: *sie hat eine Figur wie ein ~ mit zwei Erbsen; sie is' hint' wie ein Laden und vorn wie ein ~* she's all bones without bulges, she looks the same coming and going, *AmE a.* she's as flat as a board, she's a slabsides. – (b) a graphic warning to a miser: *warum so aufs Geld aussein? – du hast in sechs oder acht ~n auch noch Platz!* why be such a money-grubbing lot? – shrouds have no pockets (*or,* you can't take it with you)! → **2.** *sports* mostly pl. *~(n) colloq.* a pair of skis [ski:z] (Schi[er]): boards, woods, *AmE a.* slats ‖ the first lines of a spirited skiing song –

Zwoa Brettln, a g'führiga Schnee, juchhe!
Des is' halt die höchste Idee.

*Two boards, snow to dash through in glee, yippee!
What greater delight can there be?

phr.: zum ersten Mal im Leben auf (den) ~n stehen to be on skis for the first time in one's life; *jedes Schihaserl wird bald merken, dass sich die ~n beherrschen lassen* any snow bunny will soon learn that the boards can be controlled; *ich bin heuer im Winter fast jedes Wochenende mit den ~n weggewesen* I was away (*or,* I went) skiing nearly every weekend this winter. – **II.** *theat.* a theatre producing satirical revues (*Kleinkunstbühne*): intimate theatre, cabaret [ˈkæbəreɪ].

brẹttl ... [see preceding entry, I. 1] in cpds. – **~breit,** dial. **~brat, ~broat** *adv,* often used with a tinge of disapproval – **1.** taking up (unusually) much space: full-length, full out; *der müde Bruder hat sich ~ auf das Sofa geschmissen* (that *or* our) Tired Tim flopped down (*or,* sprawled out) full-length on the couch; *genussvoll lehnt sie sich ~ zum Fenster* *hinaus – was kann denn da ihren Luchsaugen noch entgehen?* she relishes to plant herself, elbows apart, on the sill of the open window – what can then escape her eagle eyes? – **2.** said very directly, or even rudely: point-blank, fair and square; *er hat ihm ~ gesagt, wie es ausschaut* he told him point-blank what the situation was. – **~eben,** dial. **~ebm** *adj* said of some country areas – very flat or unusually flat: (as) flat as a pancake; *ähnlich dem englischen Norfolk ist das Marchfeld, nordöstlich von Wien gelegen, zumeist ~* Marchfeld [mʌrx-] Plain, northeast of Vienna, not unlike Norfolk in England, is largely as flat as a pancake. – **≈rutscher** *m* -s/- *colloq.* = *Schifahrer* ↓; *AmE a.* slatrider, ski bum. – **≈salat** (or *Spitzelsalat*) *m* -(e)s/pl. rare: -e *hum.* or *sarc.* one or several ski tips sadly dislocated (*abgebrochene Schispitze*[*n*]): "ski shard salad"; *einen ~ bauen* to break or wreck one's ski(s): "to make ski (tip) salad"; *er ist mit einem ~ nach Haus gekommen* he returned home with only the wreckage of his skis.

Briefadel, or **Dienstadel** *m* -s *soc. hist.* in Imperial Austria, officially used until April 3, 1919: lower (*or* lesser) nobility (as opposed to *Hochadel* ↓), a society in which titles were earned by recent service to the Crown; the ranks conferred, in descending order, read *Freiherr*, *Ritter*, *Edler*, and the simple *von*.

Bries *n* -es/-e [< Early NHG *brüs* < *brus*, surviving in NHG *Brosam* and *Brösel* – the animal gland in question has the appearance of being crumbly, of easily breaking into small pieces] *cul.* the thymus gland, a small organ from a young cow or sheep, esp. as used for food *(innere Brustdrüse bei jungen Schlachttieren,* [*Kalbs-*]*Milch*): sweetbread.

Bringungsweg *m* -(e)s/-e *min. (Förderstrecke)* haulage road.

brodeln[1] *v/t colloq. (trödeln)* to waste time, esp. by stopping often in the middle of doing something: to dawdle, to dillydally; *brodel nicht so!* stop dawdling!

brodeln[2] *v/i* [< Max *Brod,* 1884–1968, a well-known German-Jewish novelist and theatre critic, member of the Prague School of Expressionist Writers in the 1920s] a pun on *brodeln* 'to bubble' to show evidence of noticeable literary activity by, or in the manner of, Max Brod: rare, except for the happily sustained nonce accumulation of surname derivatives, *es kafkat, es werfelt, es brodelt, es kischt.*

Brösel *n* -s/-(n) **1.** *(Krümel)* crumb; *mir ist ein ~ in den falschen Schlund gekommen und ich hab husten müssen* a crumb went down my throat the wrong way, and I had to cough. – **2.** *cul.* (Ger. *Weckmehl;* cp. *Paniermehl* ↓) usu. *pl.* breadcrumbs; *alte Semmeln werden zu feinen ~n zerrieben* stale rolls are (being) ground into fine breadcrumbs.

Brot ...: ~laden *m* -s/ ... läden **1.** (a) bread drawer, still found in massive old farmhouse tables, wide and deep enough to hold a big (often home-made) loaf; (b) *sg.* only, *contp.* a person's mouth, esp. considered as an organ of speech: (fish, clam, *or* potato) trap; a peremptory call for silence: *halt deinen ~ !* shut your (fish, *etc.*) trap!, *BrE* shut your cakehole (*AmE* piehole)! – **~laib** *m* -(e)s, *dial.* -er bread loaf; *der ~ der Steiermark* a doubly effective sobriquet for the Erzberg, a well-known site of opencast ore mining near Eisenerz, whose concentric terraced workings resemble the circular welts of a well-baked loaf of bread that provides sustenance for many people; cp. *Eherne Mark* ↓.

Bruderzwist *m* -(e)/-e largely *lit. hist.* a compound well-known in Austria because encapsulated in the title of an historical drama by Franz Grillparzer, 1791 –1872, found among his literary remains, but completed about 1848: feud between brothers; *im* „~ in Habsburg" *wirft sich eine Handvoll Erzherzoge die merkwürdigsten Schandtaten vor* (Kürnberger) in *Family Strife in Hapsburg,* a handful of archdukes blame each other for having committed the strangest of nefarious deeds.

Brummer *m* -s/- *colloq.* **1.** *entom.* any insect that makes a loud noise when flying, e.g. a bluebottle or a bumblebee: buzzer, *baby talk* buzzy bee; *der ~ um mich herum macht mich ganz narrisch* that buzzer flying around me is driving me crazy. – **2.** often *pl.* scolding; *ich hab fürs Zuspätkommen meine ~ bekommen BrE* I got a ticking-off for being late, *AmE* I got harshed on for coming in late.

brunzen *v/i* [< MHG *brunnezen,* an intensive form of *brunnen* 'to piss'] *vulg.* to urinate: to (take *or* to have a) piss ‖ *phr.* a rude command, in Viennese dialect, to be silent: *red', wann die Gäns ~ !* keep your trap shut!, shut your mouth – there's a draught!; → *hunzen.*

Bschoad [pʃoat] *dial.* [< *Bescheid m* '(item of) information to be relayed'], usu. in cpds. only: **~packl** *n* -s/-(n) chiefly in Alpine use – food (and drink) for the road, taken along from home: snack for a wayside rest. – **~tüachl** *n*

Franz Grillparzer, the greatest Austrian dramatist

-s/-(n) often *hum.* a square of linen, the size of a large handkerchief or a neckerchief, with the four ends tied together, containing (1) either a titbit of food, e.g. the piece of a wedding cake brought along or sent for others to share, as a kind of token participation in the event post festum; or (2) some left-over food for one's dog or other pet animal back home: doggie bag.

Buchtel *f* -/-n [< Cz *buchta*] **1.** *bak.* a popular delicacy filled with cherry or plum jam, plum purée, or other centres, arranged with dozens or so of its "mates" in a pan and baked in the oven (*gebackenes Hefeteigstück*): (sweet) yeast dumpling, yeast dough cube, *AmE a.* sweet roll ‖ **Dukaten**~ *f* a small ducat-sized dough cube without jam

A saucepan of a "yummy" array of Buchteln *fresh from the oven*

filling: *baked ducat. → **2.** P *contp.* a large, puffy person, usu. a woman: soufflé [ˈsu:fleɪ].

Bu̯ckelkraxe *f* -/-n *colloq.;* much more common in its *dial.* form, **Bu̯cklkraxn** *f* -/- ↓ & *com.,* chiefly in Alpine areas – a wooden framework for supporting a carrier's load, a pedlar (*AmE* peddler)'s wares, a grapepicker's basket, etc. (*Traggestell auf dem Rücken*): carrying-frame; *der Senn bringt den Kas auf oana Bucklkraxn ins Tal* the Alpine dairyman takes his cheese to the valley on a carrying-frame.

Bu̲del *f* -/-n *dial.* **1.** *concr.* a narrow table or flat surface at which customers are served in a shop, bank, etc. *(Verkaufstisch)*: counter; *breiten Sie 's bittschön auf der ~ aus, dass ich mir alles gut anschauen kann!* spread it out on the counter for me to have a good look, please. – **2.** *fig. phr.* mostly used with reference to a commodity sold or bought – *unter der ~* secretly, indeed often illegally: (from) under the counter, underhandedly.

bu̯m(m) [an onomatopoeic morpheme, here used serving as an intensifier] *colloq.* ...: **~fest** *adv (ohne die geringste Bewegungsmöglichkeit)* locked in place: held tight, held fast; *die Fenster (Türen) waren ~ geschlossen* (or, *verschlossen)* the windows (doors) were tightly shut (*or,* closed tight); *der Stein sitzt ~ im Boden, den bringt man ohne Sprengen nicht heraus* the boulder is stuck fast in the ground, it won't come out without blasting. – **~voll** *adj* of a room, theatre, vehicle, etc. crowded, filled to capacity *(sehr voll)*: jam-packed, cramfull of people.

bu̯msternazi, bu̯msti or ~ **Na̯tzl (Na̯zl)** [- *nazi, Na(t)zl* < *Ignaz* 'Ignace', 'Inigo' (a Christian name made into a common noun; cp. E *guy, jack, joe*)] *interj.* in *baby talk* a friendly and sympathetic comment on a toddler "going bump", usu. a harmless little fall on its behind: (ooh) bumpity-bump!, (wh)oops-a-daisy!, *AmE* did you go boom!

Bu̯ndes...: ~kanzler *m* -s/- *polit.* Federal (*or* Austrian) Chancellor. – **~piaster** *m* -s/- [second el. < *piastre* 'a small coin or banknote in Egypt, Syria, Lebanon, and the Sudan'] *hum.* "federal piastre", Austrian shilling; cp. *Alpendollar.* – **~poldl** *m* -s [second el. < dim. of *Leopold*] *hist. sobr.* "Leo of the Austrians", an appreciative nickname for Leopold Figl, 1902 –65, a popular post-War diplomat who, as Federal Chancellor and Foreign Minister, succeeded in bringing about the Austrian Treaty (*Staatsvertrag*) on May 15, 1955. – **~rat** *m* -(e)s *polit.* **1.** no *pl.* Federal Council, i.e. the upper house of the Austrian Parliament (cp. *Nationalrat*); its fifty members are appointed by the provincial governments for indefinite terms of office. – **2.** *pl.* … räte [actually short for *Abgeordnete(r) zum ~*] Federal Councillor; *in Österreich führte der Gang der Geschichte nicht dazu, die Wahl der Bundesräte zu demokratisieren, ja er hat vielmehr allmählich die Kompetenzen dieser Körperschaft beschnitten* the course of history in Austria has not led to the democratization of the election of Federal Councillors; instead, it has gradually curtailed the powers of this body.

Burg *f* -/-en (but no *pl.* for either any of the Austrian instances listed) castle: **1.** in Vienna rarely used, except in compounds = *Hofburg.* – **2.** in Vienna *colloq.* short for *Burgtheater; leider, heut abend geht's nicht, da sind wir in der ~* (I'm) sorry, nothing doing tonight, we're going to the Burgtheater. – **3.** *phr.* only in the negated form, communicating the speaker's stubborn refusal: *nicht um die ~* not for any consideration, not if you paid me, *BrE* not on your nelly,

The Vienna Burgtheater, *the former Court Theatre, erected in the 1880s on what used to be the glacis*

AmE not for a million bucks; *sie wollte sich nicht um die ~ davon trennen* she wouldn't part with it for the world, she held on to it like grim death.

-burg *f* -/-en [second or third cp. el.] *hum.* or *iron.* a large building, or block of buildings, accommodating a mass of people temporarily huddled together for one purpose – e.g. to be cured of a common disease (→ *Husten~*), or to engage in a repetitious humdrum activity the man in the street feels some faint disdain for (→ *Tinten~*).

Bürgerschule *f* -/n *educ. hist.* "citizens' school", a three-year terminal institution after elementary school, established in 1869, which (in contrast to *Gymnasium* and *Oberrealschule*) prepared less ambitious pupils for practical life; it was replaced by the *Hauptschule* in 1927.

Burgstall *m* -s/ ... ställe [< OHG *burcstal* 'site of a castle'] *geog.* **1.** *hist.* (site of a) prehistoric hillside fort. – **2.** level patch of ground above the valley floor.

Burli *n,* rarely *m* -/- *colloq.* [dim. of *Bub,* dial. *Bua* 'boy', 'son'] **1.** term of endearment: little man, baby(-boy); *bist ja doch mein ~!* you're still my darling boy. – **2.** said to a youngster, not necessarily a relative; sometimes patronizingly, and with an undertone of discontent: kiddo, kiddie, *BrE a.* boydy-boy; ~, *du rauchst mir einmal zuviel!* kiddo, I think you're smoking too much.

Bürokretinismus *m* - [a portmanteau word made up of *Bürokratismus* 'red tape' and *Kretinismus* 'cretinism', coined by Karl Kraus, 1874–1936, an adamant moralist quick to satirize specific abuses, esp. by police authorities and judicial courts] *journalese* imbecile officialdom, esp. outrages committed by the foot-dragging of a bureaucracy whose mottoes seem to be "We are the masters here" and "We can wait"; cp. *Amtskappelton* ↑.

Buserer *m* -s/- [< *buserieren* ↓] *low colloq.* **1.** push *(Stoß)*: shove. – **2.** a (car) collision *(lautstarker Zusammenstoß [von Autos])*: crash, smash-up, wreck; *es hat einen ~ gegeben* there was a smash-up.

buserieren *v/t* [< French billiard term *pousser d'arrière* 'to push from behind'] *low colloq.* *([be]-drängen, [mit Bitten] belästigen)* to annoy, to ply insistently with a request: to pester, to plague.

Bussi *n* -(s)/-(s) *baby talk* and *joc.* in adult speech (sweet little) kiss: kissie-wissie; *gib der Tante ein ~* give Auntie a kissie-wissie; *ein dickes ~* a big kissie-poo ‖ *phr.* used as an appreciative and innocent thank-you, or greeting, from male to female who are close friends: *~ aufs Bauchi!* *I could kiss your sweet belly button!, I could give you a big kiss (on the lips)!

Buzerl *n* -s/-n [< ? Cz *buže* 'child of fortune'; or L *pusillus* 'very small'] *emot.* a very young child: kiddy, kiddiwink. **Buziwackerl** *n* -s/-n, **Buziwacki** *n* -s/-(s) [second el., a twin diminutive tacked onto the base of *wackeln* 'to waggle one's head' and/or 'to walk with short unsteady steps'] *hum.* a parent's or an auntie's affectionate form of endearment for a small child (though some mothers tend to protract the word's use into, or even beyond, the child's adolescence): toddlekins, toddles, tumble boy [lady], fiddledeflumps, polliwog, *NorBrE & ScotE* weeny little bairn.

C

C *abbr. financial hist.* the initial letter of L *Corona,* G *Krone* ‘crown’, the monetary unit current in Austria-Hungary between 1892 and 1924; St Corona, in those decades, was, therefore, venerated also as the ‘Arch Treasurer’, G *Erzschatzmeisterin.*

Cafetier [-ˈtje:] *m* -s/-s the official, dignified occupational term for a *Kaffeehausbesitzer* (cp. *Kaffeesieder* [which is definitely pejorative]): café owner.

Calafati *m -/pl.* rare: -(s) [the name of an immigré Triestino family of conjurers and who, from 1840, operated a merry-go-round in the pleasure grounds of the Vienna Volksprater for more than one hundred years; the last Calafati died in 1969.] **1.** *hist., a.* **~-Chineser** (→ *Chineser,* 2): Calafati, a popular merry-go-round or, actually, its central figure, the huge effigy of a Chinaman, impressively garbed, stern-featured, his right arm raised and lowered in imperious gestures; “Big Chinee” formed the pivot of a noisy whirl of railway seats and two locomotives (one, named “Peking”, reviving memories of the fall of that city, in 1860, during the Second Anglo-Chinese War). – **2.** *obs. colloq.* tall man: Harry Longlegs.

Capua [ˈka:pʊa] *pl.n.* [an ancient commune in Southern Italy, 19 miles north of Naples, where in 216 B. C., while in winter quarters, Hannibal’s troops succumbed to the luxury and debauchery prevalent in that city]: in ~ **der Geister** *sobr.* “Capua of the Mind”, an ambivalent laudation, in a poem by Franz Grillparzer (1843) of Vienna, the “proud Imperial City”, which tends to enfeeble the creative genius of any poet caught in her web.

Cercle [ˈserkl] *m* -s *theatre* parquet, i.e. part of the main floor of a theatre, opera house, etc., between the musicians’ area and the parterre or rear division; **~sitz** *m* -(e)s/-e seat in the parquet, stall.

Chaisen [ˈtʃe:zn] *f -/-* [< F *chaise* ‘pleasure or travelling carriage’] *dial. contp.* decrepit vehicle: crate of works, jalopy, rattletrap, wreck, *BrE* (old) banger; *was ist denn das für eine ~? BrE* what’s this crate?, *AmE* what heap of junk is that?, what’s that for a piece of metal on wheels?

Chaluppen *f -/-* = *Kaluppe.*

Chineser *m* -s/- **1.** *hum.* a mild form of reproach (1) clumsy person: *BrE* clumsy clot, *AmE* clumsy-boots, stumblebum, stumblebunny; (2) one who acts imprudently in a particular instance: silly billy; *du bist ein ~, das hättest du ja einfacher kriegen können* you are a little silly, you might have got that more easily. – **2.**

a landmark of the Vienna Volksprater adjudged an "historic monument" from 1935; usu. prefixed by *großer* or *Calafati-~* ↑: the 29-foot figure of a Chinese mandarin, portentously attired and countenance to match, the centrepiece of the Calafati merry-go-round that continued to attract young and old from 1840 to 1945, the year it was destroyed in the final holocaust of the Second World War; a smaller replica is now to be seen in the grounds.

Chrịstbaum *m* -(e)s/ …bäume *(Weihnachtsbaum)* Christmas tree; *phr.* humorously said of a woman who is gaudily dressed: *sie war behängt wie ein ~* she was decked out like a Christmas tree, she was wearing everything but the kitchen sink.

Note: Christbäume are a tradition that came from Germany in the early nineteenth century and is now widespread in Austria; such a tree adorned the feast in the family of Archduke Charles, the victor over Napoleon in May 1809, whose German wife had introduced the custom from her native Hesse in 1832. Similarly, in England, the Christmas tree found its way there through the example set by Prince Albert of Coburg-Gotha, the consort of Queen Victoria.

Chrịstenverfolger *m* -s/- only in: **moderner** ~ "latter-day persecutor of Christians", a *hum.* or *sarc.* epithet for the head of any local Church-Rate Revenue Office (G *Kirchenbeitragsstelle*), who is looked upon by some, esp. those notoriously tardy to comply, as being doggedly persevering in demanding payment.

Chrịstkind *n* -(e)s/ only in some senses *pl.:* -er < *relig.* Jesus Christ as a newborn child > **1.** *relig.* the representation of the Infant Jesus in art; a smiling baby with plump cheeks and blonde curls: Christ-child, Holy Child; *das liebe ~* (the) Baby Jesus ‖ said on or after December 25: *gehen wir (in die Kirche) das ~ anschauen in der Krippe* let's go (to the church) and have a look at (*AmE* the) Baby Jesus in the manger. – **2.** *folklore* the legendary bearer of gifts on Christmas Eve, occasionally depicted as a curly-haired child (in the German tradition, often a girl) in shining robes: *BrE* Father Christmas, *AmE* Santa Claus, Santa – a rotund and jolly, white-bearded old man in a red coat who, on Christmas Eve after all are asleep, comes in a sleigh drawn by reindeer, lands on the roof, and climbs down the chimney to put gifts under the Christmas tree and in the stockings hung by the chimney. ‖ *phr.* (a) encouraging a young child to write a wishful letter to the legendary bearer of Christmas gifts: *hast du dem ~ schon geschrieben?* have you written your letter to Father Christmas yet? (b) a parent's conventional warnings to a small child who misbehaves during the Advent season: *du* (or, *wart nur), ich sag's dem ~! BrE* just you wait, I'll tell Father Christmas!, *AmE* you better be good, Santa's watching!; *wenn du nicht brav bist, dann gibt es* (or, *dann kommt) heuer kein ~* if you aren't a good boy [girl] Father Christmas won't come (*or,* won't bring you anything) this year. (c) a mother's response to her children's question about what she would like for Christmas: *ich wünsch mir lauter ~er zu Weihnachten* I'd like a bunch of little angels for Christmas. (d) *heute abend kommt das ~* Father Christmas is coming tonight. (e) said about a gullible, simple-minded person: *er* (or, more bluntly, *der*) [*sie (die)*] *glaubt ja noch ans* ~ [s]he still believes in fairies (*or* Santa Claus), *AmE a.* … the Tooth Fairy (*or* the Easter Bunny). – **3.** (1) Christmas present: Xmas gift; *im Pfarramt wartet auf Bedürftige heuer wieder ein kleines* ~ this year once again there is a Christmas hamper waiting for the poor and needy at the parish office; *heuer gibt es nur kleine ~er, denn das ~ hat kein Geld* there won't be much under the tree (*or,* in the Christmas stocking) this year because Santa's running low on funds; *mein ~ war heuer ein Fotoapparat* this year Father Christmas (*or* Santa) brought me a camera. (2) *econ.* Christmas bonus: *BrE* Christmas lolly; *die Arbeitnehmer sind gespannt, wieviel das ~ diesmal ausmacht* the staff are wondering how much Santa Claus is going to bring them this time. – **4.** usu. only in the *phr.*: *zum* ~ (see *Christkindl,* 7 [1]) as a Christmas present (cp. *Christkindl,* 7 [2]): *heuer gibt's zum ~ einmal nichts* there'll be no Christmas presents this year for a change. – **5.** *interj.* an expression of surprise or mild dismay: *ach* (or *ja,* or *o*) *du liebes ~!* holy smoke!, holy mackerel! *BrE* o ye gods and little fishes!, *AmE* Jiminy Christmas!, holy smokes (sometimes jokingly pronounced [...ʃməuʃ])!, goodness gracious sakes alive!

Chrịstkindl *n* -s/ rarely *pl.* -(n) [in the United States this diminutive of *Christkind,* corrupted into *Kriss Kringle,* has gained some ground in or near areas of heavy German settlement; it is synonymous with Santa Claus and Father Christmas (cp. *Christkind,* 2)] **1.** *relig. & folklore* Infant Jesus: Baby Jesus (cp. *Christkind,* 1). – **2.** *appr.* any beautiful and happy little baby resembling the conventional representation in art of the Holy Child: little cherub; *das ist doch ein goldiges Kind, ein richtiges ~!* isn't [s]he the sweetest thing, [s]he's just a little angel! – **3.** mildly *iron.,* to someone for having done or said something foolish: *du bist ein ~!* (you) silly billy (*AmE a.* … goose)! – **4.** *iron.* said of a young, round-faced, naive-looking woman: *sie* (or, more bluntly, *die*) *schaut aus wie ein* ~ she's got a face like a (baby) doll (*AmE* like a kewpie [ˈkju:pɪ] doll). – **5.** Christmas present (cp. *Christkind,* 3 [1]): little Xmas gift; *emot. BrE* Christmas prezzy, *BrE & AustralE* Chrissie present. – **6.** one born at Christmas; Christmas baby; *wir erwarten gegen Jahresende etwas Kleines, vielleicht wird's gar ein* ~ we're expecting a little addition to the family towards the end of the year, it might even be a Christmas baby; *ich bin ein ~ geworden und komme so jedes Jahr um meinen Geburtstag* I was a Christmas baby, so I miss out on (*or,* never get) a real birthday every year. – **7.** usu. only in the *phr.*: *zum* ~ (1) in the Christmas season: at Xmas; *was machst du [macht ihr] zum ~?* what are you doing for Xmas? (2) as a Christmas present (cp. *Christkind,* 4): *vielleicht kriegst du das zum ~ BrE* you might get that as a Christmas prezzy (*BrE & AustralE* … Chrissie present), Santa Claus (*BrE* Father Christmas) might bring you that.

Chrịstkindlein *n* -s chiefly *StG* a sentimental or pious variant of referring to the Infant Jesus: Little Baby Jesus.

Chrịstkindl …: ~gesicht *n* -(e)s/-er (a) *appr.* said of plump cheeks and blond curls (cp. *Christkind,* 1): face like a cherub (*or* an angel), babyface. (b) *iron.* = *Christkindlkopf.* – **~kopf** *m* -(e)s/ … köpfe *iron.* of a young, round-faced, naive-looking woman (cp. *Christkindl,* 4): face like a (baby) doll (*AmE* like a kewpie [ˈkjuːpɪ] doll).

Field Marshal Johann Joseph Graf Radetzky

ciao [tʃaʊ] [< It (Venetian) dial. < StandIt *schiavo* 'slave', like obsolete Viennese *gschamster* (< *gehorsamster*) *Diener,* the remnant of a full phrase of humble submissiveness, 'I am your obedient servant': that Venetian cliché was breezily taken up by the troops of Field Marshal Johann Joseph Graf Radetzky operating in Upper Italy in the mid-nineteenth century, and quickly became a standard greeting among Austrian officers] *interj* a curt or off-hand greeting of farewell among young people today: see ya!, *AmE a.* hi!

C+M+B *abbr.* the initials, in popular belief, of the Three Holy Kings, or Three Wise Men or Magi, *C*aspar, *M*elchior, and *B*althasar, who came to Bethlehem on Epiphany (January 6) to worship the newborn Jesus Christ; actually, this is a formula, "*C*hristus *M*ansionem *B*enedicat", or "*C*ustodiat *M*ansionem et *B*enedicat [Deus]", in accordance with which, on Twelfth Night, every room of the house and the stable are sprinkled with incense, and the initials plus the figures of the New Year (two on either side of them) are chalked on the door lintels.

Note: This practice, purporting to show that the Three Wise Men have called, is also found in certain German-Austrian communities in the United States.

Colonia *local admin.* …: **~auto** *n* -s/-s. – **~fahrzeug** *n* -(e)s/-e = *Coloniawagen* ↓. – **~kübel** *m* -s/- in the backyard of town houses *(Mülltonne)*: large refuse-bin, dustbin, *AmE* garbage can, trashcan. – **~mann** *m* -(e)s … männer, … leute *colloq.* refuse-collector *(Angestellter der städtischen Müllabfuhr)*: dustman; *AmE* sanitation engineer: garbage collector, garbage man; *die ~männer sieht man eigentlich nur einmal im Jahr – wenn sie zum Neujahrwünschen kommen und dabei die Hand aufhalten* you're not likely to see the dustmen more than once a year, when they come round to wish you a Happy New Year – and extend a palm.

On January 6, in every Austrian village three younsters are dressed as the Holy Three Kings; and they go from house to house singing in rhyme what the Bible tells us about the joyful occasion

– **~system** *n* -(e)s/-e *(Müllabfuhr)* refuse collecting, *AmE* garbage disposal. – **~wagen** *m* -s/- *(Fahrzeug der Müllabfuhr)* refuse-van, *AmE* garbage truck.

Congrès *m* F *polit. hist.* short for *Le ~ Viennois* [lə kɔ̃ˈgrɛ vjɛnˈwa:] 'The Congress of Vienna' (or *Wiener Kongress*), the international conference in 1814-15 where majesties and ministers of state convened to establish a new order for post-Napoleonic Europe; however, social events were paramount, as seen in a pun made by the aged Prince Charles Joseph de Ligne, *"Le ~ danse et rien ne transpire que ces messieurs-là"* ... 'elder statesmen perspire on the dance floor, but nothing transpires through the conference-room door'.

Copa Kagrana *n* -s [a place-name blend of *Copacabana,* the fashionable beach of Rio de Janeiro, and *Kagran,* a riverside suburb of Vienna] *hum.* "Copa Kagrana", the new eighteen-mile recreation area by the Danube off Vienna, the longest inland beach in Europe.

Cottage [kɒˈtɛ:ʃ] -/ *pl.* rare: -s [the conceptual and formal roots here lie in England, which caused Austrian architects as well as city and landscape planners to found the *Wiener Cottage-Verein* in 1872] *archit. (Gartenvorstadt)* garden suburb, a fashionable residential area with tree-lined avenues and front gardens, esp. in Vienna, the oldest ones laid out to cover parts of the eighteenth and nineteenth districts of the Capital; *eine Prachtvilla im [Währinger] ~* a mansion in the garden suburb [of Währing]. – **~lage** *f* -/-n *econ.* often in real-estate advertisements: chic residential area; *luxuriöse Zweifamilienvilla in ~ zu verkaufen* two-family luxury villa for sale in fashionable dormitory area. – **~viertel** *n* -s/- = *Cottage* ↑; *in einem ~ seine Zelte aufzuschlagen, davon kann unsereins, fürchte ich, ja nur träumen* settling down in a posh suburb must remain a pipe dream for folks like me, I'm afraid. – **~wohnung** *f* -/-en (well-appointed) apartment in garden suburbia.

Cricketer *m* -s/- [the name, like that of the First Vienna Football Club, is due to the enthusiasm instilled by Britons, e.g. gardeners working on the Rothschild premises, practising their sports in Vienna about the turn of the last century] *sports,* largely *hist.* Cricketer, a player, member, or supporter, of the Vienna Cricket and Football Club; *bis 1911 waren die 1894 gegründeten ~ sogar einer der stärksten Fußballvereine auf dem Festland* until 1911, the Cricketers founded in 1894 were even among the best football clubs on the Continent.

Dableiber *m* -s/- *polit. hist., colloq.* with reference to the 1939 Hitler-Mussolini pact, under which the German population of South Tyrol (in Italian, Alto Adige) was to be resettled on the northern side of the Alps: non-optant, *colloq.* one of those "staying put", rather than "pulling up the roots" and "stirring to go" (*Geher* ↓); the reason for defying the lure stemmed from the reluctance of the largely conservative Roman Catholic population to move to areas under the sway of National Socialism, and from their distrust that complete re-acculturation (as promised) could be achieved for such a vast ethnic group of 200000 people.

Dachgleichenfeier *f* -/-n *tech. & folklore* a small snack-and-beer party given by the building owner for the carpenters, joiners, and other craftsmen to mark the erection of the roof timbers; in recognition of the courtesy shown, the men invariably put up on the roof ridge a little fir tree with gaily coloured streamers (*Dachgleiche, Richtfest*): topping-out ceremony.

daherböhmakeln, ~bömakeln *vi/t* = *zusammenböhmakeln* ↓.

Dampfplauderer *m* -s/- *iron.* a person who talks at great length without making much sense (*Schwätzer*): chatterbox, gasbag, prattler, windbag, *AmE a.* blatherskite; *das ist ein ~, der einfach kein End' findet* he's got a tongue like a dog's tail, it 's always wagging.

Dickerl *n* -s/-n *hum.* or slightly *contp.* a fat person: fatty, tubby.

Dienst...: ~adel *m* -s = *Briefadel* ↑. – **~bot** [–o:t] *m* -en/-en, **~bote** *m* -n/-n, and **~botin** *f* -/-nen, respectively, all largely *obsolescent* servant (in a rural or city household). – **~botenmadonna** *f* - *relig. & arts* in the nave of St Stephen's Cathedral, Vienna: "Virgin of the Servants", a sculpture of Virgin and Child, from the early fourteenth century, expressive both of the medieval cult of the female and timeless motherly love; the name probably derives from the fact that the statue once stood on the altar where the first daily mass was celebrated, which the servants had time to attend. – **~geber** *m* -s/- *econ. (Arbeitgeber)* employer; *~ und Dienstnehmer* employer(s) and employee(s); *Unfallhaftpflicht des ~s* employer's accident liability; *Verhältnis zwischen ~ und Dienstnehmer* industrial relations *pl.* – **~mädel,** *dial.* **~madl** *n* -s/-n *colloq.*, but a great scarcity in modern life *(Dienstmädchen)*: maid(-servant), *BrE colloq.* tween(e)y. – **~mann** *m* -(e)s/ ... männer largely outmoded odd-job man for hire, wearing a red cap:

handyman, out-porter, *BrE* commissionaire, *AmE colloq.* redcap ‖ the opening lines of a Viennese wine song, humorously setting forth what may happen even to the circumspect after a bibulous evening out: *ich hab mir für Grinzing einen ~ engagiert, / der mich nach Hause führt, / wenn irgendwas passiert* *I had myself a porter out in Grinzing one fine day, / who'd take me on my way / if things should go astray. – **~nehmer** *m* -s/- employee, *AmE a.* employe; *Mitbestimmungsrecht der ~* co-partnership of labour; *~vertreter pl.* employees' representatives. – **~sprache** *f - mil. hist.* in the Austro-Hungarian Army: language of command; *vom Major abwärts galt als ~ Deutsch, magyarische Offiziere mussten selbst dann auf ein (siebzig Wörter umfassendes) deutsches Befehlsinventar zurückgreifen, wenn sie vor einer Truppe eigener Landsleute standen* the language of command at the rank of major and below was German, and Magyar officers had to make use of a (seventy-word) German vocabulary when giving orders to a unit of their own countrymen.

Dịrndl *n* -s/-n [< *Dirn f* 'farm-girl' + intrusive consonant *-d-* + *dim. -l*] **I. 1.** P, always *apprec.* – a healthy-looking young (country) girl *(frischmunteres Mädel* [*vom Land*]*)*: (pretty) lassie. → **2.** *garm.* a popular native apparel for women, featuring a full skirt, gathered waist, and tight bodice *(Trachtenkleid)*: dirndl [ˈdəːndl] (dress). – **II.** ❦ a yellow-flowering bush or tree bearing longish red berries *(gelbblühender Hartriegel, Kornelkirsche)*: cornel (tree), cornelian tree *or* cherry, 🕮 Cornus mas.

Djụvec [–tʃ], in German spelling **Djụwetsch** *n* -s/pl. rare: -(e); also known as **Sẹrbische R̲e̲isfleisch** *n* -n -(e)s/- -(e) *cul.* cubed meat (veal, pork, beef, or mutton), stewed with tomatoes, green peppers, onions, rice, and potatoes, and boiled in meat broth – a Balkan speciality known in Eastern Austria: Serbian hotchpotch.

Dọbos [ˈdoːbɔʃ] [< József C. Dobos (1847 –1924), a famous Budapest pastry-cook]… *bak.*: **~schnitte** *f* -/-n one of a trayful, or trayfuls, of rectangular pieces cut from a multiple-layered sponge, each of the seven or eight thin bases (*Biskuitböden*) baked on a baking tray, then spread with chocolate (or mocha) buttercream, the top one sporting a glaze of crisp caramel: Dobos (*in the mouths of English-only natives, a.* [ˈdəʊbɔs]) slice. – **~torte** *f* -/-n a rich cake of the above type: chocolate layer cake, Dobos Torte [ˈtɔːta].

D̲o̲del *m* -s/-n *contp.* a slow-thinking foolish person: dork, idiot, dumb head, *NZE* dumb-bum; *so ein ~!* such an idiot!; *geh weg, du ~!* go away, dumb head! ‖ → *Haus-, Hof- und Wiesendodel.*

D̲o̲nau *f - river-name* [like the *Don* (several British rivers, of which the two most important ones are in Yorkshire and Aberdeenshire), the *Doon* (Ayrshire), and the *Rhone* (< *Rhodanus,* France), an old Celtic word for (probably, 'swift-flowing') 'water'] Danube [ˈdænjuːb], the second longest river in Europe, after the Volga, extending 2,888 kilometers, or 1,775 miles, from the Black Forest to the Black Sea. **1.** *adj colloc.: die obere ~* the Upper Danube (as far as the mouth of the River March [marx], or Morawa,

Stein on the Danube – a masterpiece by Donald Maxwell, another enthusiast for Austria

the boundary between Slovakia and Lower Austria ‖ in and around Vienna: *die Große ~*, or *der Donaustrom* ↓, the Danube proper; in contradistinction to *die Kleine ~*, or *der Donaukanal* ↓, the Danube Canal, and *die Alte ~* the Old Danube, an abandoned stretch of the river forming a series of lakes, with boating and swimming in summer, ice skating in winter ‖ *poet. & hist.* an appreciative collocation first used in the "Stille Lieder" of 1839 by Karl Beck, a German-Hungarian poet, who also wrote the text for the *Donauwalzer* ↓: *die blaue ~* the blue Danube; *eine "schöne, blaue ~"? ... nun, die Bläue liegt zumeist im Auge des Betrachters, sie ist eigentlich nur dann gegeben, wenn bei sonnigem Wetter das klare Wasser die Azurfarbe des Himmels spiegelt* a "blue and beautiful Danube"? ... well, its blueness lies mostly in the eye of the beholder, or only in sunny weather does the limpid water reflect the colour of the azure sky. – **2.** *prep. colloc.: an der ~* (1) in a concrete sense: (a) by the Danube; *der Park liegt unmittelbar an der ~* the park is right by the Danube; (b) on the Danube; *Krems liegt an der ~* Krems lies on the Danube. (2) in a metaphorical sense: with an unmistakably Danubian ring (*or* flavour); *zwar dirigierte der Deutsche auf seine Art, durch den philharmonischen Klang aber lag dann doch alles an der ~* although the German conducted in his own style, the Vienna Philharmonic gave the piece a distinctly Danubian ring; *polit. hist.: Die Wacht an der ~* [formed on the analogy of *Die Wacht am Rhein,* a provocatively chauvinist, anti-French song by Max Schneckenburger, 1840] "The Watch on the Danube", a Christian Social Party slogan of the late 1880s, warning against infiltration from non-German lands in the East and emphasizing German nationalism in Austria. – **3.** *phr.:* (1) an action considered superfluous: *Wasser in die ~ gießen* (or *schütten,* or *tragen*) *BrE* to carry (*or* take, *or* bring) coals to Newcastle, *AmE* to bring steel to Detroit, to take ice to Alaska. (2) a piece of advice against worrying about a situation (a) which may already have changed, or (b) which may do so only in a rather distant future: (a) *seither ist viel Wasser die ~ hinuntergeflossen* since then a lot of water has gone under the bridge; (b) *bis dahin wird* (or *mag) noch viel Wasser die ~ hinunterfließen* by then a good deal of water will (*or* may) have passed under the bridge, much water will (*or* may) run under the bridge before that happens.

Donau ...: **~abwärts** *adv* down the (River) Danube; *eine Dampferfahrt von Melk ~ wird oft zu einem idyllisch-geruhsamen Erlebnis* a steamboat trip downstream from Melk can be a restful experience. – **~au** *f* -/-en, often *pl.* low-lying land beside the Danube; *sich weithin dehnende ~en* miles of marshes along the Danube. – **~aufwärts** *adv* up the (River) Danube; *der Ort liegt eine Autostunde von Linz ~* the place is an hour's drive upstream from Linz. – **~becken** *n* -s *geol.* Danube Basin. – **~bus** *m* ... busses / ... busse *nav.* (Danube) water bus, a small river craft plying on the River Danube over short distances, e.g. between Melk and Krems, or Vienna and Hainburg. – **~dampfschiffahrtsgesellschaft** *f* - *nav.: Erste Donau-Dampfschiffahrts-Gesellschaft* (abbr. DDSG [ˌde:de:es'ge:]) First Danube Steam Navigation Company, established by two Englishmen, John Andrews and Joseph Prichard, in 1829 for the transport of passengers and goods along the Danube and its tributaries; *ling. hum. ~ kapitänswitwe* 'widow of a captain in the Danube Steamship Company', a multiple compound made up for the nonce in order to demonstrate the capacity of the German language to form long words (compare the heroic length of a Welsh railway-station name in Anglesey, *Llanfairpwllgwyngyllgogerychwyrndrobwll* 'St Mary's church by the white hazelpool near the fierce whirlpool'). – **~durchbruch** *m* -(e)s/ ... brüche *geol.* Danube Gorge, one of several picturesque narrow river sections, e.g. between Passau and Schlögen, or Melk and Krems, their sides often wooded or terraced to support vineyards. – **~fetzen** *m* -s/- in: *ausgschwabter ~* [< StG *ausgeschwaibt, p. pt.,* said of an old cleaning rag worn out with constant washing and wringing] *dial.* a vulgar term of abuse for a harridan *(alte Vettel)*: old hag; *sie ist ein ausgschwabter ~* she's a washed-out old hag. – **~fürst** *m* -en/-en *myth.* at Freienstein, in the Strudengau, Lower Austria, the site of a haunted castle complex, now in ruins: "Prince of the Danube", an epithet of the *Nöck,* a mischievous water sprite, said to rise from the depths of the river to kidnap virgins. – **~gold** *n* -(e)s *hist.* at Langenlebarn, Lower Austria, where there was formerly a considerable settlement of gold-panners: Danubian gold; it was laboriously dredged and sifted from the river, and can be seen today in the altar chalices in the Melk and Klosterneuburg monasteries. – **~kanal** *m* -s Danube Canal [kə'næl], an artificial waterway forming a river-loop through the centre of Vienna. – **~land 1.** *n* (e)/ ... länder *geog.* usu. *pl.* (one of the) countries through or along which the River Dan-

The Benedictine Abbey of Melk on the Danube, engraved in 1821 by three Englishmen who had then set out to minutely record in word and picture the monastic life of contemporary Austria

ube flows: Danubian countries. – **2.** *f pr.n. - sg. only* the name of a renowned book club, with its seat in Vienna, selling books to its members at a discount: *die Buchgemeinschaft ~* the Donauland Book Society. – **~lände** *f -/-n* landing-place (*or* quay) on the Danube; *am 1. März 1886 kam in Pöchlarn in einem Haus an der ~ Oskar Kokoschka zur Welt* Oskar Kokoschka was born on 1 March 1886 in a house on the Danube quay of Pöchlarn. – **~metropole** *f - journ.* Danube Metropolis, an epithet of Vienna. – **~monarchie** *f - hist.* a shorter popular way of saying *Österreichisch-ungarische Monarchie*: Danube (*or* Danubian) Monarchy; *er stammt aus der alten ~* he hails from the old Austro-Hungarian Empire. – **~muskelkraftschiffahrt** *f hum.* "muscle-powered Danube navigation", a play on the contrast to *Donaudampfschiffahrt* (cp. the quintuple compound above), referring to (1) pleasure boating and canoeing on the Danube, in general, and (2) especially, *hist.* the Roman river flotilla stationed at Comagena(e), a place of some consequence in antiquity (which is the modern Tulln, in Lower Austria). – **~mutze** *f -/-n nav.,* almost *obs.* wooden ferry (on the Danube). – **~schiffer** *m -s/- nav.,* largely *hist.* Danube bargeman (whose patron saint is St Nicholas, hence the frequency of such place-names along the river). – **~schill** *m* -(e)s/-e Danube zander *or* pike-perch. – **~schule** *f* - *arts* in early Renaissance drawing and painting, 1490–1540: Danube School of Painting, esp. Rueland Frueauf the Younger, Lucas Cranach, Albrecht and Erhart Altdorfer, the first to develop the practice of creating a landscape around a central religious subject. – **~schwall,** or **Greinschwall** *m* -(e)s *nav. hist. & folklore* like the *Donaustrudel* and *Donauwirbel* ↓, a menace to old-time navigation, downstream from Grein, Upper Austria: Danube flood-sweep *or* rapid, a sudden dash down a rugged defile caused by a treacherous tongue of land, until the mid-1850s an object of fear and legend. – **~staat** *m* -(e)s/-en *polit.* Danubian state. – **~stadt** *f* -/ … städte **1.** rare in its generic use: city on the Danube. – **2.** no *pl.* "Donaustadt", the twenty-second district of Vienna. – **3.** ~ *am Alpenrand* no *pl., sobr.* "Danubian City on the Alpine Fringe", a tourist-trade epithet of Linz. – **~strom** *m* -(es) *BrE* River Danube, *AmE* Danube River. – **~strudel** *m* -s *nav. hist. & folklore* off Werfenstein Castle, a few miles after the *Donauschwall* ↑: Seething Cauldron, strong circular currents amid chains of crags beneath the water, which made craft fall with violence and uproar through three separate channels. – **~turm** *m* -(e)s *archit.* Danube Tower, an 853ft. reinforced-concrete structure in the Vienna "Donaupark", the second-highest building in Europe. – **~walzer** *w* -s ♪ "Blue Danube" waltz, composed by Johann Strauss Jr. [ˈdʒuːnjə] (*or* the Younger)

Johann Strauss Jr., the "Waltz King": a 1999 stamp issued on the centenary of his death

1867, a piece first warmly received in Paris and London, and now long, as it were, the unofficial 'national anthem' of the country; the title on the music-sheet reads *"An der schönen blauen Donau"*, which led to the erroneous belief that the Danube sparkles blue in Austria.[1] –

[1] In many American high schools, the first four bars of the "Blue Danube" waltz are frequently used to learn German dative prepositions: *aus, außer, bei, mit, nach, seit, von, zu;* this theme is varied often enough to provide both fun and easy memorization.

~wasser *n* -s Danube water; a *colloq.* paraphrase for a real native of Vienna: *mit ~ getauft (worden) sein* *to have been christened with water from the Danube; there are similar phrases in English, e.g. "to be born within the sounds of Bow [bəʊ] bells", to be a true-

Franz Schubert, the "Prince of Songs", similarly fêted on the bicentenary of his birth

born Cockney, and the idea of christening recurs in an old metaphor for a talkative Irishman, who is said "to have been dipped in the Shannon", the immersion being regarded as an effective cure against bashfulness. – **~weibchen** *n* -s *myth.* Fair Maid of the Danube, a mermaid risen from the river mists, the companion in song and dance of the Danube fishermen; *das ~ sah seine Aufgabe darin, den Lebenden Fröhlichkeit zu schenken und der Ertrunkenen Seelen zu wahren, bis Gott sie rief* the Danube Mermaid saw her task as spreading joy among the living and preserving the souls of those drowned until God calls them to Him. – **~wirbel** *m* -s/- *nav. hist. & folklore* between St Nikola and Sarmingstein Castle, a third navigation hazard from the last century, soon after the *Donaustrudel* ↑: "Danube whirlpool", formed by the violence with which two currents of the river were hurled against each other on leaving an island, and again checked and divided by a huge rock; damming the waters for a hydroelectric power station at Ybbs-Persenbeug has finally done away with all three forever.

Dreimäderlhaus *n* -es/ … häuser **1.** group of three girls (or, *iron.*, [elderly] women): three graces; ein *vergnügtes* ~ a merry group of three graces, a merry threesome ‖ said in *hum.* surprise when encountering a group of three females: *was, ein ~!* rub-a-dub-dub, three maids in a tub! → **2.** ♪ a tune by Franz Schubert, in the final Rondo of the Piano Sonata in D major, Op. 53 (composed at Gastein in 1825): Lilac Time.

Drischel *m* -s/- or *f* -/-n [< OHG *driscil,* the umlauted stem form of *drëskan vt/i* 'to thresh' + the agent-noun suffix *-il,* which was added in order to denote a hand tool; some other such NHG word forms are *Griffel* 'slate pencil', *Meißel* 'chisel', *Schwengel* '(pump) handle', and *Waschel* ↓] *dial.*, ♩ (1) in a broader sense, an instrument for separating grain from wheat by beating it (*Dreschflegel*): flail. – (2) in a narrower sense, properly, the wooden bar, hinged or tied to a long handle, that does the actual threshing (*Schlagkolben* [*an einem Dreschflegel*]): thresher, swingle.

Duckanterl *n* -s/- [second el., a dialect diminutive variant of *Ente f* 'duck'] *ornith., colloq.* a small swimming and diving bird – so named after its striking capacity to disappear very quickly under the water's surface *(Bläßhuhn)*: coot.

Dulliäh, Dullioh [< *dulliäh* 'yip-a-dee', a cry of bibulous mirth] *colloq.* **1.** *n* -s *(Ausgelassenheit)* wild fun of a harmless type: high jinks, hi-jinks. – **2.** *m* -s *(leichter Rausch)* state of light intoxication: tipsiness; *mit einem richtigen ~ zog die Gruppe vom Heurigen wieder in die Stadt* with a real high the group left the new-wine tavern for town; **~stimmung** *f* -/-en *(lustige, ausgelassene Stimmung)* pleasant state of mind caused by drinking: merry mood, good-time feeling, feeling whoopee (*or,* whoop-dee-do); *nach einigen Vierteln geriet die Gesellschaft immer mehr in eine ~* after a few glasses the party really began to get that good-time feeling; *es war ihm später gar nicht recht, dass man ihn in ~ fotografiert hatte* later it didn't suit him at all that he'd been photographed making whoopee.

Dụmmerl; slightly stronger also **Tẹpperl** *n* -s/-n laying gentle blame, or said in laughing self-defence, nearly always affectionately, to or of a person: silly, silly billy; *du bist ein (kleines) ~, das hab' ich ja gar nicht so gemeint* you are a little silly billy, I didn't really mean it that way at all.

dụnsten *v/i* < to give off vapour > only in the *fig. phr.* **j-n ~lassen** to keep someone in suspense: to keep someone on a string; *es war nicht gerade die feine englische Art, mich so lange ~ zu lassen* it was not exactly the peak of good manners to keep me dangling for so long.

Dụnstobst *n* -es *cul.* apples etc. cooked by heating with steam (*Dünstobst*): stewed *or* steamed fruit.

Dụrchhaus *n* -es/ … häuser **1.** *archit. (Haus mit öffentlichem Durchgang)* house with a covered passageway, house given on to two streets, arcade(d house), passage house [*cp.* the Burlington and Piccadilly Arcades, in the West End of London (see also above, under *Abschneider*)]. – **2.** *fig.* (1) clearing station, transient home; *es wird behauptet, die Wiener Oper sei vor allem ein internationales ~ von Stars* it has been said that the Vienna Opera is primarily an international clearing house (*or, AmE,* way station) for opera stars. (2) social event, with a kaleidoscopic sequence of those attending: swirl of visitors; *ein Samstagnachmittag, an dem nicht, wie üblich, das ~ bei uns ausbricht, ist auch ganz schön* a Saturday afternoon without the usual swarm of visitors is also quite nice.

dụrchräumen *v/t* [< *tech.* to clear a pipe or sewer of obstructions] *fig., colloq.* said of a medicine taken to relieve constipation: to loosen *or* open one's bowels ‖ a constipated person's semi-desperate cry for such a cathartic agent: *ich bin schon seit drei Tagen wie vernagelt und brauch' dringend was, das mich durchräumt* (or, … *was zum Durchräumen*) I haven't had a road through me (*AmE a.,* I've been gummed up *or* plugged up) for three days, and badly need a loosener *or* opener.

durchwạchsen *p.p.* [literally, 'marbled', 'streaky' (meat)] ☼, *colloq.* of changeable weather: spotty, fair to middling; *der Wetterbericht sagt für morgen schwüles, gewitter~es Wetter voraus* the forecast for tomorrow is hot and humid weather, with intermittent storms.

dụschen or **tụschen** *v/i* ☼, *colloq.* to rain very hard, often for a short period only *(schauerartig regnen)*: to bucket down; *jetzt duscht's aber!* it's bucketing down, it's coming down in buckets. – **Dụscher(er)** *or* **Tụscher(er)** *m* -s/- ☼, *colloq.* a sudden, short but intensive downpour *(Platzregen)*: goose-drownder.

E

Egart *f* -/-en [< MHG *egerte, egerde* < OHG *egerda*] **1.** a tract of open ground, esp. grassland (*Grasland*): meadow-land, lea *or* ley. – **2.** land used for a few years for pasture or for growing hay, then ploughed over and replaced by another crop (*Grasland, das in anderen Jahren als Acker genutzt wird*): lea *or* ley. – **~(en)wirtschaft** *f* - an agricultural system employing, each for a few years, crop-growing, fallowing, and pasture in rotation (*Feldgraswirtschaft*): (system of) alternate husbandry, lea *or* ley farming.

Eherne Mark *f* -n [second el., shortened from *Steiermark*] *literary use* "Borderland of Brass", an epithet for upland Styria, which is rich in mineral deposits; cp. *Brotlaib* ↑.

Eier … [< pl. of *Ei n* -(e)s/-er 'egg']: **~klar** *n* -s/- *cul.* = *Eiklar* ↓. – **~nockerl** *n* -s/usu. *pl.* -n [< *Nock m* 'small hill', 'mound'] *cul.* irregular-sized small dumpling, eaten with scrambled eggs. – **~pecken** *n* -s *folklore* a children's Easter game originating from an ancient religious rite, in which an egg is firmly held in the fist and knocked against another person's egg (first by the slender end, then by the other) to see whose is stronger, and which egg eventually can score the most victories: egg bumping. – **~schwamm** *m* -(e)s/ … schwämme; more often, *dial. & dim.* **~schwammerl** *n* -s/-n a woodland mushroom having a yellow funnel-shaped cap and a faint smell of apricots; with its delightful flavour, it is many people's particular favourite of all edible fungi (*Pfifferling*): (yellow) chantarelle *or* chanterelle [ˌ(t)ʃæntəˈrɛl]. – **~speise** *f* -/- [lit., 'dish made of eggs']; more often in its *dial.* form, **~speis** *f* -/*pl.* rare: -n **1.** *cul.* eggs cooked in a pan after the white and yellow parts have been mixed together (*Rühreier*): scrambled eggs, *BrE sl.* Adam and Eve wrecked; *sag mir, kann ich dir eine Eierspeis machen?* tell me, can I make you some scrambled eggs? – **2.** *hum.* or *sarc.* a mess of broken eggs (in a basket, etc., caused, for instance, by a car ride involving sudden jerks and jolts (*Rühreier* [*im Korb*]): scrambled eggs. – **~speispfandl** or **~speisreindl** *n* -s/-n *dial. & dim., cul.* small egg-frying pan ‖ if *emot.* **~speispfanderl** or **~speisreinderl** *n* -s/-*n* (just a) little *or* wee egg-frying pan. – **~weckerl** *n* -s/-n *bak.* oval bread roll (with a notch down its middle).

Eiklar *n* -s/- *cul.* the clear, viscous substance round the yolk of an egg that turns white when cooked or beaten ([*flüssiges*] *Eiweiss*): egg white, white of egg, albumen.

Einbrenn *f* -/-en *colloq.,* less often StG **Einbrenne** *f* -/-n *cul.* a cooked mixture of flour and butter used to thicken soups and sauces *(Mehlschwitze)*: roux [ru:], thickener, thickening.

eingesprengt *adj colloq. (versessen)* enthusiastic ‖ ~ *sein für* (or, *auf*) to rave about, to be wild (*or,* crazy) about; often in negative statements: *ich bin eigentlich für moderne Dichtung nicht* ~ my heart is not really set on modern poetry, *AmE* I'm not too crazy about modern poetry.

eingraben *colloq.* **1.** *v/t* in rural use: *(begraben)* to bury; *sie haben ihn gestern eingegraben* they put him in the ground yesterday. – **2.** *v/refl* [lit., 'to dig oneself in'] with reference to one's favourite dish: to sink one's teeth (*in* into); *ich könnte mich ~ in Marillenknödel* I could eat apricot dumplings until the cows come home, *AmE a.* my middle name is apricot dumplings.

einkasteln *v/t colloq.* **1.** *jur.* to put s.o. in a prison or in a mental hospital (*einsperren*): to lock up, to put away. – **2.** 🚗 to park so near to another car that it cannot move (*einklemmen*): to box in. – **3.** to surround s.th. with a border so that it looks pleasant or can be clearly seen ([*mit einem Stift*] *eckig umranden*): to box, to frame.

Einmach *f* -/-en *cul. colloq. (lichte Einbrenn)* flour lightly fried in fat for thickening young vegetables, etc.: white sauce. – **~suppe** *f* -/-n cream soup.

Einschicht, dial. **Oanschicht** *f* - [?< on the analogy of *Einfalt* 'singleness', which is a loan translation of L *simplex* and *simplicitas,* respectively] *geog.* a very distant and lonely spot or area, often surrounded by extensive fields or forests *(Einöde)*: isolated (*or* out-of-the-way) place; *in diese ~ verliert sich selten ein Fremder* there is hardly a stranger finding his way to this lonely place; *die beiden hausen irgendwo in der ~ auf einem Bauernhof* the two live on a farm somewhere off the beaten track (*or* path), somewhere at (*or* in) the back of beyond; *ein Urlaub in der ~ eines Tiroler Bergtals* a holiday in a Tyrolean mountain valley, away from it all. – **einschichtig** *adj* **1.** *geog. (abgelegen)* isolated; *eine ~e Gegend* a lonely region. – **2.** *colloq. (unverheiratet)* single, unmarried ‖ an impromptu quip: *immer noch ~, du Weiberfeind?* still going it alone (*or,* still in single harness), you old celibate?

Einspänner *m* -s/- [< sense of 'owner-driver of a one-horse carriage': while on the stand, the cabman took only light refreshments in order to be ready for his next fare] *cul.* **1.** *(Glas Mokka mit Schlagobers)* Viennese coffee, black coffee with (a dollop of) whipped cream, served in a glass; *wenn ein Fahrgast auftauchte, war das Obers schnell verrührt, der ~ hinuntergetrunken, und es konnte losgehen* whenever a fare turned up, the cream was quickly stirred, the coffee downed, and off they went. – **2.** *(einzelnes Frankfurter Würstchen [von einem Paar])* one of a pair of frankfurters (which are normally sold together), singleton; *wünschen der Herr den ~ mit Senf oder mit Kren?* would you like your frankfurter with mustard or with horseradish, sir?

einstreifen *v/t colloq. (einstreichen)* with reference to money: to sweep in, to pick up, *sl.* to scoop up, to pull down; *er* *streift bei diesem neuen Job* [tʃɒp] *einen Haufen Geld ein* he is raking in the dough at his new job.

Eintropfsuppe *f* -/-n [< *eintropfen* 'to pour in drop by drop'] *cul.* a clear soup with egg(-paste) drops: egg-drop soup.

Ẹmmentaler *m* -s/- [actually, a(n originally Swiss) cheese which is hard and has large holes], also **Ẹmmentalerin** *f* -/-nen *vulg.* a promiscuous woman: one playing musical beds; *sie ist ein Emmentaler [eine Emmentalerin], und denkt als solche am besten weiterzukommen* she thinks that playing musical beds is the best way to go ahead.

Ẹnd *n* -(e)s/-en *colloq.* for *Ende* 'end' ‖ *hum.* said in pseudo-resigned deference to fate, and with a quirky volte-face into crass materialism: *alles hat einmal ein ~, … nur die Wurst hat zwei* everything has an end, only the sausage has two; a guess at a possibility that occurs to the speaker only as an afterthought: *am ~* perhaps (as a thought that just occurs to me); *du tust in der letzten Zeit so geheimnisvoll … hast du am ~ geheiratet, oder toben bei dir gar schon kleine Schrazerln ums Haus?* you've been so secretive lately … have you given up the bachelor life, or maybe you've even got some little ones crashing around the house already?

ẹnds|lang [for dramatic emphasis, also **ends|lang** 'e:ndzlaŋ] *colloq.* **1.** *adj* very long, endless, interminable; *eine ~e Liste* a list as long as your arm; *eine ~e Fahrt* a devil of a long ride. – **2.** *adv* very long, for an unconscionably long time: for ages, *low colloq. ich habe dich [Sie] (ja) schon ~ nicht gesehen* I in haven't seen you for ages, *or* … for donkey's years [ji:əz, with a very long i: – a sound to suggest the unusual length of a donkey's ears].

Ẹngerl *n* -s/-n [a telescopic conflation of *Engel* 'angel' dim. *-erl*] *emot.,* often *dial.* **1.** *R.C.,* used when gently and caressingly speaking to young children: a member of God's three choirs of ministering spirits in Heaven above, pictured as dressed in white, with wings: (sweet) little angel; *die ~n im Himmel werden sich freuen, wenn du das machst* the little angels above will be happy to see you do that. – **2.** in respect of human beings – (1) a loving address to, or mention of, one's young daughter or son: (*mein*) ~ my little angel, honey, sugar, sweetie-pie, toots ‖ a coaxing request: *geh, sei ein ~ und bring* (or, *geh, bist du [m]ein ~ und bringst d') uns aus der Küche zwei Löfferln, ja?* (will you) be a sweet and get us two little spoons from the kitchen, will you? ‖ found in epitaphs, e.g. at Tautendorf Cemetery, Waldviertel, Lower Austria –

Zum Gedenken an	In memory of
unser kleines Engerl,	our darling little angel,
geb. 9. Jänner 2000,	born January 9, 2000,
gest. 4. Feber 2000.	died February 4, 2000.

(2) a man's adoring epithet for the woman he loves: *mein ~!* my spotless angel!, my lovely lamb! – **3.** *hum. phr.* (1) in a rhyming couplet, a chipper group of people setting out on a day trip, a hike or mountain climb is shown to be little concerned about the vagaries of rain, wind, and sunshine –

Das Wetter wird es uns bald weisen,
ob heute auch die Engerln reisen.

*The weather may prove fine today,
you never know: Perhaps there will
be smiling angels, flying low.

With such lingering doubts about the weather duly dispelled, all members of the party feel happily elated, indeed arrogating to themselves angelic identities and mingling with the heavenly host –

Wenn Engerln reisen, freut sich der Himmel!

*With angels on the move, the heavens smile. The sun shines on the righteous.

(2) ♪ the opening line of an old Viennese song, according the Austrian capital a rare distinction –

Heut' kumman d' Engerln auf Urlaub nach Wean.

*Angels on leave flock to Vienna today.

(3) said of two persons – the right hand of one holding the left hand of the other, or the two people linking both arms crosswise – in either case forming a makeshift cradle, or carrycot, for a third person, e.g., a baby or one's lightweight beloved, to sit in: *j-n ~ tragen* to carry sb. carrycot (*or,* sedan-chair) fashion; der *Mann war so schwach, wir haben ihn ~ tragen müssen* the man was so weak we had to carry (*or,* cradle) him on our arms between us.

Ẹnglische Fräulein *n pl.* -n - *relig. & educ.* a R.C. order of women for the higher education of girls, orig. of noble descent (hence the name "Fräulein"), founded by Mary Ward, a Yorkshire noblewoman, in 1609 at Saint-Omer, France: Institute of the Blessed Virgin Mary (L *Institutum Beatae Mariae Virginis*), Mary Ward's Sisters *or* Nuns.

Ẹnglische Gruß *m* -n -es [first word < *Engel* ↑] *R.C.* a prayer based on the salutation of the angel Gabriel to the Virgin Mary and the words of Elizabeth to her (St Luke 1: 28, 42): Ave Maria [ˌɑːvɪ məˈrɪə] Ave Mary [ˈeɪvɪ ˈmɛərɪ], Hail Mary.

Ẹrdapfel *m* -s/ …äpfel [in view of unsophisticated man's agile mind, with his rich treasure bag of multicoloured metaphors strapped to his side (holding among others such dialect beauties as G *Grundbirne* and *Erdbirne,* E *Irish apricot* and *bog orange*), it is little wonder that poets writing in English should sometimes have avoided their darkly uncommunicative standard word *potato* in favour of a sense-stimulating loan from another level of speech, or indeed from another tongue – Peter Viereck, a German-American New Yorker, proved himself to be such a blissful and inspired gleaner when addressing himself

To a Sinister Potato

O vast *earth-apple,* waiting to be fried,
Of all life's starers the most many-eyed,
What furtive purpose hatched you long ago
In Indiana or in Idaho?

♩ a very useful and common vegetable, 🕮 Solanum tuberosum L., introduced from South America into Europe by the Spaniards in the latter part of the sixteenth century *(Kartoffel)*: potato, *colloq.* tater, spud, *sl.* murphy. – **Ẹrdäpfel,** the plural form, is the much preferred basis for a number of collocations, nominal compounds, as well as proverbs and phrases, of course largely agricultural or culinary – **1.** collocations: ~ *in* or *samt der Montur* potatoes baked with their skins on *(Pellkartoffeln, Kartoffeln in* or *mit der Schale)*: potatoes in their jackets, *BrE a.* jacket potatoes. – *heurige* ~ new potatoes. – *eingebrannte* ~ boiled potato slices in soured sauce. – *geröstete ~ (Bratkartoffeln)* fried potatoes. – **2.** nominal compounds: **~akademie** *f* -/pl. rare: -n *educ., hum.* or *contp.* any agricultural school or college: ag *or* aggie school, clodhopper college. – **~gulasch** *n* -(e)s/-e or **~gulyas** [gʊlaʃ] *n -/- cul.* potatoes in red pepper and onion sauce. – **~keller** *m* -s/- (1) rural *archit.* potato cellar. → (2) *hum.* or *iron.* = *Backhendelfriedhof* ↑. – **~knödel** *m* & *n* -s/-(n) *cul.* potato dumpling *or* ball. – **~kraut** *n* -(e)s ♩ (withered) potato stalks *pl.,* potato foliage *or* leaves *pl.* – **~nudeln** *f pl. cul.* very small oblong potato dumplings rolled in fat-fried breadcrumbs. – **~nummer** *f* -/-n ⇔ *contp.* by town dwellers – (a car with) a number plate issued by a provincial district authority *(Autozulassungsnummer für e-n Landbezirk)*: yokel licence plate. – **~puffer** *m* -s/- *cul.* potato fritter or pancake. – **~püree** *n* -s *cul. (Kartoffelbrei)* mashed potatoes *pl.* – **~salat** *m* -(e)s/-e *cul.* potato salad (prepared with onions and oil and vinegar dressing). – **~schale** *f* -/-n *cul.* (1) potato peel. – (2) of boiled potatoes, always *pl.* (in dialect speech: ~schäler) skins, jackets, peelings *pl.* – **~schmarren,** *colloq.* **~schmarrn** *m* -s/- *cul.* potatoes boiled, grated and fried. – **~teig** *m* -(e)s *cul.* a dough made of boiled and finely grated potatoes, with salt added: potato-crust paste. – **3.** proverbs and phrases: *die dümmsten Bauern haben die größten* (or, *dicksten*) ~ fortune favours fools; *or,* mugs for luck. – *die ~ rechnen sich gern zum Obst* *the low-born potatoes love to think themselves to be on a par with apples and pears. – *die ~ von unten anschauen* to be dead: to push up (*or, less often,* to kick up) the daisies.

Ẹrntekrone *f -/-* ♩ & *folklore* a magnificent device in the shape of a huge crown into which most of the major crops just reaped have been skilfully woven – an expression of gratefulness, esp. to God, for church and other festive display in early autumn: harvest crown.

Archduke Johann, a democratic ruler who rescued Styria from economic and spiritual decay

Ẹrz… [< MHG *erze-,* < OHG *erzi-* < eccl. L *archi-, arci-* < Gr *árchein* 'to be at the head', 'to preside'; in English, the same learned borrowing from Greek, with the basic sense of 'chief', has taken the form of *arch-* [a:tʃ]: **~feind** *m* -(e)s/pl. rare: -e *journ. hum.,* in sports, the word – lit., 'archenemy' – has no grim connotations whatsoever, but simply emphasizes a long tradition of friendly, good-neighbourly encounters: *im Fußball sind die Ungarn unser großer „~"* in football, the Hungarians are our great (*or rather,* good old) “archenemy”. – **~herzog** *m* -(e)s/ …zöge *hist.* a title, between 1359 and 1919, of the sovereign princes of the then ruling house of Austria: archduke. – **~herzogin** *f* -/-nen *hist.* (1) the wife of an archduke; (2) a princess of the Austrian Imperial family: archduchess. – **≈herzoglich** *adj hist.* of or pertaining to an archduke or an archduchy: archducal. – **~herzogtum** *n* -s/ …tümer *hist.* the domain of an archduke or an archduchy. – **~lauser** *m* -s/- forgivingly *hum.* a child who behaves mischievously or even badly, indeed repeatedly, but from whom, nevertheless, loving lenience is not withheld: born rascal; *er ist ein ~* he's a holy terror. – **~tepp** *m* -en/-en *pej.* a notable fool: prize idiot. – **~tratschen** *f* -/- *dial., pej.* **1.** someone who is incurably addicted to talking about other people's private lives: arch gossip; *dreimal darfst du raten, von welcher ~ ich das habe* you may have three guesses who was the champion tongue-wagger (*or* gossip-monger) to tell me. – **2.** if that penchant-cum-faculty is already well developed at the infant and juvenile stages: rattle-baby, tellingest of telltales, *AmE* … of tattletales.

ẹs [e:s], **ö̱s,** often shortened to **'s** [historically known as *Dual(is)* ‘dual number’, once a special word form addressing two people (and not one, nor more than two)] *pers. pron.* you; in dial. speech: yous, yaz [jʌz] – as seen, for instance, in a humorous inscription often found near the bar (AusG *Schank*) of rural inns, and also sung as a chatter ditty *(Schnadahüpfl)*:

Geht's, Leutl, es wißt 's ja,
der Wirt braucht sei' Ruah;
bis zwölfi, so moan i',
habt 's g'soffn grood gnua!

Your landlord needs rest, folks,
Sup up, with a will!
By twelve you might all well
Have guzzled your fill.

ẹxtrig *adj* & *adv* [blending adverbial StG *extra* with the adjectival suffix *-ig* (related to E *-ic*; cp. L *-icus* and Gr -iˈkos) *colloq.* **1.** *adj* (1) additional: extra, one more; *soll ich ein ~es Paar Socken einpacken?* shall I (*or,* d'you want me to) pack an extra (*or* another) pair of socks? – (2) unusual: out-of-the-line, *BrE a.* out-of-the-way; *es müssen aber schon ~e Sachen sein, die das Weitersagen lohnen* (or, *es muss schon was ≈es sein, das das Weitersagen lohnt*) it must surely be something beyond the run-of-the-mill that is worth passing on, *or* … something to write (*or* wire) home about. – **2.** *adv* exceptionally: *was ~ Gutes* [*Schönes, Schmackhaftes* etc.] anything extremely good [fine, tasty, etc.]: something super *or* fabulous, something to have to tip one's hat to, *sl.* the cat's pyjamas *or* whiskers, the bee's knees; *der Ochsenschwanz braucht zwar immens lang zum Kochen, ergibt aber dafür eine ~ feine Speise* oxtail meat takes a rare old time to cook, but it will end up a tasty dish of rare distinction.

F

fad *adj colloq.* **1.** said of or by persons: (1) *(langweilig)* dull, boring, flat; Viennese *dial.: ein ~es Aug haben (sich langweilen)* to be bored (stiff); *(schläfrig sein)* to be sleepy; *einen ~en Magen haben* to have heartburn: to have a queer (*or* funny) feeling in one's stomach; *(ängstlich)* timorous: timid as a mouse; *trau dich einmal, sei nicht so ~!* don't be such a scaredy-cat – show a little courage! – **2.** said of things, or referring to abstract nouns: (1) *(geschmacklos)* tasteless: *die Suppe schmeckt ~* this soup tastes like water. – (2) *fig. (emotionsarm)* insipid; *an das eher ~e Spiel der berühmten Wolter hat man sich schließlich gewöhnt* people eventually got accustomed to the rather insipid acting of the celebrated Wolter.

Faden *m* -s [< Romany *fádin* 'chill'] *colloq. (Kälte):* cold, low temperature: chilly weather; *heut früh hat es aber einen ~!* there's quite a nip (*or,* bite, chill) in the air this morning!

fadisieren *colloq.* **1.** *v/t* to make s.o. feel bored *(langweilen)*: to bore. – **2.** *v/refl* to get tired and impatient because one does not think something is interesting, or because one has nothing to do *(sich langweilen)*: to get bored; *sich bis zum Gehtnichtmehr ~* to get bored stiff (*or,* … bored to tears, … to death, … out of one's mind).

fallweise *adv* **1.** *(von Fall zu Fall)* as required by the individual case; *wir müssen dann ~ entscheiden* we must then decide each case on its own merits. – **2.** *(gelegentlich)* from time to time, occasionally ‖ *(in unregelmäßigen [Zeit-] Abständen)* at irregular intervals; *einige Zeitschriften erscheinen (bloß) ~* some magazines are published at irregular intervals.

Falott, Fallot *m* -en/-en [? < F *falot* 'insignificant, foolish, ridiculous', or < It *fa lotto* '(he, she) plays the numbers pool'] *contp. (Gauner)* scoundrel, rascal, villain; *dieser ~ ist mir noch immer einen Haufen Geld schuldig* this scoundrel still owes me loads of money.

Fangeisen *n* -s/pl. rare: - [actually, a hunting term referring both to a gin trap and a boar-spear] *hum.* or *sarc.* an engagement or a wedding ring (the mention of which, as a metaphorical "*man*trap", of course immediately conjures up visions of a matrimonially inclined female on the prowl): handcuff.

Fangerl in: **~ spielen** *v/i East Austrian* a children's game: to play touch *or* tig (tick), to play touch-and-run, *AmE a.* to play tag. – **Fangerlspiel** *n* -(e)s/-e game of touch *or* tig (tick), *AmE a.* game of tag.

faschieren *v/t (durch den Fleischwolf drehen) cul. BrE* to mince, *AmE* to grind (meat). – **Faschiermaschine** *f* -/-n *(Fleischwolf) BrE* mincing machine, mincer, meat chopper, *AmE* meat grinder. – **faschiert** *p. p. & adj* of meat: *BrE* minced, *AmE* ground; *~es Laibchen BrE* rissole, Viennese steak, *AmE* meatball, hamburger; *~er Braten* or *Strudel* meat loaf, loaf of minced meat cooked in the oven. – **Faschierte** *n* -n **1.** *(das durch den Fleischwolf Gedrehte)* food, e.g., meat, vegetables or soaked white rolls, minced. – **2.** *(Hackfleisch;* Ger.: *Hackepeter)* minced meat, or dishes made from it (see above, under *faschiert*).

Fasching *m* -s/pl. rare: -e *folklore* carnival, Shrovetide, *AmE sl. a.* carn(e)y, carnie. – **~dienstag** *m* -s/-e *(Fas[t]nacht)* Shrove Tuesday, *BrE a.* Pancake Day (*or* Tuesday), a day of high festival for schoolchildren, *AmE* Mardi Gras (< F [ˈmaːdɪ ˈgraː]), celebrated in New Orleans [ˈɔːlɪənz], Louisiana, with special festivities.

Faschings ...: ~kostüm *n* -s/-e carnival dress. – **~krapfen** *m* -s/- *cul.* carnival doughnut, a light yeast pastry fried in hot oil, eaten in carnival time, "that apotheosis of the doughnut" (Monk Gibbon) ‖ a piece of rustic weather wisdom, quite comparable in Austria and Great Britain: *~ in der Sunn, / z' Ostern d' Oar* [die Eier] *in der Stubn* March in Janiveer, / Janiveer in March, I fear! – **~montag** *m* -s/-e (Ger.: *Rosenmontag*) Shrove Monday, *AmE* Rose Monday. – **~scherz** *m* -es/-e carnival joke (*or* antic). – **~treiben** *n* -s, **~umzug** *m* -s/ ... züge *folklore* at Bludenz, Vorarlberg: Shrovetide Carnival pageant, with old carved wooden masks and decorated carriages featuring in the procession.

Faschismus *m* - *polit. hist.* usu. qualified by *grüner ~* or *Austro~* Austro-Fascism, a term of opprobrium for the right-wing authoritarianism exercised by Chancellor Engelbert Dollfuss in the early 1930s.

Fassl *n* -s/-(n) [dim. of *Faß n* 'barrel'] **1.** (little) cask, keg, *ScotE* knag. – **2.** *emot.* and *hum.* **a.** huge barrel: tun, *colloq.* whopper; **b.** obese person: tubby, tubs, *AmE* fatso, *contp.* tub of lard. – **~rutschen** *n* -s *folklore* on St Leopold's Day (November 15) at Klosterneuburg, Lower Austria, with reference to an 11,000-gallon tun there: "Sliding-down-the-Barrel" (built in 1704 by a Viennese woodcarver), a popular entertainment during their New Wine Festival.

fassonieren *v/t* in regard to hairdressing and eyebrow shaping: to trim and style; *nicht schneiden heute, bitte nur ~!* not a complete cut, just trim the ends, please!

Carnival doughnuts are a seasonal delicacy

Fatsche *f* -/-n *med.* bandage, medical band. – **fatschen** *vt/i* to wrap (one's arm, leg, etc.). – **Fatschenkind** *n* -(e)s/ … kinder *hist. (Wickelkind)* baby in swaddling clothes.

Faulenzer *m* -s/- [actually, 'lazy person'] *colloq.* paper with heavy lines on it, used to guide a writer's handwriting on a blank sheet placed above it *(Linienblatt)*: ruling paper; *ohne ~ hätten ihre Zeilen wie eine Berg-und-Tal-Bahn ausgeschaut* if she hadn't used that ruling paper her writing would have just swooped up and down (*AmE* just rollercoastered) all over the page. – **~krankheit,** also **Schwänzeritis** ↓ *f - school sl. hum.* = *Tachinose* ↓. – **~stricherl** *n* -s/-(n) [second el., dim. of *Strich m* 'stroke', 'dash'] an editing mark to save time and space when writing; either a line over an 'm' or 'n' to indicate two of the letter, or ditto marks to indicate repetition in a written column or vertical list: "lazy mark(s)".

Faust …: ~busserl *n* -s/-(n), **~watschen** *f* -/- *low colloq.* a punch in the face: knuckle sandwich; *nach seinem [seiner] ~ sind ihr die Lippen ganz angeschwollen* her lips swelled up after he's given her a smack in the kisser.

Feber *m* -s/- *(Februar)* in Eastern Austria: February.

Feder *f* -/-n feather; *~n haben sl.* to be afraid *(Angst haben)*: to be shaking in one's shoes, *BrE a.* to be showing the white feather, *AmE a.* to have the shakes. – **~pennal** *n* -s/-e *educ. (Federkasten)* pen-box, pencil box (*or,* -case). – **~weiß** *n* -es *(Talkpulver)* talcum powder.

Feinspitz *m* -es/-e *colloq.* **1.** chiefly *cul. (Feinschmecker)* connoisseur [kɒnɪ'sə:] of delicacies, gourmet ['guəmeɪ], epicure; *das ist was für den ~!* that's something for fastidious palates. – **2.** *(wählerischer Mensch)* picky chooser.

Fels *m* -en/-en *geol.* **1.** *(felsiges Gestein)* rock; mass of stony matter; *die Straße ist aus dem ~ gehauen* the road is cut out of a cliff ‖ *durch Wind und Wasser verwitterte ~en* rocks weathered by wind and water; *guter, griffiger ~* sound rock with good handholds; *schlechter (*or *brüchiger) ~* unsound (*or* rotten) rock; *in brüchigem ~* on unsound rock. – **2.** = *Felsblock.* – **3.** *in comp.* **~abhang** *m steiler ~* = *Felswand.* – **~band** *n* band, ledge. – **~berg** *m* **1.** rocky mountain (opp. *Latschenbuckel)* **2.** = *Kletterberg.* – **~block** *m* piece (*or* lump) of rock, boulder; *erratischer ~* = *Findling* ↓. – **~fenster** *n pl.* rock outcrops. – **~formation** *f* rock formation. – **~geher** *m* (skilled) rock climber, cragsman, *BrE. a.* cliffsman. – **~geröll** *n* = *Geröll.* – **~grat** *m* rocky ridge. – **~kanzel** *f* "pulpit", a very small plateau in a rock face. – **~katze** *f sl.* = *Felsgeher* ↑. – **~klettern** *n* rock-climbing. – **~kluft** *f* (rock-)cleft, chasm. – **~kolk** *m* water-worn rock, pothole. – **~nadel** *f (nadelförmiger Gipfel)* needle-like mountain peak, aiguille ['eɪgwi:l], crag. – **~spalte** *f* crack, crevice, rift. – **~spitze** *f* peak. – **~sturz** *m* rockfall, rockslip, *AmE a.* (rock)slide; *die Straße ist durch einen ~ verlegt* the road has been closed due to fallen rock. – **~technik** *f* rock technique [tek'ni:k]. – **~tour** *f* rock tour, *AmE* (rock) climbing trip; *Ausgangsort für ~en* climbing base; *eine kombinierte Fels- und Eistour a* combined tour. – **~vorsprung** *m* ledge. – **~wand** *f* wall of rock, cliff, precipice;

eine glatte ~ a sheer (rock-)face. – **~zacken, ~zahn** *m* jag of rock.

Fẹlsen…: ~aurikel *f* -/-n ⚘ mountain cowslip. – **~bad** *n* -es/ … bäder *baln.* "rock bath", often an outdoor swimming-pool, e.g. the one at Bad Gastein, Salzburg, maintaining a water temperature of 35° Centigrade. – **~theater** *m* -s/- *theat.* "rock(y) theatre", esp. the one in the park of Hellabrunn, Salzburg, one of Austria's most interesting historical open-air stages.

Fẹnster *n* -s/- *school jargon (Freistunde)* free period; *heuer hab ich einen miserablen Stundenplan, fast jeden Tag ein oder zwei* ~ this year I have a dreadful timetable (*AmE* schedule), with one or two vacant class periods almost every day.

Fẹnsterl *n* -s/-(s) [dim. of *Fenster*] *colloq.* **1.** *(Fenster[chen])* (little) window; a line from a famous "trysting" folksong: *geh mach dei ~ auf, i' wart' scho' so lang drauf* your window open wide, / long have I stood outside. – **2.** *folklore* "Little Window", a figure in the Steiregger Folk Dance.

fẹnsterln *v/i colloq. folklore* an Alpine custom practised by young men: *(das geliebte und begehrte Mädchen nachts am [oder durchs] Fenster besuchen)* to pay a nightly window visit to one's lover, to woo one's girl under her window at night (and, if successful, gain the right of entry through the opened window). – **Fẹnsterln** *n* -s (SwG *Kiltgang*) window courting.

Fẹnster…: ~balken *m* -s/- *(Fensterladen)* shutter, blinds *pl.* – **~gucker** *m* -s/- *arts* "Window Peeper", the sculptured figure of Anton Pilgram looking gravely out of the window under the staircase of the pulpit in St Stephen's Cathedral, Vienna, a masterpiece created by him in 1510. – **~schnalle** *f* -/-n handle, window catch. – **~schwitz** *m* -es/ *pl.* rare: -e *hum.* or *contp.* weak, inferior beer: dishwater, bilgewater. – **~stock** *m* -(e)s/ … stöcke window frame.

Feri̱al…: ~kurs *m* -es/-e *(Ferienkurs)* vacation course. – **~tag** *m* -es/-e *([arbeits- etc.] freier Tag)* holiday, day off.

Fẹrner *m* -s/- [< *Firn* 'coarse granular snow in the process of changing into ice'] *geog.* the local term in the Stubai, Ötztal and East Silvretta area, with a few outliers in the Zillertal and Riesenferner groups *(Gletscher)*: glacier (*BrE* [ˈglæsjə], *AmE* [ˈgleɪʃə]).

Fẹrsenschmäh *m* -s/-(s) *ftb., colloq.* the act of deliberately shaking off an opponent player by suddenly kicking the ball with one's heel, rather than with one's instep, thus giving it an altogether different direction (*Hackentrick;* → *Schmäh* 10): heel feint.

fẹrtig *adj gastr.* – in Western Austria, said of a main dish or one of its trimmings, listed on the menu but no longer available *(ausgegangen)*: out; *(die) Speckknödel sind leider* ~ I'm sorry, we're all out of bacon dumplings.

fẹsch *adj* [by sound substitution and shortening < E *fashionable*] Viennese *colloq.* **1.** elegant: smart, dashing; *ein ~er junger Mann* a dashing young man. – **2.** accommodating, friendly: pally; *geh, sei ~!* oh, be a sport (*BrE a.* pal *AmE a.* honey).

Below Bad Gastein, the river forms a fine Felsenbad, *of which E. Harrison Compton, our artist, was an enthusiastic habitué.*

This fine engraving of Salzburg, by G. Lewis and W. R. Smith in 1821, foreshadows the rôle that scenic jewel and cultural centre was to play as a major Festival City one hundred years later

Feschak *m* -s/-s [< Czech *fešák* = AusG *fesch* + Slav suffix *-ák*] *colloq.* **1.** either in appreciation or in slight contempt: **a.** *appr. (elegant gekleideter Mann)* fashionably dressed man: spiffy *or* snappy dresser, dreamboat, Beau Brummel, *AmE a.* flashy guy; *wozu braucht der ~ die Intelligenz?* so what does a snappy dresser need a mind for (*or,* to think for, with a mind)?, with his looks, what does he need brains for? **b.** *contp. (Schönling)* dandy, clothes-stand, pretty-boy, Adonis, Little Lord Fauntleroy, Beau Brummel, bachelor of hearts, answer to a maiden's prayer. – **2.** *(Kamerad, der überall mittut)* good friend: good sport, *AmE* bud, good guy.

Festspiel ...: ~stadt *f* - Festival City, a sobriquet of Salzburg, the seat of the well-known *Salzburger Festspiele.* – **~städter** *m pl. ftb. journ.* any of the City of Salzburg clubs, e.g. *S. K. Austria-Salzburg,* occasionally referred to under that name when playing an away match (... *wenn sie ein Auswärtsspiel bestreiten*).

Feuchtblattern *f pl.*, **Schafblattern** *f pl. med. (Windpocken)* chicken pox; *~ sind eine verbreitete Kinderkrankheit* chicken pox is a common childhood disease.

Feuer *n* -s/- fire ‖ in the rhymed proverb, with its close Scottish parallel: *ein großes ~ verzehrt, ein kleines nährt!* better a wee fire to warm us than a mickle (['mɪkl] 'big'; related to G *Michel*) fire to burn us!

Feuer ...: ~fleck *m* -(e)s/-en, or **~flecken** *m* -s/- *cul.* a popular dish at rural festivals in Eastern Austria – "fire patch", a piece of bread dough rolled out thin in roughly circular shape, done on a hot stove plate and coated with sour cream and garlic. – **~halle** *n* -/-n *(Krematorium)* crematorium, crematory. – **~mauer** *f* -/-n *(Brandmauer)* firewall. – **~wehr** *f* -/-en **1.** fire brigade, *AmE a.* fire department; *das Spritzenhaus der Freiwilligen ~ ist am Ortsausgang* the engine house of the Volunteer Fire Brigade (*AmE* Department) is at the end of the village. – **2.** *fig.* said of one person, or a body of persons, expected to remedy a difficult situation: trouble shooter[s], *AmE a.* trouble (*or,* search and rescue) man [men]; *das hab ich schon gern, du bringst alle Leute aus dem Häusl, und ich soll dann ~ spielen!* you nettle all the people, and I am supposed to pour oil on the waters!, *AmE a.* great – you rile everybody up, and then I have to play peacemaker!

Fiạker [fɪ'akə, 'fi:akə] *m* -s/- [< *Fiacrius,* the Latinized name-form of a pious Irishman (ca. 670) who is said to have worked many miracles in France: one thousand years later, in Hôtel St Fiacre, one of the houses in Paris bearing the name and image of the saint, there lived a privileged hackney-coachman whose carriages came to be known a 'voitures de St Fiacre', and the expression soon spread abroad] **1.** (*zweispännige [Miet-] Kutsche*) fiacre [fɪ'a:kr], two-horse open carriage, a cherished relic of olden times still in demand by tourists for sightseeing trips through Old Vienna, and by native Austrians for weddings or for taking godchildren out after their confirmation. – **2.** ([*Miet-*] *Kutscher*) (fiacre) cabman, *colloq.* cabby.

Fiạker ...: ~kutscher *m* -s/- = *Fiaker,* 2; **~lied** *n* -(e)s *mus.* 'Fiacre Song', a once popular, and now only slightly obsolescent, Viennese folk-song by Gustav Pick, glorifying the cabman and his 'two dashing horses'; **~wein** *m* -(e)s/-e *vinicult., colloq. (Schankwein)* 'coachmen's special', vin ordinaire ['vɛ̃ ɔ:dɪ'nɛə], a cheap, yet unadulterated type of wine preferred by coachmen and drivers, the knowledgeable clientele of simple inns.

An old fiacre against the big Prater Wheel – Viennese bonhomie and joie de vivre for ever

Fịlz *m* -es/-e [< MHG *vilz* < OHG *filz;* like E *felt* actually 'wool and fur (or hair) worked into a compact substance'; cp. G *walken* and *E* to *walk* 'to full', i.e. to thicken cloth by a special process in manufacture] **1.** *geog.* a tract of open, peaty wasteland in alpine areas (note the place names *Filzmoos,* SW of the Dachstein Massif, and *Filzstein Alp,* above the Krimml Waterfalls) common where drainage is poor (*Hochmoor*): highland moor; *in einigen ~en kann die Torfmächtigkeit sechs und mehr Meter erreichen* in some of the moors, the peat can reach down to a depth of seven yards or more. → **2.** *cul.* (*nicht ausgelassenes Bauchfett des Schweins*) pork belly fat, not yet rendered down. → **3.** *pol.*, usu. aggressively *contp.*, in that sense often preceded by the 'colour' word of the respective major political party (*der rote ~, der schwarze ~*, etc., pillorying the 'unholy' dominance of the Socialists, or the People's Party, etc., respectively) – a political party's firmly secured interests in one or several organizations of the State (such as the Labour Exchange network, the Railway and the Postal Services, the National Airline AUA, and Vienna's Communal Housing), with that party having long arrogated to itself the privilege of filling vacancies from its own rank and file: party-membership domain, vested incumbency; *es ist höchste Zeit, mit diesem ~* (or, *mit dem Parteien≈*) *Schluss zu machen* it is high time to put an end to that vile system of party-membership domains.

Fịlzpatschen *m* chiefly *pl. (Hausschuhe aus Filz)* (felt) slippers, felt houseshoes.

Finạnzer *m* -s/- [< It *guardia di finanza* 'customs guard'] *colloq. (Zollbeamte)* customs officer, *AmE* customs guard (*or* inspector), customs man, Treasury man.

Fịndling *m* -s/-e, **~sblock** *m* -(e)s/… blöcke *geol. (vom einstigen Inlandeis verschleppter Gesteinsblock)* erratic block, glacial boulder.

fịrmen *v/t relig.* said of a R. C. bishop: to confirm, to administer the Holy Sacrament of Confirmation to a young member of the Church; *der [die] Gefirmte = Firmling.*

Fịrm…: ~göd *m* -s/-e *dial. relig. = Firmpate; colloq. schwitzen wie ein ~* to perspire freely: to sweat like a horse (*or* a pig, *or* a prize bull), *AmE a. …* like a prize hog (*or,* like a June bride). – **~gödin** *f* -/-nen *dial. relig. = Firmpatin.*

Fịrmling *m* -s/-e *relig.* Confirmation child, confirmee, godchild [godson; goddaughter]; *colloq. essen wie ein ~* to eat greedily: to fork it in, to lay it in, to eat like a horse.

Fịrm…: ~pate *m* -n/-n *relig.* sponsor, (Confirmation) godfather, *in adolescent or familiar speech* godpa(pa); *~ sein* to stand godfather to a Confirmation; *er war mein ~* he stood godfather to my Confirmation. – **~patin** *f* -/-nen [cp. preceding entry] godmother, *colloq.* godmamma.

Fịrmung *f* -/-en *relig.* Confirmation ceremony.

Fịrmungs…: ~uhr *f* -/-en Confirmation watch, the customary present received by the godson from his sponsor. – **~wagen** *m* -/- Confirmation car *or* fiacre [fɪˈaːkr], decorated for the occasion with flowers and streamers of white and pink tissue paper. – **~zeit** *f* -/-en Confirmation time (*or* season), i.e. Whitsuntide; *zur ~* at Confirmation time, in the Confirmation season.

Fịrn *m* -(e)s/-e [< OHG *firni* 'old'] **1.** ☼▮ *& geog. (grobkörniger Altschnee)* granular, compacted snow, in the process of changing into ice: firn (snow), névé [*BrE* ˈneveɪ, *AmE* neɪˈveɪ] ‖ loosely, = *Gletscher.* – **2.** *vinic.* said of a fully-developed wine: maturity.

Fịrner *m* -s/- a variant form of → *Ferner.*

The Sulzenau Snowfield with the Zuckerhütl ('Sugar loaf Mountain' [11 507 ft.]) forms an impressive background to the pastoral scene of Neustift in the Stubai Valley – an engraving dating from 1877

Fịrn ...: ~feld *n* -(e)s/-er field of granular snow, above the permanent snowline, from which the glaciers are fed. – **~gleiter** *m* -s/mostly *pl.- skiing* snow gliders, i.e. short, wide skis, used in springtime skiing for downhill runs on bumpy snowfields and in steep ravines. – **~wind** *m* -(e)s/-e *(Gletscherwind)* glacier wind; *der ~ kann einem schon eiskalt ins Gesicht blasen* the glacier wind can blow frosty cold in your face.

fịscheln *v/i colloq.* only in: *es fischelt* there is a fishy smell; *die Butter (Milch, etc.) fischelt* the butter *etc.* has a fishy taste.

Fisole *f* -/usu. *pl.* -n *cul. (Stangenbohnen)* string beans, *BrE* runner beans, French beans, *AmE* green beans; *geschnittene ~n (Schnittbohnen)* French-cut beans.

Flạnkerl *n* -s/-(n) *colloq.* **1.** *(Staubflocke; Fussel, Faserstückchen)* on someone's clothes, etc.: speck of dust, bit of lint, piece of fluff (*or* fuzz); *nimm doch ein frisches Tuch zum Abtrocknen, da sind lauter ~(n) auf dem Geschirr* use a fresh dish towel to dry off with, the dishes are coming out all linty (*or* fuzzy)!; *das Zuckerl war voller ~(n) von der Rocktasche, in der er es uneingewickelt ge-*

tragen hatte the sweetie (*AmE* candy) was covered with lint because he had carried it unwrapped in his coat pocket; *die Schreibfeder hat ein ~, schau, wie sie schmiert!* there's a hair in the pen, look how it's smearing! ‖ *Ruß≚* particle of soot *pl. ≚n* Ulster *dial.* colley, Cheshire *dial.* collow. – **2.** on the floor of rooms seldom cleaned (syn. *Waukerl*): often *pl.* fluff, fuzz, *AmE a.* woolies, house moss, dust bunnies, dust mice.

Flẹckerl *n* -s/-(n) [dim. of *Fleck*] *colloq.* **1.** small patch of cloth, etc.; *Hawaii≚ hum.* bikini, abbreviated swimming shorts *pl.* for men. – **2.** small piece of ground; *ein reizendes (süßes,* etc.*) ~* a sweet (*AmE a.* cute) little spot; *ein schattiges ~* a shady spot. – **3.** *cul.* (*quadratisches Teigstück*) pastry square, square noodle; e.g., *Kraut≚, Schinken≚.*

Flẹckerl…: ~akademie *f* -/-n *hum.* for *Lehranstalt für gewerbliche Frauenberufe* school of dressmaking and allied professions (cp. *Greißler-, Knödelakademie* ↓). – **~patschen** *m*, **~patscherl(n)** *n pl.* rag slippers; *Viennese* low *colloq. ich hab mich auf ~ zerwuzelt* I laughed fit to burst, *Glaswegian dial.* I laughed my socks off. – **~suppe** *f* -/-n *cul.* clear soup with flat square noodles (*or* paste squares). – **~teppich** *m* -(e)s/-e *(Fleckenteppich)* **1.** rag rug (*or* carpet), crazy carpet. – **2.** *fig.,* often *hum.* or slightly *contp. (Flickwerk, bunte Sammlung)* patchwork, omnium gatherum; *vom Flugzeug bieten sich die Felder wie ein ~ dar* the aerial view presents a patchwork (*or,* … resembles a huge patchwork quilt) of fields; *unsere grammatische Terminologie ist ein ~, an dem zwei Jahrtausende gearbeitet haben* our grammar terminology is an odd mishmash which has been worked over for two thousand years. – **~walzer** *m* ♪ "stay-where-you-are-waltz", a Viennese specialty danced on one spot, turning only to the left.

Fleischlaberl or **Fleischloaberl** *n* -s/-n [second el., < *Laib m* 'loaf'] *cul.* beef and pork finely ground, minced with one egg, one onion, two cloves of garlic, some parsley, marjoram, salt, and black pepper; to be eaten with mashed potatoes and green salad *(Frikadelle): BrE* rissole, *AmE* meatball, hamburger.

Flịtscherl *n* -s/-n *contp.* a promiscuous girl or woman: floozy, -zie, -sie.

Foam [foɑm] *m* -s [< MHG *veim* 'froth' – extinct in StG except in *ausgefeimt* 'devoid of any frothy head forming in the glass once the beer has been freshly poured out', hence 'subject to suspicion', 'arrant'; the English cognate of AusG *Foam* is, of course, *foam* [fəʊm], but the word, one of the notorious "false friends", is inapplicable to beer] *dial.* a white mass of small bubbles formed on a glass of beer (Schaum [in e-m Glas Bier]) froth; *des Bier hat koan ~* there's no froth on this beer, this beer has no head, this beer is flat.

Fọgosch *m* -(e)s/-e [< Hung. *fogas* lit., 'toothed' (so named after its long, pointed teeth)], also known as **Schịll** *m* -(e)s/-e 🐟 a large predatory freshwater perch native to northern and central Europe, where it is a valuable food fish (*Zander*): pike-perch, zander ['zændə], 🕮 Stizostedion lucioperca, family Percidae; *cul. ~ gebraten* fried pike-perch.

Föhn *m* -(e)s/pl. rare: -e [< Romansh *favugn* < L *(ventus) Favōnius* '(the Roman personification of) a warm westerly wind, in mid-February, interpreted as a sign of approaching spring'] ☼ the warm, dry wind which blows down the valleys of the leeward side of a mountain range, esp. on the northern slopes of the Alps, and often has an enervating effect on the human tissues) – comparable to the *Schirokko* 'sirocco', blowing from northern Africa, and to the *Chinook* [(t)ʃɪˈnʊk], descending the Rocky Mountains to the coastal regions of Oregon and Washington: föhn *or* foehn [fəːn], föhn wind. – **~fische** *m pl.* a conspicuous element of the dry, gusty air stream from the south at times sweeping down on Western Austria: lenticular fleecy föhn clouds. – **~mauer** *f* - the well-marked line of difference between the humid grey air at times rising from the Italian Plain (holding as it does menaces of violent winds, some rain and snow [as well as sudden thaw and avalanches in spring]), and the beautifully clear skies between: wall of heavy föhn clouds.

fọrtwursteln [-ʃtln] *colloq.* [the Austrian term, and its English equivalents "muddling through", "log-rolling without policy", etc., owe their popularity to Count Eduard Taaffe, the Austrian Prime Minister and Minister of the Interior in the 1880s; profoundly sceptical of all ideologies, and moved by an invincible sense of humour, he was concerned to have round him men who could see a joke and take the problems of each day as they arose, rather than men who tended to base their large ideas on woolly social, economic and constitutional theories] **1.** *v/i (ein Unternehmen mühsam und notdürftig fortsetzen)* to muddle through, to plod along. – **2.** *v/refl* = 1. *er wurstelt sich (so) fort* he just manages to keep his head above water (*or,* … to squeak by, to break even, to muddle through).

Fr̥akkele *n* -s/-n [dim. < F *flacon* '(wine) bottle'] a liquid measure (1/8 of a litre [0.22 pint]), and a glass for brandy: jigger.

fra̱tscheln *v/i colloq.* **1.** *(tratschen)* to gossip: to chitter-chatter. → **2.** *(indiskret [aus]fragen)* to pry: to ask nosy questions.

Fra̱u̱entragen *n* -s *R. C. & folklore* = *Marientragen.*

Fre̱u̱nderl *n* -s/-(n) [dim. of *Freund*] *colloq.* **1.** *emot.* good old friend, *BrE colloq.* pal, chum, *AmE colloq.* buddy; uttered, for instance, in a carefree drinking spirit: ~, *ist es nicht schön, dass wir heut bei einem Glaserl Wein beisammensitzen können? … so jung kommen wir ja nimmer z'samm!* isn't it nice, old boy, to be able to celebrate over a glass of wine? … after all, we won't meet at our present "youthful" age again! – **2.** *iron.* (influential) friend; *er hat in allen Ministerien seine ~ sitzen* he has his "boys" in all the Ministries. – **~wirtschaft** *f* -/-en often *contp.* nepotism, *AmE* cronyism; *diese ~ geht einmal zu weit!* this "old-boy basis" has gone far enough!

Fridạtte *f* -/-n an unetymological, if acoustic, spelling of the following word, sometimes found on menus and in recipes; **Fritta̱te** *f* -/-n [< It *frittato,* p.p. of *frittare* 'to fry'] *cul. (Eierkuchen)* thin pancake (for soup garnish), *AmE* fritters. – **~nsuppe** *f* -/-n *(Pfannkuchensuppe)* clear soup with thinly sliced (or shredded) pancakes, beef broth with strips of pancake in it.

Friedhofs… *colloq. hum.:* **~jodler** *m* -s/- *med.* bad cough: churchyard cough. – **~spargel** *m* -s/-(n) cigarette or cigar: coffin-nail.

frọtzeln *vt/i* [< It *frizzare* 'to sting'] *colloq.* **1.** *v/t* to tease (*necken*): to pull s.o.'s leg, *BrE a.* to take the mickey out of s.o., *AmE a.* to josh, to razz. – **2.** *v/i* to joke *or* jest about s.o. *or* s.th. (*sich über j-n* or *etwas lustig machen*): to make fun of s.o. *or* s.th. – **Frotzelei**, **Frotzlerei** *f* -/-en *colloq.* a playful, or at times malicious, attempt to make a fool of a person by calling him nicknames, copying him, telling him something that is not true, etc. (*Hänselei*): leg-pull, *BrE a.* mickey-taking, *AmE a.* razzing, giving the needle.

Fuß *m* -es/Füße foot; leg – *phr.* **1.** a hostess's jovial way at dinner of asking permission to hand a guest an item of food straightaway across the table, without the formality of serving cutlery (*Vorlegebesteck*): *darf ich dir [Ihnen] das (Stück) zu ~ reichen?* you don't mind my using the boarding-house reach, do you? – **2.** a bitter comment on having had to, or perhaps still having to, wait for an unduly long time: *da stehst du dir* (or, *man sich) die Füße in den Bauch!* you can wait till the cows come (*ScotE* … till the kye comes) home. – **3.** ways of typifying a character as being too easily put upon, trusting, unsuspicious, incapable of imagining that anyone could mean him (or her) any harm: *an dir [Ihnen] können sich wahrlich alle Leute die Füße abwischen!* you're a regular doormat, you would let people just walk all over you. – **4.** a *dial.* euphemism to describe a man's carnal desire for female company: *der lebt mit'm ~ über d' Haxn* he's a great one for legover situations.

Fụsserl, also **Hạxerl** *n* -s/-n [first el., ? < Germ. **hanhsenawo* 'tendon by which a slaughtered animal is hung up'] *emot.* a child's, or a woman's small, foot: tootsie *or* tootsy, tootsie-wootsie.

Fuzel *m* -s/- [a variant of *Fussel f* < MHG *visel* 'fibre', 'loose thread'] *dial.* **1.** a soft light piece of thread or wool that has come off cotton, wool, or other material (*Fädchen oder Faserstückchen von Kleidung, Stoffen o. ä.*): *BrE* bit of fluff, *AmE* bit of lint; *schau einmal her, von dem Pullover gehn die ~ nur so runter!* just look – that sweater is going bobbly all over. – **2.** a very small piece of something, e.g. (1) of food (which the speaker would like to sample merely); *BrE* eency-weency-bit, *AmE* bitsy-witsy, little-bitsy thing; or (2) of dust or dirt: speck. – **Fuzelei** *f* -/pl. rare: -en *dial., contp.* a small (and untidy) writing that is difficult to read: scribble in a (god-awful) puny hand; *diese ~ ist eine Zumutung!* what a cheek forcing one to get to grips with such a cramped and puny scrawl. – **fuzeln** *v/i dial.,* often used critically of some handwriting that proves a strain on the eyes of the reader because it is very small (and often also untidy and spidery): to scribble in a puny hand. – **Fuzerl** *n* -s/-(n) [< *Fuzel* ↑ + dim. *-erl*] *dial.* **1.** = *Fuzel* 1 and 2. – **2.** often used critically – a piece of paper too small for the intended written note it is supposed to bear: scrap; *jetzt gehst d' aber, so ein ~ ist ja nix zum Schreiben!* get awa' wi' ye, that's just an apology for a sheet of paper to write on!

G

Gabel *f* -/-n fork ‖ *phr.* (1) a humorous plea for adopting the "direct method" at meals, dispensing with cutlery: *mit der ~ is' 's a Ehr, / mit den Fingern kriegt man mehr!* *use a fork if you want style, / but the fingers get the pile!; similarly, in common speech: fingers were made before knives and forks! (2) jocularly said in defending one's neglect of table manners: *Jesus sprach zu seinen Jüngern: „Wennst ka ~ hast, isst d' mit den Fingern!"* God created (*or,* made) fingers before forks!, hands were made before knives and forks.

Gabel ...: ~bissen *m* -s/- savoury snack, a small plastic plate containing a piece of fish or sausage, slices of egg and gherkin, and mayonnaise, with the whole thing covered and surrounded by jelly. – **~frühstück** *n* -(e)s/-e (in Germany often: *Frühstück[sbrot]*) used by townspeople (cp. *neunern*) mid-morning snack, (snack) lunch, usu. consisting of small helpings of goulash made of beef or lamb, hashed lung meat served with a dumpling, a portion of warm pork with a vinegar-and-horseradish sauce, or a pair of frankfurter sausages.

Gaden *m* -s/- *archit.* **1.** stone building, used for storing agricultural produce (hence, e.g. *Milch~, Zehr~*). – **2.** floor level; *ein Stockhaus hat zwei ~* a one-storeyed house has two floors.

Galerie *f* - [< its standard use of '(people in) the highest and cheapest seats in a theatre, concert-hall, etc.'; hence, the have-nots and outcasts, as opposed to the well-to-do, who occupy seats in the boxes and stalls] *criminal sl. (Gaunergesellschaft [von Wien])* criminal world: the bad element, the people on the wrong side of the law, those on the wrong side of the tracks. – **Galerist** *m* -en/-en *([Wiener] Ganove)* criminal, esp. a burglar: *AmE* second-story man.

Galt ... *anim. husb.* [< MHG *galt* 'yielding (yet) no milk', 'barren'; cp. E *gelding* 'castrated horse']: **~alm** *f* -/-en mountain pasture for young cattle. – **~kuh** *f* -/ ... kühe heifer. – **~vieh** *n* -s *(Jungrinder)* young cows and bulls *pl.*

Ganslspitze *f* -/-n *tech. & hum.* "roast goose summit", the annual peak consumption of city gas in the early noon hours of 25 December, due to the roasting of the traditional Christmas goose in many households of Vienna.

Gant *f* - [< MHG *gant* 'auction', 'selling to him who bids most' < L *inquantum*] *dial. (Krida)* insolvency ‖ *phr.* said of real property for which excessive debts have been incurred: *auf die ~ kommen* to come up for auction; *das Geschäft ist auf der ~* the business is up for auction.

gar *colloq.* **1.** *adj* [< MHG *gar* < OHG

garo 'prepared', 'finished', 'complete(d)'; with the same meaning, OE *gearu*] (1) said of food consumed *(aufgezehrt)*: eaten up, all gone, at an end; *das Brot ist ~, kein Bröserl ist mehr da* the bread is all gone, not a crumb's left ‖ *phr.* found in a cheerfully resigned four-line ditty to echo the sentiment of a Continental 'Old Mother Hubbard' who also, on trying "to fetch her poor dog a bone", discovered that "the cupboard was bare":

Aus is 's	*All o'er,
und gar is 's	What a bore –
und schad is 's,	Ain't we sore
dass 's wahr is!	There's no more!

(2) said of material, merchandise, etc. given away or sold out *(aufgebraucht)*: used up, all gone, at an end (*or* spent); *unser Geld ist ~* our money is at an end, we are broke. – (3) said of something immaterial, e.g. a theatre performance *(am Ende)*: at an end, over; *das Stück ist ~* the play is over. → **2.** *adv* [a sense development of the former] an intensifier (1) preceding negatives *(überhaupt)*: at all; *~ nie* never at all, never ever ‖ the opening couplet of a famous dialect lyric by Franz Stelzhamer (1802–1874):

Allweil kreuzlusti
und trauri gar nia,
I steh da wia da Kerschbam
in ewiga Blüah.

*All the while merry
and no whit in gloom:
here I stand like a cherry
tree ever in bloom.

(2) preceding adverbs and indefinite pronouns *(sehr)*: very; *das schmeckt ~ gut* that tastes delicious; *~ so schwierig ist das ja nicht, gell?* it isn't that difficult, is it?; *~ mancher hat das auch gemeint* many a man thought so too.

Garçonniere [–ˈjɛə] *f* -/-n [–ˈjɛəren] [< F *garçonnière*] *archit. (Junggesellenwohnung)* bachelor flatlet (*AmE* apartment), i.e. a small bed-sitting room complete with kitchen and bathroom.

garteln *v/i colloq. (Gartenarbeit aus Liebhaberei verrichten)* to potter (*AmE* putter) about in the garden.

Garten *m* -s/ Gärten *hort.* garden ‖ in conjunction with the name of a province, the word is often used to give an appreciative label to an area famous for growing fruits and vegetables: *der ~ Wiens,* Lower Austria; *der ~ der Steiermark,* the Deutschlandsberg area, SW of Graz; *der ~ von Vorarlberg,* the stretch of country between Rankweil and Klaus.

Note: In English-speaking countries, "Garden" plays a very similar rôle: "The Garden of England", Kent, Worcestershire; "The Garden of South Wales", the southern division of Glamorganshire; "The Garden of Ireland", Co. Wicklow; "The Garden of Ulster", Armagh; "The Garden of Shetland", Uist, the most northerly isle; "The Garden of the West", Illinois; "The Garden of California", Alameda.

Garterl *n* -s/-(n) *emot.* little garden; *ein sauberes ~* a neat (*or,* tidy) little garden, *AmE* a cute (*or,* quaint) little garden.

Gatehose, also **Gatjehose, Gattehose** *f* -/-n [< Hung. *gatya* '(long) drawers'] *colloq.* in Eastern Austria: *(lange Unterhose)* long pants, to be tied round the ankles.

Gatsch *m* -(e)s *colloq.* **1.** ☼ very wet earth in a sticky mass *(aufgeweichte Erde):* mud; *durch den ~ soll ich da durch? da werd ich ja ganz dreckig und rutsch hundertmal aus!* I am supposed to walk through all that muck?! I'll get totally muddy and slip and slide all over

Freestyle ram-wrestling in the Tyrol: two combatants butting their heads together at full tilt

the place ‖ a *hum.* or only slightly impatient suggestion to go away at once: *hupf in [de]n ~ (und schlag Wellen)!* go jump in the lake!, take a long walk off a short pier!, go climb a rock!, *AmE juvenile sl. a.* be like a banana and split!, be like dandruff and flake off!, be like a ghost and vanish!, be like a bee and buzz off!, make like a tree and leave!, drum and beat it!, (put an egg in your shoe and) beat it!, take a rope and skip it! – **2.** ☼ partly melted snow: slush, sludge. – **3.** *cul. contp.* viscid food mixture whose ingredients are a blend of mystery, overboiled and hence disintegrated *(weiche, breiige Masse)*: goo, goop, mush, mixed mullish, *AmE a.* goozalum, stickum, mung; *und diesen undefinierbaren ~ soll ich essen?* and I am supposed to eat this mystery mullish?, *räum den ~ da von meinem Teller!* get this mung off my plate! – **gatschig** *adj colloq.* said of soft and wet ground, of boots covered with thick mud, etc.: muddy, slushy, *BrE a.* squidgy.

Gauderfest *n* -es/-e [first el., the name of an old farmhouse where the event originally took place; now with overtones of *Gaudi* 'merrimakings'] *folklore* at Zell am Ziller, on the first weekend in May: "Gauder [ˈgaudə] Festival", the oldest and biggest feast of the Zeller valley, with singing, dancing, wrestling (→ *Rangelfest*) and, not least, barrelfuls of specially brewed, strong beer.

Gebärklinik *f* -/en *med. (Entbindungsheim)* maternity home.

gefinkelt *adj (schlau, durchtrieben)* clever, sharp, witty; *als im vergangenen Monat dem Hotel der Strom abgedreht wurde, fand der ~e Geschäftsführer schnell einen Ausweg* when his hotel's electricity was switched off by the power company last month, the clever-minded manager quickly found a way to remedy the situation.

Geher *m* -s/- *colloq.* in the political history of South Tyrol: = *Optant* ↓.

Gemüt *n* -es soul, heart; *hum.,* said in praise of a favourite drink, etc.: *etwas fürs* ~ something to cheer the inner man, just what the doctor ordered, something to warm the cockles (of one's [*or,* the] heart).

gemütlich *adj* **1.** said of objects and circumstances: snug, cosy; with reference to a secluded nook, possibly furnished with one or two easy chairs and a standard reading lamp: *eine ~e Ecke* a cosy corner; *ein ~es Stüberl* a cosy little room, a cubby(-hole), a snuggery; *ein ~es Stadterl* a charming and quaint little town; in praise of an inn, etc., with wood panelling and dim lights: *da ist's* ~ there's a homey atmosphere about the place. – **2.** said of persons and human qualities: *er ist ein ~es Haus* he's a pleasant and easy-going chap; *wir Österreicher haben (nun einmal) etwas übrig* (or *über) für ~es Beisammensein* we Austrians (*AmE* just) love friendly get-togethers; **~keit** *f* - cosiness, charm; of an old inn, etc.: (genial) atmosphere; *was dem Gasthof an Komfort fehlen mochte, glich er durch seine ~ mehr als aus* what the inn may have lacked in the way of amenities, it more than made up for in atmosphere; in indignation: *da hört sich aber die ~ auf* that's where the fun ends, that's the limit, that's going too far.

Genagelte *m* -n/usu. pl. -n [the nominalized p.p. of *nageln* 'to nail', 'to put metal points on the sole of a shoe or boot'] hobnailed (*or* nail-studded) shoe *or* boot, iron(-shod) shoe *or* boot; *der Bergwanderer wäre nicht tödlich abgestürzt, wenn er statt gewöhnlicher Straßenschuhe ~ angehabt hätte* the mountain walker would not have fallen to his death if he had worn studded climbing boots instead of ordinary walking shoes.

genạnt [ʃeˈnant] *adj* [< F *gênant* 'troublesome'] *colloq.* with reference to circumstances: *(peinlich)* embarrassing, awkward; *dass ich vergessen habe, Sie anzurufen, das ist mir so ~, Sie wissen gar nicht wie!* I'm so embarrassed (or, I feel so mean, I feel about two inches high, I could sink through the floor) for not ringing (*AmE* calling) you; you just can't imagine!

Gendạrm [ʃan-, less often ʃã-] *m* -en/-en [< F *gendarme* < pl. *gensdarmes* < *gens d'armes* 'armed men'] one of a body of (orig. mounted) policemen, organized, armed and drilled as soldiers (established during the mid-nineteenth century in all sixteen Crown Lands and Kingdoms of the then Austro-Hungarian Monarchy), to do duty in country areas *(Mitglied der Landpolizei)*: rural policeman, *BrE a.* rural constable. – **Gendarmerie** *f* -/ … ien **1.** rural police, *less often* gendarmery [ʒʌnˈdaːmərɪ], gendarmerie [ʒʌndʌməˈriː]. – **2.** rural police station; *wo ist die nächste ~?* where is the nearest police station? – **~posten** *m* -s/- = *Gendarmerie,* 2.

Genierer [ʃeˈniːrə] *m* -s *colloq. (Scheu)* bashfulness, reserve; *wenn ihm etwas nicht passt, dann sagt er's schon, da kennt er keinen ~* if he doesn't like something, he comes straight (*or,* right) out and says it (… he doesn't beat about

[*AmE* around] the bush); as far as that's concerned, he's got no inhibitions (*or,* he's not shy in the least).

Genụßspecht *m* -(e)s/-e *colloq. (Genießer)* one who knows how to enjoy life, a hedonist: happy camper, good-time Charlie; *er ist ein ~* he lives life (up) to the hilt, he enjoys life to the fullest.

Gẹrm *f* [?< L *germen* 'sprout', 'shoot'; or a contraction of Late MHG *gerben* & MHG *gerwe,* derived from *gern = gären* 'to ferment'] *bak.* a greyish-yellow substance obtained chiefly from fermented beer, used as a fermenting agent to raise bread dough (*Backhefe*): baker's yeast.

Gẹrm ...: ~knödel *m* & *n* -s/-(n) *cul.* yeast dumpling – filled with a plum, plum jam, or a cherry, rolled in breadcrumbs, and sprinkled with hot butter and finely granulated sugar. – **~krapfen** *m* -s/- yeast doughnut. – **~teig** *m* -(e)s dough made with yeast, yeast dough.

Gerọ̈ll *n* -(e)s/pl. rare: -e ⛰ **1.** an area of small loose broken rocks on the side of a mountain: scree. – **2.** a mass of large stones or pieces of rock: boulders *pl.* ‖ in cpds. **~halde** *f* -/-n scree (slope). – **~schutt** *m* -(e)s = *Geröll* 2.

geschnạppig *adj dial.* [kʃ-] *(schnippisch)* flippant: cocky, *AmE a.* snippy; *ein ~es junges Ding* a cocky young thing.

gespịtzt p.p. (< *spitzen* 'to point') *colloq.* of a p.'s face: (*abgemagert*) peaked, peakish, peaky; *er schaut ~ aus* he has a pinched face.

gesprịtzt *p.p. & adj colloq.* said of wine and cider: mixed with soda-water; *ein Achtel ~ ist gut gegen den Durst* an eighth of a litre (of wine) mixed with soda-water is good for the thirst. – **Gesprịtzte** *m* -n/-n wine diluted with soda-water.

Gestẹck *n* -(e)s/-e any ornamental accessory for a lady's dress or one's hat, e.g. a brooch, feathers, or a chamois brush: posy, nosegay; *200 Orchideen~e für den Wiener Opernball* 200 orchid corsages for the Vienna Opera Ball.

Gewụ̈rzsträußerl *n* -s/-(n) *folklore* a minor but deeply symbolic item of regional home culture (often with a paper frill), pleasing to the senses of sight and smell: posy of spices; *ein ~ sein eigen zu nennen, wirkt nach dem Volksglauben in mehrfacher Hinsicht segensreich – Nelken und Muskat bringen Frohsinn ins Haus, Weinbeeren und Mandeln schützen vor Krankheit, und Pfefferkorn würzt den Ehestand* a posy of spices, in popular belief, is a domestic blessing in more ways than one – clove and nutmeg invite gaiety into the home, grapes and almonds shelter from illness, and peppercorn adds fragrance to the state of wedded bliss.

Gịftler *m* -s/- *colloq. ([Rauschgift-]Süchtiger)* drug addict: dope-fiend, drug (*or,* needle) freak.

Gịgerizpa̱tschen, less often **Kịkerizpa̱tschen** *n* -s/pl. rare: – [lit., '(where) a cock-a-doodle-doo and indoor slippers (make up about the two most exciting essentials of humdrum country living)'] *hum.* or slightly *contp.* any somnolent village or small town – sometimes indeed a mere figment of the speaker's or writer's imagination – far removed from the mainstreams of life and the comforts of modernity = *Hintertupfing* ↓.

Gịpfel *m* -s/- ⛰ **1.** the top of a mountain: summit; *wieviele ~ hast du denn in den Ostalpen schon bezwungen?* how many summits in the Eastern Alps have you under your belt? – **2.** a sharply pointed top of a mountain: peak; *diese ~ sind fast alle ganzjährig verschneit* most of these peaks are covered with snow all the year round.

Gịpfel… ⩓: **~buch** *n* -(e)s/ …bücher visitors' book (kept in a safe box on a mountain peak for climbers to make brief entries in and sign). – **~kreuz** *n* -es/-e [largely unknown in English-speaking countries] a cross marking a mountain peak, usu. erected by the local or other section of the Austrian Alpine Club (with a dedication service held on erection or renewal): summit cross. – **~pyramịde** *f* -/-n a monumental mound of rough stones (or, sometimes, shaped masonry) with a square base and sloping sides that meet in a point at the top, to serve as a conspicuous landmark: summit pyramid. – **~sieg** *m* -(e)s/-e successful mountain climb. – **~steinmann** *m* -(e)s/ …männer a mass of boulders roughly poised among loose shale to mark a mountain top: summit cairn [keən]. – **~stürmer** *m* -s/- *colloq.* a passionately enthusiastic and successful mountain climber: summit hero.

Girạrdihut *m* -s/ -hüte [named after Alexander Girardi [ʃɪˈrardɪ], 1860–1918, a popular Austrian comedian and vaudeville singer in his day, who fancied that type of hat] a man's narrow-brimmed hard straw hat with a flat top: boater, *AmE a.* sailor('s straw).

glạttstreifen *v/t (glattstreichen)* of cloth, paper, etc.: to smooth (down); *der Kellner streifte das Tischtuch glatt* the waiter smoothed (*or,* unwrinkled) the tablecloth.

Glọ̈ckler *m* -s/- *folklore* bell-ringer. - **Glọ̈cklerlaufen** *n* -s/pl. rare: - an ancient Halloween custom in the Ischl area of Upper Austria – young men in groups of up to thirty, wearing white smocks with bells attached, going round from house to house at a steady pace, in step, on their heads transparent shapes, like chapels, fish, crosses and ships, all illuminated from within: Bellmen's (*or* Bell-ringers') Parade.

The summit cross on Mt Grossglockner, the highest mountain of Austria (3789 m [12 461 ft])

Gmiạt, Gmüạt [dialect spellings] → *Gemüt.*

Goịserer *m* -s/- [< *(Bad) Goisern,* a market-town in the Traun Valley, Upper Austria, N of Lake Hallstatt – a centre for the manufacture of mountaineering boots, as well as a mountain health resort and a starting-point of expeditions up the Dachstein Massif] **1.** (if female, **~in** *f* -/-nen) a native, or inhabitant, of Bad Goisern: man [woman] from Goisern. – **2.** ⩕ usu. pl. (*Bergschuh[e] mit Flügelnägeln*) (a pair of) climbing, or mountaineering, boots (reinforced by iron clamps on either side of the sole (*Schernken* ↓): cleated mountain climb ing boot[s].

Gọldene Dạchl *n* -n -s *hist. arts & archit.* a finely ornamented loggia with a gilded copper roof, in the City of Innsbruck, built in 1500 as a stage box from which Emperor Maximilian I and his Court might watch the players (English among them) who performed in the street below: Golden Roof.

Gọld ...: ~fasan *m* -(e)s/-e [named after a long-tailed native Asian bird, *Chrysolophus pictus,* conspicuous for its brilliantly coloured plumage] *mil. sl., iron.* a senior officer of the Austrian Army, bearing the distinctive red stripes and other ornaments of his rank on the cuffs, lapels and trouser legs of his uniform: golden pheasant. – **~hältig** *adj* containing or bearing gold (*goldhaltig*): gold-bearing, auriferous, aurous. – **~haube** *f* -/-n *EastAus folklore* the picturesque heirloom headgear worn on festive occasions by native girls and women of the Wachau (the scenic stretch of the Danube in Lower Austria between Melk and Krems), of Upper Austria, and Western Styria: gold-lace *or* gold-embroidered bonnet. – **~rübe** *f* -/-n [so named from the yellow-orange root of the widely cultivated plant] ♩ *(Karotte)* carrot.

Gọscherl *n* -s/-(n) [dim. of *Gosche(n) f,* vulg. for 'mouth'] *emot.* **1.** *(Mündchen)* ([dear] little mouth); said to a child or, playfully, to an adult: *mach's ~ auf, kriegst ein Zuckerl!* open your mouth, and I'll pop in a sweetie! – **2.** appreciatively, mostly with reference to a beautiful girl or young woman *(Mündchen)*: sweet little mouth; *sie hat ein herziges ~* she has an adorable little mouth. – **3.**

The two-storeyed Goldene Dachl *is one of the outstanding sights of Innsbruck, bearing in fine stone relief the Imperial coats-of-arms*

hum. or *sarc. (Mundwerk)* sharp tongue, acid tongue; *sie hat ein ~* she has a sharp edge to her tongue, she can give you a tongue-lashing.

Gradl, less often **Gradel** *m* -s **1.** *tex.* a hard-wearing herringbone twill weave of linen and cotton, to be made into working garments, etc. (*Drell, Drillich*) – for jean and overalls: drill, denim; for mattresses: ticking. – **2.** *tech.* a loose aggregation of small water-worn or pounded stones; or a mixture of such stones with coarse sand, used for paths and roads and as an aggregate (*Kies*): gravel.

Grąnd *m* -(e)s/-e [< It *gronda* 'gutter'] ✓ a long, narrow open container, chiselled of wood or stone, and placed near the farmhouse or by the roadside for animals to drink out of ([*Brunnen-*]*Trog*): trough.

Grąndl, less often **Grąndel** or **Grąnl** *f* -/usu. pl.: -n [< L *granum* 'a single grain of a cereal' + dim. *-l*] *hunt.* a prized trophy to display on a huntsman's traditional costume (*Eckzahn im Oberkiefer* [*beim Rotwild*]): upper eye-tooth (of a deer).

Grąnt *m* -(e)s [< *Grand m* 'coarse gravel'] *dial.* (a fit of) temper, sulky behaviour (*üble Laune*): peeve, huff, huffiness; *einen ~ haben* to have the grumps; *hast du deinen ~ schon immer oder geht der einmal vorbei?* were you raised on sour milk to show such a peeve, or is it a passing affair?; *lad' deinen ~ gefälligst woanders ab, aber net bei mir!* go and dump yer load of huff somewhere else, if you please, but not with me. – **grąnteln** *v/i dial.* to be ill-humoured (and offer running confirmation of this state of mind by always bickering about trifles): to peeve, to grouch, to grouse. – **grąntig** *adj dial.* ill-humoured: peeved, ratty, shirty, *BrE a.* narky, niggly. – **Grąntigkeit** *f* - *dial.* = *Grant.* – **Grąntscherm** *m* -s/- [second el. < *Scherben f pl.* 'broken crockery'] *dial.* an (as it were, congenitally) ill-humoured, complaining person (*mißvergnügter Mensch, ‚Sauertopf'*): grumble-guts *sg.*, sourpuss.

Grasausläuten *n* -s *folklore* in the Lower Inn Valley, on St George's Day (23rd April), after which the cattle are allowed to graze on the village common again: "Ringing out the Grass", one of the noisy fertility rites performed to expel Winter and to encourage the grass to grow; a procession in which a dairyman (complete with milking-stool and other paraphernalia), boys ringing chimes and cowbells, a root-digger, and a raggedly dressed whip-cracker march gaily through the meadows.

Grätzel *n* -s/-(n) → *Gretzel.*

Grausbirnen *f pl.* only in the *colloq.* phr. *mir steigen (dabei) die ~ auf (ich ahne Schlimmes)* I shudder at the thought: I get goose flesh (*or,* the shivers [*or,* the shudders], *AmE a.* goose bumps) when I think of it; *mir steigen die ~ auf, wenn ich nur an die kommende Mathematikschularbeit denke* thinking of the forthcoming maths test just gives me the creeps (or, the heebie-jeebies).

Greißler, rarely **Greisler** *m* -s/- [? < *Gräußler, Gräuß* – being the dim. of *Grauß,* MHG *grüz,* 'granule', or *Griesler* 'retail merchant who received goods from river barges'] **1.** *obsolescent,* in Eastern Austria: *(Lebensmittelhändler)* grocer; *ob man das beim ~ um die Ecke* *auch wirklich kriegt?* do you think I could even get that at the grocer's around the corner (*AmE* at the store around the corner)?; → *Greißlerei.* – **2.** *contp. (Kleinigkeitskrämer)* stickler for detail; *bei dem ~ geht nichts weiter!* (he's so bothered about little things that) he never gets anything done!, *AmE* he gets so stuck on little things that he never gets off the ground (*or,* … on details that he never gets anything done)! – **3.** *colloq. phr.* in a mildly impatient reproach – a person who is a slow and simple thinker: Simple Simon.

Greißlerei, rarely **Greislerei** *f* -/-en *obsolescent,* in Eastern Austria: *(kleiner [Kram-]Laden)* grocery, *AmE* dime store, *AustralE* smallgoods shop; *in der ~ nebenan* at the grocer's next door.

Greißler …: ~akademie *f* -/-n school & student *sl., hum.,* rarely *contp.* any commercial school or college of Secondary or Higher Education: ec *or* eccie school, *AmE a.* sellocution college. – **~lehrling** *m* -(e)s/-e *com.* an apprentice to a dealer of general supplies: grocery boy. – **~rechnung** *f* -/pl. rare: -en *contp.* an oversimplified way of calculation *(Milchmädchenrechnung)*: case of naive reckoning, rash way of putting two together.

Grenadiermarsch *m* -(e)s/… märsche *cul.* fried potatoes with onions and noodles.

Grętzel, Grętzl *n* -s/- [< MHG *gereize*] Viennese *dial. (näherer Umkreis des Wohnorts)* locality where a person lives: hangout; *aus welchem ~ kommst denn (du)?* where do you hang out [with the mental reservation, here supplied for the etymologically interested: … your washing]?; *in meinem ~* in my neck of the woods; *in diesem ~ gibt es keinen einzigen Schuster* there isn't a single cobbler in this area (*or,* neighbourhood); *in dem ~ möchte ich nicht zuhause sein* I wouldn't like to be stuck in that part (*or,* corner) of the world.

Grieß *m* -es/-e *cul.* semolina. – **~auflauf** *m* -(e)s/ … läufe semolina soufflé. – **~knödel** *m & n* -s/-(n) *(Grießkloß)* semolina dumpling, a typically Upper Austrian side dish to accompany smoked meat, made from semolina and roasted bacon and smoked-meat soup. – **~koch** *n* -s *(Grießbrei)* boiled semolina, semolina pudding. – **~nockerl** *n* -s/-(n) little semolina dumpling; *~suppe f* -/-n clear soup with little semolina dumplings. – **~papperl** *n* -s/-(n) *baby talk = Grießkoch;* often *emot.* (good old) semolina pudding, the traditional baby food. – **~schmarr(e)n** *m* -s/- **1.** mashed semolina omelette. – **2.** *fig.: Liebe und ~* two domestic attributes, linked in partial assonance, connoting married bliss: kisses and caresses, *AmE* hugs and kisses; *alles war wieder Liebe und ~!* said of husband and wife after having settled their marital differences in an amicable way: everything was just wonderful (*or, colloq.,* kissie-wissie) again! – **~urlaub** *m* -s/-e *colloq.* "semolina holiday", a leave of absence financed by trade unions for underweight apprentices, during which they are "nourished" through the consumption of semolina and other calorie-rich food.

Grųmmet *n* -s [a contracted *dial.* form of *Grünmahd*] ♩ the second, and often last, crop of hay harvested in late summer (when the meadows, once a riot of colourful flowers in spring, are a uniform 'green' when 'mown'); cp. *Heu* ↓.

Note: In Western Austria, the third crop, if any, goes by the meaningful name of *Pofel m.*

grüß... [optative to begin a greeting formula invoking (though now largely sense-depleted) the blessing of God, whose name is either mentioned or understood to be supplied] *R. C. & folklore, colloq.:* ~ **dich!,** with its frequent dialect variants, **grüaß di'** [*pl.* **enk**]!, formally **grüaß Eahna!** a casual, sometimes rather distant mode of salutation: hello (there)!, *AmE* hi!, hey! – ~ **dich [Sie] Gott!** a warm greeting of recognition and welcome: *usu.,* God save you kindly! – ~ **enk Gott alle miteinander!** a collective greeting of joyous welcome, which owes its popularity to the lively opening song from Karl Zeller's *Der Vogelhändler* ('The Bird-Seller' [1891]), making Tyroleans readily think of Imst, once the flourishing trading centre of itinerant hawkers of singing birds: may the Lord bless you all and sundry! – ~ **Gott!** the almost universal salutation in the Tyrol, whose sturdy mountaineers of German stock would not submit to the Spanish ceremonial of *„Küss' die Hand"* and *„Habe die Ehre"* lingering on in Vienna through her Imperial Court traditions: hello!, good day!

Gschaftl *n* -s/-(n) [*Geschäft n* 'business' + dim. *-l*] *colloq.* little job; *vor lauter ehrenamtlichen ~n kommt man zu gar keiner richtigen Arbeit* all those voluntary offices on the side keep one from getting down to real work. – **~huber** *m* -s/- a meddlesome person *(Wichtigtuer)*: Jack-in-office, busybody, fusspot, *AmE a.* fuss budget; *du bist mir ein ~!* you're a regular fusspot! ‖ as a fictitious name: *Herr ~* Mr. Busyman, Meddlesome Mattie, *Frau ~* Mrs. Mixin. – **~huberei** *f* -/-en fussiness, meddlesomeness.

Gscherte, G'scherte [ˈkʃeːətɛ] *m & f* -n/-n [lit., 'close-cropped (bonds)man', the historical background being that, until about two centuries ago, feudal serfs had to wear their hair close-cut (cp. the nickname 'Roundheads', for the side opposing the 'Cavaliers' in the English Civil War of the 1640s)] *contp.,* sometimes *hum.,* always said, or purported to be said, by natives of Vienna – person from the provinces, provincial (iron. *Provinzler*): country bumpkin, local yokel; *AmE a.* country hick, hillbilly.

Gschertien [ˈkʃeːətjən], **G'schertien** *n* -s mostly *contp.* the provinces *(Provinz; Bundesländer)*: the backwoods; when hearing an unknown, or vaguely known, place-name mentioned: *das muss irgendein Nest in ~ sein* that must be somewhere in the back of beyond, *AmE* that must be a hick town (*or,* cow town) off in the sticks.

Gschisti-Gschasti, Gschisti-gschasti *n* -s *colloq.* (*Getue*) fuss; *mach nicht so viel ~-~!* don't make such a fuss about it! don't fuss around like that! don't be (such) a fuss-pot!

Gschnas *m & n* -es *colloq. & contp.* something worthless: trash, junk, *BrE* rubbish, *AmE* garbage; *was kaufst du für ein(en) ~? das ist doch zu nichts gut!* why are you buying such a piece of trash? it's not good for anything! – **~fest** *n* -es/-e *arts* a Carnival masked ball put on regularly since 1870 by the Wiener Künstlerhaus, for which they create

A quaint old engraving (from the 1870s) of Schruns, then a little mountain village in the Montafon Valley, in the land of the Gsiberger, *'those beyond the Arlberg', the Tyrolese gently tease*

original works of art as decoration *(Maskenball der Wiener Künstler)*: "Junk Masquerade"; the artists – generous and broad-minded – poke fun at themselves by giving the event this name.

Gsiberger *m* -s/-, **Gsibergerin** *f* -/-nen [first el., *gsi,* for *gewesen* 'been', the (to an outsider) attention-calling past participle form of the verb *sein* in Alemannic dialect; in the second el., the basic word is obviously an echo of *Arlberg,* the name of the mountain massif between the Tyrol and Vorarlberg] *hum.* a nickname made up by the Tyroleans, who speak a variant of South Bavarian, for their Alemannic countrymen separated from them by a barrier not merely orographic: man [woman] from Vorarlberg, *hum.* *Ale(m)arlberger.

Gspusi [ˈkʃpuːzɪ], variously spelt **G'spusi, Gschpusi, Gespusi,** *n* -(s)/- [< *Gespons m hum.* 'bridegroom', 'husband' < L *sponsus* 'fiancé'] *colloq.,* often slightly *iron.* **1.** regular boy [girl] friend: flame, heartthrob; *ist sie dein ~?* is she your sweet thing (*AmE a.* … your cuddlebug)?; *der Hans ist ein verflossenes ~ von mir* Jack's an old flame of mine. – **2.** a sexual relationship between two people not married to each other, esp. one that lasts for some time: affair, steady flirt; *sie hat mit dem besten Freund ihres Mannes ein ~* she's having an affair with her husband's best friend; *die haben schon jahrelang ein munteres ~ (miteinand[er])* theirs has been a steady whirl for years; *er hat alle zwei Wochen mit einer anderen ein ~* he goes with a different girl every other week; *fang dir mit der kein ~ an* don't you go and give that one a whirl.

Gstanzl [ˈkʃt-], *n* -s/-n [*g(e)-*, a collective prefix often elided in Southern German, and the dim. suffix *-l* here surround and aptly modify the base *-stanz-* (< LateL *stantia* 'stay', 'habitation', which [as a loan translation < Arabic *bait* 'room'] in once Arab-occupied Sicily combined the meanings of 'room' and 'verse')] ♪ a popular rhyming couplet, broken into four lines in print, often improvised and usu. making teasing fun of someone (*neckender Vierzeiler*): merry ditty *or* jingle, chatter ditty.

For a copious array of such ditties, see pp. 255ff.

Gugerschecken or **Guckerschecken** *f pl.* [lit., 'cuckoo spots', the small irregular brownish and white patches of colour with which the cuckoo *(Kuckuck)* is speckled, or spotted *(gescheckt),* on its belly for mimicry] *colloq.* freckles *(Sommersprossen)*: angel kisses, sun kisses.

Gulasch; also, with its near-Hungarian spelling, **Gulyas** [ˈgʊlaʃ] *n,* less often *m* -(e)s/-(e) [< Hung. *gulyás* (that dish, however, in Hungary being known as *pörkölt*)] **1.** *cul.* a stew highly flavoured with a Hungarian red pepper or paprika sauce and garnished with tomatoes, onions, and potatoes (*scharf gewürztes Fleischgericht*): spiced meat stew, goulash [ˈguːlæʃ] ‖ in cpds.: *Rinds*≗ ragout [ˈræguː] of beef, beef goulash; *Schweins*≗ pork goulash; *gemischtes ~* goulash with (bits of) beef and pork. → **2.** *fig. phr.* in Viennese low *dial.,* threatening to beat one's opponent up very badly: *aus dir mach' i' a ~!* I'm gonna make mincemeat of you!, I'll thrash the (living) daylights out of you!, I'll knock the stuffing (*or,* filling, *or* inside, *or* lining, *or* wadding) out of you!

Gulasch … *cul.:* **~kanone** *f* -/-n *mil. hum.* a portable cooking equipment for troops, or the place where it is set up (*Feldküche*): field kitchen, *AmE* field mess. – **~suppe** *f* -/-n a highly spiced soup, featuring small cubes of beef or pork, often served as a separate item in the evening (in good companionship with beer and wine): goulash soup *or* broth.

Gupf *m* -(e)s/pl. rare: -e [a monosyllabic variant of *Gipfel* ↑, with vowel gradation] *dial.* **1.** pile, mountain (of food, etc.). – **2.** something forming, or added to form, a head, e.g. on a freshly filled

Emperor Ferdinand the Gentle-minded

glass of beer; *noch einen ~ Schlagobers (*or *Schlagsahne), bittschön!* another dollop of whipped cream, please. – **3.** rounded end (of an egg).

Gụrgelpropeller, Krọpfpropeller *m* -s/- *hum.* [so called from the distinctive 'air-screw' shape of neckwear] *tex.* = *Mascherl* ↓1.

Gü̲tnand der Fẹrtige *m* -s des -n [a playful spoonerism] *hist.* *Ferdinand the Mental Giant, a malicious topsy-turvy improvement on *Ferdinand der Gütige* 'Ferdinand the Gentle-minded', a jocular euphemism among the Viennese prior to March 1848 for Emperor Ferdinand I, whose progressive debility made it necessary for a State Council (among them Prince Metternich) to take over the reins of government.

Gụsto *m* -s *colloq. (Appetit, Neigung)* craving: yen; *ich hätt jetzt ~ auf ein riesiges, knuspriges Wiener Schnitzel, das über den Tellerrand hängt* I'm yearning to devour (*or,* I wouldn't half mind getting outside of) a huge, crispy veal cutlet that expands beyond the edge of my plate ‖ a Viennese version of the Latin saying, 'de gustibus non est disputandum': *~ und Watschen sind verschieden* to each his own (*or, BrE* … tastes differ), said the man as he kissed his cow.

Gụsto… *colloq.:* **~katz** [–kɒts] *f* -/-en, **~mensch** *n* -s/-s *dial. & vulg.* luscious young woman: babe, chick. – **~menscherl, ~spatzerl** *n* -s/-n pretty young girl: sweet young thing. – **~stückerl** *n* -s/-(n) *cul. & fig.* one's favourite thing: favourite piece (*or [if meat]* cut), personal favourite; *sind Hendlhaxln auch deine ~?* are drumsticks also your favourite part of the chicken?

Gwạndl [–ʌ–] *n* -s/-n [< *Gewand n* (< *winden v/t* 'to wind [something round one's body']) 'clothes' + dim. *-l*] *colloq.* a man's, or boy's, (festive) suit; *prov.* either a slightly malicious, and perhaps also envious, comment on a person who is felt to be not really matching up to his or her clothes; or laughingly, with a pretence to modesty, said by the wearer when being praised for looking so neat and trim: *das ~ macht's Mandl* fine feathers make fine birds.

Gwạndlaus *f* -/pl. rare: **…läus** *contp.* an annoyingly intrusive person *(lästiger Zeitgenosse)*: obnoxious pest, gatecrasher; *if male, a.* Meddlesome Mattie.

Haberer *m* -s/ [< Yid. *chaver* 'friend', 'partner' + G suffix *-er*] *colloq.* **1.** *(Verehrer, Freund [e-s Mädchens])* steady boyfriend: steady; *sie hat schon wieder einen neuen ~* she's got a new steady again. – **2.** *(Freund, [Zech-]Kumpan)* best friend: pal, *BrE a.* chum, *AmE a.* buddy, bud; *das sind meine beiden ~, mit denen gehe ich heut abend auf Gaudee* those are my two pals; we're going to hit the town together tonight.

Habsburg 1. *f geog. & hist.* [a contraction of *Habichtsburg* 'hawks' castle'] the castle built in the eleventh century near the junction of the Aar and the Rhine, in what is today the Aargau Canton in north-central Switzerland, by Werner, Bishop of Strassburg, whose nephew, Werner, was the first to assume the title of "Count of Hapsburg": Hapsburg. → **2.** [in the following sense never to be used with an article] *polit. hist.* the name of the famous dynasty which established a hereditary monarchy in Austria in 1282 and secured the title of Holy Roman Emperor from 1452; Austrian and Spanish branches were created when Charles V divided the territories between his son Philip II and his brother Ferdinand – the "western" Hapsburgs ruling Spain between 1504 and 1700, and those in Austria ending their rule with the collapse of Austria-Hungary in 1918: Habsburg, or Hapsburg.

Habsburger *m* -s/-; **Habsburgerin** *f* -/-nen *hist.* a member, now rarely also a staunch admirer, of the House of Hapsburg: Habsburger.

Habsburger…: ~gruft *f* - = *Kapuzinergruft* ↓. – **~lippe** *f* - *hist. & med.* a hereditary physical deformity of the royal family of Hapsburg (said to have been derived through marriage with a daughter of the Lithuanian-Polish dynasty of Jagello) – a heavy hanging lip, the lower jaw monstrously protruding beyond the upper: Hapsburg *or* Austrian Lip. – **~reich** *n* -(e) realm of the Hapsburgs; *wer sich für die Geschichte des großen ~es interessiert, darf in Wien an den riesigen Sammlungen des Völkerkundemuseums auf keinen Fall vorbeigehen* those interested in the great realm of the Hapsburgs, the enormous collection of objects in the Ethnographic Museum of Vienna is a must.

Hafen *m* -s/ Häfen, less often **Häfen** *m* -s/- *dial. ([großer] Topf)* (large) pot.

Hagmoar *m* -s/-e [lit., 'the one ranking first (< L *maior*) in the enclosed (cp. German *eingehegt*) field of competition'] *dial.* winner, champion (in a wrestling competition [→ *Rangeln* 2]).

Halawach(e)l *m* -s/- *emot.,* a term of good-natured abuse, invariably levelled at males only – unreliable person *(unzuverlässiger Mensch)*: scatterbrain, chucklehead, chowderhead, *BrE* scallywag, *AmE* scalawag; *jetzt hat er schon wieder den Regenschirm vergessen, der ~!* now he's gone and forgotten his umbrella again, the scatterbrain!

ha̩lbpart *adv colloq.* with each person, usu. two, contributing (paying, etc). equal shares: halvesies, halvers, even Stephen, fifty-fifty; *machen wir ~* let's make it halvesies, let's go halvers, let's go on (*or,* to) the halves, let's go snacks.

hali̲-halo̲ [< the huntsmen's well-known sound of horns reinforcing (with pleasing vowel gradation) the very conventional cry to attract attention] *interj* a popular style of greeting: hi-de-hi! – often eliciting the response, ho-de-ho! (showing the same up-and-down vowel alternation as the German).

Emperor Frederick III (1415–93) was known to have borne a fleshy lower lip and an aquiline nose – facial characteristics that have indeed recurred in the Hapsburg Family for centuries

ha̩lt *adv* [< MHG *halt,* orig. a comparative, as seen in Goth *haldis* and OIcel *heldr* 'rather'; probably related to the OHG *hald* family, with the basic sense of 'inclined', 'sloping' (cp. NHG *Halde* 'slope', 'hillside')] *colloq.* an emotive particle, always in unaccented position, capable of adding several connotative shades to the core meaning of an utterance – among them **1.** gentle, unobtrusive advice: *so geh ~, es wird schon nicht so schlimm sein, wie du meinst* well, go then; I'm sure it won't be as bad as you think. – *wir müssen 's ~ probieren* we'll just have to (have a) try. – **2.** a plea for understanding the other side: *mach dir keine Gedanken* (or, *mach ihm keine Vorwürfe), er wird ~ Wichtigeres zu tun gehabt haben* don't you worry (*or,* don't blame him), he may have had more important things to attend to. – **3.** a broad-minded offer for one's interlocutor to decide things: *komm, wann du ~ kannst* (or, *wann dir ~ danach ist*) come whenever you can (*or,* … whenever you feel like it; *or,* … whenever you have a mind to). – **4.** winding up a point of discussion, a good-natured acceptance of what seems to be the consensus of opinion: *also dann komm' ich ~ um eins* all right then, I'll come at one. – **5.** a good-natured acceptance of a fact, whether unpleasant or not: *ja mei, das ist ~ so* (or, *so ist es ~* [*einmal*]), *gegen die Dummheit ist kein Kraut gewachsen* ah well, it's just like that (*or,* that's just the way it is; *or,* I'm afraid, it can't be helped), there is no remedy for stupidity.

– *ich bin ~ dumm und bleib's auch, was kannst (du) da machen?* I am a fool, and I'll stay one – there's nowt you can do about it! – *ich habe es ~ vergessen* I just (*or* simply) forgot (it). – *es hieß ~ zu Fuß gehen, da ließ sich nichts machen* it was simply a case of having to walk (*or, low colloq.*, to hoof it), (there was) nothing to be done about it. – a fatalistic folk wisdom tinged with piety –

> *Es gibt halt immer was,*
> *das den Himmel halt't,*
> *dass er net obafallt.*
>
> *There's always something keeps
> Good Heaven propped up there …
> fat chance to have a share.

6. a glimpse of the speaker's experience, claimed to be based on well-reflected, or intuitive, logic: *das war saftig – man spürt ~ gleich, dass du ein Advokat bist* that was certainly something – one is sure to see right off that you're a lawyer. – **7.** an expression of mounting irritation at someone's immobility, specifically his delayed response as a driver when the traffic lights have turned green: *fahr ~!* get a move on! – *geh ~, was rührst du dich nicht vom Fleck?* get going, why don't you budge? – **8.** in an expanded form, showing one's unwillingness, or inability, to go into further details; or indeed one's point-blank refusal to comment: *wir hatten da eine Reportage, Wiener Unterwelt, und so ~* we had to do an on-the-spot report – you know, the Viennese underworld, and that kind of thing (*or,* … and so on). – A: *warum magst du nicht?* B: *so ~! A:* why don't you want to? *B:* just because.

Hąluschka, Hąluska *f* -/ Haluschken, Halusken [< Slovak *haluschky*] *cul.* short for *Topfenhaluschka* ↓.

Hąndkuss *m* -es/…küsse **1.** *hist.* kiss on the hand, originally part of the Spanish court ceremonial of the Hapsburg emperors (reflected to this day in the formal ending of Spanish letter, 'S. S. Servidor q.b.s.m.' [= Su seguro servidor que basa sus manos]). → **2.** in *colloq.* phrases: *mit ~* gladly, with the greatest pleasure; *der Händler nimmt Ihnen die Golddukaten mit ~ ab* the dealer will be only too willing to buy the gold ducats ‖ *zum ~ kommen* to come to grief: to be in for trouble (*or,* for something); *der Motorradfahrer ist bei dem Unfall zum ~ gekommen* in the accident, the motorcyclist got the thin end of the wedge, … it was curtains for the motor-cyclist.

A little note on an unfortunate Austrian, ensnared in and confused by his traditional upbringing which (as we all know) can make us go into acts gestural and verbal:
As a special honour, that Austrian was received in audience by the Pope. Although naturally flustered, he did act according to the instructions previously given to him and the other visitors by the Papal Master of Ceremonies. In fact, his self-assurance was such that, on leave-taking, instead of bending low and going through the motions of kissing the Pope's "Fisherman's Ring", the one symbolizing His Sanctity's right of succession to St Peter the Apostle (who had been a fisherman by occupation), he blithely stretched out his right hand to the Pope, who smilingly clasped it. The Papal MC, standing behind His Sanctity, frantically gestured by hand that our Austrian, for Pete's sake, was to kiss that ring. But he, his Austrian background reasserting itself, duly blurted out, while still clasping the Pope's hand, "… *Und einen schönen Handkuss an die Frau Gemahlin!"*

Hąngerl *n* -s/-(n) *colloq.* **1.** *(Schlaufe, Aufhängsel)* of a coat etc.: loop, hook, tab. – **2.** *(Lätzchen)* bib; *dem Kind beim Essen ein ~ umbinden* to tie a bib around the baby's neck when eating. – **3.** *(Geschirrtuch; Wischtuch [des Kellners])* dishcloth, dishtowel, dishrag, *dial.* dishclout; *~ritter m* -s/- *hum.* waiter: knight of the napkin, *AmE a.* soup jockey. – **4.** *([Fall-]Klappe [am Schlüsselloch])* (keyhole) drop.

Hạnsl *m* -(s)/-n [dim. of *Hans* 'John': 'Johnny', 'Jack'] *colloq.,* sometimes slightly *iron.* or *contp.* a man: feller (*or* fella), guy, *BrE a.* bloke; *von den erwarteten zehn ~n sind bloß drei aufgekreuzt* just three fellers turned up of the ten expected.

hạntig *adj* [< MHG *handec* 'bitter', 'sharp'] *colloq.* **1.** said of food or drink that has a sharp, biting taste, e.g. asparagus or unsweetened coffee *(herb)*: bitter. → **2.** said of a person's gruffly uncooperative manner of speaking *(unwirsch)*: snappish, catty; *was bist du denn heute gar a so ~?* what on earth makes (*or* are) you such a crosspatch today?

Hạrfe, *dial.* **Hạrpfe** *f* -/-n [actually, a harp] ↓ a huge rack used for drying hay *(Heureiter)*: hayrack, drying rack.

Hạscher *m* -s/- [< MHG *haeschen v/i* 'to sob'] *colloq. (bedauernswerter Mensch)* poor creature, poor thing; if male, also: poor chap, poor fellow, *AmE* poor guy; *der arme ~ ist schon wieder bei der Prüfung durchgesaust* or *durchgerasselt* the poor devil flunked his exam again. – **Hạscherl** *n* -s/-n [dim. of *Hascher*] *emot. (armes Würstchen) armes ~!* poor little thing! poor little worm!, *BrE a.* poor poppet!, *ScotE* puir wee craitur, *AmE a.* poor bunny!; *im Vergleich zu deiner hohen Stellung bin ich nur ein (armes) ~* compared with your dignified position I am only a lowly mouse.

Häusel, Häusl *n* -s/-(n) [dim. of *Haus*] *colloq.* **1.** *(Häuschen)* small house: little house, cottage ‖ *emot.* (1) said in appreciation: sweet little house, *AmE a.* cosy little cabin (*or* cottage); said in understatement: old shack; *ein Schrebergarten≗[*or *Wochenend≗] wäre halt meine höchste Idee* an allotment garden [weekend] house is the thing I fancy most. (2) in contempt: hovel, miserable hut, (miserable) hole. – **2.** *prov. & fig.*: *ein kleines ~ ist oft wärmer und der im großen ist oft ärmer!* better a little fire that warms nor (*or* than) a mickle (*or* a big one) that burns ‖ *aus dem ~ sein* to have momentarily lost one's mental equilibrium (1) out of nervousness and uncertainty: to be all in a dither, to be hot and bothered, *AmE* to lose one's cool, to be all shaken (*dial.* shook) up; *sie ist ganz aus dem ~ vor Schreck* she is frightened out of her wits, she is scared stiff; with some overwhelmingly piece of positive news: to be wild with joy; *aus dem ~ bringen* to confuse completely: *BrE* to flummox, *AmE* to confusticate; *aus dem ~ geraten* to get in a tizzy (*or,* a tizz) ‖ as an invitation to resume one's walk, search, or other, line of activity, after a pause has been made for rest or thought: *gehen wir (jetzt,* or *halt) ein ~ weiter!* well, let's get a move on (for another space, *or* another leg)!, let's get cracking again! – **3.** *(Toilette)* bathroom: lav., loo, little boys' [girls'] room, *AmE a.* john, can, crapper; if outside: *(Landklosett)* wooden shanty, outhouse, end, *AmE a.* backhouse, *NZ & AustralE* the little house; *aufs ~ gehen müssen* to have to go to the loo, *etc.* ‖ a person thus intentioned may be heard quoting a famous couplet of Grillparzer's *Die Ahnfrau* – in parody of the title heroine's final words: *öffne dich, du stilles Kläusl* [a nonce diminutive of *Klause* 'hermitage', 'retreat'], / *denn die Ahnfrau geht aufs ~* open up your still retreat, / the Old Dame's now to take her seat ‖ as a crude allusion to being constipated: *ich bin seit einer Woche wie vernagelt, da rührt sich nichts bei mir mehr am ~* I'm all plugged up, I haven't had a movement for a week, *BrE* low *colloq. a.* I haven't had a road through me for a week. – **4.** as a term of good-natured abuse – silly person *(rechter Dummkopf)*: big silly, ninny, clot, *AmE* dumbbunny, dummy, nim-num, jerk; *du bist ein ~, warum hast du den Strudel anbrennen lassen?* you're a such a scatterbrain, why did you let the strudel burn?

Häus(e)l … *colloq.*: **~bauer** *m -s/- apprec.* or mildly *iron.* one who intends, or has managed, to build himself and his family a cottage, or possibly more than one: home-builder. – **~besen** *m -s/- (Klosettbürste)* lavatory brush, toilet brush; *wenn das wahr ist, fress' ich einen ~!* I'll damn well eat my hat (whole) if that's a fact! – **~brille** *f -/-n* toilet seat: loo seat. – **~frau** *f -/-en (Wartefrau)* female attendant in a public lavatory: loo attendant (*or* woman), john-keeper. – **~geruch** *m -(e)s/ …gerüche (Geruch von den Toiletten)* toilet odour: toilet smell ‖ said in disgust, in a restaurant, beer garden, etc.: *setzen wir uns von da weg, der ~ ist einmal zu stark!* let's move over to another table, it smells like a sewer here! – **~muschel** *f -/-n* lavatory pan *or* bowl: loo pan. – **~papier** *n -(e)s (Klosettpapier)* toilet paper: loo paper, *BrE a.* bumf, *AmE* ammunition, flypaper; *eine Rolle ~* → *Häus(e)lrolle.* – **~poet** *m -en/-en hum.* the always anonymous author of rhymed and ribald philosophy found on the walls and doors of public conveniences: bathroom lyricist (of whom it is said, by a rival gutter colleague of the pen, "One would think, with all this wit, / Shakespeare had been here to shit"). – **~rolle** *f -/-n (Rolle Klosettpapier)* toilet roll: *BrE* roll of bumf, *AmE* crap roll. – **~steuer** *f -/-n (Benützungs- und Räumungsgebühr für Unratsanlagen) BrE* sewerage rate, *AmE* sewerage tax. – **~tschick** *m -s/-s* soggy cigarette-end, as found deposited in a toilet bowl or urinal: *BrE* soggy fag-end, *AmE* soggy (cigarette-)butt ‖ said in disgust of one who is extremely drunk: *angesoffen* (or *voll*) *wie ein ~* absolutely pissed, (as) tight as a tick, *AmE a.* wasted, loaded (to the gills), (as) drunk as a skunk. – **~witz** *m -es/-e (Zote)* ribald jest: smutty joke, piece of bathroom (*or,* outhouse) humour; *~e reißen* to tell dirty jokes, to talk smut; *er* *hat nichts als ~e im Kopf* he's got a mind like a sewer.

Haus-, Hof- und Wiesendodel *m* -s/-(n) [cp. *Dodel*] *hum.* in rural Eastern Austria, said in laughing self-depreciation by a farmer, innkeeper, etc. or his wife (who may in fact carry out neither of these duties) – factotum: general servant; *ich bin halt da der ~* (ah) well, I'm the head (*or* chief) cook and bottle-washer in this place, *AmE* I'm Mister [Missus] Fix-it(-all) around here.

Hẹld *m* -en/-en **1.** hero ‖ a satirical pun on the private cemetery and memorial grove of Heldenberg ('Heroes' Mount') at Groß-Wetzdorf, Lower Austria; laid out by Joseph Gottfried Pargfrieder (Parkfrieder), a rich purveyor of army equipment between 1805 and 1863, it displays the busts of 147 famous generals from Austrian military history, and holds the monumental graves of two comrades-in-arms, Field Marshal Radetzky ↓, Pargfrieder's hero incarnate, and Field Marshal Baron Maximilian von Wimpffen, as well as that of the initiator himself: *Hier ruhen drei ~en in ewiger Ruh', / Zwei lieferten Schlachten, der dritte die Schuh'* *Three heroes lie here till it God someday suits; / Two dealt blows in battles, the third dealt in boots. – **2.** *colloq.* a term of gentle reproach for an act of clumsiness or oversight, as when a wrong key was forced into a keyhole, and duly got wedged, or when an unsuitable purchase was made at the grocer's: clumsy clot, silly billy; *du (bist [mir] ein) ~!* you are a one!

Hẹmd *n* -(e)s/-en shirt ‖ low *colloq.* as a judgement of value when tasting sour wine or fruit: *da musst d' dein ~ halten!, da zieht's dir das ~ rein!* *that stuff's so strong it could take the starch out of your shirt!

Hẹnderl *n* -s/-n [first el., < *Henne f* 'female of the common domestic fowl'] **1.** *zo.* & *cul., apprec.* a young hen: chicken, chick. – **2.** *zo., emot.,* often **Pipi**≈ *n* the nursery name for a chicken: chickabiddy. – **3.** *iron., hum.* a lean, skinny person, usu. male: flyweight scrag.

Hẹndl *n* -s/-(n) [< rural dial. *Henn'* 'hen' + intrusive *-d-* + dim. *-l*] *dial.* **1.** *zo.* (1) an adult female chicken (*Henne, Huhn*): hen, chicken. – (2) a young chicken during its first year of laying eggs (*junge [Lege-]Henne, Kücken*): pullet, chick; *die Anklageschrift bezeichnet mit leichter, liebevoller mundartlicher Einfärbung die beiden jungen, dem Bauern entwendeten Legehühner als „~"* in the bill of indictment, allowing for a touch of jovial dialect ease, the two young laying hens pilfered from the farmer are dubbed 'chicklings'. ‖ → *Kärntner ~.* – **2.** *fig. contp.* a person, usu. an elderly adult male, of rather slight build: runt, lightweight, *AmE a.* canary (kid), cream puff. – **3.** *phr.* animal similes bring into focus (1) people who regularly go to bed early at night, and those who get up very early in the morning: *er geht mit den ~n schlafen* he goes to bed with the dickeybirds; *sie steht mit den ~n auf* she's an early bird, she gets up with the lark, *NorBrE a.* she's up before the crows. – (2) someone who appears to be utterly bewildered: *er rennt herum, wie wenn ihm die ~n das letzte Brot weggefressen hätten* he's running about like a chicken with its head cut off. – (3) someone

An East Tyrolean God's Corner – fruits of the fields devoutly offered to the Crucified, the hearts of Mary and Jesus open to the faithful

whose sanity, irony has it, is to be seriously doubted: *ein verrücktes* ~ a crazy bird; *verrückt wie ein* ~ crazy as a bedbug, mad as a March hare, *NZE a.* mad as a maggot. → **4.** in *comp.* **~brust** *f* -/pl. rare: ... brüste (1) *med.* a malformed projection of the human breastbone: chicken breast, pigeon breast *or* chest; *er hat eine* ~ he's chicken-breasted (*or* pigeon-breasted). – (2) *fig., contp.* any slightly-built person = *Hendl,* 2. – **~dreck** *m* -s low *colloq.* (1) *euphem.* the body waste of barnyard fowl: chicken-dirt. → (2) *fig. contp.* any insignificant or petty person: (piece of) chicken-shit, flyspeck, *AmE a.* minus quantity ‖ in graphic elaboration of the slur: *das ist dir doch ja grad ein aufgestellter ~!* why, he's just an abbreviated piece of nothing. – **~farm** *f* -/-en = *Hühnerfarm.* – **~friedhof** *m* -(e)s/... höfe, **~grab** *n* -(e)s/ ... gräber = *Backhend(e)lfriedhof.* – **~gupf** *m* -(e)s/-e *folklore, hum.* for *Goldhaube* ↑. – **~jagd** *f* -/-en *hunt.* = *Rebhendljagd.* – **~steign** *f* -/- = *Hühnersteige.*

Hẹrrgottswinkel *m* -s/- [though old as a devotional arrangement, the word itself was coined by Peter Rosegger (1843–1918), the most famous regional writer and poet of Styria] *relig.* a space provided with a crucifix (often ivy-clad and a treasured heirloom) as well as with other religious objects, and devoted to worship, the figure of the Crucified leaning into the room in a protective attitude: God's Corner; *der ~ ist mit Palmkatzerln geschmückt, die der Priester am Palmsonntag geweiht hat* the God's Corner is decorated with pussy willows which were blessed by the priest on Palm Sunday.

Hẹrrschaft *f* -/-en **1.** *hist.* one of a number of communes, owned and governed by nobility, that continued to exist after the abolition of serfdom and feudal dues in the nineteenth-century Austrian Empire – often headed by a once feudal lord now turned simply great landowner, trying to evade the authority of the communal administration and to preserve his independence by making himself responsible for the maintenance of public order and the upkeep of roads on his land: noble domain; e.g., *die ~ Frohnsdorf* 'the Frohnsdorf Estate' (at the eastern extremity of Lower Austria, almost on the frontier of Hungary, where the traveller of today can still see the escutcheons of the proprietor, the Comte de Cahmbord, the last king of France ['Henry V'], who had spent his melancholy years of exile there).→ **2.** *pl.* only; a courteous or even reverential way of addressing, or speaking of, a group of people, e.g. one's dinner guests: *meine (hochgeschätzten) ~en!* (my revered) ladies and gentlemen!; *dürfen wir nunmehr die ~en nebenan zum Abendessen bitten?* will you now please honour us with your good company at supper next room? *haben die beiden ~en heute nacht gut geschlafen* (or, with consummate formal courtesy, … *gut geruht)?* did sir and madam have a good night's sleep (*or,* … rest)?

Hẹrrschafts(seiten [by way of annoyed emphasis added to by **noch einmal**])!, in *EastAus* sometimes also **Hẹrrschafts Laudon!** *interj* [the former a *euphem.* shortening and alteration of *Herrgotts Seiten* 'by Lord Jesus' side [wound]', equivalent to the once common English interjections "by God's wounds" (or "swounds", "swouns", "zounds" for short); the latter similarly substituting the name of an Austrian general under Empress Maria Theresa, Baron Gideon Ernst Laudon, 1716–1790, who had greatly distinguished himself in the battles, both against King Frederick the Great and against the Turks] *colloq.* exclamations to give vent to the speaker's astonishment or slight consternation (which, however, do not altogether keep him from seeing the bizarre or even funny side of the new situation): by all saints (*or,* oh ye gods) and little fishes!, Holy Godfrey!, *AmE a.* holy cats!, holy cow!

herụm …: ~brodeln *v/i colloq.* to potter about, *AmE* to jerk around. – **~gurken** *v/i colloq.* to wander around aimlessly: to drift (around), *AmE sl.* to bum around. – **~klezeln** [-e:-] *v/i dial.* to try to remove unwanted pieces from, esp. with a finger; *lass die Wunde gut verheilen, klezel nicht herum!* let the wound heal properly, don't meddle with the scab!; *wirst du aufhören, an der Nase herumzuklezeln!* will you please stop poking your nose! – **~kugeln** *v/i colloq.* to wait or stay in one place in enforced idleness: *BrE* to hang about, *AmE* to hang around; *schlaflos im Bett ~* to toss and turn in bed (all night): *die Anschlüsse nach X sind leider sehr schlecht, da musst du fast den ganzen Tag auf der Bahn ~* the connections to X are very poor, I'm afraid, one's got to dawdle about (*or* around) at train stations nearly all day long. – **~schustern** *v/i colloq.* to monkey around. – **~stierln** *v/i dial. (herumstochern)* to rummage about; *was stierlst du denn im Coloniakübel herum?* what are you poking around for in the dustbin (*AmE* garbage can)? – **~störzen** *v/i* Alpine *dial.s (vagabundieren)* to tramp about, to lead a vagabond life, to vagabondize. – **~strabanzen, ~strawanzen** *v/i dial. (sich herumtreiben)* to loaf (about), to ramble ‖ *er strabanzt herum* he is on the loaf; *wir sind in der Stadt herumstrabanzt* we were roaming over the city; *nach der Schule wird nicht herumstrabanzt!* no roving about after school (is over)! ‖ → *strabanzen.*

Herz-Jesu- …: ~ Fẹst *n* -(e)s; **~ Monat** *m* -(e)s; **~ Sọnntag** *m* -s R.C., in the Tyrol – a religious festival in June offering special devotion to the physical heart of

The Heart of Jesus: A mural painting in a Tyrolean Village (Oberperfuss, WSW of Innsbruck)

Jesus Christ, as a symbol of His love and redemptive sacrifice: Feast [Month; Sunday] of the Sacred Heart.

Hetschepetsch *f* -/- [< Cz *hečipeč* < *heksipeč* < G *Heck(e)* + Cz *sipeče* 'dog rose'] ⚘ *(Hagebutte)* (rose) hip; **Hetscherl** *n* -s/-n *colloq.* = *Hetschepetsch;* **Hetscherltee** *m* -s *pharm.* rosehip tea; **Hetschipetschi** *f* -/- *colloq.* = *Hetschepetsch.*

Hetz *f* -/ rarely: -en [< *hetzen* 'to bait': animal baiting, i.e. the worrying of bulls, bears, wolves and foxes by whips and vicious bulldogs, or by setting them against each other or some harmless prey, was a popular form of entertainment in eighteenth-century Vienna; a special arena, the *Tierhetztheater* in the third district (where there is still a *Hetzgasse* to commemorate the site), was erected for these brutal fights and continued to draw the masses until the early 1800s] *colloq.* **1.** *(Spaß)* fun (of it); *aus ~, wegen der ~* just for a laugh, just for a giggle; *es ist eine ~ und kostet nicht viel* a set *phr.* accounting for the silliness of a pastime one happens to indulge in at the moment: it's a lot of fun and doesn't cost a thing; it's great fun, and free, too! – **2.** *(Jux)* playful or mischievous trick, prank; *wir haben uns nur eine ~ erlaubt, wir haben nur ~ gemacht* we were (just) skylarking, we were only out for kicks, we just did it for a joke.

hetzhalber *adv colloq.* (just) for kicks, for fun; *ich hab es ja nur ~ gesagt* I was just kidding, I only said it (just) for kicks (*or,* … to tease you).

Heu *n* -s hay; in a narrower sense, the first crop of hay (usu. harvested in June; cp. *Grummet* ↑) ‖ *colloq. phr.: wir haben das ~ nicht im gleichen Stadel* he (*or,* she) is not my cup of tea, *IrE* we don't dig with the same foot.

Heu… ↓ : **~baum** *m* -(e)s/ … bäume *(Wiesbaum)* hay-pole, binder (to weigh down a cart-load *[Fuder]* of hay. – **~boden** *m* -s/- hay loft. – **~geige** *f* -/-n **1.** = *Heubaum.* – **2.** *colloq.* lanky person: beanpole, *BrE a.* hop pole, lamppost. – **~harfe,** *dial.* **~harpfe** *f* -/-n *(Trockengestell [für Heu])* (wooden) drying rack. – **~hüpfer,** *dial.* **~hupfer** *m* -s/- = *Heuschreck.* – **~mahd** *f* -/-en *(Heuernte)* hay-harvest, hay-making (season). – **~markt** *m* -(e)s/ … märkte (e.g. in Vienna), **~platz** *m* -es/ … plätze (e.g. in Klagenfurt) an historic place name, with sundry analogues elsewhere (e.g. in London and Chicago): Haymarket. –

~raufe *f* -/-n hay-rack. – **~reiter, ~reuter** *m* -s/- tripod for drying grass. – **~schlitten** *m* -s/- *IrE* hay slipe. – **~schober** *m* -s/- hayrick, haystack. – **~schreck** *m* -(e)s/-e *dial. (Heuschrecke)* grasshopper. – **~stadel** *m* -s/- (log) hay-hut (*or,* hay chalet) away out in the meadows.

heuen *dial.* **heign** *vt/i* to make hay; a Tyrolese proverb: *~ muss man, wenn die Sonne scheint* (or, *wann's [Heu-]Wetter ist*) make hay while the sun shines. – **Heuer** *m* -s/-, **~in** *f* -/-nen haymaker.

heuer *adv* [< OHG *hiuru, hiu jāru*] *(in diesem Jahr)* (in) this year.

heurig *adj* this year's, of this year; *der ~e Wein = Heurige,* 1; *~e Erdäpfel, Heurige (neue Kartoffeln)* new potatoes; *colloq. ein ~er Hase = Heurige,* 3.

Heurige *m* **1.** -n *vinicult. (Wein der jüngsten Lese)* wine of this season's vintage, the year's new wine, young wine. – **2.** -n/-n *vinicult. & soc. hist. ([gemütliches] Lokal, in dem mit behördlicher Genehmigung der Wein aus den eigenen Weingärten ausgeschenkt wird)* new-wine tavern, (open-air) wine garden(s), Heuriger, heuriger; *Nobel~* (swanky *or* top-notch) new-wine restaurant. – **3.** -n/-n *colloq. (unerfahrener Neuling)* inexperienced newcomer: greenhorn, *AmE a.* tenderfoot; *ich bin ja kein ~* I wasn't born yesterday, I didn't come down with the last shower, I'm no amateur, *BrE a.* I'm not a learner (any more), *AmE a.* I'm no spring chicken.

Heurigen… [always with reference to *Heurige,* 2]: **~abend** *m* -(e)s/-e new-wine party; *einen ~ veranstalten* to give *or* hold (*colloq.* to throw) a new-wine party. – **~besuch** *m* -(e)s/-e visit to a new-wine tavern; *von diesen ewigen ~en habe ich schon restlos genug* I'm sick and tired of this never-ending business of dropping in on new-wine taverns. – **~buschen** *m* -s/- hung on a pole over the entrance of a new-wine tavern: *(Rebenbusch)* wine bush, i.e. a bunch or tuft of evergreen(s), usu. a pine-branch on the outside of a tavern, as a sign that new wine is available there. – **~casanova** *m* -s/-s *colloq.* small-time casanova, who tries to pick up women visitors at a new-wine tavern. – **~kranz** *m* -es/ … kränze, **~kränzl** *n* -s/-(n) new-wine wreath, variously made of straw or oak leaves (and dangling strings of wood-shavings). – **~lied** *n* -(e)s/-er (sentimental) wine-drinking song. – **~musik** *f* - wine-garden music; often = *Schrammelmusik.* – **~ort** *m* -(e)s/-e wine-producing village (around Vienna). – **~packerl** *n* -s/-(n) package of food taken along and eaten at a new-wine tavern: picnic supper. – **~sänger** *m* -s/- (semi-professional) singer of wine-drinking songs. – **~schank** *m* -(e)s/ … schänke, **~schenke**

An East Tyrolean mountain chalet for storing hay

f -/-n = *Heurige,* 2. – **~seligkeit** *f* - winey cheerfulness; *voller* ~ full of (*or,* mellow with) the spirit of new wine, feeling very merry from the new wine; *in seiner ~ hat er den Herrn Minister auf die Schulter geklopft* feeling great from (*AmE a.* flying high on) the new wine, he pounded the minister on the back. – **~stüberl** *n* -s/-(n) small, cosy room in a new-wine tavern, snug. – **~wirt** *m* -(e)s/-e (vintner and) proprietor of a new-wine tavern.

"Come sit with me in the shade of those trees, And drink the drink spelling mirth and ease!"

Hieb *m* -s/-e <cut> *colloq.* **1.** only in the *phr.* denoting a person considered foolish: *er hat einen* ~ he is cracked, *or* off his rocker. – **2.** [< the 'cutting up', in 1861, of the Vienna municipal area into districts] often said with an aggressive or condescending overtone – any of the twenty-three local districts of Vienna, esp. one with an overwhelmingly working-class population such as the tenth or sixteenth *(Wiener Gemeindebezirk)*: section; *aus welchem ~ kommt der Mensch denn?* well, which side of town is the chap (*or, AmE,* guy) from?; *er wohnt im zehnten* ~ he hangs out in the tenth (district).

hierbleiben *v/i (nachsitzen)* of pupils, by way of punishment: to be kept in ‖ ~ *lassen* to keep in, to detain; *die Lehrerin hat die ganze Klasse ~ lassen* the teacher made the whole class stay behind after school.

hinhocken *v/refl colloq. (sich hinsetzen)* to sit down: *AmE* to cop a squat, to make a lap.

Hinter ...: ~arlberg *m* -s [a nonce word formed by contrast to *Vor*arlberg 'the land before the Arlberg (as you travel east)'] *polit. sarc.* "the land behind the Arlberg", the westernmost part of Austria, the body politic to which a good many "Gsiberger" ↑, proud of their Alemannic otherness, see themselves only grudgingly attached. – **≃fotzig** *adj & adv,* low *colloq. (heimtückisch)* insidious: sneaky, sly; *i' sag dir, das ist ganz ein ≃er!* for your information, he's a sneaky slimeball!, *AmE* I'm telling you, he's an underhanded jerk!; auf *~e Art* in a sneaky manner, underhandedly. – **~fotzigkeit** *f* -/-en low *colloq. (Hinterhältigkeit)* insidiousness: sneakiness, slyness; *vor dem seiner ~ musst du dich in acht nehmen!* you need to watch out for his underhandedness. – **~stinkenbrunn** *m* low *colloq.* = *Hintertupfing.* – **≃tückisch** *adj* [a telescoping of *hinterlistig* and *heimtückisch*] in Alpine *dial.* speech: = *hinterfotzig;* a Tyrolean snarl: *du ~er Tuifi du!* you underhanded no-good devil you. – **~tupfing** *n* -s/- *hum.* or *sarc.* an out-of-the-way, and therefore behind-the-times, village or small country town: *BrE* Little-Puddle-in-the-Mud, Much-Binding-in-the-Marsh, *AmE* Hickville (, U.S.A.), Podunk, Timbuktu; *er ist in ~ zuhaus* he lives somewhere in the sticks (*or,* back of beyond). – **~türl** *n* -s/-n *colloq.* **1.** *(Hintertür)* backdoor; *der Einfachheit halber geh ich gleich durchs ~ raus* it's easier for me to go out the backdoor. – **2.** *fig.* *(heimlicher Ausweg)* loophole; *sich ein ~ offenlassen* to leave a backdoor open for oneself.

Hirn *n* -(e)s/-e brains; *cul.* *~ mit Ei* calf's brain with eggs ‖ *colloq. phr.*: *mir steht das ~! (ich bin ganz verwirrt)* I am lost (in a fog), I'm all fussed up, I don't know where I'm at, I don't know whether I'm coming or going; *vulg.* apologetically for a man's carnal love affairs: *beim ~ kann er's ja nicht herausschwitzen!* he can't get it out of his system by the brains, can he?

Hirn ...: ~kastl *n* -s/-(n) *colloq.* brainbox; *streng dein ~ an!* think hard!, *sl.* tap your thinking-tank!, put your thinking-cap on! – **≁rissig** *adj colloq.* of an idea: *(hirnverbrannt)* crazy, *sl.* cracked, cockeyed; *wo hast denn du diese ~e Idee her?* where did you get that hair-brained idea (*or, AmE* ... did you come up with that cockamam[e]y scheme)? – **~schöberlsuppe** *f* -/-n *cul.* clear soup with brain squares. – **≁teppert** *adj* low *colloq.* very crazy; *wie kann man nur so ~ sein?* how can somebody be so bird-brained (*AmE* ... frazzled, wacky)?

Hochadel *m* -s, *or* **Aristokratie** *f* - *soc. hist.* in Imperial Austria, officially used until April 3, 1919: higher (*or* upper) nobility, peerage (as opposed to *Briefadel* ↑), the descendants of former sovereign families, whose holdings had been mediatized in 1806 taking precedence over those whose ancestors had never ruled a principality of the Holy Roman Empire; members of the higher nobility bore the title *Fürst*, *Graf* or, if belonging to the royal family, *Erzherzog* ↑, and were addressed as "*Hochgeboren*".

Hochalm *f* -/-en ♩ & *econ.* a high-lying dairy-hut and meadows the cows, goats, and sheep are moved up to by the farmhands from the *Niederalm* ↓ in late spring: upper mountain pasture.

Hofrat *m* -(e)s/ ... räte [lit., (member of the) 'court council' of the Holy Roman Empire; still widespread even in modern post-Imperial times, it is justified, as would-be etymologists have it, by reference to the supreme law-courts bearing the name *Hof* in present-day Austria, e.g. the Oberste Verfassungsgerichts*hof*, Oberste Verwaltungsgerichts*hof*, and Oberste Rechnungs*hof*, where indeed many justices of the title *Hofrat* are employed] **1.** *hist.* aulic councillor, one of about twenty members of the *Reichshofrat,* or Imperial Court Council, an organ originally intended for executive work but acting chiefly as a judicature from 1498 to 1806, exercising the Emperor's judicial powers on his behalf. – **2.** *hist. & admin.* fully, *Vortragender ~,* once the distinctive rank for the man in authority immediately below that of Minister, the name being due to the fact that he was received in audience by the Sovereign to present his Ministery's business; now, too, the senior official, outranked only by the Governor, in the

Provincial Government of Lower Austria (whose counterpart in the Civil Service is a *Sektionschef*). – **3.** *admin.* fully, *Wirklicher* ~, a senior rank in a central authority concerned with labour, building, etc. – **4.** *admin.* any bearer of an honorary title often conferred on a civil servant after a certain number of years, e.g. on a head teacher or inspector in a secondary school system, or a head of social services. – **5.** *colloq.* often slightly *contp. (vornehm-umständlicher Mensch)* man of genteel and lackadaisical manners: languid fuddy-duddy, Gentleman Bumble ‖ *Beschwichtigungs*~, or ~ *Rücksichtl*, one who tries, often with little success and even less acclaim, to put at ease either of two contending parties: Pussyfoot Peacemaker.

Hofrat...: ~deutsch *n* -(s) *hist. ling.* 'Court Council German', a dialect-tinged standard German affected by senior civil servants in Old Austria. – **~sektion** *f* - ⛰, *hist. & hum.* 'Court Council branch' of the Austrian Alpine Club, founded in 1874, in whose committees many university-trained members played a prominent role. – **~stil** *m* -(e)s/-e *hum.* or slightly *contp.* "Court council efficiency", the awkwardly ceremonious procedure said to be typical of a senior civil servant in Imperial Austria ‖ *sports,* as a critical comment on a football match: *der Angriff agierte im* ~ the forwards had about as much life in them as an elderly group of civil servants.

hölzeln *v/i colloq.* to speak as though with "a little stick of wood" in one's mouth *(lispeln)*: to (have a) lisp, *iron.* to lithp.

Hölzl *n* -s/-n [dim. of *Holz n* '(piece of) wood'] *colloq.* (little) stick ‖ *fig. ein* ~ *werfen* to give verbal assistance (e.g., in an examination): to give a clue, to drop a hint.

Hörndl *n* [dim. of *Horn n*] -s/-(n) (small) horn of animals, etc. ‖ *fig.* said of a young person, a new holder of office, etc., who, while behaving wildly at present, is expected to calm down in good time: *er wird sich schon noch rechtzeitig die ~(n) abstoßen* he will sow his wild oats in good time (, don't you worry).

Hörndl... ** *colloq.*: **~bauer *m* -n/-n one who breeds and fattens cattle for slaughtering, or who rears cows for producing milk *(Hornviehzüchter* [opp. *Körndlbauer* ↓]*) cattle* (*or* beef, *or* livestock) farmer, dairy farmer, grazier, pastoralist. – **~schlitten** *m (Hörnerschlitten)* sledge (*or,* sleigh) with long horn-shaped runners.

Hubertusmantel *m tex.* = *Lodenmantel* ↓.

Huchen *m* -s/- 🐟 a splendid fighting fish found in the larger Austrian rivers: huchen, land-locked (*or* Danubian) salmon ['sæmən].

hudeln *v/i* [this is the verbal derivative of a plural noun, now obsolete, which denoted 'a pile pushed together in disorderly fashion', 'a heap of rags': our verb, therefore, basically means exactly the same as its English cognate – *to huddle* 'to crowd together confusedly'] *colloq.* **1.** *(übereilt agieren)* to act in a hasty manner: to rush (through) things; *nur nicht ~!* never hurry!, no good thing is done in a hurry!, keep your hair (*AmE a.* hat) on!, what's the rush?, we mustn't run before we can walk!, *IrE* fine day, no hurry!, *specif.* we'll come to that all in good time! – **2.** *(nachlässig arbeiten)* to scamp: to botch things; *so etwas Gehudeltes!* what a botched piece of work!

hudriwudri *adv. dial.* of a (usu. cleaning) activity done quickly and superficially: higgledy-piggledy, *IrE* throughother; *du hast das ~ gemacht* you did this in a slapdash fashion. – **Hudriwudri** *m* -s/-s, **Hudriwusch** *m* -s/-e *colloq.* an agitated, unsettled person who cannot concentrate *(Schussel)*: harum-scarum [ˈhɛərəmˈskɛərəm] flibbertigibbet [ˈflɪbətɪˈdʒɪbɪt], fidget, *AmE* fidgeter, kittle-cattle.

Hufschlag *m* -(e)s/ ... schläge *nav.* = *Treppelweg* ↓.

Hühner ...: ~haut *f* - *(Gänsehaut)* goose-flesh: goose pimples, *AmE a.* goose bumps; *eine ~ kriegen* to get goose pimples. – **~junge** *n* -s *cul. (Hühnerklein)* giblets *pl.* – **~steige** *f* -/-n ↙ *(Hühnerleiter)* chicken ladder.

hunzen *v/t* [lit., 'to call one' (later on also, 'to treat one like') 'a dog'] *colloq. (rücksichtslos behandeln)* to treat roughly and cruelly; *wer mag schon den Chef, der einen bei der Arbeit hunzt?* who would take kindly to a boss who gives you a rough deal (*or,* what for) during working hours? ‖ a sampling from a collection of ribald verses covering the whole alphabet, each couplet of which links two words whose beginnings are identical, yet the innocence of the first line stands in fierce contrast to the blatancy of the second: *der Marabu lässt sich nicht ~, / die Mädchen gehen paarweis brunzen* a marabou's no modest freak, / coy maids pair up to take a leak.

Hunzerei *f* - *colloq. (Plackerei)* **1.** a hard and usu. uninteresting piece of work: grind, sweat, *BrE a.* fag. – **2.** hard work done for little or no pay, or because one is forced to do it: slave labour.

hupfen *v/i dial.* to move by jumping on one foot (*hüpfen*): to hop, to jump; *hupf nicht so rum im Zimmer, die Leut' unter uns werdn glei' explodiern* don't skip around in the room so much, the folks downstairs are going to be up in the air in a minute ‖ *phr.* **1.** said in annoyance, or sometimes even anger, rudely telling a person to go away at once: *hupf' in 'n Gatsch (und schlag' Wellen)!* (go) jump in a lake!, *BrE a.* hop it!, take a running jump at yourself!, *AmE a.* go chase yourself! – **2.** used to say that it does not matter which of two things one chooses, because neither is clearly better – *das ist gehupft wie gesprungen* it's as broad as it's long, it's six of one and half a dozen of the other, it's much of a muchness, *in an AmE word-play a.* there isn't a diff of bitterness.

Hupfer *m* -s/- *dial.* **1.** a quick light stepping and jumping movement (*[kleiner] Sprung*): hop, skip; *geh, hol' mir bittschön ein Packerl Zigaretten – zur nächsten Trafik ist's bloß ein ~* go get me a packet of cigarettes, willya? it's but a skip and a jump (*AmE a.* two whoops and a holler) to the nearest tobacconist's (shop; [*AmE* tobacco store]). – *sein Herz schlägt nicht regelmäßig, es macht oft einen ~* his heart (*or* pulse) rate is irregular, it often skips a beat. – **2.** P often *junger ~* usu. *contp.* (1) a young man thought to be overly confident and lacking in respect to older people (*Grünschnabel*): little whippersnapper, young pup. – (2) definitely *pej.* a relatively young man, or adult, who achieved preferment in office over others with greater seniority (*Streber*): pushy upstart. – **3.** ⇔ *hum.* often *kleiner ~*; with an endearing undertone, also **Hupferl** *n* -s/-(n) [< *Hupfer* ↑ + dim. *-l*] *hum.* or slightly *contp.* a small car (*Kleinwagen*): midgie, kiddie car, puddle-jumper, *BrE a.* sardine tin, *AmE a.* pupmobile.

hupfert *adj* [< stem of *hupfen v/i* ↑ + suffix *-ert*] *dial.* tending to skip about madly: nervy ‖ *phr.* describing **1.** a person's outburst of anger: *wie ich das Durcheinander in seinem Zimmer gesehen hab, bin ich ~ wordn* I went hopping mad as soon as I saw that mess in his room. – **2.** a non-alcoholic drink with bubbles of gas: *~(e)s Wasser* fizzy drink.

Husaren ...: ~streich *m* -(e)s/-e or **~stück** *n* -(e)s/-e [first el., < *Husar m* 'hussar' [hʊˈzɑː] (related to *Korsar m* 'corsair'), a member of a light cavalry unit in the Imperial Austrian Army; some of these regiments or squadrons distinguished themselves by their lightning attacks and extraordinary feats of bravery, dashing across hundreds of miles sometimes to raid enemy headquarters and returning unscathed, such as in their sorties towards Milan (1702), Kamenz (1745), and Berlin (1757)] **1.** *mil. hist.* daring exploit (in line of old Hussar tradition). → **2.** *fig.*, now often *hum.*, and always *apprec.* any comparable action demanding determination, stamina, and unusual bravery: deed *or* act of derring-do. – **~tempel** *m* -s *mil. hist.* on the summit of Kleine Anninger, near Mödling, Lower Austria, affording an extensive view of the wooded heights to the east, as far as the Leitha Mountains: "Temple of the Fallen Hussars", a stately war memorial and burial site erected in grateful memory of the regiment of hussars who, in the Battle of Aspern (1809), had courageously cut their way through the French troops and thus saved the life of Prince Johann I of Liechtenstein (whose ancestral castle happens to stand not far away, close to Vorderbrühl).

hussen *v/i colloq. (hetzen)* to speak maliciously about an absent person or persons: to backbite, *AmE a.* to blow poison gas; *er husst immer gegen seine Arbeitskollegen* he's always running his co-workers down (*or*, into the ground).

Hustenburg *f* -/-en *hum.* or *iron.* a tuberculosis sanatorium *(Lungenheilanstalt)*: *"cough castle", phlegm factory.

Hütten ... ⩓: **~bummel** *m* -s/- casual hut-to-hut stroll. – **~schuhe** *m pl.* moccasocks. – **~tourist** *m* -en/-en hut-to-hut walker. – **~wirt** *m* -(e)s/-e caretaker *or* keeper of a mountaineering hut. – **~zauber** *m* -s "mountain-hut magic": **1.** gay houseparty-like atmosphere at an Alpine chalet or ski-lodge. – **2.** gay chalet party; *heut abend gibt's ~ mit Klampfn und Zither* there'll be a cosy get-together tonight, with guitar and zithern.

Hutze *f* -/-n [< MHG *hutzel, hützel*] *dial. (Dörrobstschnitz)* slice of dried fruit.

Hutzel ... *dial.*: **~brot** *n* -(e)s/-e *bak.* bread made, usu. for special occasions, from rye-meal and containing an assortment of dried fruit such as pears, apples, plums, raisins, and figs: fruit bread, spiced currant bread; *ein ~* a fruit loaf. – **~weiberl** *n* -s/-(n) *emot. (altes Weiblein voller Runzeln)* dear old wizened (*or* wrinkled) woman.

I

Identitätsausweis *m* -es/-e *(Personalausweis)* identity card, identification papers.

Idiotenhügel *m* -s/-, **~wiese** *f* -/-n *skiing hum. (Anfängerhügel)* nursery slope.

IHS [ˈi:ha:ˈes] *R.C. abbr.* a message always reverential if slightly variable in content, to be found on belfries and elsewhere on sacred ground; the tradition of those initials, often shown in a setting of golden rays, was established in the Eastern Alps from the fifteenth century onwards after the preaching of St Bernard of Siena: < LateL < Gr *IHΣ,* short for *IHΣOYΣ* 'Jesus' (*H* here is the Greek eta, an upper-case letter symbolizing the vowel sound of [e:]), or L *Iēsus Hominum Salvātor* 'Jesus Saviour of Men'; alternatively, with reference then to the Holy Cross, < L *In Hōc Signō [Vincēs]* 'in this sign shalt thou conquer', or < L *In Hōc Salūs* 'in this is salvation'.

Indian *m* -s/-e [reference is to the country, or city, in Asia where that bird is supposed to have been imported from; hence formerly also known as *indisches, kalkutisches,* or *türkisches Huhn*] *zo. & cul.* a large domesticated bird, *Meleagris gallopavo L.,* often kept on farms for its meat, which is eaten esp. at Christmas, and in the United States at Thanksgiving *(Truthahn)*: male turkey, turkey-cock: *ScotE* bubbly-jock, *AmE* gobbler.

Indianerkrapfen *m* -s/-, **Indianer** *m* -s/- **mit Schlag** *bak. (Mohrenkopf)* chocolate(-covered) sponge bun (filled) with whipped cream.

Inkassant *m com. (Kassierer)* bill-collector, collector of money who goes to the debtor's house.

Innerösterreich *n* -s *hist.* (1) a collective name for the former duchies of Styria, Carinthia, Carniola *(Krain),* and the county of Gorizia *(Görz);* (2) in Tyrol and Vorarlberg, a collective name also for the rest of Austria: Inner Austria ‖ cp. *Vorderösterreich* ↓.

Inquisitenspital *n* -s/-spitäler *jur. med. (Krankenabteilung der Justizvollzugsanstalt)* prison hospital (*or,* infirmary).

Inspektor [–ʃp–] *m* -s/ … toren *Herr ~,* the customary form of address by a pedestrian or a motorist to any rank of policeman, esp. one on duty; *Herr ~, wie komme ich bitte am einfachsten zur Oper?* excuse me, sir (*AmE a.* officer [as a joke: ossifer]), which is the easiest way to get to the Opera?

I-Tüpfel, I-Tüpferl dot over the i; *bis aufs ~ genau sein* to be accurate (in every detail): to dot the i's and cross the t's.

J

Jạnker *m* -s/- *garm.* a short coat, usu. reaching to the hip, heavily fulled *(Jacke, Joppe)* – **1.** or *Bauern*~, used for everyday wear, esp. in Austrian mountain areas: loose (Alpine *or* Tyrolean) jacket. – **2.** if part of a distinctive regional suit worn on festive occasions (fully known as *Trachten*~): traditional *or* regional jacket.

Jạ̈nner *m* -s/- *(Januar)* January.

Jạss [jʌs] *m* -(en)/-(e) [? < Cz *jasny 'positive'*, 'sure'] *colloq.,* always used appreciatively – an expert at doing or knowing something *(Könner)*: ace, *BrE a.* dab (hand); *der Rolf ist im Schachspielen ein* ~ Ralph is a fantastic (*or,* a crack) chess-player, Ralph is a wizard at chess.

Jauk *m* -s [< ? *Jauche f* 'liquid manure': if correct, the word may originally well have been intended as an insult to the Slovenes] ☼ Carinthian *dial.* a warm southerly wind blowing over the Karawanken and the Julian Alps, elsewhere known as *Föhn* ↑: jauk [jaʊk].

Jause *f* -/-n [< Slov. *južina* 'lunch'] *gastr. (Zwischenmahlzeit)* snack, "quick pick-me-up".

Jọchgeier *m* -s/- [< *Joch n* 'saddleback' (between two mountains); *Geier m* 'vulture'] *ornith.* the largest European bird of prey, 🕮 *Gypaetus barbatus,* ranging in the Alps and preying on lambs *(Lämmergeier)*: lammergeier *or* lammergeyer, bearded vulture, ossifrage ‖ *fig. colloq.* gen. only in the negative comment on a person's unpleasantly harsh and piercing voice: *schreien* or *plärren wie ein* ~ to screech as if possessed.

jodeln *vt/i* ♪ [like *johlen* 'to howl or bawl for joy or triumph', < *jo* [jo:], a mountain dweller's loud and lively shout – comparable to a plainsman's *hey!* in English – to attract and hold someone's attention] to sing or shout melodiously while frequently changing from one's ordinary to a very high voice and back again: to yodel, *less often* to yodle *and* jodel [ˈjəʊdl]. – **Jodler** *m* -s/- ♪ **1.** and **~in** *f* -/-nen, respectively – a person who yodels: yodeller. – **2.** a song or a sound made by yodelling: yodel.

This is what Frances Trollope, a famous traveller to Austria in the 1830s, had to say about this, to her, weirdly fascinating but also mystifying mode of native self-expression and communication (*Vienna and the Austrians* [London: Richard Bentley, 1838, Vol. I, p. 69]):

It was [in Austria] that we first heard that peculiar falsetto, called, in the language of the country, *Jodeln,* and by the rest of the world, *Tyrolese singing.* I hardly know why the ear takes pleasure in it, for it is a mere trick, and no more like the legitimate notes of the human voice than it is like a jew's harp. The truth is, I believe, that we are accustomed to associate it in our minds with ideas of Alps and chamois hunters, picturesque hats and embroidered jerkins, and therefore kindle at the sound, as if listening to it would bring one nearer to the mountains. Something like this was, I am certain, my own feeling as I hung out of my window [that night], to catch the sounds of a voice which had little in it worth listening to, except to serve as a call between one mountain top and another. Nevertheless, I did listen to it with unwearying perseverance for nearly an hour.

Jonas [ˈjo:nas] *pr. n.* [< Franz Jonas, Mayor of Vienna, between 1952 and 1965] *hum.* in cpds **~-Grotte** *f* "Jonas('s) Grotto", a nickname for the *Opernpassage* [-paˈsa:ʃ], an underground passageway and shopping area, below the crossing of the *Ring* and the *Kärntnerstraße*. – **~-Reindl** *n* "Jonas('s) Bowl", a nickname for the *Schottenringschleife,* a city terminus (*AmE* downtown terminal), of several tramlines, next to the University, in the form of a loop below street level. – **~-Wurm** *m* -s/Würmer "Jonas('s) Worm" [wə:m], a facetious reference to one of the modern articulated trams of Vienna Transport.

Josefi *m* gen. sg. [< L *Josephus R.C.* March 19, honouring the husband of St Mary, the mother of Jesus – the patron saint of Styria, Carinthia, Salzburg, and the Tyrol: St Joseph's Day; *zu* ~ on St Joseph's Day || an Austrian weather-day saying:

Wenn 's zu Josefi hell und klar,
bringt reiche Früchte dann das Jahr.

*St Joseph's Day, if bright and clear,
Bids fair to bring much fruit that year.

juchazen *dial.,* **juchzen** *colloq.* [< MHG *jūchezen* (from *jūch* 'hurrah', an interjection conveying a person's joy and delight about something)] *v/i* to shout and cheer (*jauchzen*): to yippee, to hurrah (*or* hurray, hooray).

Here is an Alpine chatter ditty briefly spotlighting a high, and its consequent low, in the erotic mindscape of a herdsman from the mountain pastures:

Håb oamoi nur gjuchazt, mei, schee woa die Alm…
und hiaz hån i' wieda die Hebamm' zan zahln.

I yippeed but once on our alp, what a day!
And here is that midwife again wants her pay.

Juchhe *n* -s/-s [from the shout of triumph given by mountaineers upon reaching the peak] *theat.* the seats high up at the back of a theatre: *BrE* the gods, *AmE* peanut gallery, peanut heaven; *am* ~ *BrE* (a seat) in the gods, *AmE* … at nosebleed height.

Juleber [ˈju:l–e:bə] *m* -s/- *cul., folklore* "Yule boar", a roast pork served in some mountain districts as Christmas supper after the farm people's return from midnight mass.

Jungfern … [*-fern-* in the following two compounds is derived from different roots, in the first from MHG *farh* 'pig' (as in NHG *Ferkel* 'piglet'), in the second from *Frau(en)* 'woman's']: **~braten** *m* -s/- *gastr. (Lendenbraten aus Schweinefleisch)* roast loin of pork. – **~sprung** *m* pl.n. Maiden's Leap, a name given to certain conspicuous cliffs (e.g., in Carinthia, near Landskron Castle [Lake Ossiach] and a few miles south of Heiligenblut), down which, according to legend, an innocent girl is said to have jumped to escape her pursuers.

Note: In English-speaking countries, this same basic concept of flight to death is embodied in the common cliff name of "Lovers' Leap".

Justitia regnorum fundamentum *hist. phr.* "Justice is the foundation of empires", the Latin motto of Emperor Francis I. of Austria, 1804–35.

K

Kabskutscher *m* -s/- [< *hist.* driver of a two-wheeled dust-cart] in *phr.: fluchen wie ein ~* to swear like a trooper (*AmE* ... like a truck driver, ... like a redneck); if female, *BrE:* ... like a fishwife; *du führst einen Spruch wie die ~* your language is straight out of the gutter.

Kaffeetscherl *n* -s *emot.,* in praise of a cup of coffee (cp. *Teetscherl* ↓): (some) delicious coffee; *das ist ein ~, da muss man „Sie" dazu sagen!* that's a coffee that you have to bow down to!

Kaiser *m* -s/- [< L *Caesar*] **1.** emperor; *~ von Österreich* Emperor of Austria, the hereditary title assumed by Emperor Francis in 1804; cp. the name of several first-class hotels with Hapsburgian associations, e.g. at Bad Aussee. – **2.** *colloq. phr.* largely on the basis of the counting-out formula, *„Kaiser, König, Edelmann / Bürger, Bauer, Bettelmann": da war ich ~!* I was tops! ‖ a *sarc.* or resigned observation that nobody is exempt from life's trials and tribulations: *es sind schon ~ gestorben* even kings have to die some time ‖ a withering verdict on a self-important person: *der kommt sich vor wie der ~ von China* he thinks he's the emperor of China ‖ said in resignation, or in gallows humour, at being confronted with a material void (as when the refrigerator is empty or the newspaper is undelivered): *„wo nichts ist, (da) hat der ~ sein Recht verloren"* *even the Kaiser can't demand his share of nothing, "where nothing is the King must lose his right", you can't stake a claim in cloudland; "and when she got there the cupboard was bare, and so the poor doggie had none". ‖ a euphemism for a trip to the toilet: *ich geh jetzt, wohin selbst der ~ zu Fuß geht* *I'm off to where even the Kaiser has to go on foot, I have to see a man about a dog. – **3.** ⛰ *colloq.* short for *Kaisergebirge,* a climbers' paradise in the Tyrol; *im ~ gibt es großartige Klettermöglichkeiten* there is some excellent rock-climbing in the Kaiser (mountains).

Kaiser ... (in cpds. sometimes adding little more than a generally appreciative sense; cp. E 'king [-size]'): **~bart** *m* -(e)s/ ... bärte **1.** *(Vollbart)* full beard [Note: E 'imperial' = G *Knebelbart*]. – **2.** *vulg.* female pubic hair: (rose-)bush, muff, thatch, *ScotE* sporran. – **~birne** *f* -/-n *(Butterbirne)* thin-skinned (juicy) butter pear. – **~-Ferdinands-Nordbahn** *f* - "Emperor Ferdinand's Northern Railway", the first railway line in Austria opened in 1837, under a charter of Emperor Ferdinand (1835–48), between Floridsdorf and Deutsch-Wagram.

The Danube bridge for the pioneer Austrian railway line to Deutsch-Wagram, northeast of Vienna

– **~fisch** *m* -(e)s/-e = *Saibling* ↓. – **~fleisch** *n* -(e)s *cul. (geselchtes Bauchfleisch)* fatty smoked pork chops (from the breast), a high-quality meat without bones. – **~frühstück** *n* -(e)s/-e *colloq.* a lavish breakfast: royal breakfast. – **~gebirge** *n* -(e)s [< *Kaser,* 2] "Kaiser Alpine Range", near Kitzbühel, on the Bavarian border of the Tyrol, naturally divided into the *"Wilder Kaiser",* with jagged limestone peaks, and the 'meeker' *"Zahmer Kaiser".* – **~gelb** *n* -s = *Schönbrunnergelb* ↓. – **~groschen** *m* -s/- *hist. numis.* groat, a monetary unit, the equivalent of three Kreutzers (hence *Dreikreutzer*), in circulation between the sixteenth and nineteenth centuries. – **~gruft** *f* - in Vienna – "Imperial Crypt", = *Kapuzinergruft.* – **~haus** *n* -es Imperial family.

Kaiserinmutter *f* – *hist.* "Emperor's Mother", the contemporary appellative of Archduchess Sophie, 1805–72, daughter of King Maximilian I of Bavaria, who was extremely ambitious for her son, Emperor Francis Joseph I; she thus brought about his betrothal to Elisabeth, a marriage between first cousins, which helped to cause the mental instability of Crown Prince Rudolph.

Kaiser…: ~jäger *m* -s/- *mil. hist.* (*sg.* member of one of the four) *pl.* elite mountain regiments in the Hapsburg monarchy, 1816–1918, whose rank and file were recruited from Tyrolean stock ǁ on the Berg Isel, Innsbruck: *~-Museum,* a regimental museum with flags, uniforms, weapons, portraits, war pictures, and the 'Tyrol Roll of Honour'. – **~koch** *n* -(e)s/-e *cul.* "Emperor's pudding", a rice pudding flavoured with almonds. – **~melange** [-meˈlɑ̃:ʃ] *f* -/- *cul.* often chosen as a cure for a hangover: strong coffee, added to an egg-yolk mixed with two tablespoonfuls of boiling cream, a dash of cold water and two tablespoonfuls of sugar (plus an optional jigger of cognac). – **~mischung** *f* - *cul.* in Lower Austria: a drink of wine, soda water, and raspberry syrup: *AmE* wine spritzer. – **~park** *m* -s *hort.* on the slopes of the Jainzenberg, Bad Ischl: → *Kaiservilla.* – **~quartett** *n* -(e)s ♪ Emperor's String Quartet, Op. 76, written by Joseph Haydn, 1799, with variations on *Gott erhalte Franz den Kaiser* 'May God Save Emperor Francis', the old Austrian national anthem by the same composer. – **~saal** *m* -(e)s/… säle *archit.* in monasteries, e.g. at Melk, Kremsmünster, and St Florian: "Emperor's Hall", a spacious setting amid glories of baroque or rococo architecture for audiences, receptions, etc., worthy of princes of the State when being entertained by the princes of the Church. – **~schinken** *m* -s/*pl.* rare: - *cul.* smoked ham. – **~schmarr(e)n** *m* -s/- *cul.* pancake torn into small pieces and fried, with sultanas or raisins added: shredded flapjack, *AmE a.* griddlecake; this is sprinkled with castor (*AmE* powdered) sugar and served with a compote, usually cranberries, which may be mixed in or eaten on their own. – **~schnitzel** *n* -s/- *cul.* a speciality of the Vienna "Alte Hofkeller": cream cutlet (with grated lemon peel), for which prime-quality meat is used (→ *Kaiserteil*). – **~schöberl** *n* -s/-(n) *cul.* an ingredient used for garnishing clear soup: fried mixture of flour, minced veal, and beaten egg whites, cut into squares. – **~schütze** *m* -n/-n *mil. hist.* (*sg.* a member of the) *pl.* "Imperial militiamen" (1910–18), a unit created from the *Landwehr* militia, drawing its members from all parts of the Austro-Hungarian Empire (cp. *Kaiserjäger* ↑). – **~semmel** *f* -/-n *cul. (Brötchen [mit fünf Strahlen])* "Emperor's roll", a round, crispy baked good with a five-armed pinwheel pattern on top; the name goes back to Emperor Frederick III who, in 1487, had such rolls made with his portrait stamped on them, and gave one to each of the children called together at the Vienna city moat. ǁ *colloq. phr.* to be completely without money: *krachen wie eine ~* to be beanless, to have no cabbages (*or,* potatoes) in the patch, to be flat as a pancake, *AmE* to have no bread (*or,* dough). – **~stadt** *f* - *hist.* a sobriquet of Vienna, as the civic centre of the Austro-Hungarian Empire: Imperial City. – **~stiege** *f* -/-n *archit.* in monasteries, e.g. at Altenburg, Geras, and Göttweig, all in Lower Austria: "Emperor's Staircase", Grand Staircase, a spacious flight of stairs, most often lavishly decorated with painted ceilings, etc., meant to impress Imperial visitors when walking up to their chambers (*Fürsten-*

Some 180 years ago, monastic libraries throughout Austria were opened to T. F. Dibdin, a prominent British historiographer, where he was welcomed over Kaiserstiegen *and into* Kaisersäle, *while his companions got in touch with the humble laity, here shown at the foot of Göttweig Abbey, a straggling group of pilgrims on the way to Mariazell, to the "Magna Mater Austriae"*

or *Kaiserzimmer)*. – **~teil** *m* -(e)s/-e *cul.* *(Kalbsschale [vom Schlögel])* prime-quality thigh cut of veal. – **~trakt** *m* -(e)s/-e *archit.* in monasteries, e.g. at Klosterneuburg and Melk: Imperial suite (of rooms). – **~villa** *f* - *archit.* "Emperor's Villa", a country house standing in parkland *(Kaiserpark)* just on the outskirts of Bad Ischl, Upper Austria, the favourite summer residence of Emperor Francis Joseph from 1854 to 1914; King Edward VII visited him there in 1907 and 1908. – **~walzer** *m* -s "Emperor's Waltz" **1.** ♪ a composition by Johann Strauss, Jr. in 1888, the most chaste and royal of his dances, written to honour the monarch on the fortieth anniversary of his accession to the throne. – **2.** *vulg.* sexual intercourse *(Geschlechtsverkehr)*: mattress jig, dancing in the sheets, doing the bed dance, *AmE* doing the tube steak boogie. – **~wein** *m* -(e)s *vinic.* "Emperor's wine", an excellent type of wine from the Dinstlgut Vintners' Society at Loiben, in the Wachau, originally proffered by Dr. Karl Lueger [luˈeːgə], then Mayor of Vienna, to Emperor Francis Joseph and his entourage at the "Ball of the City of Vienna". – **~wetter** *n* -s ☼ *colloq.* traditionally fine weather, as though by appointment, in order not to mar a ceremonial occasion: King's [Queen's] weather, royal weather, weather fit for a king [queen]. – **~zimmer** *n* -s/- *archit.* in monasteries, old palace hotels, etc.: → *Kaiserstiege.*

kajolieren [-ʒ-] *v/t* [< F *cajoler* 'to flatter'] *j-n* ~ to speak or write flattery to sb.: to butter sb. up, *AmE a.* to give sb. soft soap, to soft-soap (*or,* soap) sb.; *dein ewiges ~ reicht mir schon langsam!* I've had it up to here with your smooth talk.

Kalabreser *m* -s/- [actually, 'man from Calabria', Southern Italy] in Eastern Austria, said in mild reproach of somebody one considers to have acted awkwardly: (1) if imprudent: duffer, oaf, *BrE a.* Silly Billy; (2) if unskilful: clumsy clot, butterfingers *sg*; *das ist ein ~! BrE* what a silly old boot!, *AmE* he's a silly old coot.

Kalụppe *f* -/-n [< Cz *chalupa* 'modest little house'; 'hut'] *contp.* *(baufälliges Haus)* dilapidated old house: shanty, old hovel, ramshackle affair; *in so einer ~ möchte ich nicht wohnen, und wenn man mir sie schenkt!* I wouldn't want to live in a tumbledown shack like that even if they gave it to me as a present (*or,* … even if they paid me).

Kaminfeger *m* -s/- *(Rauchfangkehrer)* chimney-sweep, sweep.

Kanalgitter *n* -s/- [actually, 'grating of a manhole or drain cover'] Viennese *vulg.*, in a verbal threat: *ich passier' dich durchs ~!* I'll make pulp of you!, *AmE a.* I'll run (*or,* put) you through a meat grinder!

Kạnevas *m* - *hist.* [a nonce formation < *kann er was?*] "What's he good at?", "Is he any good?", a nickname given by intimates to Franz Schubert, 1797–1828, who is said to have raised the question of talent whenever a new man was to be presented to his circle of gifted friends.

Kapuziner *m* -s/- **1.** *R. C. relig.* Capuchin [ˈkæpjuʃɪn], a Franciscan friar of the new rule of 1528. – **2.** *cul.* *(Kaffee mit wenig Milch)* coffee with a drop of milk, dark brown like a Capuchin friar's habit: cappuccino; *versoffener ~* "inebriated friar" *(Grießauflauf mit Weinbeerüberguss)* semolina soufflé, with almonds and currants, over which wine has been poured. – **3.** *med.,* low *colloq. (Schleimpfropf [beim Raucherkatarrh])* wad of phlegm [flem], the secretion of a heavy smoker suffering from tracheal catarrh: *er hat einen ~ geschluckt, er bringt den ~ nicht raus* he's choking on his brown gob (*AmE* … his own loogie).

Kapuziner… *R. C. relig.:* **~gruft** *f* - on the Neuer Markt in Vienna: Capuchin Vault, the crypt of the Capuchin Church, with the sarcophagi [saːˈkɒfəgaɪ] of 140 Hapsburgs. – **~kirche** *f* -/-n church of the Capuchins, Capuchin church. – **~kloster** *n* -s/… klöster Capuchin friary.

Karfiol *m* -s [like its English equivalent, < It *cavolfiore*] ♆ and *cul. (Blumenkohl)* cauliflower; *zwei Stück ~* two head of cauliflower; *~ mit Butter und Bröseln* cauliflower with brown butter and breadcrumbs ‖ an instruction from a cookerybook: *den ~ putzen und kurz in Salzwasser legen, damit vorhandene Schnecken herauskriechen* wash cauliflower and put in salt water for a short while, so any snails will crawl out.

Karfreitagsratsche *f* -/-n, *dial.* **Karfreitagsratschn** *f* -/- **1.** *relig.* "Good Friday rattle", a clapper used in Roman Catholic areas instead of bells on the Friday and Saturday preceding Easter. – **2.** *fig. hum.* or *iron.* talkative or gossipy

"The Capuchin Vault on the Neuer Markt contains the bones of twenty-seven emperors and empresses of the House of Hapsburg. (A steel engraving by W. H. Bartlett and E. I. Roberts, about 1850.)

woman: yackety-yack, gasbag, *BrE a.* washerwoman ‖ a slur on two women seen talking together for some time: *schau hin, da sind jetzt zwei Karfreitagsratschen zusammengekommen! BrE* look at those old gasbags nattering over there!, *AmE* ... jabbering away like jays.

Karnten *n* -s (rare) *dial.* = *Kärnten.*

Kärnten *n* -s *geog.* the most southerly federal province of Austria, cupped between two mountain ranges (→ *Sonnenbalkon Österreichs*), and rich in scenic lakeland attractions: Carinthia ‖ *das Paradies von ~ sobr.* the Lower Lavant Valley, in the eastern part of the province, a fertile area producing much wheat and fruit: "The Paradise of Carinthia". – **kärntisch** *adj* = *kärntnerisch.*

Kärntner 1. *m* -s/- Carinthian (boy or man) ‖ two instances of popular lore, also documenting the feeling of rivalry among neighbours – (1) an inane and groundless taunt: *der ~ wird mit fünfzig Jahr' gscheit, der Tiroler nie!* the Carinthian will be wise when he reaches fifty, but never so the Tyrolean. – (2) a light-hearted quatrain sung by Carinthians with rollicking pride in possessing rich mineral deposits of lead (from which, among others, the ubiquitous figures of Christ – in churches and chapels, on wayside crosses, and in devotional corners of farmhouses – can readily be made):

Der Kärntner – lei, lei! –
hat an Herrgott aus Blei;
und der Steirer wa' froh,
wann er hätt' an aus Stroh.

*The Carinthian, you bet,
Shapes his Lord out of lead;
But the Styrian – poo-paw! –
Can't e'en have one of straw.

Note: – Such harmless verbal darts are, of course, aimed at ethnic groups the world over; one instance is the English rhyme,

Taffy was a Welshman,
Taffy was a thief;
Taffy came to our house
And stole a leg of beef.

2. *adj* used in set collocations (similar to 'Scotch' in English): Carinthian; → *kärntnerisch* ‖ ~ **Blume** *f* – ❦ *sobr.* = *Wulfenia* ↓. – ~ **Hendl** *n* -s/-n *cul.* said in self-ridicule, or mockingly by non-Carinthians (cp. in England, 'Welsh rabbit', for a dish of toasted cheese – with the implication of a similar quip (though now faded) on the poor, meatless diet of one's Celtic neighbours = *Sterz* ↓. – ~ **Messe** *f* -/pl. rare: -n ⚲, also known as *Österreichische Holzmesse,* held every summer in Klagenfurt: Carinthian Fair, the most important timber fair in Central Europe. – ~ **Reindling** *m* -s/-e *bak.* a gastronomical speciality of the province, named after the large covered dish in which it is baked – a yeast pastry filled with raisins, cinnamon, finely chopped walnuts, and other fancy ingredients, offered as an Easter present or as a gift to one's godchild: "Carinthian Casserole." – ~ **Rigi** *m* - -(s) ⛰ *sobr.* the Dobratsch plateau near Villach which, like the mountain mass in central Switzerland, commands an excellent panoramic view: "Carinthian Rigi" [ˈriːgɪ]. – ~ **Seen** [ˈseː(ə)n] *m pl.* "Carinthian Lakeland"; *die Ufer der ~ ~ mit ihrem südlichen*

A 30-page information bulletin for the British Occupation Forces in Carinthia (this number from 1946). The cover features a trio of Irish bagpipers against the background of the Karawanken Range.

No. 10

PUBLISHED BY WELFARE AND EDN. 38 (IRISH) INF. BDE/CARINTHIA AREA

Klima und zumeist beständig schönem Wetter gelten als die österreichische Riviera the Carinthian lakes, with their southern climate and rather dependable fine weather, are called the Austrian Riviera. – **~ Vọlksabstimmung** *f - - polit.* an ascertainment of opinion, made in 1920, returning an overwhelming vote of holding on to the border territories (with a Slovene majority) which Yugoslavia had claimed after Austria losing the First World War: Carinthian Plebiscite [ˈplebɪsɪt].

kạrntnerisch *adj* used in a more general sense than attrib. *Kärntner* (similar to 'Scots' and 'Scottish' in English): Carinthian, typical of Carinthian life and manners.

Kạrren[1] *m* -s/- cart; wheelbarrow ‖ *fig.* use: *den ~ fahren* to rule the roast, to be at the helm of affairs, to have the innings; *der ~ ist verfahren* we are [etc.] up a tree, *AmE a.* … up the creek; *jetzt will er einen Dummen finden, der ihm den ~ aus dem Dreck zieht* now he wants to find some stupid bloke (*AmE* dumb jerk) gullible enough to save his hide. – **~weg** *m* -(e)s/-e cart track, country track, dirt road, unsurfaced road; *diese Straße ist ein besserer ~* this road is merely a glorified cart track.

Kạrren[2] *pl.* ⛰ & *geol.* clefts *(Kluft~)* and grooves *(Rinnen~)* in limestone rock. – **~feld** *n* -(e)s/-er fissured plateau of limestone rock, an expanse of knife-edged ridges and grooves due to erosion, e.g. the karst tract in the Loferer Steinberge and in the Dachstein massif.

Kạrst *m* -es [< the Karst mountain range, near Trieste] *geol.* bare and fissured mountain area, karst. – **~erscheinungen** *f pl.* rugged stone formations and phenomena due to disintegration and porosity of limestone, e.g. clefts and grooves *(Karren),* shallow troughs *(Dolinen),* steep craters, caverns, and subterranean streams.

Kaser *m* -s/- *dial.* **1.** [< *Kas m* 'cheese'] *occupational name* (1) also **Käser** *m* a man who works in a mountain dairy or at a valley farm making cheese (*Käsebereiter*): cheese dairyman, cheese-maker. – (2) a man who sells cheese, butter, or other dairy products (*Käsehändler*): cheesemonger. – **2.** [< VulgL *casearia* 'cheese dairy'] in the Tyrol *(Almhütte im Gebirge)*: alpine dairy hut ‖ this word is also encapsulated in the geographical names *Kaisergebirge, Kaisertal,* as well as in *Wilder* and *Zahmer Kaiser,* two parallel mountain ranges of the North Tyrolean Limestone Alps, east of Kufstein, wildly beautiful and ideal for climbing – no misprints these, but popular etymology good and proper, and no link whatsoever with anything 'imperial'. – **~mandl** *n* -s/pl. rare: -n – in Carinthia, **Wịntersenner** *m* -s/pl. rare: - *folklore* a mischievous spirit who seizes possession of an alpine dairy hut after the summer folks servicing it have gone down with the cattle to the valley farm in autumn: dairy-hut goblin.

Kạsperl [-ʃp-] *m & n* -s/-(n) [< *Kasper m,* the traditional name of one of the Three Kings, in English *Caspar* or, more often, *Jasper,* + dim. *-l*] **1.** *theat.* the stereotyped merryman of centuries-old popular comedy shows, who still survives in marionette plays all over Austria (*Hanswurst*): Clown, Fool, Buffoon. → **2.** mildly *iron.* or *contp.* any person behaving in a ridiculous but often amusing manner (*Hanswurst*): clown; *er ist unser Klassen~̽* he is the professional jester in our class. – **~theater** *n* -s/- **1.** *theat.* a puppet show presented on the miniature stage of a tall collapsible booth traditionally covered with striped canvas (*Kasperletheater*): Punch and Judy (show). → **2.** *fig. contp.* the ridiculous behaviour of one member or, more often, the whole ensemble of a public body, such as a parliament during certain sessions (*Harlekinade, Hanswurstiade*): act *or* scene of buffoonery, Punch and Judy show; *da trommelten doch Abgeordnete auf die Pulte, so dass das vom Sprecher Gesagte ungehört verhallte, andere bliesen die Trompete oder schrillten mit ihren Pfeiferln los – das „~“ oder „Narrenhaus“ war da, und so hatte denn das Parlament beim Volk diesen Namen los* some Members of Parliament banged their desks to drown the speaker's voice, others blew upon trumpets or activated shrill penny whistles – a perfect take-off of a "Punch and Judy show" or "madhouse", the choice terms given to Parliament by the man in the street.

Kạtzel …: ~berger (rare), **~macher** *m* -s/- [first el. < *cazza* 'wooden ladle' in Venetian dialect; such kitchen utensils were made in the cottage industries of Val Gardena (and elsewhere in South Tyrol), and hawked throughout Austria by Italian pedlars] often *contp.* Italian: spaghetti-eater, spaghetti-bender; after the First World War, the Italians, because of their about-turn in joining the Allies, were very unpopular in both Austria and Germany, and a macaronic doggerel, circulating widely then, expressed this contempt: "Italiano, / nix in la mano, / caccelimacca, / drecco in sacca". – **~̽munter** *adj* [first el., dim. of *Katze* 'cat': kitten] *colloq.* **1.** fully awake: bright-eyed and bushy-tailed, as chipper as a sparrow, as chirpy as a bird, *AmE a.* fresh (*or* crisp) as a brand-new dollar. – **2.** very lively: full of life, bouncing off the walls, *AmE* hyper.

kạtzeln *v/impersonal, colloq.: es katzelt* there's a smell of cat about (*AmE* around).

Kạtzen …, *dial.* also **Kọtzn …** [first el., *Katze f* 'cat'] *cul.:* **~gschraạ** [kʃrʌː] and **~gschroa** [kʃrɔə] *n* -s/-, in Viennese *dial.,* and elsewhere in Eastern Austria, respectively [second el., < *Geschrei n* 'prolonged, piercing scream' – the well-known meat dish being given that name (people say) because any domestic feline observing the chunky pieces being nicely chopped up into small portions to be conveniently seized and chewed with ease, but then realizing that those – to the cat's taste – prize portions are cruelly whisked off for human consumption, is bound to break out into wauly lamentations] a plain but popular fare, esp. met with in wine-growing areas of Eastern Austria – a vintners' stew prepared from bits of home-slaughtered pork or veal (usu. from the shoulders, then also from livers, kidneys, and brains), cubed, as well as onions, garlic, peppercorns, marjoram, thyme, caraway seeds and other ingredients, to be eaten with brown bread or potatoes (*Fleischeintopf*): "caterwaulers' speciality". – **~zunge** *f* -/-n a tea-time favourite – chocolate biscuits covered with dairy milk chocolate: milk finger.

Kees *n* -es/-e *geol.* in some parts of the Tyrol, esp. in the Ziller Valley (cp. *Ferner* ↑): glacier. – **~wasser** *n* -s/- (*Gletscherbach*) glacier stream.

Kekserl *n* -s/-(n) [dim. of *Keks n* 'biscuit'] *bak. BrE* biscuit, *AmE* cookie: *BrE* biccy, bikky, *AmE* (little) cookie; *willst* (or, *magst) ein ~?* would you like (*or* [d'you] want, *or* how about) a biccy (*AmE* cookie)? – **Keksi** *n* -s/-(s) *baby talk* biscuit: *BrE* biccy-wicky, *AmE* cookie-wookie.

Keller *m* -s/- short for *Wein*~: wine cellar. – **~dorf** *n* -(e)s/ - ... dörfer, **~gasse** *f* -/-n in wine-growing areas of Eastern Austria: vintners' lane, rows of small houses, on the edge of townships and villages, with subterranean vaults where wine is made and stored. – **~partie** *f* -/-n *colloq.* in wine-growing areas of Eastern Austria: a wine-drinking spree, where cold meat, smoked ham, sausage and home-made bread, either brought by the people or offered for sale by the vintner, is eaten at trestle tables in front of, or inside, a private wine cellar on the outskirts of the village; *eine ~ machen* to go on a wine-drinking spree. – **~stiege** *f* -/-n cellar stairs; *colloq.* in wine-growing areas of Eastern Austria: *der Wein ist auf* (or, *unter*) *der ~* (*dial. ~n*) *gewachsen* "the wine has grown inside the wine cellar under the staircase", i.e. it was adulterated with water there. – **~stüberl** *n* -s/-(n) **1.** (Ger.: *Trinkstube im Keller)* in a restaurant, monastery, or private country home: small and cosy underground bar. – **2.** in wine-growing areas in Eastern Austria: snuggery, a small room, at road level, in a (private) wine cellar where the wine that has been made on the premises is drunk. – **~wirtschaft** *f* **1.** -/-en underground restaurant. – **2.** - *vinic. (Weinerzeugung)* wine-making.

Kellnerenglisch *n* -s *colloq.* waiters' pidgin English, heard from low-class members of the catering trade with a record of long service in English-speaking countries, marked by fluency but also by what seems to be an eternally lingering Austrian pronunciation and syntax; cp. *Kuchelböhmisch* ↓.

Keppelmonolog *m* -s/-e *colloq.* usu. with reference to the verbal outburst of a cantankerous wife: naggy curtain lecture. – **keppeln** *v/i colloq.* ([*ununterbrochen*] *schimpfen*) to nag (persistently) (*mit j-m* at s.o.), *AmE a.* to bitch; *du kannst nichts als an mir herum~* you nag, nag, nag at me all the time; *ich kepple doch nicht* I'm not nagging, please. – **Keppel ...: ~weib** *n* -(e)s/-er *colloq. (dauernd keifende Frau)* scold, battleaxe (*AmE* battleax). – **~zähne** *m pl.* "nagging teeth"; said in anger: *einmal muss man ihr die ~ ausreissen* somebody 's got to put a sock in her bickering bitchy mouth one day. – **Kepplerin** *f* -/-nen *colloq.* = *Keppelweib.*

Kiberer or **Kieberer** *m* -s/-; in Viennese *dial.* also, **Kieberant** *m* -en/-en [< MHG *kīben* 'to get angry'] *contp.,* sometimes just *hum.* a plain-clothes detective *(Kriminalpolizist*): (cop) eye, *BrE* CID man; *da war ein ~ da, der hat dich gesucht* some cop eye was around looking for you.

Kind *n* -(e)s/-er **1.** child ‖ *colloq. phr.* (1) in most mountain areas, illegitimate children give proof to the marriageability of the parent and are therefore not looked down upon – hence the following statement, made by a father or mother sorting out a heterogeneous offspring, is facetious rather than bitter: *meine ~er, deine ~er, unsere ~er!* (these are) my children, (these are) yours, and (these [eventually] are) ours! – (2) an injunction jocularly applied to a group of persons when the speaker is about to expose himself to certain risks for the benefit of the rest: *~er, tut's beten, der Vater geht stehlen!* say your prayers, kids, your dad is off to steal!, *~er, seid's ruhig, der Vater schreibt sein'n Namen!* be quiet, kids, your dad's trying to sign his name. – **2.** Tyrolean *dial.* girl; this specialization has its historic English parallel, e.g. in the phrase 'Was it a boy or was it a child?' (Byron).

Kịnder…: ~bewahranstalt *f* -/-en *(*Ger.: *Kleinkinderbewahranstalt)* day nursery, crèche [kreɪʃ]. – **~dorf** *n* -(e)s/…dörfer children's village, a self-contained community of some ten or fifteen houses built and run by a private welfare organization for the benefit of deprived children; *cp.* in Britain the British Pestalozzi Children's Village Association, and in the U.S., Father Flanaghan's Boys Town; → *~betreuerin f* -/-nen, *~mutter f* -/-…mütter housemother, a housekeeper and foster-mother in charge of one of the houses, with up to ten children, in a children's village. – **~freund** *m* -(e)s/-e friend of children, child lover; → *~e pl. polit. pr.n.* Socialist Children's Welfare Organization, established in 1908. – **~land** *n* -(e)s, fully: *Demokratische Vereinigung ~* a child-and-parent organization of the Austrian Communist Party, established in 1946. – **~limousine** *f* -/-n *hum. (Kinderwagen)* perambulator: *BrE* pram, *AmE* baby buggy. – **~moden** *f pl. (Kinder[be]kleidung)* children's wear. – **~segen** *m* -s *(Kinderreichtum)* abundance of children; *colloq. das ist ja ein ~* that's quite a quiverful! – **~übernahmsstelle** *f* -/-n in Vienna, since 1925: municipal child clearing centre, a welfare station run by the Municipality of Vienna for infants and young children in need of care, before they are committed to charity or foster-parents. – **~verzahrer** *m* -s/- [the dial. spelling and pronunciation of -*verzieher ([Kinder-]Verführer)* 'seducer'] *hum.* said to a man courting a girl much younger than himself: *du bist ja*

Hermann Gmeiner (Alberschwende 1919–1986 Innsbruck), the pioneer of the Children's Village Movement after the Second World War

ein ~! you're robbing the cradle; *du gehörst ja als ~ eingesperrt!* they ought to put you in jail for statutory rape (*or,* child molesting)!

Kịnds ...: ~koch *n* -(e)s/-e *cul. hist.* "children's soft pap", hot milk brought to a boil and thickened by adding flour and sugar, commonly prepared by rural families in the 1930s. – **~tauf** *f* -/-en *colloq.* **1.** *(Kindstaufe)* christening (of a child). – **2.** *hum. (Fußbad)* ring of beer, coffee, etc., made by filling to overflowing or by jostling the glass or cup; an apology, mostly heard at a party, from the server who inadvertently spills the drink: *jetzt habe ich aber eine ~ gemacht* "I'm sorry to have christened the baby", the popular belief being that the runnel points to the father or mother of the next baby to be born.

Kịrtag *m* -(e)s/-e, fully *Kirch(weih)tag* **1.** *R. C. relig.* the anniversary of the consecration of a church: patron saint's day, on which a festival is held. – **2.** *colloq.* (1) *prov.: wenn die Katze aus dem Hause ist, dann haben die Mäuse ~* when the cat's away, the mice will play; (2) *wenn ich mir in der Schule was hätt' zuschulden kommen lassen, dann hätt' daheim der Hintern ~ g'habt* if I had run into trouble in school, my behind would have got a good polishing (*AmE* ... they would have walloped my fanny) at home.

Kịttelfalte *f* -/-n, *dial.* **Kịttelfalt(e)n** *f* -/- skirt pleat ‖ *phr.* of a child or an adolescent that is unduly dependent on an elderly woman, usu. one's mother; *j-m an der ~ hängen, j-m auf der ~ sitzen* to be tied to (*or,* to hang on to) sb.'s apron-strings, not to be able to let go of sb.'s apron-strings; *schau nur, wie sich das Angsthaserl hinter der Mutter ihrer ~ versteckt!* just look at that fraidy-cat hiding behind mummy's skirt!

Klạmm *f* -/-en *geol.* a deep narrow valley with sheer rock walls (*Felsenschlucht [mit Wasserlauf]*): gorge, ravine, *AmE a.* canyon; *in den Alpen gibt es so manche ~, durch die sich über Felsstufen hinweg ein Bergbach wild schäumend seinen Weg bahnt* in the Alps, there is many a ravine through which a mountain torrent boils and seethes and swirls in a series of cascades.

Klạmpfe *f* -/-n [rare in this standard form] usu. **Klạmpfen** or, following the dialect pronunciation, **Klạmpfm** *f* -/- [related to LowG *Klamp* and E *clamp* 'a device that holds things together'] *dial.* **1.** ♪ a guitar, having a long fretted neck and six strings to be plucked with the fingers *(Gitarre)*: gitbox, tickle-box. – **2.** *archit.* a metal bar bent at both ends used for holding together pieces of wood, metal, etc. *(Bauklammer)*: cramp (iron).

Klạpotetz *m* -es/-e, *dial.* -(e)n [< Slov. *klapotec*] *vinic.* a wind-driven scarecrow wheel, one of many harvest-time landmarks in South Styrian vineyards, four long wooden slats pinned together in a circle to activate a hammer to strike on a sounding board in quick succession – its loud clappety-clap, combined with the erratic motion of the wheel (rotating on a high vertical post) effectively scares birds away from looting the luscious bunches of grapes (*hölzernes Windrad*): windwheel rattle.

Klein ...: ~häusler *m* -s/- (**~häuslerin** *f* -/-nen) a man (woman) holding a small farm of a barely subsistence character:

(very) small farmer, *ScotE* crofter. – **~richter** *m* -s/pl. rare: - [lit., 'retailer (< *ausrichten* 'to tell or send a message') of small news'] *admin.* in rural areas of Burgenland – someone employed to leisurely perambulate the streets of a village or a small town, announcing official news and/or warnings on the drum *(Austrommler):* town crier. – **≗weis** *adv colloq.* by degrees, gradually (*nach und nach*): bit by bit, in little bits and bobs, in dribs and drabs. – **≗wụnzig** *adj* [a tautological variant of *winzig* (of which *wunzig* is the result of vowel gradation)] *adj colloq.* very tiny: teeny-weeny, teensy-weensy, weenchy; *ich hab' dich schon gekannt, da warst du noch ein ~er Stöpsel* I knew you when you were a teeninecy little thing (*or,* … when you were just knee-high to a grasshopper).

klẹschen *vt/i* [imit.] *colloq.* **1.** *v/t* to strike a blow; as a verbal threat: *ich klesch' dir gleich ein paar!* I'll smack (*or,* sock) you one in a minute! – **2.** *v/i* to strike a surface, causing a high and resounding note or noise; *wir haben gar nicht weiterfahren können – so (sehr) hat der Regen gegen die Scheiben gekleschst* we couldn't go on driving because the rain was pounding so hard against the windscreen (*AmE* windshield); *ich schmier' dir gleich eine, dass es nur so klescht!* I'll give you a slap that they'll hear a mile away.

Klẹscher *m* -s/- [imit.] *colloq.* **1.** any loud smacking noise, like the burst upon impact of a fully inflated paper-bag, or of a plastic bag filled with a liquid: *das hat einen ~ gegeben* (or, *gemacht), dass wir alle wie verrückt hochgefahren sind* there was such a loud pop (that) we jumped out of our skins. – **2.** a blow struck with the flat palm of one's hand: *ein paar ~ links und rechts – und dann wirst d' sehn, wie das Bürschchen spurt!* a few slaps (*or,* smacks) right and left, and there you'll see how nicely that youngster behaves!, *AmE* give him a couple of slaps, and that kid is sure to straighten out fast!

Kletterei *f* -/pl. rare: -en ⛰ *colloq.,* sometimes used with a tinge of pride, fear, or contempt – (rock) climbing; *das war eine wüste ~!* this was some stiff climbing.

Klẹtterer *m* -s/- ⛰ climber, cragsman.

klẹttern *v/i* ⛰ *(Hochtouristik betreiben)* to climb, to alp; *auf einen Berg ~* to scale a mountain; *(mühsam steigen)* to clamber, to scramble.

Klẹtter… ⛰**: ~berg** *m* -(e)s/-e often *apprec. ein* (*ausgesprochener* or *richtiger*) ~ a peak (ideally) suited for climbing. – **~eisen** *n pl.* climbing-irons, climbers, crampons, claws, grapplers (*all pl.*). – **~garten** *m* -s/ … gärten, *hum. a.* **~palästra** *f* -/ … stren often *apprec.* (ideal) training ground for mountaineers; *der Röthelstein, die Kletterpalästra der Grazer, weist leichteste und sehr schwere Kletterwege auf* the Röthelstein, the magic playground for climbers from Graz, offers the whole gamut of difficulties, from the easiest route to the very exacting one. – **~partie** *f* -/-n = *Klettertour.* – **~schuhe** *m pl.* light climbing shoes of rope and canvas: rock-climbing shoes, rope-soled espadrilles, kletterschuhe (*all pl.*). – **~schule** *f* climbing school. – **~seil** *n* -(e)s/-e climbing rope. – **~steig** *m* -(e)s/-e climbers' *or* climbing trail; *ein ~ mit festen Sicherungen* a climbing route with artificial aids. – **~tour** *f* -/-en climbing expedition, scramble; *eine zweitägige ~ durch die Gesäuseberge der Steiermark* a 48-hour scramble across the Gesäuse Mountains in Styria. – **~zeit** *f* -/-en **1.** climbing season. – **2.** years of climbing *pl.; seine ~ ist schön langsam vorbei* he's drawing near the end of his high-climbing days.

Kl̨etze *f* -/-n, often *dial.* **Kl̨etzn** *f* -/- [< MHG *klœzen* 'to split' – the proper verbal expression to choose since the pears, the staple ingredient of this type of bread, are *split* into small pieces before drying] *gastr.*, chiefly in rural use – (a slice or all of a[n oven-]) dried pear. – *fig.*, in a left-handed compliment for a robustly healthy, though definitely elderly, person (often a female); alternatively, the witticism may also come out of the mouth of the senior citizen herself (or himself), and should then rather be taken as a coquettish piece of self-praise for bearing one's advanced age so well: *wann die Birn' a Kletzn wird, is' s' nimma zum Umbringen!*

*A pear, once shrunk and shrivelled dry,
For inward strength will never die.

Kl̨etzenbrot *n* -(e)s/-e *bak.* a bread dough, spiced, rolled, and filled with small slices or cubes of dried pears and figs (prunes, walnuts, pine kernels [*Pignoli*], and some grapes being optional extras), all sprinkled with rum and/or brandy, mixed, left to stand, and then baked like any other bread (*dunkles Brot mit gedörrten Birnen und Gewürzen*): (loaf of) fruit bread.

kli̲eben, kliebte/klob, hat gekliebt/gekloben *v/t* [cp. E *to cleave*] with reference esp. to wood: *(spalten)* to split. – **Kli̲ebhacke** *f* -/-n *(schwere Spalthacke)* axe.

Knä̲uschen *n* -s/- [a dim. adjustment of the surname of Dr. Hermann *Knaus,* 1892–1970, a Carinthian gynaecologist, who together with his Japanese colleague, Dr. Kiusako Ogino, 1882–1975, closely investigated the human female cycle of fertility; the word had much earlier come to be widely known as a rhyming diminutive in "Hansel and Gretel", a famous fairy tale by the Grimm Brothers, in which the two children, who had completely lost their bearings in the big forest came to the cottage of the Old Witch and, for sheer hunger, began to nibble some gingerbread tiles off her roof, duly causing her to shout, „Knusper, Knusper, *Knäuschen,* / wer knuspert an meinem Häuschen?"] *hum.* or *iron.* a nonce "baptismal" name bestowed on a child who was given birth to against the parents' wishes who had tried, in their case unsuccessfully, to use the anti-conception method devised by Drs. Knaus and Ogino.

Kni̲e… *colloq.*: **~schnackler** *m* -s/- *med.* knee-ache caused by walking downhill for a long time: sore knees, aching knees; *(den) ~ kriegen [haben]* to get [to have] sewing-machine leg; *nach dem Abstieg hab ich einen richtigen ~* my knees feel just like jelly after walking down the mountain. – **~schwamm** *m* -(e)s, **~schwammerl** *n* -s/- **1.** = *Knie-*

Understandably, the Knieschnackler, *or "wobbly-knees syndrome", is felt by many a mountaineer after his long and wearisome descent from the Gross Glockner to Heiligenblut – two focuses of scenic delight here brought together by E. Harrison Compton*

E. HARRISON
COMPTON

Speckknödel – *a Tyrolean delicacy … but can outsiders wrap their tongues round the throaty word?*

schnackler. – **2.** numb legs due to a sudden shock: *ist es ein Wunder, wenn ich bei der Aufregung den Knieschwamm hab?* I'm not a bit surprised that my knees have gone all rubbery with excitement.

Knödel *m & n* -s/-(n) [dim. of *Knoten* 'knot'] **1.** *cul. (Kloß)* dumpling ‖ *phr.* (1) *iron.*, if the product turns out hard: ~ *sind das, die kann man über neun Dächer werfen!, mit den ~n da kann man ja Fußball spielen (*or, *Fenster einschmeißen)!* marvellous dumplings these – you could play tennis (*or,* football, *BrE a.* cricket, *AmE a.* baseball) with them!, these are great dumplings – they go down like lead (*or,* they'll sink straight to the bottom of the ocean; *or,* you could use them to sink the Titanic with)! (2) an adult's patronizing remark to a minor lacking in strength: *da musst du noch viele ~ essen!* you'll have to eat a lot more spinach (*or,* porridge, greens, *BrE a.* rice pudding, *AmE a.* Wheaties) before you can do that! – **2.** low *colloq.* (short for *Roßknödel*) mostly *pl.* (round) horse manure: horse apple, road apple. – **3.** Viennese *football sl.* football: pill, leather; *X hat das einzige ~ eingeschossen* X bagged the only goal. – **4.** any pliable object, e.g. a scrap of paper or small piece of linen, crumpled into a ball: lump; *das ist ja ein ~ von einem Kopfpolster; den musst du ordentlich aufbeuteln!* why, that's a lumpy pillow you've got there; you'll have to give it a good shake (*or,* … fluff it out properly)! – **5.** a roguish type of physical assault –

a person's knee ramming the victim's posterior *(Knödelreiter ↓)*: knee bump; *in Hintertupfing aufgewachsen, hatten wir im Dörfl nur ein wackeliges Kino auf einer Wiese stehen; da die Filme fast immer Jugendverbot waren, bohrten wir Bürscherln Löcher durch die dünne Holzwand, warfen auf das jenseitige Geschehen ein sehnsüchtiges Auge, und das in arg unbequemer Haltung, immer gefährdet, von einem Vorbeikommenden ein ~ in den Hintern gestoßen zu bekommen* grown up in Little-Puddle-in-the-Mud, we had but a wobbly cinema to go to; and since the films shown were nearly always for adults only we young hopefuls drilled peepholes through the thin boarding – standing at an uncomfortable crouch, one eye glued to the scene beyond, we always ran the risk of getting kneed in the backside, good and proper, by anybody passing. – **6.** *fig.* feeling of pressure caused by emotion: lump in one's throat; *ich brachte kein Wort heraus, ein ~ steckte mir im Hals, und ich hatte Tränen in den Augen* I couldn't say a word, I had a lump in my throat (*or,* I was all choked up), and there were tears in my eyes.

Knödel… *colloq.:* **~akademie** *f* -/-n *educ., hum.* or *contp.* (1) domestic science school: dough school; (2) domestic science college: dough college. – **~bauch** *m* -(e)s/…bäuche, **~friedhof** *m* -(e)s/…höfe *hum.* or *iron.* a prominent abdomen: pot-belly, beer-belly, belly-barrel, corporation; *der kriegt ja die Hosen nicht mehr über seinen ~!* he can't get his trousers done (up) over his big fat paunch! – **~reiter** *m* -s/- usu. in the *phr.: j-m einen ~ geben* to knee s.o. in the backside (*AmE* … in the rear [end]). – **~tenor** *m* -s/…tenöre *or* …tenore ♪, *iron.* **1.** a deep bass voice: bull-fiddle voice. – **2.** a singer with a deep bass voice: bullfrog. – **~tresor** *m* -s/-e *hum.* = *Knödelbauch.* – **~würger** *m* -s/- *iron.* a blunt table-knife: *dumpling-strangler.

knödeln *v/i iron.* **1.** to speak indistinctly: to have a mushmouth; *er (*or, *der) knödelt ja!* he talks as though he's got marbles (*or,* pebbles, *or AmE a.* marshmallows) in his mouth. – **2.** to sing in a strangled voice: to gargle; *sie (*or, *die) knödelt ja beim Singen* she gargles when she sings, she croaks like a frog.

Knoschpen [the dialect spelling of *Knospen,* lit. 'buds'] *f pl.* ♩ sturdy wooden shoes, with nailed-on leather uppers, used for stable work: clogs, clodhopper shoes, clodhoppers.

Knusperhäuschen *n* -s/- *hum. euphem.* (*Toilette;* actually, "little gingerbread house" [in Grimm's fairy tale of *Hansel and Gretel*]) toilet: little boys [girls]' room, Poet's Corner, throne room, *AmE a.* Chamber of Commerce; *wo ist denn hier das ~? BrE* may I see the geography (of the house)?, where is the (*or,* your) indoor plumbing?, *ScotE* whaur's the wee hoose?

Köchelverzeichnis ['køxəl-] *n* -ses [first el., < Ludwig von Köchel (in E pron. often ['kɜːʃl]), 1800–77, a nobleman from Krems-Stein, Lower Austria, who in 1862 brought together Mozart's musical estate, which had been widely scattered and in great disorder at his death], *abbr.* **KV** [kaː'fau] ♪ Köchel Catalogue (*or,* Listing) of Mozart's music, *abbr.* K., to this day the accepted standard work of its kind, systematically ordering that composer's creations in 626 items; *kommt über den Rundfunk die Ansage, sagen wir, „Sinfonie Nummer 40 in G-Dur, ~ 550", schwingt auch leise das Echo der Lebensarbeit eines hingebungsvollen Musikgelehrten mit* whenever one hears over the radio the announcement, let us say, "Symphony Number 40 in G Minor Köchel Listing 550", you are also hearing the faint echo of a scholar's devoted lifework in music.

Ko̲fel *m* -s/ Köfel [< Late MHG *kofel,* pron. -ŏ-; further origin unknown) a hill or mountain, frequently cone-shaped and rocky in parts; as the second element of compound names, chiefly found in the Northern and Southern Limestone and Dolomite Alps, e.g. in *Gartner~* (*[Berg-]Spitze*): peak.

Ko̲gel *m* -s/ Kögel [< L *cucullа* 'a monk's large loose hood' (cognate and synonymous with E *cowl*); our word of the Eastern Alps is also related to *Kugel* 'ball or any other solid rounded mass', as well as to *Keule* and E *cudgel,* both denoting 'a heavy tapering stick which is thick at one end'] **1.** a small (dome of a) hill (*[Berg-]Kuppe*): mound, knoll. – **2.** a cone-shaped top of a hill with a well-defined summit and approach ridges, broad or narrow, in all though with a rounded profile; similar in general to a *Kofel* ↑, but often lower in altitude: dome-shaped hill *or* mountain.

Kọlarič, Kọlaritsch *m* -/-(e) [a generic use of a Slav family name, esp. prevalent in Serbia, Croatia, and Slovenia] *colloq. (Gastarbeiter)* foreign worker: Mister (*or,* Mr.) Alien Labour.

Komforta̲bel, *colloq.* **Komforta̲bl(er)** *m* -s/- [< F *confortable* (showing the *n* assimilated to *m* before the labial *f*): the form in parentheses is a later variant with a German ending] *hist.* **1.** a horse-drawn carriage used for hire: hackney carriage. → **2.** the (owner-)driver of such a carriage (cp. *Einspänner* ↑): cab-driver, cabman, *colloq.* cabby, cabbie.

Konsumatio̲n *f* -/-en *(Verzehr, Zeche)* consumption of food and/or drink in a public restaurant; **~szwang** *m* -es in a nightclub, etc.: obligation to consume food and/or drink.

Kọpfnuss *f* -/... nüsse *colloq.* a sharp, but affectionate rap, or rub, on the head with one's knuckles: *AmE colloq.* noogie.

Kọ̈rberlgeld *n* -(e)s [first el., 'little basket (intended to act as a woman's minor private, and often secret, savings bank to go back to as her heart desires)'] *colloq.* **1.** a small money allowance granted to, or little sums earned by, a woman for dress, the odd personal necessity, etc. (*Nadelgeld*): pin-money. – **2.** a small sum of money saved by a woman for future use (not yet decided upon at the time being): nest-egg; if set aside for some spontaneous, unscheduled expenditure, usu. on pleasure: mad money. – **3.** small sums of money retained by the wife from the household money, without the husband's knowledge (*kleine, harmlose Veruntreuungen*), also known as **Schmu̲geld**: something (*or,* some shekels) on the side.

Kọ̈rndlbauer *m* -n/-n one who grows crops for sale, such as wheat for bread, barley for brewing or for animal feed, and sugar beet for sale to the sugar factories *(Getreide-, Ackerbauer* [opp.

Hörndlbauer ↑]: cereal grower, arable farmer.

Korrespondẹnzkarte *f* -/-n *(Postkarte)* postcard (often with a printed stamp).

Krạcherl *n* -s/-(n) [< *Krach m* 'any loud, explosive noise' + dim. *-erl*] *colloq.* an effervescent soft drink in a bottle which, when its top is quickly removed, produces a loud noise (*Brauselimonade, Sprudel*): (1) *gen.,* fizzy drink. – (2) *if flavoured with ginger,* (ginger-) pop.

Krạftlackel *m* -s/-(n) *contp. ([geistig unbemittelter] Muskelprotz)* person noted rather for his muscles than his brains: musclehead, (big) ox, *AmE a.* heavyweight, Tarzan; *er ist ein ~ ohne viel Hirn* he is all brawn and no brains.

Kragen *m* -s/- or Krägen (*Hals*) neck ‖ a drastic dialect rhyme from Fließ, near Landeck, poking fun at unnatural phenomena, and delighting the folklore comparatist with neat parallels from both sides of the Atlantic, while at the same time showing students of the history of English that consonantal loss in the infinitive ending also massively occurs in some areas of the Tyrolean vernacular: *wenn d'Madla pfeifa und d'Henna kra-a, / soll ma bead da Kraga umdrah* [Scotland:] fustlin maidens an craain hens is nae lucky aboot ony man's place; [South Carolina:] a whistling girl and a crowing hen / will bring this world to no good end (*or,* will land this world in the devil's den).

Kramuri *f* - *colloq. (Kram, Gerümpel)* old, disused objects: junk, *BrE a.* lumber; *mit dieser* (or, *der*) *~ kann man nichts mehr anfangen, sie* (or, *die, das*) *gehört einfach weggehaut* you can't do a thing with this junk, it simply wants throwing away.

Kranawett, Kranewit *m* -s ❦ *(Wacholder)* juniper (tree). – **Kranewitter** *m* -s *(Wacholderschnaps)* (juniper) gin.

Krawạttl *n* -s/-(n) *colloq. (Krawatte)* (neck-)tie ‖ *beim ~ haben* (*a. fig.*) to grab (a person) by the neck; *ich werde dich gleich beim ~ haben!* as a threat; quite often used, however, in good nature: I'll give you a proper shaking in a minute! – **~tenor** *m* -s/-e (*or,* … tenöre) P *contp.* (*Tenor mit Fistelstimme*) tenor with an unusually high and thin voice.

krawụtisch *adv* [a dialect corruption of StG *kroatisch* 'Croat', 'Croatian' – a name encapsulating reminiscences of acts of violence long past, committed by Croatian constabulary during the War of the Austrian Succession, 1742–45] *dial.* by sheer force, with unbridled energy – as in the lusty invitation to resolute physical action, either jointly or by the speaker only, say when an unwieldy piece of furniture is to be lifted and moved: *(hiaz) pack ma's ~!* it's brutal strength that does it – here we go (*or,* now or never)!

Kren *m* -(e)s [< Slav *krenu*] **1.** ❦ *& cul. (Meerrettich)* horseradish; *ich habe mir ein Paar Würstel mit ~ und nicht mit Senf bestellt* I ordered a pair of wieners with horseradish, not with mustard. – **2.** *colloq., iron.* an unsolicited comment *(unerwünschter Kommentar [e-s Wichtigtuers])*: precious wisdom; *musst du denn auf alles* (or, *zu allem) deinen ~ geben?* do you have to get your bit (*AmE* your two cents' worth) in about everything? ‖ *Mandl mit ~ = Krenreißer,*

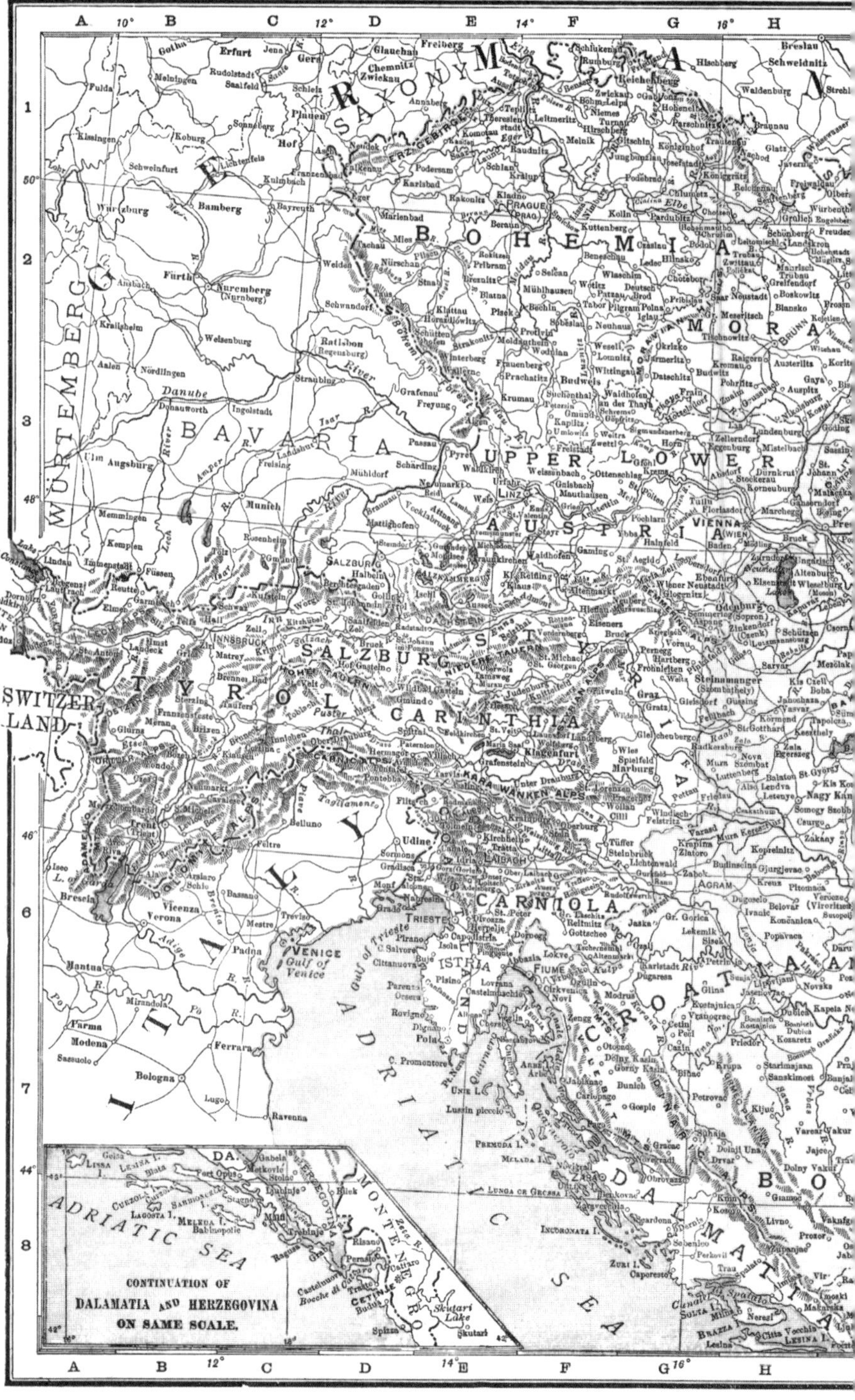

SAXONY
BOHEMIA
MORA
BAVARIA
WÜRTEMBERG
UPPER
LOWER
AUSTRIA
SALZBURG
TYROL
CARINTHIA
STYRIA
CARNIOLA
ISTRIA
CROATIA
DALMATIA
ITALY
ADRIATIC SEA
SWITZERLAND
LIECHTENSTEIN
PRAGUE (PRAG)
VIENNA (WIEN)
INNSBRUCK
LINZ
TRIESTE
LAIBACH
VENICE
Gulf of Venice
Gulf of Trieste
FIUME
AGRAM
Munich
Nuremberg
Augsburg
Danube
ERZ GEBIRGE
NIEDERE TAUERN
HOHE TAUERN
KARA WANKEN ALPS
CARNIC ALPS
DOLOMITE ALPS
CONTINUATION OF
DALAMATIA AND HERZEGOVINA
ON SAME SCALE.
ADRIATIC SEA
HERZEGOVINA
MONTENEGRO
Skutari Lake

AUSTRIA-HUNGARY
SCALES
Statute Miles, 63 = 1 Inch.
0 10 20 30 40 50 60 70 80 90 100
Kilometres, 101 = 1 Inch.
0 10 20 30 40 50 60 70 80 90 100
Rand McNally & Co.'s New 11 x 14 Map of Austria-Hungary.
Copyright by Rand McNally & Co.
Longitude East from Greenwich.
K 20° L M 22° N O 24° P Q 26° R
RUSSIA
GALICIA
HUNGARY
TRANSYLVANIA
BUKOWINA
ROUMANIA
SERBIA
CARPATHIANS
TRANSYLVANIAN ALPS
TATRA MTS.
Lemberg
Cracow
Przemysl
Czernowitz
Debreczen
Grosswardein
Klausenburg
Kronstadt
Hermannstadt
Karlsburg
Temesvar
Szegedin
Arad
Belgrade
Danube
Tisza
Dniester
Vistula

one who allows himself to be exploited: sucker.

Kre̲n…: ~fleisch *n* -es **1.** *cul. (gekochtes Schweinefleisch von der Brust oder vom Bauch)* boiled breast or belly of pork, sprinkled with horseradish, and served with salt potatoes. – **2.** *fig.* a verbal threat: *wenn du mir noch einmal unter die Augen kommst, mache ich ~ aus dir!* don't you get in my way again, or I'll make mincemeat of you! – **~reißer** *m* -s/- **1.** *cul. (Meerrettichraspel)* horseradish grater. – **2.** *contp. (Angeber)* braggart, swaggerer: show-off; *er ist ein ~, wie er im Buch (*or, *im Büchl) steht* he's the world's worst for blowing his own horn.

Krịppen…: ~dorf *n* -(e)s/ … dörfer *R. C. & folklore* "crib village", one of several rural communities around Innsbruck, esp. Thaur, where the art of carving and composing crèches (which often take up a whole farmhouse parlour from Christmas Eve until mid-January, or sometimes until Candlemas) has been developed to perfection. – **~schauen** *n* -s *R. C. & folklore* a Christmas custom observed since the Counter-Reformation: "crib visiting", the viewing and admiring, in churches as well as in private farmhouses, of Nativity scenes, when the eye can behold a host of elaborately carved angels, shepherds and animals paying homage to the infant Jesus.

Krispịndl [-ʃp-] *n* -s/(n) [< dim. of *Crispinus,* the patron saint of tailors (who, in popular belief, are always thought to be emaciated)] *contp.* a person of slight build: runt, twig, puny wimp; *was stellst du denn dir vor, das ~ kann doch so einen schweren Koffer nicht tragen!* what are you thinking, that runt can't manage such a heavy suitcase!

Preceding double spread: A detailed map of the Dual Monarchy (New York, 1917) – only a year after, the initials k.u.k., *and whatever they stood for, had passed on to history*

Kro̲i̲gerl *n* -s/usu. pl. -n *med. dial.* mucus secreted by the eyelid (*Augenbutter*): sleepy-seeds.

Krọpfpropeller *m* -s/- *hum.* = *Gurgelpropeller* ↑.

Krụmmholz *n* -es/ … hölzer & a collective term for the stunted bushes and recumbent trees battling for survival in high mountain altitudes: crook-timber, *AmE* scrub timber. – **~gürtel** *m* -s/pl. rare: - the belt of rugged arboreal growth above the timberline (cp. *Krüppelgrenze* ↓): scrub zone. – **~kiefer** *f* -/-n = *Latsche* ↓.

Krü̩ppelgrenze *f* -/pl. rare: -n the last woody growth above the timberline (*oberste Grenze der verkrüppelten Bäume)*: crook-timber line.

Krụzitü̩rken [an ethnic name blend < *Kuruzzen,* lit. 'crusaders', a Hungarian peasant movement in the sixteenth century rioting against the Turks; a name then adopted by Hungarian Protestant aggressors against the Hapsburg regime (pillaging the Marchfeld and penetrating even as far as the suburbs of Vienna in 1703–04) + *Türken* 'Turks', whose long-standing inroads on Austria had then barely come to an end] *interj* chiefly in Eastern Austria – a euphemistic swear term: dang it all!, what the dickens!; *~ noch einmal!* o ye gods and little fishes!

Kụchel…: ~böhmisch *n* -s [first el., the dialect form of *Küche* 'kitchen', a hint

Princess Elizabeth of Wittelsbach, who was to become Empress of Austria and Queen of Hungary

of the rough-and-ready lingo at home in the nether household regions] *colloq. ling. hist.* pidgin Czech, resorted to after about 1880 by the Germans of Prague, who refused to master the native tongue of their servant personnel and simply fitted badly pronounced Czech words into their own native syntax; cp. *Kellnerenglisch.* – **~grazie** *f* -/-n *hum.* or *iron.* female cook: lady of the ladle. – **~mensch** *n* -es/-er low *colloq.* kitchen maid: kitchen wench.

Kufenstechen *n* -s [first el., *Kufe f* 'hoop'] *folklore* "pierce (*or* spear) the ring" tournament, a horseriders' competition held annually at various places in Carinthia, when country lads charging at full gallop have to spear a wooden ring on the point of a lance.

k. u. k. ['ka:ʊnt'ka:] *abbr., mil. hist.* a venerable, and once ubiquitous, shortening of *kaiserlich und königlich* 'Imperial and Royal', a formula by 1889 placed before the respective name of any military unit or office throughout the Monarchy: to the modern reader about Austrian history, too, this verbalizes the fact that after the lost war of 1866 against Germany The Compromise of 1867 (*Ausgleich* ↑) indeed gave Hungary an equal position in the Dual Monarchy, with Emperor Francis Joseph duly crowned King, and "The Imperial Army" becoming "The Imperial and Royal Army."

Kuttel *f* -/usu. *pl.* -n; **~fleck** *m* -(e)s/usu. *pl.* -e [< MHG *kutel(vlec),* possibly related to OE *cwið* 'belly', 'bowel'] *gastr.* the edible inside parts of an animal, esp. its bowels (*eßbare Eingeweide;* in regional G dials., *Kaldaunen, Löser, Pansen, Rampen*): entrails *pl.* – of a cow: tripe; of a pig: chitterlings *pl., AmE* chitlings *pl.* – **~kraut** *n* -(e)s ❦ a plant used for giving food a special taste *(Thymian)*: thyme [taɪm].

kutz-kutz ['kutskuts] *interj.* an imitative word, expressing solicitous empathy with somebody who has a coughing fit: oh, have you got a little coughie-whoffie?

KV, K.V., K–V ♪ *abbr.* = *Köchelverzeichnis.*

L

La̲berl *n* -s/-n [dim. of *Laib* 'loaf'] **1.** *bak.* roll in the shape of a miniature round loaf; → *Schuster~.* – **2.** *cul.* (meat-)ball → *Fleisch~; ich hab das Faschierte ausgepackt und angefangen, es zu ~n zu formen* I unwrapped the ground meat and began to shape it into patties.

Lạcher *m* -s/- *sarc.* laugh (as an outburst of bitterness or contempt, made when faced with the ridiculousness of an assertion: *das kostet mich einen ~* * that doesn't even deserve a laugh; *er hat mir für den Mercedes 2000 geboten – das hat mich nur einen ~ gekostet* he only offered me 2000 for the Mercedes – of course, I just laughed in his face.

Lạchwurzen *f* -/- *colloq.* a laughter-loving person *(fröhlicher Mensch)*: merry number.

Lạckerl [–ʌ–] *n* -s/-(n) [dim. of *Lacke f* 'puddle', 'pool'] *colloq.* **1.** *(kleine Lacke, Lache, Pfütze)* small pool of spilt liquid: puddle; *der Hund hat schon wieder ein ~ auf den Teppich gemacht* the dog 's made a puddle on the carpet again, the dog 's peed on the rug again. – **2.** *(kleine Menge [e-r Flüssigkeit])* small amount of liquid: little drop ‖ *phr.:* (1) *wenn du mir halt ein ~ Milch übriglässt, mehr brauch' ich nicht* leave a little drop of milk, that'll be enough. – (2) said by a person politely refusing a full glass: *aber nur ein ~, bitte!* just a mouthful (*or,* a wee drop), please!

Lạckl, less often **Lạckel** *m* -s/- [? < French General Ezéchiel de *Mélac* who, by order of King Louis XIV, devastated the Palatinate in 1689, reducing many towns such as Heidelberg, Mannheim, Speyr and Worms to ashes and ruins; or < *Lakai m* 'lackey' who, by definition, always does what someone else tells him to] *colloq.* **1.** *contp.* a man who uses his strength or power to hurt or frighten other people *(aggressiver Mensch)*: bully; *ein grober ~* a rough customer, *AmE a.* a roughneck. – **2.** a large heavy male *(Klotz)*: hulk, man mountain; *ein ~ von einem Mann* a hulk (*if used appreciatively,* a hunk) of a man, *AmE a.* a big bundle *or* package. – **3.** *contp.* a stupid awkward man or boy: oaf.

La̲hn, in Tyrolese dialect also **Lä̲hn** *f* -/-en [*a* contraction of *Lawine* ↓ or, rather, < OHG *lao* 'warm', 'mild' & *lāwen* 'to melt'] *dial.,* snow avalanche; *von den steilen Hängen droht die ~; wie Stundenschlag der großen Bergeinsamkeit gehen dröhnend und dumpf die Schneelasten zu Tal* the massive monster called Avalanche is a squatting menace on top of the steep slopes; and like a resounding clock striking the hours for the vast and silent solitude of mountains around, its huge bulky whiteness comes hurtling down the mountainside, with a boom and a thud. – **lahnen** *v/i* said of ice and snow changing to water by gradual warming (*schmelzen, tauen*): to melt, to thaw; *es lahnt* it is thawing. – **lahnig** *adj* **1.** said of certain stretches of ski runs that are regularly swept by avalanches when a warm dry wind is on: avalanche-prone. – **2.** said of such weather conditions fraught with avalanche danger (causing, for instance, high-altitude ski trips to be cancelled): *attrib.* avalanche-in-the-air (weather); *heut' geht leider nix, es is' zu ~!* sorry, nowt doin' today, avalanches lurkin'. – **Lahnwind** *m* -(e)s/pl. rare: -e ☼ a warm, dry wind coming off the lee slopes of a mountain range (*Tauwind*): warm spring wind, föhn *or* foehn [fə:n].

Lamentabel *n* -s *colloq. (Gejammer)* wailing; *sie macht ein ~, weil sie die Schlüssel nicht finden kann* she is moaning about not being able to find her keys.

Land ...: ~haus *n* -es *archit.* **1.** *gen.* pl.: ... häuser country house; *if small:* cottage. – **2.** *hist., polit.* usu. sg. only – the central administrative building of a provincial capital (e.g. the one in Innsbruck, built by Georg Anton Gumpp, 1670–1730, a native master of the Baroque, who successfully merged a certain strictness of tectonic design into the sense of decorative opulence he had become acquainted with in Italy): Assembly Hall of the Estates. – **~libell** *n* -s [second el., dim. < L *liber* 'book (of law)'] *hist.* an administrative regulation decreed by Emperor Maximilian I in 1513: Tyrolean Defence Law, giving the country its own defence, according to

Emperor Maximilian I, whose Landlibell *saw his beloved Tyrol well defended all around*

which the Tyrolese, holding the freedom to arm, were not conscripted for any warfare outside the confines of their territory.

Latsche *f* -/-n ✿ *(Krummholzkiefer, Legföhre)* dwarf *or* mountain pine, arven tree.

Latschen ...: ~bock *m* -(e)s/ ... böcke *zo.* solitary chamois [ˈʃæmwɑ:] buck, i.e. one hiding among dwarf pines in the daytime. – **~brenner** *m* -s/- ⚒ *a small-scale trade in the Tyrol* – distiller of dwarf-pine needle oil. – **~brennerei** *f* distillery of dwarf-pine needle oil, needle-oil distillery. – **~buckel** *m* -s/- ⛰ sometimes *contp.* a bare mountain whose prostrate arven growth prevents brisk walking: "dwarf-pine hump". – **~kiefer-Hustenbonbon** *n* -s/-s *med.* dwarf-pine drop *or* lozenge. – **~(kiefern)öl** *n* -(e)s *med.* a popular folk remedy extracted in small-scale distilleries high up in Tyrolean mountain valleys: dwarf-pine needle oil, 🕮 Oleum pini pumilionis. – **~ölbrenner** *m* -s/- = *Latschenbrenner.*

lau(b) *adj dial., cul.* said of food without much taste *(mild, wenig gesalzen)*: light, bland; opp. *raß* 1 ↓.

Laube *f* -/-n [< OHG *louba* 'canopy'] *archit.* **1.** *obs.* a hollow place, above the open hearth in old farmhouses, used to hold kitchen utensils: kitchen niche. – **2.** a structural feature imported from the South *(gewölbter Bodengang)*: arcade, covered, passageway, placed below the first (*AmE* second) floor of dwelling-houses, offering protection from inclement weather.

Laus *f* -/Läuse, *dial.* Läus [actually, a louse, i.e. a small blood-sucking animal held in general contempt] *colloq.*, in a *sarc. dial.* phrase graphically describing to what extremes of acquisitive greed a miser may be said to stoop: *der treibt die ~ nach Mariazell* [or any other rhyming place-name] *nur weng 'em Fell* he'd skin a louse, and send the hide (and fat) to market. – **~allee** *f* - *hum.* a parting in one's hair *(Haarscheitel)*: lousewalk.

Lauser *m* -s/- *colloq.* wicked boy, young scamp, *hum.* rascal; often said of one whose mischievous or irresponsible conduct causes worry or even terror: *er ist ein großer ~* (or *Erz≈*) he's a holy terror.

Lawine *f* -/-n [< Lad *lavīna* 'snowslide', 'falling ice' < MedL *labīna* 'landslide', 'avalanche'; related to L *lābī* 'to slide'. (The present English form is due to association with F *aval* 'downward', < L *ad vallem.*)]. **1.** a hurtling mass of snow, with ice and rock, descending a mountain side: avalanche ['ævəlan(t)ʃ], snow-slip, AmE *a.* (snow) slide; cp. *Lahn* ↑. ‖ as a second el. in cpds.: *Grund≈, Naßschnee≈* (heavy) wet-snow avalanche; *Staub≈* fine-snow *or* powder-snow avalanche; → *Dach≈, Schlamm≈, Stein≈.* – **2.** *phr. eine ~ auslösen* or *lostreten* to bring down *or* start an avalanche; *eine ~ geht nieder* or *zu Tal* an avalanche falls; *von einer ~ verschüttet werden* to be buried *or* overtaken by an avalanche, to be avalanched.

Lawinen ...: ~abgang *m* -(e)s/ ... gänge (descending) avalanche, avalanching; *alle Anzeichen sprechen dafür, dass die beiden Skifahrer den ~ durch das Lostreten eines riesigen Schneebretts verursacht hatten* there is every indication that the two skiers had caused the avalanche by breaking off a huge snow slab. – **≈frei** *adj* of an Alpine region, mountain slope, etc. (opp.: *≈gefährdet* ↓): avalanche-free. – **~gang** *m* -(e)s/ ... gänge path of an avalanche. – **~gefahr** *f* -/-en danger of *or* from avalanches, avalanche danger ‖ on a warning board: ~! Beware of Avalanches!; *bei jedem Steilhang besteht ~, jeder Steilhang bedeutet eine ~* any steep slope has avalanche possibilities. – **≈gefährdet, ≈gefährlich** *adj* exposed, liable, or prone to avalanches, avalanche-infested, avalanche-swept (↑ *lahnig*); *zu gewissen Zeiten, die dann immer angeschlagen sind, können Teile des Geländes ≈ sein* at certain times, which are always posted, parts of the area can suffer from avalanche danger; *launisches Wetter hat heute die Suche nach zehn Skifahrern behindert, die in*

An avalanche disaster: a dramatic scene, drawn by F. H. Hurd, London

einem ~en Gebiet vermisst werden freak weather today hampered the search for ten skiers missing in an avalanche-infested region. – **~hang** *m* -(e)s/ … hänge avalanche(-prone) slope. – **~hund** *m* -(e)s/-e = *~suchhund* ↓. – **~kegel** *m* -s/- avalanche cone, debris [ˈdeɪbriː] of an avalanche. – **~schneise** *f* -/-n avalanche lane *or* line; *hie und da unterbricht den Wald eine schotterige ~, deren Bahn die Waldarbeiter gern für den Bau ihrer Holzriesen nützten* sometimes the forest is broken by a gravelled avalanche lane, which lumberjacks were often fond of converting into skid roads to haul tree-logs along. – **~schnur** *f* -/ … schnüre avalanche cord. – **~schutz** *m* -es protection against avalanches, avalanche prevention; *~bauten m pl* anti-avalanche structures *pl,* avalanche defences *pl.* – **≃sicher** *adj* of an Alpine region, mountain slope, etc. (opp.: *≃gefährdet* ↑): safe from avalanching, not prone to avalanches; *der Skihang ist ~* skiing is safe on that slope. – **~sonde** *f* -/-n one of many steel rods used by a rescue team to search the debris of an avalanche for buried victims: sounding rod, avalanche probe. – **~strich** *m* -(e)s/-e = *~schneise* ↑. – **~suchhund** *m* -(e)s/-e search dog for avalanche disasters, avalanche (rescue) dog; *manchmals werden ~e mittels Fallschirm(s) abgesetzt, um Verschüttete aufzuspüren und zu retten* search dogs are sometimes parachuted to sniff out survivors of avalanches. – **~suchtruppe** *f* -/-n : (*eine von Suchhunden begleitete*) ~ (a man-and-dog) avalanche rescue team. – **~unfall** *m* -(e)s/ … fälle accident caused by an avalanche; *pl.* accidents due to avalanches (*or* avalanching). – **~unglück** *n* -(e)s avalanche disaster. – **~wald** *m* -(e)s/ … wälder protective forest (shielding exposed mountain farms). – **~warnung** *f* -/-en warning of avalanches; *die Behörden haben heute für den gesamten Alpenbereich ~ ausgegeben* the authorities today issued a general warning of avalanches throughout the Alps. – **~wind** *m* -(e)s the wind produced by an avalanche, sometimes causing destruction at a considerable distance: avalanche wind *or* blast.

lawinös *adj* ⩕ = *lawinengefährdet* ↑.

Leber … *gastr.:* **~käs,** *dial.* **~kas** [-kɑːs] *m* -es/pl. rare: -e, **~käse** (the StG form, which is very rare) *m* -s [first el., < *Laib* 'loaf' (because it is offered for sale in long cube-like loaves at butchers' and grocers' shops) meat loaf; *der ~ besteht aus durchgedrehtem Rind- und Schweinefleisch, sogenanntem Brät* a meat loaf consists of finely ground beef and pork, or what is known as 'sausage meat' ‖ *fig.* in a piece of abusive speech imputing utter stupidity: *dem habm s' ja das Hirn raus- und a Stück warmen ~ reinoperiert!* they must have gouged his brains out and filled the cavity with blubber (*or,* … with fat [cheese, mush, sawdust])! – **~knödel** *m* & *n* -s/-(n) liver dumpling, made of minced (*AmE* ground) liver, bread and onions, cooked and served in soup; **~suppe** *f* -/-n liver-dumpling soup.

Leberlein *n* -s/pl. rare, and only for sense 1: - [< *Leber f* 'liver' + dim. suffix *-lein*] *colloq.* **1.** *cul., apprec.* (delicious piece of) liver; *schau, was du heute kriegst – ein ~, deine Leibspeis!* look what you're getting today – liver, your favourite dish(ie)! – **2.** *phr.* a solicitous question directed at someone who looks miserable or depressed: *(ja, sag einmal,) was ist dir denn über's ~ gelaufen?* (now tell me,) who's stolen your cookie (*ScotE* ... your scone)?

Leib ...: ~fiaker *m* -s/- *hist.* coachman-in-waiting, private cabman of royalty or a titled family; *Josef Bratfisch war der ~ des Kronprinzen Rudolf* Joseph Bratfisch was the cabman in attendance on Crown Prince Rudolph. – **~speis(e)** *f* -/-n *colloq.* (*Lieblingsspeise*) favourite dish; *Zwetschkenknödel sind meine ~ AmE a.* (in the food line,) plum dumplings are my middle name.

Leich *f* -/-n [< *Leiche f* 'corpse', 'dead body'] low *colloq.* or *dial.* **1.** *phr.* in which the very word form clearly reveals that the death of the person concerned has had little or no impact on the speaker: *Montag ist die ~* the funeral will (*or,* is to) be on Monday; *auf die ~ gehen* to go to the funeral. – **2.** *hist. phr.* reflecting the Viennese bourgeoisie's more or less pronounced insistence on, and indeed often "ghoulish delight" (Barea) in, a pompous funeral, a trait they had adopted from the privileged great and rich in the Biedermeier Age, and continued to show until the decades between the two World Wars: *ich möcht' eine schöne ~ habm!* mine shall be a lovely funeral. – **3.** *fig.*, a *hum. phr.* expressing someone's (say, a rural innkeeper's) light-hearted resignation when trying to swat flies populating his dining room: *eine bringst (du) um, und hundert kommen auf die ~!* you kill one, and a hundred come to the funeral.

Leintuch *n* -(e)s/... tücher *domestic economy*] a large, thin, rectangular piece of linen or cotton cloth serving, with a mattress underneath, as a basic article of bedding (*Bettlaken* or *-tuch*): (bed) sheet ‖ low colloq. *phr.* a crude, since near-desperate, flash of grim insight that parental procreation has launched the speaker into a "life of froth and bubble", an act which could have easily been forestalled if coitus interruptus had been resorted to then; English prefers the metaphor of the man-in-question leaving his train shortly before the terminus, always with due mention of the penultimate stop, in Australia, for instance, Redfern, on the line to Sydney Central Station – and here, in a felicitous double entendre, Edge Hill, the penultimate station before Lime Street, the terminus of the London-Liverpool line: *ich wollte, mein Vater hätte* (or, *meine Eltern hätten*) *mich aufs ~ gesetzt* I wish my father had got off at Edge Hill.

leinwand, leiwand *adj & interj (ausgezeichnet)* excellent: jolly good; *(das ist) ~! ([das ist] großartig!)* (this is) grand!; *alles wieder ~! (alles wieder in Ordnung!)* everything's great again.

Leopold ['le:opɒlt] *m* **1.** *pr.n.* -s/-e Leopold ['lɪəpəuld], Margrave of Austria, patron saint of Vienna, Lower and Upper Austria (15 Nov.). – **2.** only *sg.* in child use in Eastern Austria: ~, or *Lepold* the sanctuary of certain catching games: home, den ‖ *~! Lepold!* the cry of a child claiming exemption from pursuit in such a game: *BrE* kings!, pax!, *AmE* home free!

Lẹpschi [< Cz *lepši* 'something better (than work)'] in the *hum. phr.: auf ~ gehen (Liebesabenteuer suchen)* to be amorously inclined: to be out on the tiles, to go (out) on the make.

E HARRISON
COMPTON

Ligist *n* the name of a small market town WSW of Graz – used in a *hum.* pun based on the regional phrase *liegen gehen* 'to go to bed': *gehn wir auf ~!* let's go to bed!, let's go to Bedfordshire!

Linz [-ts] *n place-name* the capital of Upper Austria, on the River Danube, a commercial and manufacturing city || *phr.* the sequence *~ an der Donau* 'Linz on the Danube' (rather more ear-catching than others, for sorting-out's sake, because of the presence of another *Linz* on the Rhine, NNW of Koblenz) has encouraged the coinage of two playful substitutions: (1) *~ an der Tramway* [ˈtrʌmvaɪ], reminding us of the fact that, in the early nineteenth century, Linz was the starting point of the first "railway" line ever constructed in Europe – a horse railway, not a steam railway – along which carriages used to be drawn with passengers on their way north to the Mühlviertel country and on to Bohemia. – (2) *~ an der Torte,* a sweet-toothed gourmet's quirky analogy perhaps at first, drawing added attention to the tasty apricot jam and almond tart (mentioned below) bearing the name of the city.

Linzer [ˈ-tsə] *adj:* **~ Augen** *n pl. bak.* two biscuits made of rich egg pastry *(Mürbteig),* circular and about 5 cm, or 2 ins. in diameter, stuck together with a layer of jam; before, the top biscuit has allowed the pastry cutter *(Ausstechform)* to model two goo-goo eyes into it, giving the whole the semblance of a human moonface: Linz eyes pl. – **~ Bua** *m* -m/-m *dial.* (an appreciative epithet for) a boy or a young man from Linz: laddie from Linz; often used collectively for a local group of singers, a football team, etc.: *die ~ Buam.* – **~ Madl** *n* -s/-n *dial.* (an appreciative epithet for) a girl or a young woman from Linz: lassie from Linz. – **~ Sinfonie** *f* ♪ the nickname of Wolfgang Mozart's Symphony in C, K. 425, composed at Linz for and first performed by the orchestra of Count Thun, in 1783: Linz Symphony. – **~ Torte** *f* -/-n *bak.* a crisp, round layer cake made of a rich pastry dough composed of chopped almonds, butter, flour, cocoa, sugar, eggs, and spices, filled with a fruit-jam or preserves (thus far comparable to a 'Washington pie' in the US) and topped with a lattice of baked dough; its recipe is authenticated to have been in existence as early as 1718, and that speciality has professionally been made at Linz (and been sent abroad from there to all parts of the world) for the past one hundred years: Linz lattice (*or* trellis) jam cake.

When painting the main square of Linz, in about 1930, E. Harrison Compton duly paid much attention to its tall Trinity Column

Liptauer or **Liptauerkäse** *m* -s/- [< *Liptau,* a former Hungarian administrative district on the left bank of the Danube, flown through by the River Váh (G *Waag*), now part of Slovakia] *gastr.* a soft, creamy and highly flavoured cheese spread, orig. made in Hungary, seasoned with caper sauce, anchovy paste, finely cut onions, and sprinkled with paprika: Liptau cheese.

Loden *m* -s/- [< MHG *lode* < OHG *lodo* 'coarse woollen material'; an English cognate is the first element in *Lawn Market,* the name of a place downhill east from Edinburgh Castle, where the *lawn,* or cloth, sellers of the Scottish capital once had their booths] *tex.* a thick dark green, brown, grey, or (in recent times, also) dark blue woollen cloth, hairy or feltlike – the proper type of clothing to be worn by gamekeepers, huntsmen, and hikers (to brave the elements), but also by tradition-conscious people, esp. when attending a local or regional festive event: fulled woollen cloth, frieze, loden (cloth); *~ aus Österreich ist weltbekannt* Austrian loden is known all over the world (*or,* … the whole world over).

Loden…: ~cape [-e:-] *n* -s/-s loden cloak. – **~kostüm** *n* -s/-e woman's two-piece loden suit. – **~mantel,** also known as **Hubertusmantel** *m* -s/… mäntel waterproof woollen coat, loden coat. – **~rock** *m* -(e)s/… röcke **1.** *for men:* waterproof woollen jacket. – **2.** *for women:* waterproof woollen skirt. – **~stoff** *m* -(e)s/-e loden material. – **~tracht** *f* -/-en *cost.* traditional loden costume; *als österreichische Nationaltracht hat sich die graugrüne ~ in zahlreichen örtlichen Abarten herausgebildet* the Austrian national garb, while allowing for a number of regional variants, is basically the grey-green loden costume. – **~umhang** *m* -(e)s/ … hänge = *Lodencape* ↑; ~ (*mit Kapuze*) sleeveless (hooded) loden cloak; *sie hatte ihren ~ um die Schultern gelegt* she had slung her loden cape over her shoulders. – **~walker** *m* -s/- [second el., < *walken* 'to full', 'to felt', i.e. to roll out, shrink, and mat together a textile by heat, pressure, and moisture; *to walke* was its corresponding verb in Middle English, and *walker* its parallel occupational name, in the sense of 'fuller' (e.g., in the Wyclif Bible, Mark, ix. 2)] loden miller, fuller. – **~walkerei** *f* -/-en **1.** loden milling, fulling; *die ~ blüht seit alters in den Gebirgsgegenden, vor allem in denen von Kärnten* loden milling has been flourishing in the mountainous areas, especially in those of Carinthia, since (*or* from) time immemorial. – **2.** loden mill.

Luller *m* -s/- *colloq. (Schnuller)* rubber teat for a baby: dummy, *AmE* pacifier, passie.

Lungen…: ~braten *m* -s/- [first el. < L *lumbus* 'loin'] *cul. (Filet-, Lendenbraten)* undercut of sirloin *or* fillet, *AmE* tenderloin, the best cut of beef. – **~haché, ~haschee** *n cul.* = *Beuschel* ↑. – **~strudelsuppe** *f* clear soup with slices of rolled paste stuffed with meat.

Lurch *m* -(e)s *colloq.* down particles which collect under beds and furniture *([Ansammlung von] Staubflocken)*: dust bunnies *pl.,* (if smaller:) dust mice *pl., AmE a.* beggar's velvet, house moss, slut's wool; *der ~ da herin ist schon so dick, dass man ihn riecht* the dust in here is so thick it nearly chokes you; *unter den Betten ist ein Haufen ~* there's a lot of fluff under the beds, *AmE* the space under the beds is full of dust balls. – **~wuzelwahn** *m* -(e)s *hum.* a woman's tendency to spend a lot of time on keeping her house or apartment clean and tidy, perhaps too much so *(Putzfimmel)*: mania for cleanliness.

M

magistra̲tisch *adj* [< *Magistrat m* 'municipal council'] in large towns: of, or belonging to, the city council; *jeder Bezirk Wiens hat sein ≈es Bezirksamt, in welchem die örtlichen Verwaltungsstellen der Stadt untergebracht sind* each district of Vienna has its Municipal District Hall, in which the local administrative agencies are housed.

Ma̲i̲...: **~butter** *f* - *gastr., dial. (Schlagsahne)* whipped cream. – **~säss** *n* -es/-e [lit., 'May residence'] ✓ & *econ.* in the Upper Bregenzerwald of Vorarlberg = *Niederalm* ↓.

Mạkart *pers. n.* el. [< Hans Makart, 1840 –1884, a neo-Baroque painter, whose presentation on huge canvases of riotous scenes in sensuous colours created a temporary furor in the Vienna of the 1870s and 80s]: **~bukett** *n* "Makart bouquet", a bunch of rushes and reeds, dry flowers and palm-leaves, an ornamental fitting favoured by the nouveaux riches of the day. – **~-Farbe** *f* "Makart hue", any garish colour, esp. red, favoured by Makart and his imitators in painting and in fashion design. – **~-Hut** *m* "Makart hat", a wide-brimmed plumed lady's hat of the period. – **~-Rot** *n* → *Makart-Farbe*. – **~-Zimmer** *n* "Makart Salon" ['sælɒn], any contemporary drawing-room decorated in the lavish and gaudy style of Hans Makart, esp. the study of Nikolaus Dumba, a patron of the arts, on Parkring.

Mạlakofftorte *f* -/-n *bak.* sponge-finger cake, *AmE* lady finger cake.

Ma̲lerwinkel *m* -s/- *geog.* & *arts* the decorative epithet for any scenic outlook point (in the province of Salzburg, for instance, the entry to the Kötschach Valley, east of Badgastein) that has long tempted artists to stop and capture the views it affords on canvas: Painters' Corner; *wer mit offenen Augen durchs Österreicherland streift, heimst sich leicht hundert, ja tausend ~ als geistige Wegzehr für die fernere Lebensfahrt ein* anybody roaming open-eyed through beautiful Austria will readily find a hundred, or indeed a thousand, Painters' Corners, to delight and spiritually strengthen him on his pilgrimage through life.

Mạmlas *m* gen. sg. rare: -es/-e [< Hung. *mámlász* or Cz *mamlas* 'idiot'] *contp.* **1.** a mentally dull person: dumbo. – **2.** a miserable, depressed (and depressing) person: sad sack; *so ein ~ – steht da, als ob ihm die Hendln das Brot weggefressen hätten!* him, what a picture of misery, as though somebody had stolen his cookie! – **3.** a sulky, discontented person: grouch.

Mander [ˈmɒːndə], **'s isch Zeit!** [a rallying cry, in Tyrolese dialect, showing an intrusive <d> in the unumlauted plural of StG *Männer,* and the regionally characteristic palato-alveolar fricative ʃ in the <t>-less form of StG *ist*] *phr.* *men, it's high time [to rise to action]! **1.** *polit. & mil. hist.* Andreas Hofer ↑ 's rousing call to his Tyrolean countrymen, in April and May 1809, to take up arms against the Bavarian troops which, as Napoleon's allies, had held the land occupied since 1805. → **2.** *polit. hist.* an echo from Anno Neun ↑ with which, in Innsbruck on 9 March 1938, Dr. Kurt von Schuschnigg, the then Austrian Chancellor, declared his resolution to hold a plebiscite four days later for a "free and German, independent, social, Christian and united" Austria; it was a vain, eleventh-hour attempt to thwart Hitler's plan to bring about the *Anschluss* ↑. → **3.** *hum.* a timely warning, usu. uttered in a relaxed mood, to call sleepers to wake (and get ready for a mountain hike, etc.) or to break up a past-midnight party: time to hit the road (*BrE* folks, *AmE* guys)!

Marẹnde, also **Merẹnde** *f* -/-n [< It *merenda*] *cul. (Zwischenimbiss am Nachmittag)* mid-afternoon snack. – **marẹnden,** also **merẹnden** *v/i* to take a snack break in the afternoon.

Marientragen *n* -s *R.C. & folklore* an Alpine custom practised in Advent-time, esp. during the nine-day period before Christmas, when a statue or portrait of St Mary's is carried by children from one farmstead to another, to be the centre of homage and prayers: Our Lady's Procession.

Marịlle *f* -/-n [a blend of It *armenillo, armellino* 'apricot' + *Aramelle, Morelle* (< It *amarelia, amarena, amaresca* 'morello [cherry]')] ✿ *(Aprikose)* apricot.

Marịllen ...: ~knödel *m* -s/- *cul.* apricot dumpling (made of potato-flour dough). – **~likör** *m* -s/-e *bev.* apricot liqueur. – **~marmelade** *f* -/-n *cul.* (*Aprikosenkonfitüre*) apricot jam. – **~schnaps** *m* -es/ … schnäpse *bev.* apricot brandy.

Maroni *f* -/- [the pl. form < It *marrone* 'edible chestnut'] *cul. (Edelkastanie)* Spanish *or* sweet chestnut. – **~brater** *m* -s/-, **~braterin** *f* -/-nen chestnut vendor; *auch heute noch gehört an einem Wintertag der Maronibrater zum Straßenbild der Stadt, zu ihm lockt die Wärme des Ofens, der Duft der röstfrischen Köstlichkeiten; schnell sind zwei bis drei*

Selling hot southern delights on a chilly day. A watercolour by Gustav Zafourek (1893)

A stern memento in most scenic surroundings

davon, das Ganze um einen Schilling, in ein Stanitzel getan und später genüsslich schnabuliert even today chestnut vendors are part of the street-scene on wintry days: how tempting, the warmth radiating from their little stoves and the odour of freshly-roasted delicacies – only a moment, and two or three are put in a paper bag, all for one Austrian shilling, to be nibbled at leisure later on.

Mạrterl *n* -s/-n [< *Marter f* (< OHG *martyra* < Gr *martyrion* 'martyrdom', which ancient Christians had often sacrificed themselves to for their faith, and in whose honour Pope Leo III, as early as 779 A.D., expressly recommended memorial columns and expiatory stones to be erected) + dim. *-l* and, in Vorarlberg, *-le*] *R.C. & folklore* **1.** esp. in Alpine areas, usu. made fast to the bole of a tree or a rock face – a simple board with a crude painting and inscription drawing wayfarers' attention to somebody's sudden death there, often through an accident *(Gedenktafel mit gemalter Darstellung eines Unfalls)*: memorial tablet.

O Wanderer, den Schritt halt an!
Mit Steinwurf hat dem braven Mann
der list'ge Tod ein End gemacht.
Wer hätte wohl daran gedacht?

My friends so dear, as you pass by,
This goodly man was here to die.
A rock hurled from Death's wily clutch –
Indeed who would have thought as much?

2. if on a pedestal, also known as **Martersäule** – a wooden or stone pillar, with a niche [nɪtʃ] holding a crucifix or a saint's image *(Pfeiler mit Nische für Kruzifix oder Heiligenbild)*: wayside shrine.

Maschạnsker *m* -s/- *(Borsdorfer Apfel)* golden pippin, a kind of small, round apple; *sl. Glatzen*≈ P bald-headed man; *sl.* bald coot, baldy, cue ball, skinhead, turret top.

Mạsche *f* -/-n *tex.* a knot of cloth or string with a curved part on either side, used esp. for decoration *(Schleife)*: bow [bəʊ]. – **Mạscherl** *n* -s/-n [< *Masche f* ↑ + dim. *-erl*] **1.** *concr., tex.* a short bow whose loops and ends are spread like a butterfly's wings; often used for formal wear (*Fliege, Smokingschleife*): bow tie, butterfly-bow. – **2.** *fig.* (1) *sl.* a nickname for Dr. Wolfgang Schüssel, the present Federal Chancellor of Austria (in office since February 2000), an enthusiastic wearer of bow ties (to the exclusion, nearly, of any other formal neckwear) – *das* ~ Mr (*or* Mister) Bow Tie. – (2) *colloq.* a distinctive sign or emblem making someone or something possessing it clearly conspicuous: telltale mark ‖ *prov.* saying that the sight of a (usu. huge) sum of money offers no clue to its provenance, the source quite possibly being odious, disreputable, or immoral – the Austrian variant of L *non olet* and G *Geld stinkt nicht: Geld hat keine ~n* (or, in Viennese *dial., … hat ka ~*) money does not smell, money tells no tales. – (3) *colloq.,* usu. pl., always in a negative sense – one, or usu. several, unnecessary but embellishing features of an object or arrangement: frills; *Ferienreisende sind in unserem ja wunderschönen, aber schwer erreichbaren Gretzel gern mit einer einfachen Unterkunft zufrieden, die keine ~n aufweist* holidaymakers in our neck of the woods – a most beautiful area, though difficult of access – are willing to accept a simple accommodation without (*or,* with no) frills. – (4) *colloq. phr.* used of the stages of an action which are well coordinated, like beads pleasingly threaded on a string (*wie am Schnürchen*): (*das läuft ja*) *wie am* ~ (it is) shipshape, (it goes) like clockwork.

Mạschekseite, Mạschikseite *f* - [< Hung. *a másik* 'the other (one)'] *colloq.* **1.** *(Rückseite)* rear side; *wenn vorn nichts zu lesen ist, dreh's um, vielleicht steht was auf der* ~ if there's nothing to read on the front side, then turn it over and try the back ‖ *phr.* an advice to someone having difficulty in handling an awkward piece of furniture, etc.: *wenn's so nicht geht, nimm's halt von der ~!* if it won't go like that, then try it from the other side (*or,* from another angle). – **2.** *(Schattenseite)* seamy side; *sie ist halt auf die ~ gefallen* well, she just ended up on the shady side of the street.

mạtsch [-ʌ-] *adj* [actually, a cardplayers' term (based on It *marcio* 'soft', 'lazy') for one who has not made a single trick in the game] *colloq.* exhausted: dead beat, done for, done in, *BrE a.* fagged ‖ although used only as a predicative adjective in ordinary speech, *matsch* here twists a banterer's verbal kaleidoscope to offer a playful little quatrain:

> *Zwei Burschen krochen auf den Gletscher,*
> *der eine matsch, der andre mätscher;*
> *da ächzt' der Mätschere zum Matschen,*
> *„Geh, tean ma wieder abehatschen!"*
>
> *Two lads slogged up an ice-bound hill –
> One, fagged; the other, faggeder still.
> Then wheezed the faggeder of the twain,
> "I say, let's slog downhill again!"

mạtschkern *v/i colloq.* **1.** [–ʌ–] *(schmatzen)* to eat noisily: to chew with one's mouth open; *AmE a.* to smack (one's lips); *hör auf mit dem ≗!* don't eat with your mouth open!, don't chomp your food!, *AmE* close your mouth when you chew!, *hum.* cut out the sound effects! – **2.** [–ɒ–] (1) *(brummig reden)* to mumble, to mutter; (2) *(schimpfen, maulen)* to grumble, to complain: to grouse, *AmE a.* to grouch, to gripe, to bitch; *er matschkert immer, ganz gleich, was für eine Arbeit man ihm gibt BrE* whatever job you give him, he always finds something to go on about, *AmE* … he's always got something to bellyache about.

M<u>au</u>t *f* -/-en *admin.* tax due for the use of certain highways or bridges: toll, turnpike money. – **≗frei** *adj* toll-free. – **~gebühr** *f* -/-en toll charge; *eine ~ einheben* to levy a toll charge. – **~haus** *n* -es/ …

häuser tollhouse. – ≗**pflichtig** *adj* subject to toll; *diese Brücke ist* ~ there is a toll required for this bridge, this is a toll-bridge. – **~schranken** *m* -s/- toll-bar, tollgate. – **~stelle** *f* -/-n tollbooth, toll station. – **~straße** *f* -/-n toll-road, turnpike (e.g., the motorway across the Brenner Pass).

Melange [meˈlɑ̃ːʒ] *f* / n [since about 1830 < F *mélange* 'a mixture; medley'] **1.** *concr., bev.* coffee with more than half milk or cream (*Milchkaffee*): coffee with milk, *BrE a.* white coffee; *Herr Ober, bitte eine ~!* waiter, one coffee with milk, please. – **2.** *fig.* a person in whom the human qualities and faculties are felt to be properly represented and well mixed: good Mister Average, jolly Tom Mix ‖ an informal thumbnail description by Dr. Wolfgang Schüssel, the present Federal Chancellor of Austria, a native of Vienna, about himself: *ich bin 1,72, ein durchaus ansprechendes Mittelmaß; weder besonders stark noch besonders gut – ich bin ein guter Wiener Durchschnitt … eine Wiener ~* I stand 5 ft. 8 in., which is as fair an average as any; nor am I particularly brawny or physically fit – just good Viennese average … a proper Vienna mélange, half coffee, half milk.

Melanzani *f* -/- [< It *melanzana*] ❦ a plant (📖 Solanum melongena) allied to the potato; its large smooth ovoid fruit is eaten as a vegetable, usu. cooked (*Aubergine* [obɛrˈʒiːnə], *Eierpflanze*): *BrE* aubergine [ˈəʊbəʒiːn], *AmE* eggplant.

Mezzanin *n* -s/-e [< F *mezzanine* < It *mezzanino,* a dim. of *mezzano* < L *mediānus* '(placed *or* lying) in the middle'] *archit.* an intermediate storey between two main storeys of a building, usu. between the ground floor and the first floor (*Halbgeschoss; Hochparterre*): mezzanine [ˈmezəniːn, ˈmetsə-], entersol [ˈentəsɔl, ˈɐntrəsɐl]. – **~wohnung** *f* -/-en *archit.* mezzanine apartment.

Michel Glattweg *m* – a fictitious name for a plain-spoken person: Honest John; *er ist ein ~* he does not mince matters (*or,* his words), he calls a spade a spade.

Millimetternich *m* -s [a portmanteau word 'telescoping' *Millimeter* and *Metternich*] *hist.* "Pocket(-sized) Chancellor", a political gibe at Dr. Engelbert Dollfuss, the Austrian Chancellor from 1932 – 1934, a verbal blend punning at once his autocratic rule and the smallness of his figure (1.64 metres, i.e. 5 ft. 4½ in.).

Milz *f* -/-en *anat.* spleen; **~schnittensuppe** *f* -/-n *cul.* clear soup with spleen on croutons ([ˈkruːtɔ̃z] = small pieces of fried bread). – **~schöberl** *n* -/-n *dial. cul.* used to garnish a clear soup: fried mixture of minced spleen and rolls, duly cut into squares; → *Schöberl.*

mir bleibt nichts erspart! *phr.* (oh,) I am spared nothing! **1.** a mournful complaint in 1898 by Emperor Francis Joseph I on hearing of his wife Elizabeth's assassination, one of a string of disasters in his private life. – **2.** *hum.* also used playfully: that's too much (of a good thing)!

Mohn…: ~kipfel *n* -s/-, **~kipferl** *n* -s/-n *bak.* poppy-seed crescent. – **~nudel** *f* -/usu. pl. -n *cul.* potato-dough noodle(s) covered with ground poppy seed. – **~semmel** *f* -/-n *bak.* poppy-seed roll. – **~striezel** *m* or *n* -s/- *bak.* braided (*or* plaited) yeast pastry covered with ground poppy seed. – **~strudel** *m* -s/- *bak.* rolled cake filled with poppy seed and raisins.

– **~zuzler** *m* -s/- [lit., 'one who sucks poppy' second el., < *zuzeln* 1 ↓] a Waldviertel regionalism based on the fact that opium poppy has, in some parts of that North Lower Austrian area, long been cultivated both for its oil and medicinal purposes; the plant is also known there for its property of inducing drowsiness (🕮 *Papaver somniferum)* **1.** P, largely *hist.,* a young baby given a makeshift comforter – a little poppy-filled cloth bag – to suck or bite upon in order to keep it quiet: poppy sucker. → **2.** P, *iron.* or *contp.* (1) an adult (claimed to have) fallen for the habit of "sucking" poppy – opium addict: hop-head, poppy head. – (2) a dull-witted person *(Dummkopf)*: dope, num(b)skull; *schau, was du jetzt angestellt hast, du ~!* look, what you've done now, you dope (*AmE a.* ..., you stupor man)! – **3.** *bak.* a yeast-dough pastry filled with poppy seed and one brandy-soaked prune (in it an almond for a fancy nipple), and rolled into a small ball: poppy-seed bun.

Mọhr *m* **im Hẹmd** *cul.* a warm sweet dessert: steamed chocolate pudding with whipped cream.

Molkerei *f* -/en **1.** ✓ dairy, creamery. → **2.** *vulg. hum.* large female breasts: jugs, knockers; *mei, hat die eine ~ (beisammen)!* wow, would you look at the jugs on that woman!; oh my, what a pair of knockers she has!

mọllert ['molət] *adj. dial.* of a person, chiefly female – (pleasantly) round and fat (*mollig*): (well-)rounded, buxom, roly-poly.

Momẹnterl *n* -s/-(n) [dim. of *Moment m*] *colloq.* any brief period of time: half a second, sec; said when having been invited to sit down for a little while: *ich setze mich ein ~ nieder* I will sit down for a few ticks ‖ *(ein) ~!* **1.** asking for a little patience: half a mo!, half a tick!, (I'll be ready in) two ticks (*or,* in two shakes of a dog's tail [*or,* lamb's tail])!, I'll be with you in a sec! – **2.** raising an objection: wait a minute!, (now) just a minute!, hang on a sec!

Monats ...: ~erdbeeren *f pl.* ✿ everbearing strawberries *pl.* – **~schlössel** *n* -s *archit.* at present a folklore museum in the Hellbrunn Castle grounds, near the City of Salzburg: "Little Castle of a Month", "Month's Castle", owing its name to the fact that it was built by Archbishop Marcus Sitticus, in 1616 within one month as a surprise for a returning guest; there was at the time a popular belief that he was assisted in the accomplishment of what was, at all events in those days, a wonderful feat by Satan himself. – **~zins** *m* -es/-e *(monatliche Miete)* monthly rent.

Moosbeere *f* -/-n ✿ *(Heidelbeere) BrE* bilberry, *AmE* blueberry.

Moräne *f* -/-n [< F dial. *morena* (1) in Savoy: 'boulders deposited by a glacier'; (2) elsewhere, and in Sp: 'stack of wood', 'sheaf of grain' < pre-Romance **murro-* 'jutting mountain top', < orig. 'animal snout'] ⛰ (1) an accumulation of boulders, stones, sand, and silts, carried down and deposited in areas where two glaciers join or where one flows around rock islands in the valley floor – typically as ridges at its edges or extremity: moraine [mə'reɪn]; **~nschutt** *m* -(e)s moraine debris ['debriː]. – (2) types of moraines: **End**~ *or* **Stịrn**~ end-moraine, terminal moraine; **Mịttel**~

medial *or* central moraine; **Rạnd~** or **Se̲i̲ten~** lateral moraine; **Grụnd~** ground moraine.

mọrdstrumm [indeclinable] *colloq. adj* huge: great big, *AmE sl.* humongous [hjuˈmʌngəs]; *der Hans hat eine ~ Nase* Jack has a humongous nose.

mü̲a̲chteln; for *hum.* emphasis also, **mụ̈rchteln** *v/i* [< OHG *smiohan*] *dial.* said with disapproval of a room or house or object with a damp and unpleasant smell, because it is old and has not been ventilated for a long time (*muffeln* ↓) – *da müachtelt's wia net gscheit!* pooh! what a foul and musty smell in here!; *pfui, dei ganzes Gwand müachtelt – häng 's raus!* ugh! all your clothes really pong – go and air them! – **Mü̲a̲chtler;** for *hum.* emphasis also, **Mụ̈rchtler** *m* -s *dial.* dampness or mould offending a person's sense of smell (*schlechter, muffiger Geruch*): must, pong; *der Eiskasten hat einen schiachn ~!* there's an awful pong in the fridge!

mụffeln *v/i (abgestanden riechen)* to smell unventilated; *es muffelt in dem Zimmer, weil die Fenster schon wochenlang bummfest zu sind* it smells very musty in this room (*or,* this room smells very musty) because its windows have been shut fast for weeks.

Mu̲gel *m* -s/-(n) *colloq.* **1.** *(Berg[rücken] kleinerer Art)* minor ridge *or* hill, rather round. – **2.** small, round elevation in the terrain: hillock, mound, *AmE a.* mogul [ˈməugl]. – **3.** *skiing* usu. *pl.* small man-made snow mounds on a ski run which make the descent more difficult and challenging: *AmE* mogul; *die Abfahrt mit den vielen ~n liegt mir nicht, sie schaut mir zu gefährlich aus* I don't feel like taking the ski run with all the moguls because it looks too dangerous.

Mụlatság, in phonetic spellings **Mụllatschag, Mụllatschak** [ˈmu:latʃak] *m* -s [< Hung. *mulatság* 'fun', 'merriment', 'pastime'] *colloq.* in Eastern Austria: riotous feasting (at the end of which glasses, crockery, and household utensils are being smashed with a vengeance: pot-smashing, hullabal(l)oo, hicockalorum. – **mulatti̲e̲ren, mullati̲e̲ren** *v/i* [< Hung. *mulattat* 'to amuse, entertain, divert'] *colloq.* to celebrate exuberantly: to be on the ran-tan (*or,* razzle-dazzle), at the end of which slam-and-smash-things is standing operating procedure.

Mu̲re, *dial.* **Mu̲r** *f* -/-n ⛰ a torrent of mud and debris [ˈdebri:] in high mountain areas (*Schutt- oder Schlammstrom*): torrential wash, mudflow, rock stream; débâcle [deɪˈba:kl]; *nach einem gewaltigen Wolkenbruch ging eine ~ nieder und riss einen Streifen durch den Wald* after a heavy cloudburst, a rock stream formed cutting a lane of debris through the forest. – **Mu̲rbruch** *m* -(e)s/ … brüche rock flood. ‖ → *vermurt, Vermurung.*

Mụss a conversion of the auxiliary denoting 'must', 1. and 3. pers. sg. present tense, into a noun; it occurs in two proverbial contexts: **1.** *n* in a protest against a verbal demand formulated, in the opinion of the speaker, too peremptorily, esp. through an overuse of such verb forms such as *muss* and *müssen*: *das ~ ist eine harte Nuss;* **2.** *m* in a warning that the force of circumstances is "a mighty lord" to resist whom would be idle: *der ~ ist ein großer Herr* – in English, both: must is a king's word.

nącht *adv* the preferred form after another adjunct of time *(nachts)*: night; *heute ~* tonight; *Samstag ~* (on) Saturday night.

Nącht...: ~essen *n* -s/- Vorarlberg *dial.* = *Nachtmahl.* – ***~kästchen*** *n* -s/-, *colloq.* **~kast(e)l** *n* -s/-(n) *(Nachtschränkchen, Nachttisch)* bedside table, *AmE a.* nightstand; *~ladel n* -s/-(n) *colloq.* drawer in the bedside table. – **~mahl** *n* -(e)s/-e *or* ... mähler *(Abendessen)* dinner; *gehen wir am Freitag in der Stadt feudal wohin zum ~?* shall we go out and have a posh meal (*BrE a.* slap-up meal, *AmE* fancy dinner) in town on Friday night? – **≚mahlen** *vt/i (zu Abend essen)* to have (for) dinner (*AmE a.* ... supper); *ich habe heute schon zweimal genachtmahlt* I already had dinner twice tonight; *Hummer ~* to have lobster for dinner.

Nachzipf *m* -s/-(e) *school sl.* a pupil's re-examination at the beginning of a new school year, in September, whose end-of-year report showed him, or her, to have failed in a core subject (*Wiederholungsprüfung*): re-exam [ˈriːɪgˌzæm], re-do; *ui je, ein ~ in Mathe! da wirst (du) aber den ganzen Sommer fei arg strebern müssn* eek, a re-do in maths – seems to me you'll have to do a lot of swatting (*or* cramming) all summer.

Nąndl – a *colloq.* doublet of Christian-name diminutives in both languages: **1.** *f* -/-n [through faulty agglutination < mei*n*(e) *An*na + intrusive *-d-* + dim. *-l*] a popular name form of *Anna,* widespread in rural Western Austria: Nance, Nancy, Nanny. – **2.** *m* -s/- *hist.* a truncated form of Ferdi*nand* + dim. *-l,* best known from a gibe at Emperor Ferdinand of Austria (1835–48), a good-natured, pathetic epileptic, and hence a mere puppet ruler of his country *(→ Gütnand der Fertige)*: *der gute alte ~* 'good old Ferdy'.

Nationalrat *m* -(e)s *pol.* **1.** no *pl.* National Council, i.e. the lower house of the Austrian Parliament (cp. *Bundesrat*); its 165 members are chosen in a general election for a four-year term of office by all Austrians having the right to vote. – **2.** pl. ... räte actually short for *Abgeordnete(r) zum ~* National Councillor.

Nębbich *m* -s/-e, **Nebochąnt** *m* -en/-en [of uncertain origin, probably Polish or Yiddish] *colloq. (minderwertiger Mensch, Nichtskönner)* ignoramus: good-for-nothing, know-nothing, numskull, bonehead.

Netsch *n,* usu. pl. only: - [< Hung. *négy* 'four', 'four-kreutzer coin' (an old divisional monetary unit, valid in Austria-Hungary till 1892)] *colloq.,* often *hum.* small change *(Kleingeld)*: the needful, shekels, *AmE & CanE a.* chicken-feed; *was du für die Sache lockermachen müsstest, wären doch nur ein paar ~* it'd be only chicken-feed you'd have to cough up (*or* fork out) for the thing; *ich werde halt meine letzten ~ zusammenkratzen* ah well, I'll scrape the bottom of the barrel, then.

neunern *v/i gastr. (gegen neun Uhr vormittags eine Jause einnehmen)* to have a light morning snack at about nine o'clock (in BrE, this break is appropriately known as 'elevenses').

Niederalm *f* -/-en ♪ & *econ.* a lonely farmstead halfway between the valley and the mountains, populated by the Alpine dairymaid (*Senn[er]in*), or dairyman (*Senn[er]*), with the animals in spring, and then again towards the end of summer – an intermediate station, as it were, between the valley farm and the high mountain dairy (*Hochalm* ↑), the two end points of a nomadic shepherd's and cowherd's existence, the one place lived at in winter, and the other in July and August (*Frühlingsbergweide*): lower mountain pasture.

Nipperl or **Schluckerl** *n* -s/-n a very small amount of a drink: little sup, wee sip, sippie; *ich brauche nur ein ~ Wasser oder Tee, um die Tablette runterzukriegen* all I need is a little sup of water or tea, to get the tablet down.

Nixerl *n* -s/-(n) [a dial. noun diminutive of *nix* < indef. pron. *nichts* 'nothing', 'nil'] *colloq.,* often *contp.* **1.** an unimportant or unimpressive person: nobody, *sl.* zero; *im Vergleich zum Vater ist der Kerl ein ~* that wretch isn't a patch on [his] father. – **2.** any object or matter of little or no substance: a mere nothing ‖ *hum.* (1) *ein ~ von einem Bikini* a teeny-weeny (*or,* an apology for a) bikini. – (2) a mischievous answer in the negative for an obtrusive child or lover, asking *„Sag, was hast du mir denn (Schönes) mitgebracht?"* 'What kind of goodie have you brought me, I wonder': *ein ~ in einem goldenen Büchserl* [-ks-; better still, *dial.,* to make the rhyme pure: ˈbɪksərl] *a little bit of nowt stuck in a piggy's snout.

Nudel ...: ~drucker *m* -s/- **1.** *hist., tech.* an antiquated kitchen appliance (still on view in some rural folklore museums) which was used to squeeze noodle dough through a sieve: noodle press. → **2.** P slightly *contp.* or *hum.* a parsimonious person *(Geizhals)*: skinflint, penny-pincher, *AmE a.* dough-pincher, tightwad. – **~druckerei** *f* -/pl. rare: -en a miser's prime characteristic: cheeseparing, penny-pinching. – **~suppe** *f* -/-n **1.** *cul.* a bouillon garnished with noodles: noodle or vermicelli [ˌvəːmɪˈselɪ] soup. – **2.** only in a *phr.* irately denying being unsophisticated, lacking common sense, and being ignorant about the ways of the world – *ich bin ja nicht auf der ~ dahergeschwommen!* I wasn't born yesterday, *BrE a.* I didn't come here on a banana boat, *NZ & AustralE* I didn't come down in the last shower; *wir Österreicher haben es satt, uns vorschreiben zu lassen, welche Regierung wir wählen oder nicht wählen dürfen, und sind schließlich nicht auf der ~ dahergeschwommen!* we Austrians are fed up with being dictated to which government to choose or not; after all we were not born yesterday. – **~walker** *m* -s/- [second el., < MHG *walgen* 'to roll out s.th. (flat and thin)'] *cul.* a long tube-shaped piece, usu. of wood, for rolling out dough before cooking *(Nudelholz, -rolle)*: rolling-pin.

O

Oberg'scheite, Überg'scheite *m* or *f* -n/-n *dial.,* said with malice or in anger – someone who annoys others by trying to sound clever and claiming to know everything *(vermeintlich Kluge[r], Neunmalkluge[r])*: smart aleck, smarty-pants, *BrE a.* cleversides *sg.,* clever dick, *AmE a.* slick boots *sg.,* Mr. [Miss] Smarty.

Oberländer *m* -s/- inhabitant of the Upper Inn Valley, west of Innsbruck *(*opp.*, Unterländer* ↓*).*

Obststeige *f* -/-n a fruit box made of narrow wooden slats: fruit basket.

Ohrenschliefer *m* -s/- [< the mistaken belief that this harmless insect creeps into the human ear] *entom.* earwig *(Ohrwurm, Ohrenkriecher)*: *BrE dial.* lugwig, twinge, twitch(y)-bell, (s)kutchy-bell, forky-tail.

Ohrwaschel, often **Ohrwaschl** *n* -s/-n [second el., Germ. *wat-skō* 'to wash quickly with water, often running water, by rapidly pulling the piece of laundry to and fro', 'to rinse'; the word was early applied also to the quick and twitchy motion a number of quadrupeds are known to give to their ears ‖ for the derivative suffix *-el,* see under *Drischel* and *Waschel*] *dial.* **1.** *human anat.* (1) also **Ohrwangl** *n* -s the outside part of the ear (*Ohrmuschel*): (outer, *or* shell of the) ear, *BrE colloq.* earhole, lug(-hole), listener. – (2) also **Ohrlapperl** *n* – the soft piece of flesh at the bottom of a person's ear (*Ohrläppchen*): ear lobe. – **2.** *concr. phr.* verbal threats of physical action – (1) to mete out punishment: *du kriegst gleich ein paar hinter die ~(n)!* I'll sock your ears for you (*BrE a.* I'll give you a clip round the earhole) in a minute. – (2) to rid a person of his or her silly ideas: *i nimm di' bei die Haar und ~(n)!* I'll shake (*or* beat) the living daylights out of you. – **3.** *fig. phr.* (1) a sharp reprimand to one for failing to hear, or for misunderstanding what he had been told before: *mach* (or *sperr*) *gefälligst deine ~n auf, wenn ich dir was sag!* prick up yer ears, will ya, when I'm telling you things. – (2) a rude query when hearing no reaction from somebody spoken to: *ja, sitzt du auf den* (or, more dial., *auf die) ~(n)?* (why, aye, man), are you deaf or something? – (3) an indignant comment when being faced with a refusal to make the slightest effort to help, etc.: *nicht ein ~,* or *sich nicht mit einem ~, rühren* not so much as stir a finger (*or,* … lift a hand); *die Bürgermeister haben das Land um Aufschub der Straßenarbeiten ersucht, doch die Hofräte dort oben rühren kein ~* the mayors have asked the provincial government to stay these road repairs pro tem, but the aulic powers in being upstairs have not deigned to budge an inch. – (4) an impertinent, or at best carelessly cheerful, reply to a question where one is going (the implication being that such nosiness deserves no answer) – A: *wo gehst du denn hin?* B: *der Nasn nach und zwischn d' Ohrwaschl durch!* A: where are you going? B: where the crow flies and where my feet decide to carry me. – (5) *contp.* said of a feckless person, often when thus characterizing a henpecked husband: *steht sein Weib hinter ihm, lasst sich unser Held prompt beim ~ heimführen* with his wife standing behind him, our hero lets himself be dragged off home by the lug-hole.

Optạnt *m* -en/-en, *colloq.* **Gẹher** *m* -s/- (opp., *Dableiber* ↑) *polit. hist.,* in the 1940s often used with bitter sarcasm: optant, *colloq.* one of those "opting out", two key words from a cluster of references, and often personal slurs, following the 1939 Hitler-Mussolini pact on the resettlement of South Tyrolean Germans north of the Alps, chiefly in what was then the *Ostmark* ↓ provinces of Greater Germany; the reasons for such a "voluntary" mass emigration lay in the repressive measures taken by Fascist Italy (like the threat of enforced exile to areas south of the River Po) and in the hope of preserving one's ethnic integrity as well as simultaneously solving the nagging problem of widespread unemployment.

Ọstmark *f polit. hist.* "Eastern March" **1.** parts of the former provinces of Noricum and Pannonia, which were placed under a margrave (*Markgraf* 'guardian of the border') by Charlemagne, to defend the rest of the German Empire against the Avars and other tribes in the East. – **2.** the cultural and political centre of those mid-European regions which were united under the Hapsburg dynasty. – **3.** the name given to Austria between 1938 and 1945, after her annexation *(Anschluss* ↑*)* by Adolf Hitler into Greater Germany.

Ọttoman *m* -s/-e [< F *ottomane* 'Turkish couch'] *obs.* a sofa-like lounge on short legs, with a low head-rest and no back, often also used as a box for storing bedding (*Ottomane: niedriges Sofa*): ottoman.

Ọ̈tzi *m* - [shortened from *Ötztal,* the name of a southern branch of the Inn Valley, in the Tyrol, some 25 miles west of Innsbruck, + dim. *-i*] *hist.* the form of endearment for a mummified Stone Age body of a mountaineer, released in 1991 by the glacier in the Oetztal Alps, on the Austro-Italian border; that prehistoric find, on the analysis of skin and bone samples, can be dated at around 3300 B.C. (and is now the rarest of all possible exhibits in Bozen's Museum of Archaeology): Ötztal Ice Man.

Oxdrahdium *n* -s [a *dial.* imperative (lit., 'ox, turn around!') coined for the occasion and made into a noun] *hum.* on April Fools' Day, or whenever a prankster is feeling his oats – a fictitious item some potential "victim", naive and unsuspecting, is asked to go and buy (or otherwise get), couched in phrases like *geh, hol mir ein (Flascherl, Packerl, eine Portion* etc.) ~! *BrE* go get me a yard of pump-water, *AmE* … a dime's worth of strap oil (*or,* ten cents' worth of radium)!

P Q

Packel<u>ei</u> *f* -/-en chiefly *polit., contp.* the act of meeting in a small group for secret (inter-party) discussions (*heimliche Übereinkunft*): hush-hush get-togethers, underhand *or* hugger-mugger dealings *pl., BrE a.* jiggery-pokery (*less often,* jackery-pokery); *der leidgeprüfte Bürger fragt sich, warum denn die Roten und Schwarzen in den vielen Jahrzehnten ihrer Zusammenarbeit – manche sagen auch: ~ – nicht annähernd in die Tat umgesetzt haben, was sie in abertausend Sonntagsreden angekündigt hatten: so ein Gerede hat keine Arbeitsplätze geschaffen, ja die Arbeitslosenzahl ist größer als je zuvor* the sorely tried citizens are asking themselves why these Reds and Blacks, throughout their many decades of collaboration – some also say, collusion – have not nearly materialized what they had promised in their speechifying: their constant streams of 'hot air' did not create new jobs, in fact the figure of those unemployed is bigger than ever before. – **pạckeln** *v/i* [lit., 'to crowd together, forming a solid parcel'] chiefly *polit., contp.* to confer in a small group, away from other people, in order to plan something, esp. something disreputable (*etwas* [*heimlich*] *aushandeln*): to be in, *or* to go into, a huddle.

Pạckerl *n* -s/-n [< *Pack m* + dim. *-erl*] *colloq.* a smallish paper or cardboard container, typically one in which goods are packed to be sold; or a small assortment of eatables, conveniently wrapped up to be taken along with ease (*Päckchen*): packet, small parcel; *ein ~ Zigaretten* a packet of cigarettes ‖ in cpds.: **~suppe** *f* -/-n, *dial.* **~suppm** *f* -/- *cul.* a dehydrated soup mixture in the form of powder, artificial flavourings, solid small dried pieces of herbs and vegetables, sometimes also of croutons and other ingredients, to be prepared by simply adding hot water (*Fertigsuppe*): instant *or* ready-made soup; → *Heurigen*≟.

Palatschịnke *f* -/-n *cul.* a very thin egg-batter pancake, filled with jam etc. (→ *Topfen*≟) and rolled up *(gefüllter Eierkuchen)*: crepe *or* crêpe, flapjack.

Pạllawatsch *m* -(e)s Viennese *dial.* [< It *balordaggine* 'confusion'] said of a disorder caused by clumsiness or lack of coordination: *(Wirrwarr)* muddle; *so ein ~!* what a mess!, what a mix-up!, *BrE* that's a fine kettle of fish!

Pan<u>ier</u> *f* - **1.** *cul. (Masse aus Ei und Semmelbröseln als Hülle von Fleisch)* coating of egg and breadcrumb (in which cutlets, etc. are fried). – **2.** low *colloq. (Kleidung)* one's clothes: togs, *AmE sl.* threads; *sie klopfen ihm begeistert auf* *die Schulter, dass es ihn fast aus der ~ haut* they slap him so heartily on the shoulder that his togs nearly fall off. – **panieren** *vt/i cul.* to coat with egg and breadcrumb, to (bread)crumb, to bread. – **Paniermehl** *n* -s *(Brösel[n] ↑)* breadcrumbs.

Paradeisapfel *m* -s/… äpfel [once considered to be an aphrodisiac, and hence also called "fruit of temptation" or "love apple" in English; the fruit was duly felt to be the one with which Eve had tempted Adam in Paradise] rare, only in the Tyrol and Vorarlberg: = *Paradeiser* ↓.

Paradeiser *m* -s/- **1.** ⚘ *& cul. (Tomate)* tomato; *~ ziehen* to raise tomatoes; *gefüllte ~* stuffed tomatoes; *die ~ zerteilen und mit den Paprikas zu der Zwiebel geben* (to) slice the tomatoes and add to the onion and peppers; *die ~ passieren* to puree (*or* process) the tomatoes ‖ *die Störer haben den Redner mit faulen ~n beworfen* the rioters pelted the speaker with rotten tomatoes. – **2.** *fig.: rot wie ein ~* as red as a turkey-cock (*or,* a peony [ˈpiːənɪ], *or AmE,* a tomato); *Fräulein Mizzi wurde rot wie ein ~* Miss Molly turned crimson (*or,* blushed to the ears, *or,* went as red as a beet[root]).

Paradeis… *cul.:* **~mark** *n* -(e)s tomato paste; if of a thinner consistency: tomato pulp, tomato puree [ˈpjuəreɪ]. – **~salat** *m* -(e)s tomato salat. – **~sauce, ~soße** *f* -/-n tomato sauce. – **~suppe** *f* -/-n tomato soup.

Pạrte *f* -/-n, **Pạrtezettel** *m* -s/- *(Todesanzeige)* **1.** sent by post as printed matter, in the event of death: death notice; *wieviel Parten lassen wir denn drucken?* how many notices should we have printed? – **2.** published in a newspaper: obituary (notice); *eine Parte in der Zeitung? … das ist doch ein Pflanz, und gar nicht, wie's der Hans gewollt hätte!* an obituary? … that's too showy, nor would Jack have wanted it that way, surely!

Patsch [pɔːtʃ] *m* nearly always only *nom. & acc. sg.,* **Patschạchter** [paˈtʃɔxta] *m* -s/-, **Patscherl** [ˈpɔːtʃəl] *n* -s/-(n) *dial.* a person awkward in handling things, or one who is generally inept (*Tolpatsch*): clumsy clot, butterfingers, *AmE a.* stumblebum.

Patschen [ˈpɔːtʃn] *m* -s/- [< Serb. *papuča,* or F *botte* 'boot'] *colloq.* **1.** usu. *pl. (Hausschuh[e])* slipper(s) ‖ *phr.* (1) said of a person who is content with what he has already professionally achieved: *die ~ anziehen* to put one's career on the back burner, *AmE* to set one's career on cruise control. (2) *coarsely,* to die: *die ~ aufstellen* (or *beuteln,* or *strecken*) to kick it, *BrE a.* to pop one's clogs. – **2.** punctured tyre *(Reifendefekt)*: flat, *NZE* flattie; *sich einen ~ fahren* to blow (*or* catch) a flat; *er hat einen ~ und muss das Rad schieben* he's got a flat and has to push his bike.

Pẹch *n* -(e)s *(Harz)* resin. – **~mandl** *n* -s *folklore* an imaginary figure said to come to the person, often a child, on the verge of sleep: sandman; *das ~ kommt* the sandman's coming.

Pẹrcht *f* -/-en [< *Perchta* or *Berchta,* 'The Brightly Resplendent One', the name of the female leader of a traditional mummers' procession] *folklore* one of a crowded group of masked, and often weirdly dressed, men walking or gambolling through the streets of a Alpine village or town in accordance with an age-old ritual – they do this among shouts and noise-makings in the Advent, New Year, and Carnival seasons in order to drive away the evil demons of winter: masked mime *or* mummer (in an Alpine midwinter procession). – **~enlauf** *m* -(e)s/ … läufe, **~enlaufen** *n* -s, **~lspringen** *n* -s, **Berchtenspringen** *n* -s one of various such festive folklore processions held in Western Austria – among them primeval demons, devils and witches, as well as terrestrial figures of the past, be they Moors and Turks, carters and jesters: Alpine mid-winter pageant.

Pfạrrer *m* -s/- *relig.* parson ‖ in a *colloq. phr.* used when annoyed at being asked to repeat something because it was not fully heard or understood: *der ~ predigt nur einmal (am Sonntag)* I don't boil my cabbages twice. – **~alm** *f* -/en *hum.* churchyard, graveyard *(Friedhof)*: "the parson's farmland"; *auf die ~ fahren* to die: to answer the last summons, to bite the dust, *AmE a.* to buy the farm.

Pfịtschipfeil *m* -(e)s/-e *colloq.* **1.** a child's plain paper dart (*or,* aeroplane), made of a sheet of paper which is folded to resemble a delta-wing plane; *mit ~en spielen* to fly paper aeroplanes. – **2.** any other toy dart; *wie ein ~* quick as an arrow. – **3.** slightly *contp.* for the three arrows, symbol of the Austrian Socialist Party: *die drei ~e* those little Socialist darts ‖ with reference to the Austrian Labour Party practice, in Socialist-dominated areas, of decorating the windows of council flats with small red flags showing the party emblem: *ich wohne in einem Gemeindebau und bin einer der wenigen, die sich trauen, am 1. Mai nicht die drei ~e auszuhängen* I live in a municipal apartment block, and I am one of the few bold enough not to stick out those three silly arrows on May Day.

Pfu̲sch *m* -(e)s *colloq.* illicit work, for pay that does not involve the Inland Revenue Department *(Schwarzarbeit)*: work (done) on the side; *im ~ arbeiten, am ~ gehen* to work on the side, *NZE* to work at mate's rates.

Pịckerl *n* -s/-n [< *picken vt/i* 'to (be) fasten(ed) with glue' + dim. *-erl*] *colloq.* **1.** an adhesive label, with an official message on the front, generally printed or illustrated, stuck on certain articles for sale, e.g. on bananas, in order to draw attention to a specific brand (*Klebeetikett*): sticker. – **2.**, also *Autobahn~*, required on Austrian motorways and expressways since 1997 – a label, clearly displayed on a motorized vehicle, usu. on its windscreen, in order to show that, for the period of days or months specified, toll-charge has been paid (*Vignette*): (motorway) sticker.

Pịckzeug *n* -s *colloq.* an adhesive, e.g. for repairing a bicycle tyre: sticky-stuff; *ist da wo ein ~?* is there some sticky-stuff anywhere?

Pie̲pserl *n* -s/-(n) *techn. colloq.* a portable device used to alert one of messages which are received from a separate answering machine: beeper.

Plä̲tschen, Plä̲tschn, also **Ple̲tschen, Ple̲tschn** *f* -/- *colloq.,* sometimes *hum.* or *contp.* any large, flat object, e.g. a big plant leaf *(flacher, rundlicher Gegenstand)*: whopper; *vom Verputz des Hauses fallen jetzt schon ganze ~ runter* the plaster on the side of the house is coming off in big patches. – **~express** *m* -es *hum.* the tram-line operating between Kagran and Groß-Enzersdorf, on the northeastern outskirts of Vienna beyond the Danube; so called from the cabbage fields along which the tram passes on its route ([Wiener]Straßenbahnlinie 317): "Cabbage Patch Express".

Plausch *m* -es/-e *colloq. (Plauderei)* chat; *sie ist auf einen ~ zur Nachbarin gegangen* she's over at her neighbour's having a chitchat. – **plauschen** *v/i colloq. (plaudern)* to (have a) chat, to have a chin-wag (*mit* with), *AmE a.* to chew the fat. – **Plauscherl** *n* -s/- *colloq. (gemütliche Plauderei)* folksy talk: chat, chit-chat, little gossip session; *kommen Sie doch auf ein ~ (zu uns)!* do come in for a cosy chat!; *die beiden alten Damen haben sich im Kaffeehaus zu einem ~ getroffen* the two elderly ladies met in the café for a nice little chat.

plimsplams *adv* [by way of sound symbolism through ablaut modification; cp. F *cric-crac* 'noise of breaking or tearing something'] *colloq.* in disorder, mixed together without system *(durcheinander, ohne Sorgfalt)*: topsy-turvy, in a mishmash, higgledy-piggledy.

Plunderwagen *m* -s/- or, *dial.*, ... wägn [first el., *Plunder m* < LateMHG *blunder, plunder* 'household goods', 'clothing', 'linen', 'bedding', from MLG *plunde* 'clothing' – a bride's material possessions the elements of which the eye of the beholder should here see stacked high on a commodious carriage, ready for removal from the parental home] *hist. folklore* an inalienable feature of a sometime Austrian peasant wedding (BavG *Kammerwagen, Kuchlwagen*): bride's household *or* dowry wagon (*BrE a.* waggon), trousseau ['tru:səʊ] carriage – loaded with all the bride's personal possessions, inclusive of clothes and articles for the home she is about to marry into (not forgetting the bride's favourite seamstress [*Näherin*] sitting plumped on a bed among the things); in front, there is the team of draught horses festively adorned, while the bride's father's best cow, duly tied on, complaisantly brings up the rear.

Plutzer ['–u:–] *m* -s/- *dial.* **1.** ♩ (*Kürbis*) pumpkin. – **2.** (*Steingutgefäß*) narrow-necked round (*or* bulging) earthenware bottle *or* jug; *Schnaps*≗ round brandy-bottle; *if full:* round bottle of brandy ‖ *hol' uns im Zweiliter*≗ *einen Most!* go and get us some must in the four-pint jug! – **3.** *sl.* (*Kopf*) noodle, pumpkin, *BrE sl. a.* twopenny ‖ *phr. wie ich bei der niedrigen Tür (her)einkam, hab' ich mir an einem Balken den ~ angehaut* when entering by the low door I knocked my noodle against one of the wooden beams; *zieh den ~ ein!* tuck in your twopenny! – **4.** (*grober Fehler*) blunder, *sl.* howler, bloomer.

Pockerl *n* -s/-(n) [< Hung. *pulyka, pujka* 'turkey(-cock)'] *zo. & cul., dial.* = *Indian* ↑.

Polsterl *n* -s/-(n) [< *Polster m* 'pillow' + dim. *-l*] *colloq.* **1.** a small pillow often placed, along with others, on a couch or a settee for decorative purposes only: (wee) little pillow. → **2.** *fig.* something providing support or protection: padding, cushion; *wenn Sie zu schlank sind, setzen Sie tunlichst etwas Fett an, damit der Magen eine bessere Stütze, ein „~", bekommt* if you are too slim, try to put on some weight, which will give your stomach some firmer padding, and "cushion" it. – **~tanz** *m* -es/ ... tänze *folklore* a lively folk-dance featuring the use of little cushions, popular especially in rural areas (in England indeed since early Stuart times): cushion dance.

Pọlsterzipf *m* -(e)s/-e *bak.* an East Austrian delicacy, also offered at Lower Austrian vintners' festivals (*Blätterteigkissen*): puff-pastry square filled with plum or apricot jam.

Potschạmper *m* -s/- [a blend < F *pot de chambre* 'chamber pot' + Austrian dial. *Amper* (< StandG *Eimer m* 'bucket')] *colloq.* a euphemistic detour, following the English standard term, in order to avoid mentioning the functional crudity of the object (still occasionally to be found [and, when the urge is on, eagerly groped for from] under the bed at night) – chamber pot (*Nachttopf*): jerry. – **Potschạmperl** or **Potschạmberl** *n* -s/-(n) [the same blend as above + dim. *-l*] *hum.* no change in the nature of the household item, perhaps only smaller in circumference, and looked at as well as handled in a more light-hearted mood, esp. by children and their laughter-loving parents: (piddle) potty.

P<u>o</u>tschi *n* -(s)/pl. rare: – [< euphem. *Po m* (short for L > hum. G *Podex m* 'buttocks', 'posterior') + dim. *-tschi*] *nursery talk* a baby's or a small child's buttocks: bottie *or* botty, *WestIndE* botsie ‖ *phr.* a mnemonic couplet warning young children against two common health hazards, catching a cold and getting constipated – a dual reminder which, if heeded, would keep the doctor well away from getting fussily busy:

> *Mund geschlossen, Potschi offen –*
> *hat der Doktor nichts zu hoffen!*
>
> *Mouth well closed, and bottie open,
> Doc's kept twiddlin' thumbs, and mopin'.

Pọwidl *m* -s/- [< Cz *povidla* 'home-cooked plum jam'] **1.** *cul.* *(Zwetschkenmus)* plum jam, used as pie filling. – **2.** *colloq.* (1) = *schetzko jedno;* (2) in the slightly *contp.* phrase signalling indifference: *das ist mir ~!* I couldn't care less!, I don't give a hang (*or,* a rip, *or,* a tinker's dam [*AmE* ... a damn])!, I don't care a fig!, *BrE a.* I don't care tuppence! – or, more curtly: *is ~* same difference.

Pọwidl ... *cul.*: **~golatsche** *f* -/-n = *Powidlkolatsche.* – **~knödel** *m* -s/-(n) plum-jam dumpling. – **~kolatsche** *f* -/-n plum-jam square, a yeast pastry folded into the middle at each corner, and filled with plum jam. – **~tascherl, ~taschkerl, ~tatschkerl** *n* -s/-(n) little jam pocket, a potato-dough triangle filled with plum jam, and boiled in salt water.

Pragm<u>a</u>tik *f* -/-en *admin.* **1.** also **Dienst**≗ the status of defining the grade structure of the Civil Service (*Dienstordnung*): Civil Service Regulations *pl.* – **2.** (*Beamtengesetz*) the grading of civil servants: Civil Service Act.

Pragm<u>a</u>tische Sankti<u>o</u>n *f* -n - *hist.* **1.** *pl.* --en *gen.* an imperial or royal ordinance or decree that has the force of law: pragmatic sanction. – **2.** no *pl. specif.* **Die ~ ~** a document drafted in 1717 by the Emperor Charles VI providing for his daughter Maria Theresa to succeed to all his territories should he die without a son; opposition to it led to the War of the Austrian Succession (*Österreichischer Erbfolgekrieg*) on Charles's death in 1740: The Pragmatic Sanction.

Empress Maria Theresa proudly points out the old Hapsburgian crown, to which she succeeded on the strength of the "Pragmatic Sanction"

pragmatisieren *v/t admin.* to give s.o. a permanent post in the Civil Service, e.g. as a teacher (*fest in den Staatsdienst übernehmen*): to make s.o.'s appointment permanent, to tenure s.o.; *sind Sie pragmatisiert?* are you on the permanent staff?; *ich bin schon ewig lang pragmatisiert* I was tenured ages ago ‖ a dialect speaker's smug observation: *wannst d' amoi pragmatisiert bist, können s' di' net aussehau'n… es sei denn, dass d' goldene Löffl stiehlst* once you're on the permanent staff you can't be kicked out … unless they nab you pinchin' golden spoons. – **Pragmatisierung** *f* -/-en *admin.* **1.** (act of) appointment to the permanent staff. – **2.** (status of) appointment to the permanent staff. – **2.** (status of) permanent appointment; *ich habe heuer die ~ geschafft* I was given (security of) tenure this year.

Pratzen, Pratzn [-ɑ-] *f* -/often pl.: - [actually, an animal's foot that has nails or claws] *dial.* **1.** coarsely *hum.* (1) a human hand: paw, mitt; *geh und wasch dir die ~!* go and wash your dirty paws!; *die Zigaretten gehören mir, lass die ~ davon!* these are my cigarettes, get your mitts off them! – (2) said to a card-player: *ich wünsch' dir a ~ voller Trümpf'* I wish you a fistful of trump cards. – **2.** shrilly *contp.* – a female's warning not to be handled roughly in a sexual way: *(nimm) die ~ weg!* (take your) paws off (me)!; having hands trouble? you stop mauling me! – **3.** low *colloq.* (usu.) a (male's) large, heavy hand: paw, mauler; *der hat ja richtige ~!* he's got hams (*AmE a.* mutton chops) for hands; ~ [pl.] *so groß wie Abortdeckel* maulers the size of (*or,* as big as) manhole covers.

Preberschießen *n* -s/pl. rare: – [named after *Prebersee,* a small mountain lake NNE of Tamsweg, at an altitude of 1522 m (4993 ft), in the Lungau area of Salzburg Province, close to the border of Styria] *folklore* a unique lakeside shooting contest staged on the occasion of weddings, jubilees, and other festivities, requiring competitors not to aim at the conventional target rings (set up on a spit of land opposite the rifle range) but at their reflections on the singularly unruffled surface of the water – if the angle of the trajectory chosen by the marksman is correct, the bullet will ricochet from the water right into the target: Preber Riflemen's Competition.

pritscheln *v/i* to splash: splatter; *geh ins Bad, aber bitte ohne zu ~* go into the bathroom, but please don't splatter water all over the place.

Privilegium Minus *n* - - *hist.* a deed of independence granted in 1156 by Frederick Barbarossa, Emperor of Germany, to the Babenbergers, raising Austria to a duchy, granting her juridical autonomy, and endowing her with the rights of succession through both male and female lines; so, Austria held a rather unique position within the Holy Roman Empire, which eventually led to her establishment as an independent state: Minor Privilege of Precedence [ˈpresɪdəns].

Prügel *m* -s/- (at Retz, Lower Austria, near the Czech border), or **~torte** *f* -/-n (in Brandenberg Valley, Tyrol, north of Kramsach-on-the-Inn) [< *Prügel m* 'cudgel: a thick stick used as a weapon'; here: 'a cudgel-like log (wrapped in greaseproof paper)', the *pièce de résistance* round which the time-honoured

A "Cudgel" to feast one's eyes and palate on

cake (here documented for places hundreds of miles apart) is baked by constantly turning it over a beechwood fire] *bak.* a long, thick, slightly gnarled confection made up of successive layers of rich dough, at last to be coated in lemon or raspberry icing – standing on end and lasting for weeks, it is a popular rural wedding or birthday present, a staple diet at church fairs and wine-drinking parties … and, surprisingly, never gets hard enough to serve as a real cudgel: cudgel cake.

Prusik… [< Karl *Prusik,* 1896–1961, a Viennese mountaineer who devised this method of climbing (and in whose honour the very difficult Prusik Peak [ˈprʌsɪk piːk], in the State of Washington, USA, has been named] ⩓: **~knoten** *m* -s/pl. rare: – a type of knot by which a prusik sling is attached to a rope (*Seilklemmknoten*): prusik (*or* Prusik) knot. – **~schlinge** *f* -/-n a type of rope sling attached to a climbing rope, which grips firmly when carrying weight, but when unweighted can be moved up the rope: prusik (*or* Prusik) sling; *mit (Hilfe von) ~n klettern* to climb, or raise (oneself) up, on two such slings: to prusik.

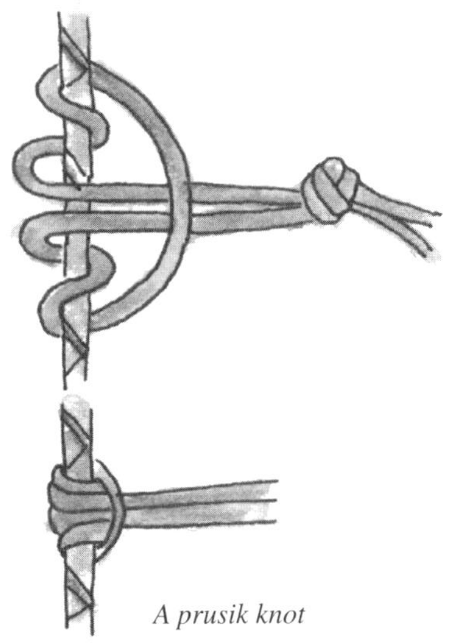

A prusik knot

Pudelhaube *f* -/-n [first el., < the frizzy hair of the poodle] *(Pudelmütze)* thick woolly cap, ski cap; if with the tip hanging down past the ears: stocking cap.

Pulver…: ~schnee *m* -s ⩓ loose, dry, newly fallen snow: powder, powder snow, powdery snow. – **~turm** *m* -(e)s/ …türme *mil. hist.* a landmark at Innsbruck, Krems, and other medieval cities (with their counterparts often to be found in the British Isles and the United

States of America) – a massive round tower, in former centuries storing arms, ammunition, explosives, and provisions for defensive use in military operations: powder magazine.

pumperlgesund *adj colloq. (kerngesund)* thoroughly healthy: fit as a fiddle, *AmE a.* healthy as a horse; *schau mich nur an mit meinen sechzig Jahren, nie krank und ~! AmE* just look at me, sixty years old, never been sick, healthy as a horse.

Pupperl *n* -s/-n [dim. of *Puppe* 'doll'] *colloq.* **1.** *(Püppchen)* little doll: dolly. – **2.** *(süßes Mädchen)* (baby) doll ‖ as a form of endearment: popsy(-wopsy), pet, sugar, honey. – **3.** *(Geliebte)* sweetheart: flame. – **4.** *(leichtes Mädchen)* frivolous creature: merry bit, merry-legs *sg.*, push-over, *AmE a.* easy make, easy number. **~hutschen** *f* -/- ⊡ *(Soziussitz)* pillion (seat): *BrE* flapper-bracket, *AmE* buddy seat; *ich sitze für mein Leben gern auf der ~* I simply love riding pillion.

putzen *v colloq.* **1.** *v/t* said of clothes, material, etc. to be cleaned with chemicals instead of water ([*chemisch*] *reinigen*) to dry-clean; *kannst du denn nicht ein bissel mehr aufpassen? Jetzt muss ich das Kleid von dir da schon wieder ~ lassen!* can't you take a little more care? here I am having to go and get your dress dry-cleaned again (now). – **2.** *v/refl* to leave, esp. in a hurry *(abhauen)*: to make tracks ‖ often used in the imperative, to a person whose presence is not desired: *putz dich!* beat it!, buzz off!, go jump in the lake!, *AmE a.* scram!, get lost!

Putzerei *f* -/-en *com.* a shop where customers' clothes are (taken to be) cleaned with chemical solvents rather than water ([*chemische*] *Reinigung*): dry cleaner's; *less often, since very formal,* dry-cleaning establishment; *wo ist denn die nächste ~, in die ich den Anzug von meinem Mann (zum Putzen) bringen könnte?* where is the nearest cleaner's I might take my husband's suit to?; *das Kleid ist in der ~* the dress is at the cleaner's; *ich habe deine* [*Ihre*] *Krawatten zur* (or *in die*) *~ gegeben* I sent your ties to the cleaner's.

Quargel *m* & *n* -s/-; *f* -/-n [< Cz *tvaroh* 'cottage (*or* curd) cheese'] **1.** *comest.* an orange-coloured, strong-smelling curd cheese, shaped as a small round piece and sold in a cellophane pile of four or six (*Olmützer Stinkkäse, Harzer Käse* or *Roller*): Harz (Mountain) cheese. – **2.** *fig. colloq.* rubbish, piffle, tripe; *der redet einen ~ daher* (or *zusammen*)*!* he's talking a load of rubbish, he's talking through his hat (*or,* … through the back of his head). – **~stecher** *m* -s/- *Viennese contp.* someone who pays too much attention to small and unimportant points of faults (*Pedant, Nörgler*): nitpicker. – **~sturz** *m* -es/pl. rare: … stürze *tech.* (*Käseglocke*) cheese(-dish) cover; *fig. iron.* in a phrase characterizing someone's over-solicitous attitude towards a child, consort, etc.: *wenn es nach ihr ginge, würde sie ihn am liebsten untern ~ stellen* she would rather cushion him round in cotton wool if she only could.

Quetschn *f* -/- ♪ *colloq.* a small, portable, keyed wind instrument in which the wind is forced upon free metallic reeds by means of a bellows *(Ziehharmonika)*: squeeze-box, pleated piano, *BrE a.* squiffer, *AmE a.* stomach Steinway.

R

Radẹtzky *m* -s/- [a playful extension of the proper name, whose most illustrious bearer was Field Marshal Count Johann Josef Wenzel Radetzky (1766–1858), a very popular Austrian commander in his time (for his portrait, see p. 64)] *schoolboy sl. (Radiergummi)* (india-)rubber, Indiarubber, *AmE* (rubber-)eraser.

Radmähen *n* -s *folklore* "circle-mowing" **1.** in Upper Austria, when a farmer has neglected the mowing of his field, his neighbours may chide him by mowing a huge wheel in it. – **2.** generally, the mowing of a holy sign (e.g., a cross in the Lungau area of Salzburg province) at the beginning or end of a job or project.

Ramasuri, Remasuri *f* - *colloq.* **1.** *(gründliches Aufräumen)* thorough clearing-up: clean-up, *AmE* mop-up, k.p. [short for 'kitchen patrol']. – **2.** *(großes Durcheinander; Wirbel)* chaos, confusion: hurly-burly, rumpus, hullabal(l)oo, *AmE a.* ruckus; *gottseidank läuft nach dieser ~ alles wieder schön am Schnürl* thank heavens everything's nice and neat again after all that hurly-burly, *AmE a.* ... back to normal again after all the chaos. – **3.** *(ausgelassenes Vergnügen)* exuberant gaiety: fling, spree, *AmE* whoopee.

Rạnd [rɒnd] *m dial. (Weile)* chiefly in: *einen (ganzen) ~ warten* to wait a (good) while; *setzen wir uns hin und rasten wir einen ~! SouAmE* let's sit here and rest a spell.

Rạnderl [ˈrʌndərl] -s/-(n) *colloq.* **1.** [dim. of *Rand* 'space (of time)'] *(Weilchen)* little while; *wollen wir nicht ein ~ verschnaufen?* shall we take a wee breath?, *AmE* how about a minute's break (*or,* ... a "take five")? – **2.** [a short form, with a dim. ending, of F *Rendezvous*] *(Stelldichein)* rendezvous, date; *du hast also ein ~ mit einem süßen Käfer und kannst darum nicht kommen!* so, you have a date with a sweet little peach and can't come to see us!

Rạndi *n* -s/-(s) *dial. & fam.* = *Randerl,* 2 ↑.

Rạndkluft *f* -/...klüfte ⛰ crevasse between moving and fixed ice.

Rạngel..., Rạnggel... *folklore* at the *Gauderfest* ↑, on the Hundstein, east of Zell am See, Salzburg, and elsewhere in the Alps: **~fest** *n* -es/-e "wrestling festival", an annual competition of local amateur wrestlers, involving certain catches and throws – "brawling according to rules", as it were. – **~konkurrenz** *f* -/-en, **Preisrang(g)eln** *n* -s competitive wrestling (in the Alpine style), wrestling contest. – **~platz** *m* -es/ ... plätze wrestling area.

rạngeln, rạnggeln 1. *v/i* to wrestle in the Alpine peasant style. – **2.** *≈n* in Western

Austria: wrestling contest. – **Rangler, Ranggler** *m* -s/- peasant wrestler.

raß *adj* **1.** *cul.* said of certain foods, e.g. goulash *(scharf gewürzt)*: spicy, hot; opp. *lau(b)* ↑. – **2.** said of an irritable person: *er ist ein rasser Mensch* he blows his top easily, he's got a hot temper.

ratschen *vt/i* [< *ratsch,* an interjection formed through sound imitation of the long sharp tear when quickly made into cloth, paper, etc.] *colloq.* **1.** *v/t* also, **herunterratschen** – to perform s.th. quickly, often mechanically: to rattle off *or* through (a poem, a prayer [e.g. the one chanted by the clapper boys before Easter]). – **2.** *v/i* (1) to use a baby rattle. – (2) to use a clapper; *die Buben freuen sich schon drauf, am Karfreitag durch den Ort ~ gehen zu können* the lads are already looking forward to the chance of jangling their clappers through the place on Good Friday. – **3.** *v/i* (1) to converse in a friendly informal manner *(plaudern)*: to chat, to chitchat, to have a chinwag, *AmE a.* to chew the fat (*or* the rag), to shoot the bull (*or* the breeze); *er ratscht ganz gern, aber er ist ein lieber Mensch* he's a friendly, chatty sort of person. – (2) to be an exaggerated talker: to wag the tongue; *es haben schon zu viele geratscht, als dass die Sache noch vertraulich bleiben könnte* too many tongues have been wagging for the matter to remain confidential any longer.

Rätien [-ts-] *n* -s *hist., geog.* Rhaetia [ˈriːʃjə], an ancient Roman province in Central Europe, comprising what is now Tyrol and Vorarlberg. – **rätoromanisch** *adj ling.* Rhaeto-Romanic, Rhaeto-Romance; das ≈e Rhaeto-Romanic, Rhaeto-Romance, a group of closely similar Romance languages, comprising Swiss Romansh, Tyrolese Ladin, and Friulian.

raunzen *v/i* [an extended stem form of *raunen* 'to whisper', already documented as OHG *rūnezōn* 'to whisper one's discontentment'] *dial.* to complain in a subdued but effectively annoying way, esp. by mimicking a voice of misery, and all without good reason (*weinerlich klagen, nörgeln*): to grumble, to moan, to niggle, *AmE a.* to bellyache; *sie hat wegen jedem Posten in der Rechnung geraunzt* she niggled over every item in the bill. – **Raunzer** *m* -s/- *dial.;* Viennese *dial.* also, **Raunzen, Raunzn** *f* -/- grumbler, moaner, niggler, *AmE a.* bellyacher; *if said of a child, a.* whineybird; *wer hätte gedacht, dass der* (or *das*) *so eine Raunzen sein kann?* who would have thought him to be such a niggly moaner? – **Raunzerei** *f* -/-en *dial.* (act[s] of) continual grumbling *or* moaning *or* niggling; *hör auf mit der (ewigen) ~!* cut out all this (wailing and) moaning.

Rauschkugel *f* -/-n *contp.* someone who drinks a lot of alcohol (*Trunkenbold*): *BrE* pisshead, *AmE* boozehound, stiff.

Redaktrice [-s] *f* -/-n *(Redakteurin)* woman editor.

refundieren *v/t (rückvergüten)* to refund, to pay back; *die Portospesen werden Ihnen refundiert* you will be refunded the cost of postage.

Regendach *n* -(e)s/pl. rare: …dächer [here and elsewhere, the native vernacular tongue often prefers a simple and descriptive word or phrase to the learned and foreign-born term used in standard speech] West Austrian *dial.* an umbrella *(Schirm)*: shower-stick.

Reh ...: ~filet *n* -s/-s *cul.* fillet of venison ['venzn]. – **~fleisch** *n* -(e)s *cul.* venison. – **~häutel, ~häutl** *n* -s/- *colloq. (Rehleder [zum Fensterputzen]; Ger.: Fensterleder)* doeskin, chamois ['ʃæmɪ] leather, chamois cloth. – **~ledern** *adj* deer-skin (e.g., gloves). – **~rücken** *m* -s/- *cul.* **1.** a meat of game (*Rehziemer*): saddle of venison. – **2.** a cake: chocolate cake with blanched almonds. – **~schlegel, ~schlögel** *m* -s/- *cul. (Rehkeule)* leg of venison.

Reinanke and **Rheinanke** *f* -/-n [< MHG *rīnanke*] 🐟 = *Renke* ↓.

Rein *f* -/-en [< OHG *rīna*] *dial., cul.* a rather shallow, thick-walled iron container, round or rectangular of shape, used for roasting or frying food in the oven (*größerer, flacher Pfannentopf*): (iron) pan, casserole. – **Reindl** *n* -s/-n [< LateMHG *reindel, reydl;* its elements, however, definitely being *Rein* ↑ + dim. *-l* (with an intrusive *-d-* for natural ease of pronunciation)] *dial.* **1.** *concr.: cul.* small (iron) pan. – **2.** *fig.,* in a humorous *phr.* accompanying, for didactic emphasis, an appropriate clockwise motion of one's forefinger: *so schmiert man das ~ aus!* that's the way to clean the pot! – **~frisur** *f* - *hum.* or *contp.* a primitive haircut effectively brought about (or jeeringly suggesting to have been brought about) by using an inverted soup bowl and trimming around its edges: bowl trim. – **Reindling** *m* -s/-(e) [< *Reindl* ↑ + *-ing,* a suffix of origin (which is also quite common in English) – the compound thus, literally, meaning 'something made in a casserole'] *dial., bak.* a speciality made in Carinthia and in southern Styria all the year round, and frequently offered also as an Easter, or as a godparent's christening, present – a yeast pastry rolled up with raisins, grapes, cinnamon, and other savoury filling (*Germkuchen* [*als Festtagsspeise*]): fancy pancake.

rekommandieren *v/t ([Post] einschreiben lassen)* to register; *einen Brief rekommandiert aufgeben* to send a registered letter, to have a letter registered.

Rẹnke *f* -/-n, and **Rẹnken** *m* -s/- [< LateMHG *renke,* a contraction < *rīnanke*] 🐟 a freshwater fish of the carp family dwelling in Lake Constance (*Bodensee*) and other waters of the Alpine foothills; it has a slim body, its sides and belly are silvery white; and weighing some 300 grams, i.e. about 10–12 ounces, it is highly valued for food (*Felchen*): whitefish; ≃ *IrE* pollan ['pɔlən] (found in Lough Neigh), ≃ *ScotE* powan ['paʊən, 'pəʊən] (found in Loch Lomond and Loch Eck).

Rẹttung *f* -/-en, **Rẹttungswagen** *m* -s/- *med. (Krankenwagen)* ambulance; *wir haben den Verletzten mit der Rettung ins Spital gebracht* we took the injured man to the hospital in an ambulance.

Reuß Matthias *m* - [a playful corruption < *Rheumatismus*] *med. & hum.* rheumatism: screwmatics, rheumatics, rheumatiz.

Ribisel, Ribisl *f* -/-(n) [< Cz *ryviz* < L *ribes*] ✿ *(Johannisbeere)* currant; *rote ~* red currant, *schwarze ~* black currant ‖ *~ brocken* to pick (*or,* to gather) currants; *das Abrebeln der ~(n) ist eine langwierige Arbeit* picking the currants one by one is a laborious task. – **~garten** *m* -s/

…gärten currant field. – **~kompott** *n* -(e)s/-e stewed currants. – **~kuchen** *m* -s/- black- *or* red-currant cake. – **~kultur** *f* -/-en **1.** currant-growing. – **2.** = *Ribis(e)lgarten.* – **~marmelade** *f* -/-n black- *or* red-currant jam. – **~saft** *f* -(e)s/ …säfte black currant juice. – **~staude** *f* -/-n, **~strauch** *m* -(e)s/ …sträuche currant bush. – **~wein** *m* -(e)s/-e black- (*or,* red-)currant wine.

Riegel *m* -s/- *colloq.,* mostly of a burly male only: (*kräftiger Mensch*) he-man; *ein ~ von einem Mann* a big bear of a man; *die Fußballer waren (alle[s]) lauter ~* the football players were all big hunks.

Rinds… [< *Rind n* 'any heifer or cow, bull young or old, or ox'; its equivalent compound element in Germany is *Rinder…*] *cul.* **~braten** *m* -s/- (1) if raw: joint of beef. – (2) if cooked by prolonged exposure to heat: roast beef. – **~filet** *n* -s/-s a beef steak cut from the lower part of a sirloin (*Rinderlende*): fillet *or* filet ['fılıt] of beef, fillet steak. – **~gulasch** *n* -(e)s/-e a meat dish, originally of Hungary, cooked with a hot-tasting pepper (*Rinderhackfleisch*): beef goulash *or* gulash ['gu:læʃ]. – **~knochen** *m* -s/- long bone of beef, containing edible marrow, duly chopped up – a magic ingredient for a tasty soup. – **~leber** *f* -/-n (reddish) liver of beef, to be used for dumplings and soups. – **~lende** *f* -/-n = *Rindsfilet* ↑ – **~roulade** *f* -/-n = *Rindsvögerl* ↓ – **~schmalz** *n* -es/-e butter that has been made clean and pure by heating it (*Butterschmalz*): clarified butter.

Rindsuppe *f* -/-n *cul.* soup consisting of beef cooked in stock, with barley (or other cereals), noodles, vegetables, eggs etc. added (*Fleisch-, Rinderbrühe*): beef broth.

Rinds…: *cul.* **~talg** *m* -(e)s/-e the hard white fat on the kidneys and loins of cattle, used in making foods such as puddings, pastry, and mincemeat: beef suet *or* fat, beef dripping. – **~vögerl** *n* -s/usu. *pl.* -n slices of beef (often from the hind leg [*Schlegel*] of the animal), oiled, ham cut into small squares, bacon, onion, cucumbers, carrots (all sliced), rolled up and tied, then fried and stewed (*Rindsroulade*): stuffed beef roll, roulade of beef, *BrE a.* collared beef. – **~zunge** *f* -/-n ox tongue.

Ringlo *f* -/-(s) *colloq.,* short for next entry. – **Ringlotte** *f* -/-n [a mangled form (through popular etymology, the elements *Ring* and *Lotte*) of F *reine-claude* 'Queen Claudia', so named in honour of the consort of Francis I, King of France (ruling 1515–47)] *hort.* a kind of round plum with greenish-yellow skin and flesh, and a fine, sweet flavour (📖 Prunus insititia var. italica; Ger.: *Reneklode*): greengage, gage.

Risipisi *n* -(s)/-(s) [< It *risi piselli*] *cul.* (a dish of) rice and peas.

röntgenisieren *v/t med.* (*röntgen*) to X-ray, *AmE a.* to roentgenize; *sie muss sich den Fuß ~ lassen* she must have an X-ray taken of her leg; *er ist gerade beim ~* he's being X-rayed at the moment.

Rossknödel *m* or *n* -/s-(n) *colloq.* a ball *or* lump of horse manure (*Pferdeapfel*): alley apple, road apple; *Harry sammelt für seinen Garten ~, die sind prima fürs Düngen* Harry is collecting alley apples for his garden, it's a great fertilizer.

Rostbraten *m* -s/- *cul.* (portion of) rib of beef with roasted onions.

Röster *m* -s/- *cul. (gedünstete Früchte)* stewed fruits, fruit compote.

Rotz... [< *Rotz m* -es – this, and all the rest, low *colloq.* nasal mucus (*Nasenschleim*): snot]: **~bremse** *f* -/-n, *dial.* **~bremsn** *f* -/- *hum.* a moustache: soup-strainer. – **~bub** *m* -en/-en, *dial.* **~bua** *m* -m/-m used in anger about a badly behaved child or young person (*Rotzjunge*): snotty-nosed brat. – **~fetzen** *m* -s/- a handkerchief (*Rotzfahne, -lappen*): nose rag, snot rag. – **~glocke** *f* -/-n, *dial.* **~glockn** *f* -/- a large drop of nasal mucus, protruding from a young child's nostrils (eventually to be released through sheer force of gravity, slithering over the upper lip, or blown away in childish protest by a nasal blast of air): (pendulous) nose ball. – **~löffel** *m* -s/- = *Rotzbub.* – **~nas(l)ert** *adj* [< *Rotznase f* 'snotty nose' + *-(l)ert*, an expanded adj. suffix] *dial.* **1.** *concr.* always with reference to a child who is not very clean – filled or covered with nasal mucus (*rotznäsig*): snotty, snotty-nosed, with a snotty nose. – **2.** *fig.* used as a general term of abuse – (1) said of a young person who is childish and inexperienced: snot-nosed. – (2) said of a snob, or of a letter, showing a superior or conceited attitude: snotty, snot(ty)-nosed. – **~nigl** *m* -s/-(n) [second el., < *Nikolaus* 'Nicholas']; **~pippen**, *dial. spelling* **~pipm** *f* -/- [second el., < It *pippio* 'pert little mouth'] both *dial.* = *Rotzbub* ↑.

Rudolf der Stifter *m* -s des -s *hist.* Rudolph IV, Duke of Austria (1339–65), who richly deserved being honoured with this epithet because of the major architectural projects patronized by him, e.g. the rebuilding of Vienna's St Stephen's Cathedral in the Gothic style and the establishment of Vienna University, Alma Mater Rudolphina, in 1365.

Duke Rudolph IV, surnamed "The Founder"

Rutschepeter *m* -s/- *colloq.* restless child, esp. one impatient of inaction when seated: fidget, *AmE* wriggle-worm; *sitz einmal stad, du alter ~!* sit still (*or,* quit your squirming), you little fidget, will you!

Rutscher *m* -s/- *colloq.* a short trip (*Reise, die nicht lange dauert und leicht durchzuführen ist*): stone's throw, a skip and a jump; *ihr könntet leicht einmal zu uns auf Besuch kommen, mit dem Auto ist es doch nur ein ~* you could easily visit us some time, it's only a minute in the car.

S

Sạchertorte *f* -/-n [named after a pastry-cook who first composed the delicacy in 1832 when employed by Prince Metternich (and later owner of the de luxe Sacher Hotel in the very heart of Vienna, at 4 Augustinerstrasse, right behind the Opera)] *bak.* a world-famous cake made by carefully blending and heating melted chocolate, eggs, butter, fat, sugar, flour, vanilla and salt, a layer of apricot jam in the middle and chocolate icing on top, most often served with a dollop of whipped cream: Sacher chocolate cake, Sacher torte [ˈsʌkəˌtɔ:tə].

S<u>a</u>gschartn [ˈsɔ:gʃa:tn] *f* -/usu. pl.: - [first el., the dial. form of *Säge f* 'saw'; second el., cp. *Scharte* ↓] *dial.* a very thin strip of wood cut from a surface with a sharp steel blade, such as the one operative in a plane (*'Hobel'*): wood shaving; *a Haufn ~ aufm Bodn* a pile of wood shavings on the floor ‖ *fig.* in a piece of abusive speech imputing to somebody utter stupidity: *der hat ja lauter ~ im Hirn!* he's got a head full of sawdust, *AmE a.* he must be sawdust-brained.

S<u>ai</u>bling, less often **Sạlbling** *m* -s/-e [two *dial.* variants of *Sälmling,* a name, of course, easily linked to E *salmon* [ˈsæmən]] 🐟 a trout-like freshwater fish of the family *Salmonidae,* widely valued as a food and game fish (and therefore also known as *Kaiserfisch*): charr *or* char, 🕮 Salvelinus alpinus.

sạkramẹnt *interj.* [a stark perversion into profanity of the noun *Sakrament n* 'sacrament' which, in the R.C. liturgy, stands for one of the seven outward tokens of inward grace ordained by Jesus Christ – Baptism, Confirmation, Holy Eucharist, Penance, Extreme Unction, Holy Order, and Matrimony] an expletive, often unthinkingly capsizing grace into ungodliness, with feelings indeed ranging from violent anger and annoyance to mere amazement: Jesus Christ!, damn!; *~ noch amal, sei (endlich) stad!* for Pete's sake, (do) shut up!

sạkrisch an intensifying *dial. adv* [based on a euphem. shortening of *sakrament* ↑ + *-isch* (< OHG *-isc*)] *emot.* very, to a great degree – (1) in a positive sense: *~ stolz* mighty proud; *dein letztes Buch hat mir ~ gefallen* your latest book pleased me no end; *mir geht's ~ gut* I'm on top of the world. – (2) in a negative sense: *~ teuer* damn expensive; *das tut ~ weh* that hurts like hell; *ihnen geht's ~ schlecht* they're in an awfully bad way.

Sal<u>a</u>thund *m* -(e)s/pl. rare: -e *iron.* or *contp.* a person who prevents others from enjoying something that is useless to himself: dog in the manger.

Salonbeuschel *n* -s/- [see *Beuschel* ↑] *cul.*

(pikantes Gericht aus Kalbslunge und Kalbsherz) lungs and hearts of veal, hashed and highly seasoned.

Sạnd *m* -(e)s/-e <sand> only in the Viennese *dial. phr.* **am ~ (sein)** – **1.** (to be) in great poverty, possibly also having no work and nowhere to live: down-and-out, *BrE a.* on one's uppers. – **2.** (to be) physically exhausted: dragged out, frazzled, jiggered up, *AmE a.* pooped out, feeling like a boiled rag.

sạndeln *v/i* [< MHG *seinelen* 'to flow slowly'] *colloq. (faulenzen)* to laze, to idle, to mess about, to loaf. – **Sạndler** *m* -s/- *colloq.,* often *contp.* **1.** a lazy fellow *(Faulenzer)*: loafer, lazybones. – **2.** *([alter] Landstreicher)* (old) tramp, hobo, bum, drifter. – **3.** *(Taugenichts)* good-for-nothing, scamp: *AmE* deadbeat; *du bist mir ein ~, nicht einmal die Schuhbandeln kannst du dir richtig einfädeln!* you're hopeless, you can't even (manage to) tie your own shoelaces right.

Saumeise *f* -/-n; usu. in dial. form, **Saumaasn** *f* -/- [a fanciful combination of two animal names, jocularly suggesting that a *Meise,* or 'titmouse', though a small and acrobatic ball of a bird, is yet destined to fall prey to a 'piggy' eater] *cul.* a Lower Austrian sausage speciality, many a regional gourmet's delight in new-wine taverns and at wine-cellar festivals – pork, coarsely minced, seasoned, smoked, given a roundish shape to be wrapped up in a piece of the pig's membranous skin or in a stringed net, and thus boiled for some twenty minutes prior to eating: it is served with potatoes and sauerkraut (i.e., chopped pickled cabbage): piggy-in-hammock.

Schale *f* -/-n **1.** a small bowl-shaped container for drinking from, typically having a handle and used with a matching saucer for hot drinks (*Tasse*): cup; *die ~ (da) hat aber einen Sprung* this cup is cracked, mind. – **2.** the contents of such a container: *eine ~ Gold* a cup of yellow-brown coffee.

Schalerl *n* -s/-(n) [dim. of *Schale f* ↑] *colloq.* **1.** little cup; *der Mokka gehört (immer) in ~n serviert* mocha ['mɒka] should (always) be served in demitasse cups. – **2.** *emot.* (1) with reference to its outward appearance: sweet (pretty, cute, *BrE a.* dinky, etc.) little cup. – (2) with reference to its contents: delicious cup o' (*or* cuppa) ['kʌpə] coffee (tea, etc.). – **3.** *phr.* (1) *ich lad' dich auf ein ~ bei uns ein* come and have a spot of coffee with us. – (2) *bei einem ~ Kaffee läßt sich das alles viel gemütlicher besprechen* we may discuss all this at much greater ease over a cup of coffee. – (3) a rhymed couplet both praising the stimulating effect of coffee and the attentiveness of the hostess, who has chosen the right kind of drink:

Ein Schalerl Kaffee
hebt 's Herzerl in d' Höh'!

*Aye coffee's fine sight
Fills my heart with delight.

Schanigarten *m* -s/ …gärten [< *Schani m,* the East Austrian *dial.* form of *Johann* 'John'; frequently used to address the bus-boy, who is often told by the proprietor, *„Schani, trag den Garten aussi!"* 'Johnny, take the garden outside!'] *gastr.* a makeshift garden in front, or in the courtyard, of an eating establishment, with moveable greenery in wooden planters: "Johnny-garden",

"Merry Viennese frothblowers in their 'open-air pub' about 1890", as painted by Hans Schließmann

BrE pavement café, *AmE* sidewalk café; in Spring and Summer the guests sit here, and the bus-boy, who gets the patio ready, gave it his name.

Schar *f* - <crowd> *fig., colloq.,* often *dial.* in a slightly disparaging comment on the mediocre, or at best average, qualities imputed to a person: *ob er irgendwie auffällig ist? er geht halt mit der ~* whether he's outstanding, one way or another? no, just fair to middling, goes with the flow (*or,* swims with the tide).

Scharnierl *n* -s/-(n) [a dim. form of *Scharnier* 'hinge', but actually a pun on *Genie* 'genius'] *hum.* a joking word of praise for someone who managed to complete a minor technical operation, e.g. thread a needle or open a tin: wizard; *na so was! du bist ja ein ~, das hätte ich dir nicht zugetraut!* well, I say! you're a whiz (*or,* ... a brainy one), I wouldn't have credited you with that!

Schạrte *f* -/-n [< MHG *schart(e)* < OHG *scart,* based on *scheren* 'to cut, or clip, esp. with shears'; cp. E dial. *shard* and *sherd* 'notch' 'gap'] ⛰ a narrow saddle between two high peaks, typically affording a pass from one side of a mountain range to another (*schmaler Bergsattel*): defile, wind-gap.

Schaß *m* -es (rare)/-e *dial.,* in Vienna and Carinthia; **Schoaß** *m* -es/-e in most other provinces [< IE verbal root *skheid* 'to separate', 'to cut off'] all *vulg.,* often *contp.* **1.** an excrement, animal or human (*Scheiß* m, and *Scheiße* f): piece of shit, turd; *schnapp' dir eine Schaufel und räum' den ~ weg!* get yourself a shovel and clear up that shit! – **2.** *contp.* a detestable object, a piece of work badly executed, arrant nonsense uttered, indeed anything eliciting strong criticism and scorn (*Käse, Plunder*): crap; *was für an* [*oan*] *~ liest d' 'n da grad?* what's that shit you're reading?; *was du da hastig zusammengeschrieben hast, ist doch ein ~!* my, that's a crappy piece of work you've dashed off; *dein sogenannter Plan ist der reinste ~!* your so-called plan is a load of bullshit; *komm' nur nicht mit dem ~!* don't give me that crap. ~ – **3.** an anal wind (*Furz*): fart ‖ *phr.* (1) *einen (lauten) ~ lassen* to rip off a fart. – (2) a drastic simile criticizing a fidgety person who seems to be always on the move: *du schiaßt umadum wia der ~ in der Latern* (or *in der Hosn*)*!* you're buggering about like a fart in a bottle (*or* in a colander). – (3) a vulgar piece of bathroom humour, scabrous, rhymings brazenly passed off as part of the Proverbs of Solomon, the son of David, King of Israel –

> *Salomon der Weise spricht,*
> *„Laute Schaße stinken nicht.*
> *Doch diese, die mit leisem Zischen*
> *unbemerkt dem Arsch entwischen,*
> *vor solchen Freunden hüte dich,*
> *denn diese stinken fürchterlich!"*

> *Solomon preached things with wit:
> "Thunder farts won't stink one bit.
> But those that waft like zephyr breezes,
> Self-effacing bung-hole wheezes –
> Such fellers, mind, don't judge them wrong,
> They propagate a wicked pong!"

Schaumrolle *f* -/-n *bak.* a puff-pastry roll filled with cream: cream roll, *AmE* cream puff.

Scheibtruhe *f* -/- [first el., < MHG *schiben* 'to roll (along a surface)'; cp. *kegelscheiben* 'to play at skittles or ninepins', 'to bowl' – second el., related to E *trough* 'long, open (usu. shallow) box'] *hort.* a small cart with one wheel at the front, two legs, and two handles at the back for pushing *(Schubkarren)*: wheelbarrow, barrow, *AmE a.* (Irish) buggy, pushmobile.

Scheideblümchen *n* -s/- [first el., a double entendre playing on *Scheide f* 'the female organ discharging urine' and *(ich) scheide* '(I) am leaving (your company) briefly in order to urinate' – note the parallel homophony in English, *(to) pee* 'to urinate' and *(sweet) pea* 'a garden plant with sweet-smelling flowers in pale colours', in German "(Duft-) Wicke"] *hum.* the name of an imaginary little flower 'planted' by a squeamishly bashful female among a set of words explaining to her hiking companion, or companions, that she feels the urge to slip away behind a tree in order to urinate: *ich muss* or *ich geh' (jetzt einmal kurz) ~ streuen* I'm off (now for a minute) to do *or* plant a sweet pea.

Scheiterhaufen *m* -s/- *cul.* soufflé of white bread, sliced apples, and raisins.

Schematismus *m* -/ …ismen *admin.* *(Rangliste für öffentlich Bedienstete)* ranking list; *Beamten*~ roll of personnel.

Schemenlaufen *n* -s *folklore* at Imst, one of the most splendid and renowned Alpine carnivals, held every three or four years on a Sunday: "Phantom Procession", a lively pageant of masked figures, with elaborate headgear and bells of different sizes; some of them symbolize Winter and Spring, others represent old local trades, and still others pillory the follies that have been committed since last year's procession.

Schenk *m* -s [actually, a proper name,

short for *Mundschenk* 'cupbearer'; but here used as a pun on the imperative form of *schenken* 'to give (as a present)'] a fictitious name used in a verbal rejection of a request to get something for nothing: *der ~ ist gestorben!* *Mr Want-Something-for-Nothing is dead!, nothing's for free anymore.

Schęrnken *m* -s/usu. pl.: – ⩕ one of a set of reinforcing iron clamps on either side of the sole of a climbing boot (*Flügelnagel*): cleat; *ein Bergschuh mit ~* a cleated mountaineering boot.

schę(t)zko jędno *pred. adj* [< Cz *všecko jedno* 'makes no difference to me'] *colloq.* immaterial *(unwesentlich)*: all the same, one and the same, six of one and half a dozen of the other; *ob lila oder violett, das ist doch ~!* whether purple or violet, what's the odds (*AmE* … what's the dif[f])?

Schi, Ski [ʃi:] *m* -s/-er *or - sports* ski [ski:], *pl. colloq. a.* boards, woods. – **1.** *phr.* *~ fahren, ~ laufen* to ski (*pret.* skied *or* ski'd), *~ fahren können* to know (*or* to be able) to ski; *~ springen* to go in for ski jumping; *die ~(er) anschnallen* to put on (*or* buckle on) the skis; *auf ~(ern) wandern* to hike on skis; *einen Gipfel mit ~(ern) besteigen* to climb a peak on skis; *eine Besteigung mit ~(ern)* a ski ascent, an ascent on skis. – **2.** *cpds.* (1) as a second element – *Holz≗* wooden ski, *Metall≗* metal ski; *Berg≗* top ski, upper ski, *Tal≗* lower ski; *Innen≗* inside ski, *Außen≗* outside ski. – (2) as a first element – **~abfahrt** *f* ski run. – **~anzug** *m* ski(ing) suit, ski dress; *einteiliger Kinder≗* snowsuit. – **~ausrüstung** *f* ski outfit *or* equipment. – **~berg** *m* mountain [hill] where the slopes are ideal for skiing (on), ideal mountain [hill] for skiing on. – **~beutel** *m* a small, but very convenient, form of rucksack built into a belt and worn round the waist: bumbag. – **~bindung** *f* ski binding. – **~bluse** *f* ski blouse, anorak. – **~bob** *m* ski bob. – **~bobfahrer** *m* ski bobber. – **~bruchversicherung** *f* ski-breakage insurance. – **~dorf** *n* ski resort, *BrE* skiing centre, *AmE* ski center. – **~durchquerung** *f* ski traverse. – **~ende** *n* heel of the [a] ski (opp.: *~spitze* ↓). – **~fahren** *n* = *~laufen*. – **~fahrer(in** *f*) *m* skier (*AmE a.* skiier), ski-runner. – **~fanatiker** *m,* **~fex** *m* a person so enthusiastic about skiing that he devotes most of his leisure to it: ski fan, skiing enthusiast *or* devotee, *AmE a.* ski bum. – **~fäustling** *m* ski glove, gauntlet. – **~fliegen** *n,* **~flug** *m* **1.** ski flying. – **2.** ski-flying competition. – **~flieger** *m* ski flyer. – **~flugschanze** *f* ski-flying hill. – **~führung** *f* ski position. – **~gebiet** *n* ski(-resort) area, skiing region. – **~gelände** *n* skiing terrain, skiing grounds *pl.; ein leichtes ~* easy (ski) slopes. – **~gymnasium** *n* -s; preferred spelling, in this case, **Skigymnasium** *n* -s *educ. & sports, colloq.* at Stams, in the Upper Inn Valley, Tyrol, since the 1967–68 school year – a special type of rural arts grammar school offering, throughout winter, a de-emphasized but nevertheless full range of academic subjects plus specialist skiing expertise, and balancing the offerings out through added classroom work in spring and summer (*Aufbaurealgymnasium für Schisportler*): *BrE* skiers' rural science grammar school, *AmE* skiers' rural science high school. – **~halter** *m* -s/- *tech.* ski rack (on a car roof). – **~haserl**

The Schemenlauf *of Imst is well-known for jangling and mirroring the ugly winter spirits away*

n -s/-(n) *colloq.* **1.** *hum.* a novice on skis: ski bunny. – **2.** *erot.* a girl who frequents the ski slopes as much for the sex as for the sport: snow bunny. – **~haxen** *m* -s *med. hum.* plaster-cast leg (as a grim reminder of having had a skiing accident); *~doktor m* -s a medical practitioner, in winter sports centres like Kitzbühel and St. Anton, specializing in attending on victims of skiing slopes: skiers' plastercast merchant. – **~hose** *f garm.* ski(ing) trousers *pl., AmE* ski pants *pl.* (*sometimes construed as sg.: die ~ da ist mir zu eng* this ski pants is too tight for me). – **~hütte** *f archit.* a mountain hut, often privately owned by ski clubs or youth clubs, used during the skiing season: skiing hut, ski lodge. – **~kanone** *f colloq.,* often *hum.* skiing ace, (crack *or* top-notch) wizard on skis,

Ever since the early 1920s, St. Anton has had "the finest advanced ski courses in Austria" (Gedye)

skier. – **~kindergarten** *m* -s/... gärten ski nursery. – **~kjöring** *n,* more often **Skikjöring** [ʃi:jørɪŋ] *n* a winter sport in which a person wearing skis is drawn over snow or ice, usu. by a horse: skijoring, skiöring. – **~klub** *m* skiing club. – **~könig** *m colloq.* an expert skier who has won many races or jumping competitions: ski champ. – **~kurs** *m* ski(ing) course. – **~langlauf** *m* cross-country skiing. – **~langläufer(in** *f*) *m* cross-country skier (*AmE a.* skiier). – **~lauf** *m,* **~laufen** *n* skiing; *die Technik des ~s* the ski technique; *der Schilauf als Kampfsport* competitive skiing. – **~läufer** *m = ~fahrer* ↑. – **~lehrer** *m* ski instructor *or* teacher. – **~lehrgang** *m = ~kurs* ↑. – **~lift** *m tech.* normally operating in winter only: **1.** ski-tow. – **2.** chair-lift. – **~meisterschaft** *f* often *pl.* -en ski championship: *Alpine [Nordische] ~en* Alpine [Nordic] ski championships. – **~ort** *m = ~sportplatz* ↓. – **~paradies** *n colloq.* skiers' paradise, paradise of skiers. – **~piste** *f* an area of land on which skiers disport themselves and, in particular, race downhill: course, piste ‖ *interj.* a warning shout not to obstruct a skier's dashing approach: *aus der Piste!* gangway! – **~rennen** *n* **1.** competitive skiing, ski racing (cp. *Schilauf* ↑). – **2.** ski race, skiing competition *or* event. – **~rennfahrer(in** *f*) *m* ski racer. – **~schanze** *f,* or **Sprungschanze** *f* ski-jump hill (cp. *Schiflugschanze* ↑). – **~schaukel** *f* in a skiing centre – a network of cableways and ski lifts, enabling enthusiasts to enjoy their downhill skiing without having to do much, or indeed any, climbing in between: (skiers') swingways seesaw; *die ~ von Flachau-Wagrain hat wegen ihrer hervorragenden Pisten in schneesicherer Lage einen guten Ruf* the swingways seesaw between Flachau and Wagrain is well-known for its excellent pistes, with good snow conditions guaranteed. – **~schuh(e)** *m,* mostly *pl.* ski boots. – **~schule** *f* ski(ing) school. – **~schwung** *m* turn (on skis). – **~spitze** *f* ski tip (opp.: *~ende* ↑). – **~sport** *m* skiing; *den ~ [richtig] ausüben* to go in for [to be actively engaged in] skiing (cp. *Schilaufen* ↑). – **≗sportbegeistert** *adj* enthusiastic about skiing, *colloq.* ski-happy. – **~sportler(in** *f*) *m* hearty *or* full-blooded skier (cp. *Schiläufer* ↑). – **~sportplatz** *m* ski(ing) centre (*AmE* center), ski resort, *AmE a.* ski town, snow town. – **~springen** *n* **1.** ski jumping. – **2.** ski-jumping competition. – **~springer** *m* ski-jumper. – **~sprung** *m* ski jump. – **~spur** *f* ski tracks *pl.,* ski trail. – **~stecken** *m,* **~stock** *m* ski stick, ski pole. – **~tour** *f* ski tour, ski trip. – **~urlaub** *m* skiing holiday. – **~urlauber(in** *f*) *m* holiday skier. – **~verhältnisse** *n pl.* skiing conditions. – **~wachs** *n* ski wax. – **~wanderer** *m,* **~wanderin** *f* ski tourer. – **~wandern** *n* cross-country skiing, ski-hiking; *alpines ~* ski-touring in the mountains. – **~wanderung** *f* ski tour, ski-hike. – **~wasser** *n* in mountain hotels and shelter huts – a specific non-alcoholic drink served as a refreshment to skiers (*Himbeersaft mit Zitronenlimonade*): (a glass of) raspberry lemonade. – **~weltmeisterschaft** *f* world ski championship (competition). – **~wiese** *f* practice slope (for beginners or less experienced skiers). – **~zirkus** *m* **1.** = *Schischaukel* ↑. – **2.** *colloq.* a skiing competition in which many well-known, often professional, racers are taking part: reunion of crack skiers; *ein internationaler ~* a meet of skiing aces (*or,* of the racing élite) from many countries. – **3.** *colloq.* the period of international skiing competitions (*Rennsaison*): racing season; *für die Herren eröffnet der internationale ~ am 5. Jänner in Badgastein* on an international level, the racing season for men will start on 5 January at Badgastein.

schieberisch *adv* [an enlivening variant of *schief adj* 'not straight', 'lopsided', 'tilted' < *Schieber* or *Schuber m* 'movable element' and, as *Schubser m* 'shove', 'push', 'energetic motion (that unbalances what has so far stood straight up)' + *-isch* 'a suffix converting nouns into adjectives or adverbs'] *colloq.* at a slant, slantingly – esp. said of a hat, or another headgear, worn by a person who wishes to give himself or herself a jaunty, dashing appearance: *den Hut ~ tragen* or *(auf)haben* to wear one's hat (*etc.*) at a rakish angle.

schiech; more often, in *dial.* pronunciation and spelling, **schiach** [< MHG *schiech* (which also happens to be the basis for NHG *scheu* 'shy')] *dial.* **1.** ugly (*hässlich*): plain, *AmE a.* homely ‖ *phr.* an undisguised vote of censure on a person's features and figure: *~ wie die Nacht* (as) ugly as sin. – **2.** angry (*zornig*): mad, hot under the collar, *BrE a.* shirty; *was bist d' denn heut' so ~?* what (is it that) makes you that mad today?

Schịlcher *m* -s [< *schilchen v/i,* a dialect variant of *schillern v/i* which, in its turn, is an intensive form of *schielen v/i* 'to squint', with 'to sparkle in several tints' for a secondary meaning] *vinic.* orig. a wine blended of white and red grapes *(Schillerwein),* but now grown from a special Austrian grape (known as 'Blauer Wildbacher') indigenous to Western Styria only and producing one of the best and most idiosyncratic rosé wines, "The National Wine of Styrians", "The Mother's Milk of West Styrians" – dry, of a high acidity, very tasty; its colour varying from onion hue and candy pink to light red; and when drunk still new, the nose will inhale the freshness of grass and wood-strawberries, and the palate delight in the taste of peppers and citrus fruit: West Styrian rosé.

Schịll *m* -(e)s/-e 🐟 = *Fogosch* ↑.

Schịnkenfleckerl *n* -s/usu. pl.: -n *cul.* a popular Austrian dish *(Schinkennudeln)*: noodles with diced ham.

Schlatz *m* -es/-e low *colloq.* a mucous build-up which is brought up from the lungs and then spat out *(Schleim)*: gob (of spit), *AmE sl.* loogie. – **schlatzen** *v/i* to spit up a clot of mucus from the throat: *AmE sl.* to hawk (*or,* hork, spit) a loogie.

Schlaucherl *n* -s/-n [dim. of *schlau* 'smart, cunning'] *colloq.,* always used appreciatively or in good-natured acquiescence – shrewd person *(Schlaumeier)*: artful dodger, sly-boots *sg., AmE a.* smart cookie, shrewdy, shrewd dude.

schlegeln *v/i* [< *Schlegel m -s/-* 'something which beats'] √ *(buttern)* to make butter, to churn.

Schleich *m* -s [short for *Schleichhandel* 'illicit trade'] *colloq.* black market; *der ~ blüht* there's a boom on the black market; *im ~* on the black market: on the black, under the counter; *Karten für die heurigen Festspiele sollen nur mehr im ~ zu bekommen sein* people say you can only get tickets for this year's Festival through the backstairs way (*or,* from scalpers).

Schlịngerl *n* -s/-(n) [an overlap blend of *Schlinge f* 'loop' + dim. *-erl*] *colloq.* a small strip of material – taffeta, twill, cord, or also intertwined threads – used for suspending a piece of clothing, a towel, or a drying-up cloth (*Aufhänger*): tab, loop, hanger; *mir ist da am Nachthemd das ~ abgerissen; könntest du mir's mal bitte annähen?* look, the tab on my nightshirt has come off; could you sew it on for me, please?

Schlụckerl *n* -s/-(n) [< *Schluck m* 'mouthful (of a drink)' + dim. *-erl*] a small, but definitely welcome, swallow of a drink (*Schlückchen*): drop, *ScotE* drappie, *AmE* drinkypoo; *zu einem ~ Obstler würde ich nicht nein sagen* I wouldn't say no to a sip (*or* spot, *or NorBrE* sippie [*ScotE a.* a wee dram]), of fruit gin.

schlụpfen *v/i dial.* to move quickly, smoothly, or secretly (*schlüpfen*): to slip; *geh schlupf amal in den Mantel, und schaun ma, wie er passt* go (and) slip into that coat, and let's see how it fits. – **Schlụpferl** *n* -s/-(n) [< the stem of *schlupfen* ↑ + dim. *-erl*] *dial.* a short and narrow piece of corded cloth, taffeta, etc., or a very small and short chain, for hanging a piece of clothing, a towel, a dish-cloth, etc. up by (*Schlaufe, Aufhänger*): loop, tab.

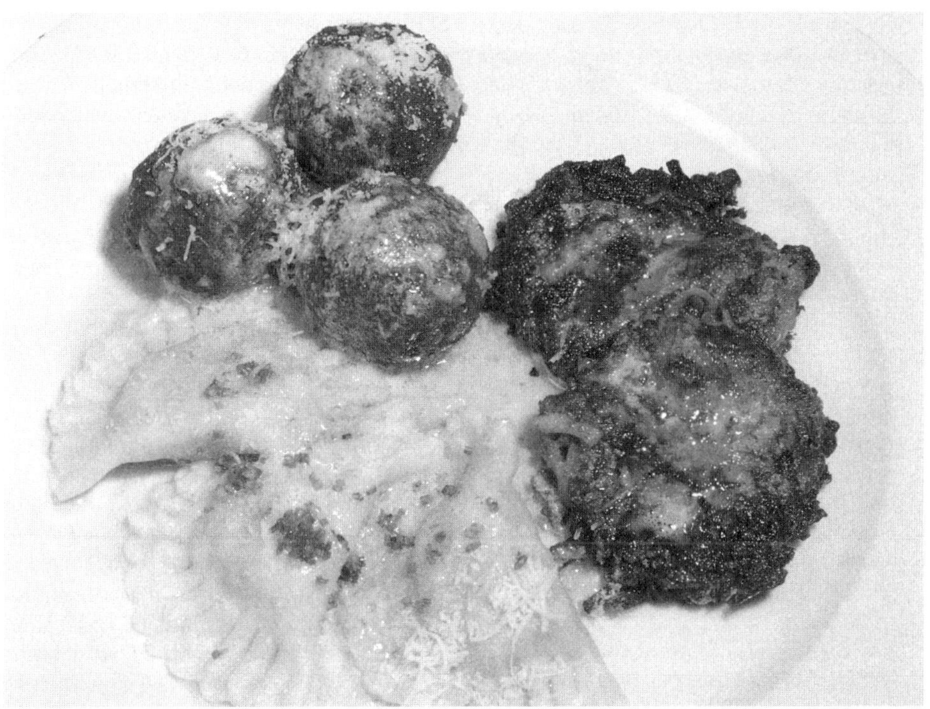

Cottage-cheese crescents, spinach dumplings, irregular-shaped (spoon-scooped) cheese dumplings – a Tyrolean threesome of gourmet delight to sink one's mind, and then of course one's teeth, into

Schlụ̈pferl *n* -s/-n [< the stem of *schlüpfen,* the StG form of *schlupfen* ↑ + *dim. -erl*] a small amount of a strong alcoholic drink: tot, sip; jigger; *jetzt wär' mir ein ~ Rum grad recht* I could do with a tot of rum now.

Schlụrf *m* -(e)s/-e [< *schlurfen v/i* 'to shuffle', 'to slouch', i.e. to walk with one's feet hardly off the ground, shoulders bent forward, giving the impression of being really and truly tired and lazy] *colloq.,* usu. *contp.; obsolescent* **1.** a male not in regular employment but who makes money by dubious business methods and who goes about smartly dressed having a good time *(Geck)*: spiv. – **2.** a young hooligan *(Halbstarker)*: *BrE* teddy boy, *AmE* dead-end kid. – **~rakete** *f -/-n sl.* a light motorcycle: iron horse, *AmE a.* gas bronco.

Schlụtzkrapfen, also **Schlịpfkrapfen** *m* -s/usu. pl.: - *cul.* a Tyrolean main dish, to be eaten with green salad: dough-and-egg crescents, filled with cottage cheese, finely chopped spinach, grated Emmental cheese (plus nutmeg, salt, and pepper to taste), and boiled in salt water.

Schmä̱h, rarely **Schme̱h** *m* -s/-(s) [of doubtful etymology, probably a coalescence in ModG of (1) MHG *smæhe* 'abusive speech', 'vilification' < OHG *smāhi* 'shame', 'disgrace', and (2) thieves' cant *Schmee* 'lie' < Yiddish *schemá* 'something (over)heard', 'rumour', 'gossip'] *colloq.*, esp. in Eastern Austria **1.** newsy conversation: ~ *führen* to sit around and talk pleasantries (*AmE* ... and shoot the breeze); *der Neusiedler Museumsdirektor Eidler genießt es, mit seinen Gästen in der wundersamen Welt zu sitzen, ein wenig "~" zu führen und ihnen ein Glas guten burgenländischen Wein zu kredenzen* Herr Eidler, the head of the Neusiedl Museum, enjoys sitting with his guests and treating them to a glass of fine Burgenland wine while gently embroidering the facts from the world of wonderment around them ‖ typical of a model company in which the participants are never at a loss for a topic: *der ~ rennt [rannte]* (1) said without guile: we are [were] having a lively chitchat; (2) said more coarsely: our gums (*or* jaws) are [were] flapping. – **2.** the quality, seemingly innate in an Austrian, of pleasant persuasion, yet without ulterior motive: *einen natürlichen ~ führen* to have the natural je-ne-sais-quoi; *der ~ des Regisseurs rennt trotz aller Konzentration, und seine Schauspieler bleiben drum auch immer bei guter Laune* the director keeps the ball rolling, in spite of all the stress, so his actors always remain in good spirits. – **3.** the act of suave persuasion: smooth talk, soft soap; said of one engaged in (obvious) flattery: *er führt einen (gesunden) ~* he's a (real) butter-upper; *sie hat ihn mit ihrem ~ dazu überredet* (or, *dazu gebracht*), *ihr zu helfen* she soft-soaped him into helping her; a piece of advice offered by a German travel guide: *nehmen Sie den österreichischen Polizisten mit ein bisschen "~" und Schmeichelei* handle the Austrian policeman with a bit of smooth talk and flattery. ‖ *Wiener ~* (the easy way of) "Vienna talk", a local manner of speaking and acting, with many a well-turned compliment being duly paid to the ladies – never quite serious, and often deliberately done in a roundabout way to achieve things. – **4.** a verbal or diplomatic prank *(Scherz, den man sich mit anderen erlaubt)*: joke, tease; *j-n am ~ halten* to pull sb.'s leg, *AmE a.* to kid sb.; *das war ein guter Scherz von Ihnen, aber ich lasse mich nicht so leicht am ~ halten* that was a good joke of yours, but I am not so easily had (*or* taken in); *ohne ~!* no joke!, no kidding!; on the adolescent level, also: for reals!, honest Injun!; *war der Attentatsversuch, von dem die zypriotische Regierung so viel Wasser gemacht hat, nur ein "~"?* was the assassination attempt the Cypriot government made such a fuss over just a hoax? – **5.** *(Ausrede)* excuse; *er hat immer einen ~ parat* (or *auf Lager*) he always has an excuse ready, he's always got a ready excuse (*or* a good fib) on hand (*or* upon stock); *mit deinen ~s kannst du bei andern hausieren gehen, nicht bei mir!* you can take your sales pitch to someone else because I don't buy it. – **6.** *([kleine] Lüge, Gefasel)* untrue statement, esp. about something unimportant: fib; ~ [pl.] *reißen* or *verzapfen* to tell fibs; *reiss (mir) keinen ~!* don't (you) fib!, *AmE* quit fibbing (, I tell you)!; *das ist kein ~!* that's no lie, I'm telling it like it is. – **7.** *(Lüge)* lie; *der ~ ist leicht zu durchschauen* I (*or* anybody) can see right through that (lie); *ein aufgelegter ~* a boldfaced (*or* flat-out, *or* down-and-out) lie, *mit dem brauchst d' mir nicht (zu) kommen!* you can't pull that (*or,* put that one over) on me!; *mach keine ~!* (1) an exhortation: don't make up any stories!, don't give me that!, don't feed me any (of your) lines!, (2) an expression of slight surprise, sometimes mingled with amused disbelief: you don't say (so)!, *AmE* no way. – **8.** *(Schwindel[manöver], Kniff)* trick; *ein gesunder ~* a smart (*or* successful) trick: a good racket; *j-n mit ~ übernehmen* to pull the wool over sb.'s eyes; *es sind mir schon andere mit diesem ~ gekommen* others have tried to pull the same gag on me, I've seen others try that line (*or,* come-on, *or* con-game) on me; *er ist auf meinen ~ voll reingefallen* he bought my story hook, line, and sinker; *auf so einen ~ fall ich dir nicht rein!* I'm not about to fall for that one! – **9.** *(Betrug)* deception; *j-n am ~ halten* to mystify sb.: to fool (*or* con) sb.; *ihn kannst du nicht am ~ halten* mind you, he's nobody's fool; *mit dem ~, er könne ihr bei der Gemeinde Wien eine Wohnung verschaffen, lockte der Gauner einer Bekannten fast alle ihre Ersparnisse heraus* with a con-game (*or* line, spiel, fairy story) that he could get her a council flat (*AmE* an apartment) from the Vienna municipal authorities, the swindler managed to cheat (*or* talk) a female acquaintance out of nearly all her savings. – **10.** *sports,* esp. in football *(Körpertäuschung)* a quick movement, or succession of movements, with one's body or legs, to shake off an opponent: trick, feint (→ *Fersen≈*); *er hat den Mittelfeldspieler mit einem ~ stehengelassen und ist mit dem Ball unaufhaltsam in Richtung gegnerisches Tor davon* he cleverly tricked the halfback with a fake and sprinted all out towards the opponents' goal.

Schmäh… *colloq.:* **~berger** *pl., m -s/-* rare = *Schmähtandler.* – **~dutteln** *f pl., vulg.* artificial breasts: fake titties, inflate-a-boobs *pl.* – **~führen** *n* -s art of unobtrusive persuasion: knack of conning people; *der Engländer ist in Wien zur Schule gegangen, hat dort viele Freunde gehabt und kennt sich im echten Wiener ~ aus* this Englishman attended school in Vienna, had many friends there, and can express himself with the smooth Viennese charm. – **~führer** *m* -s/- **1.** one who innately flatters: charmer; *das ist dir ein ~!* there's a charmer for you! – **2.** one engaged in suave persuasion: smooth talker, soft-soaper. – **3.** = *Schmähtandler,* 3. – **≈halber** *adv (scherz[hafter]weise)* on *or* for a whim, for kicks; *ich habe ~ vorgeschlagen, dass wir morgen die Schule schwänzen* just for kicks, I suggested to him that we skip (*or* ditch) school tomorrow. – **~huber** *m* -s/- rare = *Schmähtandler.* – **≈ohne** *adv* a humorous inversion, on the analogy of *zweifelsohne* and foreshortened phrases like *kopfüber, Land unter,* and *Tee mit,* of the phrase *ohne Schmäh* mentioned under *Schmäh,* 4. – **~reissen** *n* -s fibbing; *hör auf mit deinem* (or *dem*) *~!* stop fibbing!, *AmE* cut the bull! – **~reisser** *m* -s/- = *Schmähtandler.* – **≈stad** [-ʃtaːd] *adj* [second el. < MHG *staete* 'standing still', 'immobile'] (temporarily) at a loss for a proper reply (excuse, etc.): tongue-tied, *BrE a.* stymied for words or deeds; *da ist er ausnahmsweise einmal ~ gewesen* what-d'ya-know, his excuse machine broke down for once; look, he's been struck dumb; *ich bin jetzt ~* I've played my last card (*or* trump card, *or* trick), *Southern AmE* I'm losing my religion. – **~tandler** *m* -s/- [second el., 'second-hand dealer (of junk and old clothes)'] **1.** *(Possenreisser)* comedian: prankster, *AmE* great kidder, crack-up, joker, card, trickster. – **2.** *([charmanter] Lügner)* fibber, teller of tales. – **3.** *(Angeber, Wichtigtuer)* one who likes to talk to impress people: big talker; *du ~!* you're just a big talker; you just talk big!; *er ist ein ~* he's laying it on thick, he's laying it on with a shovel (*BrE a.* with a trowel). – **~tandlerei** *f* -/-en **1.** *(Possenreisserei)* playing pranks. – **2.** *([charmantes] Lügen)* fibbing. – **3.** pompousness *(Wichtigtuerei)*: *BrE* chucking one's weight about, *AmE* throwing one's weight around.

Schmạrrn, less often **Schmạrren** *m* -s/pl. rare: – *colloq.* [< ? EarlyModHG *schmerr* <MLowG *smarre* 'slash wound', 'cut'; or < MHG *smer* < OHG *smero* 'fat' (cp. Early ModE *smear* 'fat, oily substance' < OE *smeoru, smeru* 'fat', 'grease')] **1.** *cul.* a simple dish originally made in a pan from a mixture of flour, semolina or bread (curds or forest berries, sugar or cinnamon being later additions); today the dough consists of flour, milk, eggs, salt, and sugar, all fried in hot fat and duly chopped up into irregular lumps with a small iron shovel *(fett gebackene Mehlspeise)*: (dessert of) hot, torn-up pancake, scrambled pancake ‖ the variety of gustatory refinements, and hence of titular dubbings, is great, from *Apfel*~↑ to *Kaiser*~↑, and beyond. – **2.** *fig., colloq.,* often *contp. (Geringfügigkeit)* pittance; *sie kriegt, wo sie jetzt ist, einen ~ bezahlt* she gets paid a (mere) pittance in her present job; *ja, hör einmal, Schatzerl, musst du denn dein Naserl in jeden ~ neinstecken?* now listen, sweetie(pie), do you have to be poking your nose into every abbreviated piece of nothing? – **3.** *fig., colloq.,* often *contp. (wertloses Zeug)* something worthless; *das Essen ist ein ~* the food's not worth eating; *die Uhr ist einen (großen) ~ wert* the watch isn't worth a (damn) thing; *IrE* … worth a cuckoo-spit; *ich bin zu alt für so einen neumodischen ~* I'm too old for such newfangled trash. – **4.** *fig., colloq.,* often *contp. ([verbaler] Unsinn)*: nonsense: hot air, rubbish, twaddle, *AmE a.* hokum; *einen ~ zusammenreden* to be talking through one's hat; *red nicht so einen ~ daher! BrE* don't talk such rot!; *so ein ~!* get away with you!, (and) don't be silly!; *das ist doch ein (ganz großer) ~!* oh, this is just (a load of) rubbish!; *Ehrenwort, ohne ~!* on my honour, cross my heart (and hope to die)!, honest Injun! – **5.** *fig., colloq.* a rudely emphatic way of expressing negation: (1) *einen ~ macht er sich draus!* a fat lot he cares! – (2) *einen ~ hat sie ihm verziehen!* like hell she forgave him! – (3) *das geht dich einen (großen) ~ an!* this is none of your (*BrE* bloody, *AmE* goddamn) business! – (4) an energetic, yet at the same time rather mildly worded refusal to do something (, preceded by the rhetorical question, *ich soll das machen?)*: *einen ~*

werde ich das! I will – on never-never day, *BrE a.* I will – like billy-oh.

Schmạttes *m* - [< Yiddish *smartut* 'rag', esp. 'any outsize banknote in circulation during the years of inflation after the First World War] *colloq. (Trinkgeld)* tip (for service); *wieviel ~ soll ich dem Taxler geben?* how much should I tip the cabbie?

Schmiedl *m* -s/- [< its use as a proper name, a common South German diminutive form of *Schmied* 'Smith'] in the *colloq.* phrase expressing the advisability to go to the person in authority rather than to the one who is less qualified, or less informed: *lieber zum Schmied gehen als zum ~ (sich gleich an die richtige Stelle wenden)* go straight to the top (*or,* deal direct with the top dog) rather than deal with a middleman, get it straight from the horse's mouth; *BrE a.* talk to the organ-grinder, not to the monkey.

Schmierage [–ˈɑːʒ, in sense 1 often –ˈɑːʃ] *f* -/-n [a German-French hybrid, with the suffix representing (O)F *-age,* similarly pronounced in the English words *barrage, entourage,* and *sabotage*] **1.** handwriting that is hard to read: scrawl, scribble; *so eine ~ von ihm lesen zu müssen ist eine Zumutung!* who does he think he is, asking me to decipher this chicken scratch? – **2.** a badly painted picture: smearage; *die ~ könnte von meinem Hund stammen* my dog could have painted that garbage. – **3.** *hum.* make-up: goop, guck, goo; *wenn es regnet und die ~ in ihrem Gesicht kommt in Bewegung, dann gibt's eine richtige Mure* if it rains, and all that goop comes off her face, there'll be a mudslide.

Schmụck ...: ~kasterl *n* -s/-(n) *colloq. fig.* any object or layout one may be proud of, e.g. a picturesque house or a beautiful garden: gem, jewel. – **~schatulle** *f* -/-n (*Schmuckkästchen*) jewel-case, casket.

Schnạpsen *n,* or **„66"**: a popular game of cards resembling bezique (G *Bézigue*); the chief points of difference are that no groups but marriages can be declared, that each card counts a specific number in favour of the player who takes it, and that 66 scores one point towards game: sixty-six.

Schnauf *m* -s *colloq. (Atem)* breath. – **~pause** *f* -/-n *colloq. (Verschnaufpause)* a short pause for a rest: breather; *wir haben jetzt schon lang genug gearbeitet; alsdann wäre eine ~ fällig* we've been working quite a long time now: let's have (*or* take) a breather.

Schnee *m* -s [actually, 'snow'] *colloq. phr. aus dem Jahre ~* very old: as old as the hills; *ein Auto aus dem Jahre ~* a car from way back when, a car from the Dark Ages; *ich weiss das nicht mehr, das war ja im Jahre* (or, *das war ja anno*) ~ I can't remember anymore, that was way back in the year One.

Schnẹllsiede(r)... *comb.* (lit., 'instant-boiler') *colloq.:* **~kurs** *m* -es/-e crash course, quickie course (of instruction), lasting much less than the usual time provided for the same subject-matter. – **~verfahren** *n* -s/- pressure-cooker method; *ist es aber richtig, eine so wichtige Entscheidung im ~ zu treffen?* but is it the proper thing to rush such an important decision?

Schnịtzel *n* -s/- [dim. of *Schnitz* (< MHG *sniz*) 'cut', 'cut-off piece'] *cul.* a prime piece of meat to be fried: cutlet, *AmE a.*

schnitzel ‖ *Natur~* "schnitzel nature" [na'ty:r], plain schnitzel; *BrE* veal steak (*or* escalope of veal) fried in butter, fried veal cutlet; *Pariser* ~ veal cutlet covered with flour and egg and fried in butter; *Pilz~* vegetarian cutlet made with mushrooms, carrots and peas; *Rinds~* fried beef cutlet; *Schweins~* fried pork cutlet, a thin slice of pork, dipped in flour, egg and breadcrumbs, and fried in fat, fried breaded escalope of pork; *Wiener* ~ breaded veal cutlet, breaded escalope of veal, a thin slice of veal dipped in flour, egg and breadcrumbs, and fried in fat.

Schnoferl *n* -s/- [< *schnofeln,* an ablaut formation based on *schnaufen v/i* 'to breathe heavily', 'to wheeze' + dim. *-erl*: 'to distort one's face when sniffling, but also when showing one's mild disgust or reluctance to comply with an imposition'] *colloq.* a facial expression, with the lips pushed out, or one or both lips signalling disappointment and consequent sulkiness *(beleidigtes Gesicht)*: degraded facial expression: pout, sulk; *ein ~ machen* or *ziehen* to pout, to make *or* pull a face; *mit einem ~ herumgehen* or *herumsteigen* or *herumrennen* to be in the pouts *or* sulks; *wir träumen von einer Sekretärin, die uns aus der Kantine ein Sandwich holt, ohne ein ~ zu machen* we are dreaming of a secretary who will get us a canapé from the cafeteria without making a face.

Schnürl *n* -s/-(n) [dim. of *Schnur* 'length of twine'] *colloq. (Schnürchen)* **1.** (little) piece of string; *hast du ein ~ für mich?* have you got some string to spare? – **2.** *fig. jemanden am ~ haben* to have someone tied around one's little finger (*or,* … tied on the end of a string); *sie hat das ~ in der Hand, nach dem alle tanzen müssen* she pulls the strings, and everyone dances; *es muss halt alles nach deinem ~ gehen* everyone has to dance to your tune, everything has to suit your fancy; *etwas wie am ~ können* to have something at one's fingertips; *das geht wie am ~* it goes like clockwork; *das ist wie am ~ gegangen* it all ran smoothly without any snags.

Schnürl …: ~regen *m* -s, often *Salzburger* ~ ☼ "string rain", a steady drizzle typical of the Salzburg area; *schau dir nur den ~ an!* now there's a curtain of rain for you! – **~samt** *m* -(e)s *(Kordsamt)* corduroy, ribbed velvet; *dünner* ~ needlecord velvet; *~hose f -/-n (Kordhose)* corduroys, corduroy trousers (*AmE* … pants), *colloq.* cords.

schnürln *v/i colloq.* to rain in a straight, vertical downpour: *BrE* to rain stair-rods.

Schnürriemen *m* -s/- *(Schuhriemen)* shoelace, bootlace, *AmE a.* shoestring.

Schönbrunnergelb *n* -(e)s [*Schönbrunn,* the first compound el., originally only denoted (and still does today) a certain fountain in an extensive Imperial park on the western outskirts of Vienna where a splendid summer palace, almost purely Italian in style, was erected in the time of Empress Maria Theresa] *arts.* the attractive shade of yelloq adorning the whole building of Schönbrunn Palace – as well as other residences of the Hapsburg family, and since 1918 now also many administrative buildings of the State of Austria: Schönbrunn, *or* Maria Theresa, yellow.

Schopfbraten *m* -s/- *cul. (Schweinenacken)* neck of pork, best end of neck.

Schotten *m* -s *cul. (Topfen, Quark)* **1.**

curd(s). – **2.** cottage (*or* curd) cheese. – **Schọttsuppe** *f* - *cul.* *(Stoßsuppe)* whey soup, thickened by adding flour.

Schubertiade *f* -/-n [< Franz *Schubert,* 1797–1828, the famous Viennese composer + modern suffix *-iade,* derived from *Olympiade,* to denote a competition] ♪ Franz Schubert Soiree, a social evening of Schubcrt songs; thc gcnrc was started by the opera singer Johann Michael Vogl, accompanied by Schubert himself on the piano, and is still practised today in a modified form at Hohenems, Vorarlberg, and by the Vienna Society of Friends of Music.

schụmmeln *v/i colloq.* & *school. sl.* ([*leicht*] *betrügen*) to deceive: to swindle to do; said as a warning when starting a game of cards, etc.: *≈ gilt nicht!* we're not having any cheating! – **Schụmmler** *m* -s/- [? based on an acronym made up of the Hebrew initials *shin, waw,* and *mem,* for Speyer, Worms, and Mainz, the three largest Jewish communities in medieval Germany] **1.** *hist.* Jewish pedlar (*or* peddler). – **2.** *colloq.* and *school sl.* (*Schwindler*) person who deceives: cheat, jew.

Schụ̈ppel *m & n* -s/-(n) *colloq.* **1.** *(Büschel)* bunch, handful; *ein ~ Haare* a tuft of hair, *ein ~ Stroh* a wisp of straw. – **2.** *([große] Menge)* mass; *ein ~ Kinder* a quiver full of children: a quiverful, loads of children, *AmE* a whole bunch (*or,* a heap) of kids; *ein ~ Geld* a pile (*or,* bags, heaps, loads, lots, oodles, tons, wads) of money; *das wird dich ein[en] ~ Geld kosten* that'll cost you a pretty penny (*BrE a.* a packet). – **≈weise** *adv (in großer Zahl)* by the dozen, in hundreds; *ich möchte Kinder, ~* I want children, bags (*or,* loads, tons) of them; *wer weiss, vielleicht ist sie verheiratet und hat ~ Kinder!* who knows, she may be married with a houseful (*or,* loads) of kids by now!

Schụster …: ~bub *m* -en/-en *(Schusterjunge)* shoemaker's apprentice ‖ *colloq. phr.* (1) denoting heavy rainfall: *~en regnen* to rain cats and dogs, *AmE a.* to rain bullfrogs and heifer yearlings, to rain pitchforks with the tines on both ends; (2) referring to people running at great speed: *rennen wie die ~en* to tear along like mad. – **~flugzeug** *n* -(e)s/-e ⇼ *hum.* motor-assisted bicycle: buzz-bike, pop-pop bike, poor man's motorcycle. – **~laibchen** *n* -s/-, *dial.* **~laberl** *n* -s/-(n) *bak.* "shoemaker's loaflet", a small round piece of bread made of wheat and rye flour, with a small indentation in the middle, somewhat bigger than an ordinary roll (*Semmel*), at times sprinkled with caraway seeds. – **~sọnntag** *m* -(e)s/ *pl.* rare: -e *colloq. iron.* *(Nimmerleinstag)* a fictitious day on which something is supposed, or even promised, to take place (but, as the speaker and others are well aware, never will): never-never day; *er bezahlt seinen Rechnungen am ~* he'll pay his bill when hell freezes over (*or,* when pigs fly).

Schwaige *f* -/-n, *dial.* **Schwoag** *f* -/-n ⩕ *(Sennhütte)* (Alpine) dairy hut; *(Alm)* mountain dairy, alp. – **schwaigen,** *dial.* **schwoagn** *v/i (eine Alm bewirtschaften; Käse bereiten)* during the summer season, mostly from early June to mid-September: to run a mountain dairy; to make cheese. – **Schwaiger,** *dial.* **Schwoager** *m* -s/- *(Senner)* (Alpine) dairyman. – **Schwaigerin,** *dial.* **Schwoa-**

A cluster of dairy huts in the Styrian Alps, wide pastures all around, and God's peace everywhere

gerin *f* -/-nen *(Sennerin)* (Alpine) dairymaid; a folksong sets the tone of such a life on high: *wia lustig is im Winter, / wia wird's im Summer sein, / wann d' Schwoagerin auf d' Alma treibt? / ui, da wird's lustig sein!* how jolly's life in Winter! / and how 't will be in Spring? / the dairymaid goes up the alp; / what fun it's gonna bring!

Schwạmmerl *n* -s/-n **1.** 🍄 a fast-growing fungus of which some kinds are edible and duly form the basic part of delicious meals (*Pilz*): mushroom; *~n suchen gehen, in die ~n gehen* to go mushrooming || *fig.* a brash question suggesting an outbreak of mania in a person who has just said something absurd or acted in an irrational way: *ja, hat der narrische ~n gegessen?* my, did somebody hit him over the head?; why, has he gone off his rocker? – **2.** *m* & *n* -s ♪ *hist.* a nickname for Franz Schubert (1797–1828), fastened on him already by his brothers and sisters poking gentle fun at the pleasantly plump figure and features of that great Viennese composer of the Biedermeier Age: Tubby; *schon in ganz frühen Jahren war Schubert Mittelpunkt eines leichtlebigen Freundeskreises, der sich dem Gesang, Tanz und romantischen Versen verschrieb und der ohne ihr[en] ~ nicht denkbar war* from early age on, Schubert was the focal point of a circle of bohemian friends giving parties devoted to singing, dancing, and romantic verses, and there was never a real Schubertiad without their revered Tubby.

Schwänzeri̱tis *f* - *school sl. hum.* an imaginary disease, literally 'truant inflammation', from which some pupils are said to periodically suffer: = *Tachinose* ↓.

Schwe̱gelpfeife *f* -/-n, also known as *Rohrpfeife f* -/-n and *Querflöte f* -/-n [first el., > OHG *swegala* 'reed', 'flute' – our cpd.

being neatly paralleled by OE *sweglhorn*] ♪ a popular Alpine woodwind instrument to be played with one hand on three finger holes – the other hand, optionally, being free to beat a small drum: transverse flute.

Sekunderl *n* -s/-(n) [dim. of *Sekunde f*] *colloq.* any brief period of time = *Momenterl* ↑.

Selch ...: ~kammer *f* -/-n *(Räucherkammer) BrE* smoking chamber, *AmE* smokehouse. – **~karree** *n* -s/-s *(geräuchertes Rippenstück;* Ger.: *Kasseler Rippenspeer)* smoked spare(-)ribs.

Senn *m* -(e)s/-e, **Senne** *m* -n/-n, **Senner** *m* -s/- [< late L *senior*] ⛰ *(Bewirtschafter e-r Sennhütte)* Alpine herdsman *or* cowherd [ˈkauhəːd]. – **Senne** *f* -/-n rarely: mountain pasture.

Sesselleiste *f* -/-n board covering a (plaster) wall where it meets the floor of a room *(Scheuerleiste)*: skirting-board, *AmE* baseboard, mopboard [so called because it is close to the floor surface, which is cleaned by a mop].

Sezession *f* – **1.** *arts* a group of angry young painters at the end of the nineteenth century, breaking away from the artistic security of a bourgeois world, and emphasizing such decorative features as delicate faces and arms, the subtle play of colours and lines, as well as erotic themes: Vienna Secession Group. → **2.** *archit.* in Vienna, south of the Opernring – the most striking nouveau art centre in Vienna, bearing a huge openworked cupola of metal laurel leaves (in the vernacular known as *das goldene Krauthappl* 'The Golden Head of Cabbage'), designed by Joseph Olbrich in 1897–98: Vienna Secession Centre. – **~sstil** *m* -(e)s *arts* a style of art and decoration common at the end of the nineteenth century in Europe and America, using flowing lines and plant forms: art nouveau [ˈaː(*or,* ɑːt) nuːˈvəʊ], G & E Jugendstil [ˈJuːgentstiːl].

Silberreiher *m* -s/- *orn.* great white heron, the national bird of Austria, the largest European colony of which is found on Lake Neusiedl in Burgenland.

Simandl, less often **Siemandl** *m* & *n* -s/-(n) [< a fusion of *Simon,* the name of one of the disciples of Jesus, + *Man(n)dl,* a *contp.* variant of *Mann* 'man', 'husband'. (Simon is the patron saint of the *Simandlbruderschaft,* a brotherhood of married men [claiming to be] suffering under the rule of their wives; jocularly, there is also the dual warning to any married man never to contradict one's better half on St Simon's Day, October 28, and indeed to begin that fated day by rising first from bed that morning – else it will be a case of – notice the pun! – *sie Mann* 'she' being 'in command' for a full year)] *colloq.* one who is the butt of his wife's nagging (as is graphically memorialized by a fountain sculpture in the City of Krems, Lower Austria, showing a medieval couple, the man humbly kneeling before his scolding wife, arms akimbo) *(Pantoffelheld)*: henpecked husband; *er ist ein ~* he is completely under his wife's thumb; *dieser Waschlappen ist ja ein ~, wie er im Buch steht,* or ... *ist ja frank der Oberste von der Simandlbruderschaft* my, that sissy is the undoubted head of the sect of the henpecked, I can tell you.

Si̱monsbrot *n* -(e)s *bak.* slices of dark rye bread in tinfoil wrapper.

Sịmperl *n* -s/-(n) *colloq. (flaches, geflochtenes [Brot-]Körbchen)* small, woven basket of cane or straw, for holding bread, fruit, etc.

Sịngerl *n* -s/-(n) Lower Austrian *dial. (Küchlein)* (if affectively: sweet) little chicken, *AmE* baby chick, *nurs.* chickabiddy.

Sịtzerling *m* -s/-e *colloq.* someone who prefers to sit rather than walk about: sitaholic.

Solẹtti *n* -(s)/usu. pl. - (TM) *gastr.* long thin pieces of bakery made with soft wheat flour and vegetable oil, ideally nibbled at social get-togethers, when watching television, etc. – a little Austrian delicacy now being exported to some 65 countries (*Brotstäbchen, Grissini*): breadsticks; *ein Packerl ~* a packet of breadsticks.

Sọnnenbalkon *m* -s/-e [lit., 'a balcony exposed to long periods of hot sunshine'] *geog., fig. der ~ Österreichs* – an epithet for the Province of Carinthia (→ *Kärnten*), which enjoys a very favourable climate: "The Suntrap of Austria."

Spẹckbacherhut *m* -(e)s/ ... hüte [first el. < Josef Speckbacher, 1767–1820, "the Man from Rinn", a distinguished strategist and tactician in the wars against

Josef Speckbacher, Andreas Hofer's faithful lieutenant – as portrayed in Franz von Defregger's forest "Tyrolean Heroes" (1894)

Napoleon] *hist. fashion* "Speckbacher tophat", a high-crowned headgear that tapers cylindrically or conically; it was fashionable with both sexes of the Lower Inn Valley people between 1810 and 1860.

Spẹckknödel *m* -s/-(n) *cul.* "bacon dumpling", dumpling made of white bread *(Semmelknödel),* with chopped pieces of bacon or ham; *in der Dialektaussprache* [ˈʃpekx-ˌkxnø:dl] *begegnen gleich zwei angeriebene Laute; der Name dieses bekannten Landesgerichts ist so auch zum Kennwort einer lautlichen Besonderheit von Tirol geworden* the dialect pronunciation [ˈʃpekx-ˌkxnø:dl] offers (*or* holds) two affricates even; the name of this well-known regional dish has, therefore, also become a shibboleth of a phonetic peculiarity of the Tyrol.

sper *adj* [< MHG *spör(e)*] *dial.* of bread and confectionery *(trocken)*: stale.

Speisgitter *n* -s/- [first el.? < late L *spensa* < *expensa* (with elision of /n/)] *R. C. (Kommunionbank)* communion rail.

spießen *v/refl (klemmen) colloq.* to get jammed; *der Schlüssel spießt sich (ein bisse[r]l)* the key catches (... sticks a little).

Spompanadeln, Spomponadeln, Spamponaden, Spanponaden [ʃp-] pl. [< It *spampanare* 'to brag' or, rather, *Spompanada* 'horse rising up on its hind legs' – an act of dressage in the Spanish Riding School of Vienna (established in 1785)] *colloq.* **1.** *fig.* an act, or acts, of rearing up in silent protest (as it were), and then avoiding to give direct and honest answers to questions *(Umschweife, Ausflüchte)*: beating about the bush, *BrE a.* humming and hawing, *AmE a.* backing and filling, doing figure eights; *mach bittschön keine ~ und sag klar heraus, ob du für das eine oder das andere bist!* no shilly-shally shamming, please, but come out clearly in favour of the one thing or the other. – **2.** *cul.* recherché meals *(extravagante Speisen)*: quirky items of food; *in unserem Landgasthaus kommen keine ~ auf den Tisch, sondern zum Beispiel eine Petersiliencremesuppe, dann ein Lammbraten und schließlich ein Kaiserschmarrn, der die Menschen von weit und breit hierherlockt* our country inn is not one to serve freakish twiddlybits, but does offer, say, parsley cream soup, roast lamb and, at last, shredded flapjack – a delicacy making folks converge on our place from far and near.

Sprachfehler *m* -s/- *ling.* speech defect ‖ *phr.* a low or vulgar expression facetiously or maliciously impugning the moral integrity of Carinthian girls and women by accusing them of offering little resistance to a man's amorous advances: *die Kärntnerin hat einen ~, sie kann nicht 'nein' sagen* the Carinthian girl has a speech defect (*or* problem), she can't say 'no'.

sprageln *vt/refl* [related to BrE and AmE dial. *to sprag* 'to put a piece of wood between the spokes of a wheel in order to check its revolution', 'to put a wedge under a vehicle in order to prevent it from running backwards'] *dial.* to twist (*or* to get twisted) out of shape, to split; *über kurz oder lang ~ sich die teuersten Federspitzen* sooner or later, the most expensive (pen) nibs will get split, *or* become crossed.

Springinkerl *n* -s/-(n) *colloq. (komisch wehsiger Mensch)* person who seems unable to sit still or to concentrate: jack-in-the-box, jumping jack, fidget; *ein ~ sein* to have the fidgets.

Sprugg [ʃprʊk] *n* -s (rare) *place-name* the dialect form of endearment by the Tyrolese for their capital, Innsbruck [ˈɪnsprʊk]: good old Innsbruck.

Staberl [dim. of *Stab m* 'staff'] **1.** *n* -s/-(n) (1) *(Stäbchen)* thin stick, small rod, rodlet. (2) usu. *pl.* collar stiffener, either of a pair of plastic sticks used for straightening the collar of a shirt or dress. (3) usu. *pl.* chopstick, either of a pair of narrow sticks used for eating East Asian food. – **2.** *m* -s *theat. hist.* Staberl, the eternal "little man", an innocuous blunderer put on the Viennese stage during the Napoleonic years by Adolf Bäuerle in his play *Die Bürger von Wien* (1813). – **3.** *m* -s *journ.* Staberl, the pseudonym of Richard Nimmerrichter, a well-known columnist in Austria's *Neue Kronen Zeitung,* taking up the cause of the "little man" against corruption and malfeasance of office in today's political life.

stad, often **staad** adj [related to E *steady* 'firmly fixed', 'unchanging'] *dial.* & *colloq.* quiet, silent – **1.** a fine word to connote phonic associations poets have an affinity for (as in the following quatrain, with its rendering in Scottish English):

> *Im Wald is so staad,*
> *alle Weg' san vawaht,*
> *alle Weg' san vaschniebm,*
> *is koa Steigl net bliebm.*
>
> The wuds are sae still,
> A' the weys wi' snaw fill,
> A' the weys in snaw tint –
> Fient a loan leeft ye kent.

2. *attrib.* in a fixed phrase denoting 'the Advent Season', the weeks of reflexion and hushed expectation of what is about to come (namely, the birth of Jesus Christ our Saviour): *die ~e Zeit* 'the time of silence.' – **3.** *pred.* in a firm warning to stop speaking: *sei ~!* hold your peace!

Stạdt *f* -/ Städte **1.** in rural areas: (nearest [market]) town; *das kann man nur in der ~ bekommen* you can only get that in town. – **2.** in Vienna, the centre or, administratively speaking, the first district: the oldest part of the town, walled in till the late 1850s, and since surrounded by a wide street known as *Ring* and *Kai* [kɛ:]; its distinctive entity is felt by the native speaker *(Altstadt)*: City, Old-Town, *AmE* downtown (Vienna) || *phr.:* *in der ~* in the City, in town, *AmE* downtown; *in die ~* (in)to the City-centre, *AmE* downtown; a taxi-man's question to his fare: *bitte, wie soll ich fahren, über den Ring oder durch die ~?* which way would you like me to go, along the Ring or through the City [*i.e.,* do you mind risking possible delays (because of traffic) when I am taking the shorter route]? – **3.** in phrasal collocations: *~ der Lieder* "City of Songs", a sobriquet of Vienna, the birthplace and residence of many composers of popular songs (Schubert, the Strausses, etc.); *~ der Volkserhebung hist.* "City of National Rebellion", an honorary if hardly appreciated distinction accorded by the National Socialist Regime in 1938 to the City of Graz for the pro-German leanings of many of its inhabitants before the *Anschluss* ↑; the phrase is obviously modelled on older secondary names, like *Stadt der Bewegung* for Munich.[1]

[1] The practice of bestowing secondary names on big cities is, of course, widespread, and English-speaking countries also offer numerous examples, e.g., "Athens of the North" (Edinburgh) and "City of Brotherly Love" (Philadelphia).

Stạmperl *n* -s/-(n) [< *Stamm m* 'stem (of a wine glass)' + intrusive consonant *p* + dim. *-erl*] *colloq. (Schnapsgläschen)* liqueur [lɪˈkjʊə] glass, jigger; *ich könnte ein ~ vertragen* I could do with a quickie; *trinken wir ein ~ Enzian!* let's have a jigger of gentian brandy!

stạmpern *v/t colloq. (verjagen)* to chase away; *ich werde euch gleich ~, wenn ihr solchen Lärm macht!* I'll chase you in a minute if you make a racket like that! || *hunt. Hasen ~* to rouse hares.

Stanitzel, Stanitzl *n* -s/- [< *Skarnitzel,* a secondary form, now obsolete, possibly a blend of Trieste dial. *scartozo* (It standard *cartoccio*) 'paper bag' + Cz *kornut* 'triangular paper-bag'] **1.** *a. Papier*≈ *colloq.* a paper-bag pointed at one end *(spitze Papiertüte)*: paper-cone, cornet. – **2.** *cul.* ~ [pl.] *mit Schlag* cornets (filled) with ([wild] strawberries and whipped) cream.

Standschütze *m* -n/usu. pl. -n *mil. hist.* one of the home guards heroically defending the southern frontiers of the Tyrol during the First World War: Tyrolese peasant rifleman.

Staubzucker *m* -s *gastr.* **1.** a kind of white granulated sugar crushed to form fine grains, used for cooking, baking, and sweetening hot drinks *(feiner Kristallzucker)*: *BrE* caster *or* castor sugar, *AmE* powdered sugar. – **2.** a kind of sugar in the form of a very fine powder, used for icing certain types of cakes and biscuits (*Puderzucker*): *BrE* icing sugar, *AmE* confectioner's sugar, powdered sugar.

Steiger *m* -s/- *colloq.,* sometimes *contp.* a man who charms and attracts all the women he meets *(Schürzenjäger)*: ladies' man, lady-killer, Don Juan, Romeo, Casanova, *AmE a.* wolf.

Stellwagen *m* -s/- [*hist.* omnibus, a big lumbering public transport of the nineteenth century, drawn by two horses (first el. < *Gestell* 'chassis')] *Viennese phr. j-m mit dem ~ ins Gesicht fahren* to rebuke s.o. loudly and severely: to jump down s.o. 's throat, to bite s.o. 's head off, to ride roughshod over s.o., to harsh on s.o.; *wie sich das Bürscherl wegen meines amerikanischen Lieblingsautors mit mir hat anlegen wollen, bin ich ihm aber mit dem ~ ins Gesicht gefahren* when the young gent tried to cross swords with me about my favourite American author I was at him hammer and tongs; *was braucht der mir gleich mit dem ~ ins Gesicht fahren? kann man das nicht ruhig gesagt kriegen, wenn einem was nicht passt?* what did he have to jump on me like that for? couldn't he just have told me quietly that something was bothering him?

A thin pastry cornet, to be eaten together with some whipped cream and preserved cherries

Stelze *f* -/-n [< OHG *stelza* 'stilt'], or **Haxe** *f* -/-n [related to OE *hōhsinu* 'sinew of the heel'] *cul. (Eisbein)* knuckle of pork or veal, boiled and served with sauerkraut ‖ if of pork: **Schweins**≈ pig's trotter.

Sterz *m* -es/-e [< MHG *sterz* 'thick broth'; related to NHG *starr* (< OHG *ster*) 'stiff', 'rigid' and *starren* (cp. ModE *to stare*) 'to gaze fixedly'] *cul.* an unsophisticated type of farmhouse dish, prepared by pouring (a rather small quantity of) hot water or milk onto flour or semolina browned in lard or butter: thick porridge ‖ the basic ingredient from the home soil may well vary from region to region throughout Austria – *Erdäpfel*≗ or *Grumbirn*≗ potato porridge; *Heiden*≗ buckwheat porridge; *Türken*≗ maize porridge, *AmE* mush.

stimmen *vi* to be all right ‖ *phr.* in a restaurant, on payment of one's bill, to the waiter handing back the loose change: (*es*) *stimmt schon!* keep the change!

Stimmenvieh *n* -(e)s acquiescent subordinates in a large organization, e.g. in a political party (*Kopfnicker* pl.): nodding donkeys *pl.*

Stoßsuppe, more often **Stosuppe** *f* -/-n; *dial.* **Stosuppm** *f* -/- *cul.* a simple and plain type of soup, had mornings and evenings chiefly in remote country areas and on mountain farms, where the meals must be adjusted as far as possible to the yield of the land – a soup made of buttermilk (or sour milk) and flour, with black bread: curdled-milk soup, sour-milk soup.

strabanzen, strawanzen *v/i* [akin to MHG *strebeln, strabeln*] *colloq.* *(sich herumtreiben)* to roam about: to loaf (about), to gad about: *er strabanzt den ganzen Tag kreuz und quer durch die Stadt* he meanders up and down the streets of the town all day; *er strabanzt durchs Leben, statt zu arbeiten* he spends his whole life just hanging around (*or,* dinking around, putzing around, puttering about) instead of working; *wo strabanzt du denn hin?* where are you drifting off to? – **Strabanzer, Strawanzer** *m* -s/- *colloq.* **1.** *(Strolch)* vagabond: bum, tramp. – **2.** *contp.* or *hum.* (*Streuner*) gadabout; *der ~ in ihm ist nicht zu übersehen* his shoes are made of running leather. – **3.** *(einer, der sich unerwarteterweise zu spät einstellt)* prowler; *na, du ~, kommst du endlich auch schon nach Hause?* hey, you prowler, are you finally coming home?

strapaz ...: ~fähig *adj* of articles of clothing *(strapazierfähig)*: durable, rugged, *BrE* hard-wearing, *AmE* long-wearing; *~e Kleidung* heavy-duty clothing, work clothing. – ≗**schuhe** *m pl.* **1.** sturdy *or* stout shoes (boots), work boots. – **2.** *(Wanderschuhe)* hiking boots, *BrE a.* fell boots.

Straß *m* -s *or* Strasses/Strasse, **Straßstein** *m* -(e)s/-e [named after Josef *Strasser,* an eighteenth-century Viennese alchemist] *paste jewelry* a shining colourless jewel made from glass or a transparent rock and intended to look like a diamond *(Edelsteinimitation aus Glas)*: imitation diamond, rhinestone, pierre de Strass; *ein österreichisches Bijouterieerzeugnis, das seit langem im Lande hergestellt wird, sind die Straßsteine; sie sind heute in aller Welt bekannt* rhinestones, or pierres de Strass, are an Austrian speciality in the costume jewelry line, and one which has been made in Austria for a great many years; they are known all over the world.

Straube *f* -/usu. pl.: -n; *dial.* **Strauben, Straubn, Straubm** *f* -/- [< MHG *strup* 'having a rough untidy surface'; related to StG struppig 'rough', 'shaggy', 'bristly' and StG *sträuben v/refl* 'to stand on end', *fig.* 'to bristle (up)', 'to ba(u)lk'] *bak.* primarily encountered on religious holidays in the Tyrol – a batter of flour, eggs, and milk, poured through a funnel or pastry bag to form "unruly" curls (hence the name!) until filling a biggish plate; fried to even brownness, sprinkled with powdered sugar and served immediately *(krause, in schwim-*

mendem Fett gebackene Gebilde): Tyrolean ruffles.

Streif *f* - [lit., a long, narrow area of land (here taken to be the distance between the highest and lowest points of a ski run)] *geog., skiing* at Kitzbühel, Tyrol, starting at the top of Hahnenkamm Mountain – the most difficult downhill racing piste in the world: The Strip, The Vertical.

Streithansl *m* -s/-(n) [second el., dim. < *Hans* 'Jack' (Christian name; and, gen., 'everyone'] *colloq.* a person who is out to pick a quarrel, esp. about something petty or trivial (*streitsüchtiger Mensch*): squabbler; *das ist ein ~, wie er im Buch steht* he's a dyed-in-the-wool (*or* professional) squabbler.

Stricherl *n* -s/-(n) [dim. of *Strich m* 'stroke', i.e. a line made by a single movement of a pen or brush in writing or painting] *colloq.* **1.** a short stroke on paper: quick stroke, dash; *in den Kastln, wo nichts auszufüllen ist, mach einfach ~(n)* just make a quick stroke in the squares asking questions which do not apply. – **2.** *hist.* a timid, or secretive, person's mark written esp. on a letter or card, meaning a kiss: dash [*nowadays,* X] ‖ a passage from a letter sent by Emperor Francis Joseph to Frau Katharina Schratt, a highly popular actress at the Burgtheater and his constant companion since 1886: *ich schicke Ihnen so viele ~n, wie Sie mir nur gestatten* I send you as many dashes as you deign to accept.

Striezel *m* or *n* -s/- *bak.* *(längliches Gebäck in geflochtener Form)* **1.** braided egg-loaf, *AmE Yid.* chula ['xu:lə], quaelich ['kweılıtʃ]. – **2.** crisp braided (*or BrE,* plaited ['plætıd]) roll. – **Striezerl** *n* -s/-(n) *bak.* (small) braided roll; *Mohn~ (Mohnzopf)* braided poppy-seed roll, *BrE* poppy-seed plait.

A Striezel *is a yeasty glory braided by hand*

Strudel *m* -s/- *cul.* the most widely known Austrian speciality, a paper-thin pastry usually filled with fruit (apples, cherries, poppy seeds): strudel. – **~apfel** *m* -s/ ... äpfel (any kind of) small sourish apple used in making strudel. – **~teig** *m* -(e)s/-e paper-thin strudel pastry, i.e. paste rolled and pulled from underneath with one's fingers to paper thinness; *fig. colloq.,* said in irritation at some tediously lengthy matter: *die Sache zieht sich wie ein ~* this thing seems to drag on forever. – **Strudler** *m* -s/- = *Strudelapfel* ↑.

Strumpf *m* -(e)s/ Strümpfe stocking ‖ in *colloq.* phrases: **1.** *(Unsinn)* foolish talk: *red keinen* (or *nicht so einen*) *~!* don't talk such a lot of bolony! – **2.** as a mild expletive when faced with a unpleasant surprise, avoiding mention of a sacred word: *o, du ~!* my goodness!, goodness (gracious) me! – **3.** *vulg. hum.* with reference to a male: → *auswinden.*

Strụtz *m* -en/-en, **Strụtzen** *m* -s/- in Western Austria *(längliches Brot, Wecken) bak.* oblong loaf (of bread)

Stube *f* -/-n, *dial.* **Stu(b)m** *f* -/- *archit. (beheizbarer Wohnraum e-s Bauernhauses oder Schlosses;* cp. E *stove)* living-room, heated by a stove; *in früherer Zeit lagen oft zwei Wohnräume im Verbund, eine ~ mit Ofen, daneben eine Schlafkammer, die lediglich hoch oben in der Trennwand durch zwei kleine Fenster von nebenan etwas Wärme bezog* in earlier times, the rooms often came in pairs, a living-room heated by a stove and an adjoining bedroom which obtained only a little warmth from next door through two tiny windows high up in the partition wall ‖ *phr.* a friendly invitation to a person standing on the threshold: *herein in die gute ~!* step in and make yourself at home!, *AmE a.* come on in, join the party!, *ScotE a.* come into the body of the kirk!

Stụrm *m* -(e)s [lit., 'storm', 'tempest' – in euphemistic allusion to the explosive bowel movements some merry drinkers may suddenly be subjected to (disphemistically then, in low slang, referred to as *Stiegenscheißer*)] *vinic. & bev.* a cloudy grape juice, at the stage of fermenting into wine, much in favour as an annual newcomer in early autumn – it tastes like fruit juice, looks like scrumpy cider, but trickily has the hasty drinker under the table within minutes *(gärender Weinmost*: Ger *Federweiße, Sauser)*: harvest-time grape must, rebelliously young new wine, *BrE* "antenatal" (*AmE* "prenatal") new wine.

Sụlz *f* -/-en *cul.* meat from a pig's head or trotter, or from a calf's foot, boiled and pressed in a container; it is often served in thin flat pieces (*Sülze, Aspik*): *BrE* brawn, *AmE* headcheese. – **sụlzen** *v/t (zu Sulz verarbeiten)* to boil until jellified.

Sụmper *m* -s/- *colloq. (Mensch ohne höhere Interessen)* uncultured person: philistine, dimwit, *AmE a.* ignoramus.

Sụppenbrunzer *m* -s/- largely *hist.*, rustic *hum.* a wide and shapely centrally tapered glass bowl suspended from the ceiling to "do duty" over a big, well-filled tureen of soup steaming in the middle of the farmhouse dining table (for all the family and farmhands to help themselves to spoonfuls from, straight to their mouths) … the hot vapours rising, condensing into runny beads on the bowl above, and duly dropping back into the soup – concrete proof of rural frugality practised in an age gone by: *soup pisser.

Sur *f* -/-en [< MHG *sur* 'sour', 'spicy'] *cul.* a liquid (water, plus) used to preserve meat *(Beize zum Einpökeln von Fleisch)* – (1) with vinegar and spices: pickle, souse; (2) with salt: brine.

Sur …: ~fass *n* -es/ … fässer *cul. (Behälter zum Pökeln)* salt(ing) tub. – **~fleisch** *n* -(e)s *cul. (Pökelfleisch)* pickled pork. – **~haxe** *f* -/-n, *dial.* **~hax(e)n** *f* -/- *gastr.* a delicacy served roasted, grilled, or boiled, with sauerkraut as a side dish: (1) pickled leg of veal; (2) pickled pork trotter, *AmE* (pickled) ham hock.

tachinieren *v/i* [< ? Cz *táhnouti* 'to (try hard to) take French leave' (*táhni!* get off!); or *tachycardia* 'excessively rapid heartbeat', a medical term overheard during the First World War by soldiers who had purposely drunk an inordinate amount of black coffee in order to be pronounced unfit for front-line service, + German verbal suffix *-ieren,* from East French infinitives in *-ier*] *colloq.* **1.** *(sich von der Arbeit* etc. *drücken)* to malinger: to dodge work (duty, etc.), *BrE sl.* to scrimshank. – **2.** *(den Unterricht schwänzen)* to play truant: to skip (*or,* cut) school, *AmE* to play hook(e)y, to ditch *or* blow-off class(es). – **Tachinierer** *m* -s/- *colloq.* **1.** *(Drückeberger)* malingerer: dodger, *BrE sl.* scrimshanker. – **2.** *([Schul-]Schwänzer)* truant: one who skips (*or,* cuts) school, *AmE* cutter, skipper, ditcher, slacker. – **Tachinose,** rarely **Tachynose** *f* -/-n [an imaginary disease, possibly derived from the medical term mentioned in line 3, with the substitution of the pseudo-suffix *-nose* isolated from such technical terms as *Diagnose* and *Prognose*], often *chronische ~ hum.* a (sustained) morbid tendency to keep work, school, etc., at a safe distance: (chronic) case of lazyitis, indolent fever, lazyman's disease; *Frühlings~* spring(time) fever; *~ der Abschlussklassler* senioritis.

Tafel… *gastr.:* **~spitz** *m* -es/-e **1.** = *Tafelstück.* – **2.** boiled beef with sauté potatoes, vegetables and tartare sauce. – **~stück** *n* -(e)s/-e *cul. (das dem Schwanz benachbarte Fleischstück vom Rind, Hüftspitz)* aitchbone [ˈeɪtʃbəʊn], round of beef.

Tạndelmarkt *m* -(e)s/…märkte † *(Trödelmarkt)* old clothes market, flea market, *BrE* rag-fair, *AmE* yard sale, moving sale, garage sale. – **Tạndelware** *f* -/- **1.** † *(Trödelkram)* used articles, second-hand articles (*or,* goods), *AmE* junk. → **2.** *contp. (Schund)* rubbish, trash, *AmE* junk. – **Tạndler** *m* -s/- **1.** † *(Trödler)* dealer in used goods, second-hand dealer, old-clothesman, *AmE* junk-dealer. → **2.** *colloq.,* often slightly *contp. (Trödelfritze)* dawdler: slowcoach, snail, tortoise, *AmE* slowpoke.

Tạtzelwurm *m* -(e)s/ … würmer *folklore* a legendary reptile resembling a dragon, but of small size, stumpy head with glowing eyes, and short legs, capable of making long and high leaps from rock crevices to bite its victims *(drachenähnliches Kriechtier)*: Alpine dragon.

Teetscherl *n* -s *emot.,* in praise of a cup of tea (cp. *Kaffeetscherl*): (some) delicious tea; *ein ~!* a delicious cup of tea: *BrE* a delicious cuppa!, a nice cup of char!, a wonderful spot of tea!, *AmE* an orgasmic cup of tea!

Telefon, now rarely **Telephon** *n* -s/-e telephone, *colloq.* phone ‖ *football sl.* an often many-voiced, raucous shout of disapproval from the ranks of onlookers, intimating that the referee's place is not in the playing field: *Schiedsrichter ans* (or, *zum*) *~!* throw the ref out!, send the ref to the moon! – **~häuschen** *n* -s/-, *colloq.* **~häus(e)l** *n* -s/-(n) telephone callbox, telephone booth, *colloq.* phone (box); *gibt's da wo ein ~?* is there a pay phone around here (somewhere)?

Teppich *m* -s/-e [a euphemistic expansion of *Tepp* 'great fool'] *colloq.* stupid person: ninny, *AmE* dummy, dumb-bell, dipstick, darnfoolski, dumski; *mein Englischlehrer in … vergessen wir's … war ein ~* my English teacher at … ah, forget it! … was a real ninny.

Terna *f* - *univ. (Dreiervorschlag [für die Besetzung e-s Lehrstuhls])* short-list (of three candidates); *er wurde von der Kommission in die ~ für die anglistische Lehrkanzel aufgenommen* he was shortlisted by the committee for the chair of English.

Thermo… [< Gr 'hot', 'heat']: **~frater** *m* -s/- [second el., < L 'brother'] *hum.* a macaronic nonce 'translation' to denote a male homosexual, fusing two classical elements into a compound for euphemistic fun, and thus taking the sting out of the rudely unabashed German original, *warmer Bruder*: ag-fay (< a wordplay on *fag*), queer-beer (< an elaboration of *queer*), queer-vert (< a combination of *queer* and *pervert*). – **~phor** *m* -s/-e *tech. & med.* an appliance that stores heat – **1.** a bag, usu. of rubber, for holding hot water to apply warmth to some part of the body (*Wärmeflasche*): *BrE* hot-water bottle, *AmE a.* hot-water bag. – **2.** (*Heizkissen*) electric pillow *or* heat pad.

Tintenburg *f* -/-en *hum.* or *iron.* any large administrative building of a central agency, e.g. a government ministry, whose many employees are jokingly pictured as huddling over their deskwork all done (as indeed was a fact a few generations ago) by laboriously wielding quills and fountain pens: *inkspiller's scriptorium.

Tirol *n* -s the Tyrol [< F *le Tyrol,* It *il Tirolo*]; *Nord~* North Tyrol, The Austrian Tyrol; *Süd~* South Tyrol, It *Alto Adige* [ˈʌdɪdʒe].

Tiroler 1. *m* -s Tyrolean; *pl. die ~* the Tyroleans, the Tyrolese. – **2.** *adj* Tyrolean, Tyrolese: ~ **Eierspeise** *f* - *cul.* a casserole dish of hard-boiled eggs, potatoes and anchovies: Tyrolean-style eggs. – ~ **Grest(e)l,** ~ **Gröst(e)l** *n* -s *cul.* fried potatoes with small pieces of different meats. – ~ **Knödel** *m & n* -s/-(n) *cul.* "Tyrolese dumpling", made of white bread, flour and an egg, together with bits of smoked sausage, chopped herbs, and the odd caraway seed. – ~ **Leber** *f* -/-n *cul.* "Tyrolese liver", i.e. calf liver, thinly sliced, floured and prepared with a few thinly sliced onions and some bacon, to be served with rice. – ~ **Leckerli** *n* -/- *bak.* a sweet confection: "Tyrolese munchies", glazed cookies with nuts, raisins and chocolate, otherwise similar to macaroons *(Nussbusserl).* – ~ **Speckbraten** *m* -s/- *cul.* Tyrolean-style beef roast, well larded with strips of bacon. –

Two Tyrolese peasant riflemen – gorgeous from their hats to their knee-breeches and brogues

The fortress-crested rock of Kufstein, "The Gem of the Tyrol" – one of the many masterpieces by E. Harrison Compton, instancing a little "the richness and charm to be found in Austria"

~ **(Vọlks-)Tracht** *f* -/-en Tyrolean costume.

...tiroler *m* -s/- in compounds, *hum.* or slightly *contp.*: **Flạchland~** mock Tyrolean, apology for a Tyrolean, would-be Tyrolean, *AmE low colloq.* Tyrolean wanna-be: 1. one (often a North German) who, from a passing whim, dresses partly Tyrolean-style, e.g. wearing a wide-brimmed felt hat or fancy leather shorts; 2. one who lacks the stamina endurance expected of a mountaineer: *ihr ~ braucht für die Wanderung natürlich doppelt oder dreimal so lang wie ein Einheimischer* you lowlanders, you need two or three times as long as the natives for this hike. – **Ho̱f~** *hist.* "Court Tyrolean", a city-slicker, one who, though professionally attached to court and city ambience, there affects the free and easy manner, and a fondness of laughter and song, imputed to a Tyrolean; this epithet was given as a snub by some ladies at the Munich court to Franz von Kobell, 1803–92, a popular writer and professor of mineralogy, whose love of life among high mountains inspired much of his prose and poetry. – **Salo̱n~** sham *or* dandy Tyrolean, one who on festive occasions wears a real (or fake) regional costume of the Alps.

Tiro̱lerin *f* -/-nen Tyrolean (girl *or* woman); *es ist eine ~, sie ist ~* she is Tyrolese.

tirolerisch, tirolisch *adj* Tyrolean, Tyrolese; *auf ~* in Tyrolean *or* Tyrolese (vernacular [speech]); *im Tirolischen* in the Tyrol.

Tobel *m -s/- geog. (enge [Wald-]Schlucht)* in Vorarlberg: forest gorge (*or* ravine [rəˈviːn], *or* gully); *sie stürzte in einen ~ und verletzte sich dabei tödlich* she fell to her death in a forest gorge.

Topfen *m -s cul. (Quark)* curd(s), curd cheese, cottage cheese. – **~fülle** *f -/-n cul. (Füllung aus Quark)* filling of curd(s). – **~haluschka** *m pl.* [< Hung. *galuska, haluska* 'noodles, dumplings, gnocchi'] *cul. (Quarknudeln mit Speck)* boiled pastry-squares mixed with curds or sheep cheese, covered with small bacon cubes rendered down. – **~käse** *m -s cul.* cream cheese. – **~knödel** *m & n -s/-(n) cul.* curd (*or* white-cheese) dumpling. – **~kolatsche** *f -/-n bak. (Quarktasche)* a square of yeast pastry, folded into the middle at each corner and filled with curds: curd-pastry square. – **~kuchen** *m -s/- cul. (Käsekuchen)* curd cake. – **~neger** *m -s/- hum.* or slightly *contp. (nicht sonngebräunter Mensch,* Ger.: *Blassschnabel)* person without a suntan: paleface, white lily, *AmE* albino [–aɪ–]; *ein ~ sein* to have a billiard-room tan; *heuer waren wir bisher noch kein einziges Mal so richtig in der Sonne, wir werden am Strand die reinsten ~ sein* we haven't been out in the sun at all this year, as far as sunbathing goes – we're sure to be the palest ghosts on the (whole) beach! – **~negerdorf** *n* -(e)s a contemptuous name by the non-Viennese for the inhabitants of the Austrian capital: "village of palefaces". – **~palatschinke** *f -/-n cul. (Eierkuchen mit Quarkfüllung)* sweet pancake filled with curd(s). – **~strudel** *m -s/- cul.* strudel filled with curd(s), curd-cheese pastry.

törggelen [–k–] [< OHG (< L) *torcula* '(wine-)press'] *v/i* at a South Tyrolean vintner's cottage, in the harvest season: to taste the local new wine; *gehen wir ~ am Samstag?* shall we go and sample the new wine on Saturday? – **≗fahrt** *f -/-en*, **≗partie** *f -/-n*, **≗party** *f -/ …partys* or *…parties* privately arranged or run by a bus company: "wine-tasting excursion", a gregarious outing in autumn to a vintner's cottage, to sample his new produce on the site, and to eat sweet chestnuts to cushion the impact of the alcohol.

tour-retour [ˈtuːr-reˈtuːr] *adv.* [< F] *colloq., phr.* heard at the ticket window of a railway, bus, or cable-car booking office, when talk is about a possible trip there and back (*hin und zurück*): *einfach oder ~-~?* single or return?; *einmal ~-~ (Wien)!* one return, *or* return ticket, *or AmE* roundtrip ticket (to Vienna).

Tracht *f -/-en folklore* regional peasant costume; *am Marillenkirtag tragen die Spitzer natürlich ihre malerische Wachauer ~* on the day of their Apricot Festival (the) Spitzers, of course, put on the distinctive dress of the Wachau region.

Trachten… *folklore:* **~fachmann** *m -(e)s/ …leute* specialist on folklore costumes. – **~träger** *m -s/-* [**-in** *f -/-nen*] wearer of his [her] (*or,* native wearing his [her]) distinctive dress of the region or area. – **~umzug** *m -(e)s/…züge* procession of regional peasant costumes, regional costumes parade.

Trafik *f -/-en* [short for *Tabak-Trafik* 'state-operated tobacco shop'] *admin. (Tabak-*

laden) tobacconist's (shop), *AmE* cigarette store.[1] – **Trafikạnt** *m* -en/-en, **Trafikạntin** *f* -/-nen [lady] tobacconist.

[1] Note: The pitfall opened by the semantic incongruity of *Trafik* and "traffic" may best be illustrated by a little anecdote. An Austrian, on a visit to London, one day made the tour of the sights of the City. His personal vice – smoking like a chimney – was with him; and it reasserted itself on Trafalgar Square, keenly. With his cigarette case marooned in the hotel, he looked up and down for a tobacconist's shop, but all he saw was people milling around by the hundreds, and no end of cars, vans, coaches, and double-deckers. Mustering his best English, the visions of a good old Austrian *Tabak-Trafik* before his mind's eye, he politely approached a policeman. "Excuse me, please, is there no *Trafik* here?" The London bobby at first looked bewildered. But then, a big smile breaking through, he waved his hand in a wide circle, as if trying to scoop up the whirling scene in one gesture. "Traffic? Is it traffic you want, sir? Well, ..." – his hand describing another roundabout sweep – "this is all we can do for you."

Trạmway [ˈtramvaɪ] *f* -/- *or* -en *colloq.* **1.** *(Straßenbahn[zug* or *-linie]) BrE* tram (-car *or* line), *AmE* streetcar, trolley car; *fahren wir mit der ~?* shall we take a (*or,* the) tram?; *welche ~ geht denn nach Grinzing?* (I wonder) which line (*or* tram) goes to Grinzing? – **2.** *(Straßenbahnhaltestelle)* tram stop (*or,* halt), *AmE* streetcar stop, trolley stop; *wo ist die nächste ~?* where is the nearest tram (*AmE* streetcar) stop?

Trạmwayer [ˈtramvaɪə] *m* -s/- *colloq.* *(Straßenbahner)* tramway man; *die ~ streiken* the tram people (*or,* personnel) are (out) on strike.

Trạmway ...: ~haltestelle *f* -/-n = *Tramwaystation.* – **~schienenritzenkratzer** *m* -s/- *ling. hum.* like its "female" counterpart under *Donaudampfschiffahrtsgesellschaft* ↑, this "male" occupational title, made up for the nonce to parade a typical German compound construction, tickles the aural fancy of the amateur linguist: * streetcar-rail-scooper-outer. – **~station** *f* -/-en = *Tramway,* 2. – **~verkehr** *m* -s tramway traffic.

Trạnkbüttel *m* -s/- *colloq.* a person who is made out to be the one to eat the dinner remains of the family: waste-paper basket, *BrE a.* rubbish bin, *AmE a.* human garbage disposal; *du magst die Kohlsprosserl nicht? dann gib sie halt dem Papa, das ist unser ~* you don't want your brussels sprouts? ah well, give 'em to Dad, he's our family rubbish bin.

Transiteur [–ˈtøːə] *m* -s/-e *rail.* *(Zugfertigsteller)* goods waggon dispatcher (who affixes the control slips and checks them against the respective waybills).

Trauerparte *f* -/-n *(Todesanzeige)* = *Parte(zettel)* ↑.

Trauminet *m* -s/-s *colloq.* a shy, timid person lacking self-confidence: fraidy cat, scaredy cat; *dem ~ bleibt Liebe nur ein Traum* faint heart never won fair lady.

Trẹppelweg *m* -(e)s/-e *nav.* *(Treidelpfad, Leinpfad)* tow-path, towing-path ‖ on a 'forbidden' sign: *Befahren des ~es verboten!* 1. No wheeled traffic on tow-path! – 2. *generally:* No trespassing!, Trespassers will be prosecuted!

Trọpferl *n* -s [dim. of *Tropfen*] *colloq.* **1.** little drop (of water or any other liquid, often of alcohol); *emot.* tiny (wee) drop; *wie wär's mit einem ~?* what about a drinkee? – **2.** *appr.* of good wine or other liquor: *ein gutes ~* a good drop, *ScotE* a. guid drappie; *so ein ~ läßt man sich gefallen!* that's a wine to write home about! – **~bad** *n* -(e)s/…bäder *obsolescent (öffentliches Brause- und Wannenbad)* public shower (bath) for the less affluent, run by the Municipality of Vienna: "sprinkling shower hall".

Trottoir [trɒtˈwaːr] *n* -s/-e *(Gehsteig [neben der Fahrbahn]) BrE* pavement, footpath, *AmE* sidewalk; *geh (*or *steig) vom ~ herunter!* step off the curb!

Tschako *m* -s/-s [< Hung. *scáko (süveg)* 'peaked (cap)', < *scák* 'peak' < AusG *Zacken m* 'spike'] **1.** *mil. hist.* a cylindrical or conical military hat, made of felt or leather, with a peak and a plume or pompom (*Uniformkappe mit flachem Runddeckel*): shako [ˈʃeɪkəʊ, ˈʃakəʊ] (*pl.* -os). – **2.** *hum.* or *iron.* any (oddly shaped) headgear (*Deckel*): (funny) lid, cady.

Tschapperl *n* -s/-n [< (the truncated form of) Cz *cápek* 'awkward' + dim. *-erl*] **1.** *emot.* an infant (1) or an infirm old person (2) who walks with short, unsteady steps: (1) also, *süßes, kleines ~* toddlekins, toddles; and (2) also, *wackeliges, altes ~* doddery old dear, crumbly. – **2.** *emot.* a person who, through no fault of his or hers, has mostly been on the seamy side of life so far and, moreover, feels too listless and incapable of bringing about a change for the better: poor (little) mouse *or* worm ‖ cp. *Armitschkerl* ↑. – **3.** slightly *contp.,* often used in direct address – a person who is unskilled, or naturally clumsy, in handling things: butterfingers *sg.; kriegst du denn das Schloss wirklich nicht auf? – lass mich's machen, (du) ~!* can't you really get the lock open? let *me* do it, butterfingers.

Tschecherl, Tschocherl *n* -s/-n slightly *contp. (kleines Café)* small and shabby café *or* coffee-shop: *AmE* sleazy diner, greasy spoon.

Tschick, Tschik *m* -s/- [< It *cicca*] low *colloq. (Zigarettenrest)* cigarette-end, stub: *BrE* fag-end, *AmE* butt; *den (*or, *seinen) ~ abtöten* to put out one's cigarette: to squash one's cig; *~ [pl.] arretieren* to salvage discarded cigarette-ends: *BrE* to pick up fag-ends, *AmE* to scavenge (*or,* hunt) for butts. – **~arretierer** *m* -s/- low *colloq. (Kippenjäger)* collector of cigarette-ends: ciggy-butt scavenger, *AustralE* bumper-shooter.

tschinbumm *interj.* or ≙ *n* -s *colloq.* (a succession of quick) explosive noises, of a fire-arm, heavy objects hitting the ground, etc.: bang, ker-rump; crash. – **Tschinbummfilm** *m* -s/-e *colloq. ([minderwertiger] Film, in dem viel geschossen wird)* bang-bang, bang-bang-shoot-'em-up film.

Tschurtsche, Tschutsche *f* -/-n, *dial.* **Tschurtschn** *f* -/- ⚘ **1.** *(Fruchtzapfen e-s Nadelbaumes)* (pine-)cone. – **2.** = *Türkentschurtsche.*

Tuchent *f* -/-en *(mit Federn gefüllte Bettdecke)* feather-bed; *um acht (Uhr) war ich schon unter der ~* I was in my feather-bed by eight (o'clock).

Türk *m* -en/-en *dial.* Turk ‖ an *iron. phr.* derived esp. from commemorative wall paintings, e.g. at Pürbach, Burgenland, showing the effigy of a Turk (who was discovered hiding on the site after the Turkish army had retreated on its defeat before Vienna in 1683): *dasitzen wie ein angemalter* (or *angemalener*) ~ to sit motionless, without participating in the doings around him: to be sitting (there) like a lame duck (*or,* like a stuffed dummy), *AmE a.* … like a bump on a log.

Repulsing the Turks from the Löwel Bastion in 1683 – now the site of Vienna's Burgtheater

Tụrken *m* -s ↓ *(Mais)* Indian corn, maize. *AmE* corn. – **~acker** *m* -s/…äcker *(Maisfeld) BrE* field of Indian corn, *AmE* cornfield. – **~brot** *n* -(e)s/-e *bak.* a plain loaf made of corn meal: corn bread, *AmE a.* corn-pone. – **~korn** *n* -(e)n = *Türken.* – **~krieg** *m* -(e)s/ often *pl.* -e *mil. hist.* Turkish War, one of the defensive wars, esp. in 1529 and 1683, fought by Austria against her Turkish invaders, who then often ravaged large tracts of the country's eastern provinces; that standing menace is reflected to this day in several expressions, most clearly in *Kruzitürken* ↑. – **~röster** *m* -s ☼ *(Föhn)* "corn toaster", a well-known southerly wind blowing down the central Inn Valley and ripening the Indian corn, which is the staple produce of the area. – **~sitz** *m* -es *(Schneidersitz)* tailor's seat, sitting on the ground, or floor, with crossed legs; *im ~ sitzen* to sit tailor-fashion. – **~sterz** *m* -es/-e *cul.* → *Sterz.* – **~tschurtsche, ~tschutsche** *f* -/-n *(Maiskolben)* (corn-)cob; *die ~n werden unter dem weiten Vordach der Bauernhäuser gebündelt zum Trocknen aufgehängt* the corn-cobs are tied into bundles and hung up for drying under the deep eaves of the farmhouses.

U

Über…: ~fuhr *f* -/-en *nav.* *(Fähre)* ferry (-boat); *bei Spitz sind wir mit der ~ ans andere Donauufer gekommen* at Spitz we took the ferry across the Danube ‖ an *iron. phr.* aimed at an elderly woman who failed to find a husband in good time: *die ~ verpasst* (or *versäumt*) *haben* to have missed the boat, to be left on the shelf. – **~führer** *m* -s/- *nav.* *(Fährmann)* ferryman. – **~gangl** *n* -s/-(n) *colloq.* *(vereinzelte Regentropfen)* a few drops of rain (and not more): just a sprinkle, just a flock of birds flying over, just a little bird. – **~g'scheite** *m* or *f* -n/-n *dial.* = *Oberg'scheite* ↑.

überhạlten *v/t* † *(e-n zu hohen Preis verlangen)* to overcharge (*j-n* a p.); *wir werden Sie schon nicht ~!* rest assured, we aren't going to charge you too much (*or,* too highly)!

überhạpps, überhạps *adv* [< *überhaupt* 'originally' – a term in cattle trade, 'not counting in detail the heads of the animals'] *colloq.* **1.** *(ungefähr)* roughly (speaking): by hit-or-miss reckoning; *es waren ~ an die dreihundert gekommen* by guess and by God there had been some three hundred people. – **2.** *(oberflächlich)* superficially (speaking); as a casual aside: just like that; *und nun kam gleich ~ einiges bezüglich Carnuntum, das ja gar nicht im Burgenland liegt* and then, out of hand, we were chivied on to some bits about Carnuntum… which does not lie in Burgenland at all. – **Überhạppsnehmen** *n* -s *colloq.* an inexact judgment, esp. of quality, made by guessing: guesstimate; *was die Mengen der Grundzutaten zu einer Speise betrifft, so ist dem vielgeübten ~ ein energisches Veto entgegenzusetzen; Redewendungen wie „Das habe ich doch schon im Griff" oder „Was werde ich da erst viel abwägen!" sind nicht ein Zeichen besonderer Meisterschaft, sondern ein Missverstehen der Wissenschaft Kochkunst* regarding the measurements of the basic ingredients of a dish, a forceful protest should be raised against the common practice of using rough guesses; phrases like "I can tell by the feel of it" or "Why bother with a lot of weighing?" are not a sign of a particular mastery, but rather a misunderstanding in the science of culinary arts.

überknọcheln *v/refl & t sich ~* or *sich* (dat.) *den Fuß ~ med.* (Ger.: *sich den Fuß übertreten*) to sprain (*AmE a.* to turn) one's ankle; *ein überknöchelter Fuß* a sprained ankle; *ich habe mir den Fuß überknöchelt* I sprained my ankle.

Übersteigerl *n* -s/-n, less often **Überstieg** *m* -(e)s/-e ♩ chiefly found in Alpine areas – a set of wooden rungs or steps, not a gate, enabling persons on foot to get over a fence but keeping cattle etc. out: stile.

übertauchen *v/t colloq. med.* often without consulting a doctor: *e-e Krankheit ~* **1.** to survive the more serious stages of a disease: *das Schlimmste ~* to make it through the worst parts; *ich habe das Schlimmste übertaucht* I've made it over the hump. – **2.** to bypass an illness by taking preventive measures in good time: to nip in the bud; *sie hat gleich zwei Aspirin genommen und so die sich abzeichnende Verkühlung rechtzeitig übertaucht* just in the nick of time she took two aspirins and beat the oncoming cold.

ui jẹggerl, uijẹggerl, or **uijegerl** *dial. interj* [the diphthongal "upbeat" suggests the initial swish made by approaching high winds, and conjures up visions of a face distraught with grief and fear; however, such extremes, we learn from the presence of the soothing diminutive *-erl,* are not justified, a point confirmed by the euphemized form of *Jesus*] often *hum.* an inoffensive expression of gentle dismay at the sight of a minor family mishap or other irregularity or incident of forgetfulness that is part and parcel of everyday reality, such as spilling one's milk or beer, or of allowing a meal to become something of a burnt offering *(oje)*: oh (no), jeepers (-creepers), *AmE a.* shucks, by gee; *mit die Richter hat er geschimpft* (or, *die Richter hat er was genamelt*), *~!* now didn't he call the judges names, deary me!; *~, jetzt hab ich doch pfeilgrad vergessen, ob was an Post da ist!* oh my, didn't I forget to check downstairs whether there was something in the letterbox.

Umfahrung *f* -/-en or **Umfahrungsstraße** *f* -/-en a new, wide road passing round a heavily populated urban area or village, to take through traffic *(Umgehungsstraße)*: bypass *or* by-pass.

Ụnfaller *m* -s/- *colloq.* accident-prone person; *er ist ein ~* he is an accident waiting to happen.

Ụnter ...: ~länder *m* -s/- inhabitant of the Lower Inn Valley, east of Innsbruck (opp., *Oberländer*). – **~läufel** *m* -s/-(n) [< the historical sense of *Läufel m* 'messenger', 'errand-bearer'] *colloq.,* often slightly *contp.,* esp. with reference to one holding public office – subordinate *(Untergebener)*: underling; *er ist nur ein ~* he's just an underling, he's just a pawn in the game.

ụnterzünden *vt/i colloq.* **1.** *v/i Feuer* [*im Ofen* or *im Freien*], *Gas*[*flamme*] *anzünden*) to light the fire; *hast du etwas zum ~ für den Ofen?* have you(got) (*AmE* do you have) a match or lighter to get the stove burning? – **2.** rarely *v/t* to light (the stove, etc.); *das Backrohr ~* to light the oven. – **Ụnterzündholz** *n* -es kindling, small wood (for lighting a fire); *ist ~ da?* is there some kindling? is there any wood to light the (*or,* a) fire?

ụrassen *v/i* [< Gothic *ufarassus* 'abundance', *ufarassjan* 'to abound'] *colloq. (verschwenderisch umgehen)* to be wasteful, to squander; *du musst mit der Butter nicht so ~, streich sie doch ein wengerl dünner auf!* you might as well go easy on the butter and spread it a little thinner!

Venus [ˈ-e:-] *f* -/pl. rare: -se < *Roman relig.* Venus [ˈ-i:-], an ancient goddess of bloom and beauty > *prehist.* one of several, venerably old statues unearthed on the left bank of the Danube in today's Lower Austria – **1.** ~ *von Willendorf,* also known as ~ *die Erste,* found in 1908 near that village in the Wachau, possibly representing a goddess of fertility of the Aurignacian [ˌɔ:rignˈeɪʃən] peoples, at least 20,000 years old, made in oolitic limestone, only eleven centimetres (or 4.33 inches) long, and at one time seemingly coloured red; to modern ideas the lady is repellently ugly; the face was not carved at all, but there are six coils of hair above which are perfectly preserved, as is, in fact, the entire figure, with the exception of the feet, which are missing. – **2.** ~ *die Zweite* 'Venus the Second', found in 1926 quite close to the site of 'Venus the First': a slender lady with a modern figure, contrasting strongly with the swollen outlines of her female companion, carved in mammoth-tusk ivory, about 25 centimetres (or ten inches) long, and thus the tallest statue of the Ice Age. – **3.** ~ von *Langenzersdorf,* also close to the left bank of the Danube, on the outskirts of Vienna, another prehistoric female figure, estimated to be 5000 years old.

Vergelt's Gott *R.C.* a common phr. expressing appreciation for kindness, alms, or help of any kind: **1.** *interj* God reward you!, God bless you!, thank you kindly! → **2.** *n* -/- heartfelt thanks, God's Blessings in post-funeral thank-you notices in newspapers: *ein ~ der hochwürdigen Geistlichkeit für die trostreichen Worte am Grabe* heartfelt thanks to, *or* God's Blessing on, the Reverend Clergy for their comforting words at the graveside.

verhabert *adj* [pp. < *verhabern* v/refl 'to become friends (*mit* with)'; → *Haberer*] *dial.* **1.** acting as a friend, friendly (*befreundet*): *wir alle von unserer Blase sind eng ~* all of us in this gang are on close terms (with one another). – **2.** in collusion, usu. for a disreputable or deceitful purpose (*unter einer Decke* [*steckend*]): *mit j-m ~ sein* to be hand in glove (*AmE a.* to be in cahoots) with sb.: *ich bin nicht der einzige, der befürchtet, Ihre Zeitung und die Politik seien „~"* I am not the only one to have misgivings about your paper and politics being at the old game of log-rolling. – **3.** *erot.* maintaining a regular relationship: ~ *sein* to go steady.

verkühlen *v/refl* to contract a slight illness that makes it difficult to breathe through one's nose and makes one's throat hurt (*sich erkälten*): to catch (a) cold; *sich* *leicht* ~ to catch a chill; *ich habe mich schwer verkühlt* I' ve got a bad cold || a warning to the blithely unconcerned: *du wirst dich* [*ihr werdet euch*] *noch zu Tod ~!* you'll catch your death of cold. – **Verkühlung** *f* - (*Erkältung*) cold; *eine leichte* ~ a chill; *ich kann einfach* (colloq. also, *ich kann und kann*) *die ~ nicht loswerden* I simply can't get rid of my cold.

vermurt *p.p.* ⩕ said of meadows and cultivated soil: strewn with block of stone ([and other debris] carried along by torrential rains); → *Mur(e).* – **Vermurung** *f* -/-en ⩕ rock-flood devastation, damage done by a sudden rush of water carrying along blocks of stone, rubble, and sand || as a road sign in mountainous areas: *Achtung! ~en bei starkem Regen!* Watch out for sliding debris caused by heavy rain(s)!

verschnabulieren *v/t colloq. hum.* to eat with great relish: to do oneself well by, to lay into with relish; *es war sehenswert, wie die alle ihr Backhendl verschnabuliert haben!* you should have seen the lot doing themselves well by (*or,* laying into) those fried chickens of theirs with gusto.

Versenkungsrat *m* -(e)s/ … räte *hum.* or *iron.* [lit., "submersion counsellor", an imaginary title to poke fun at the Austrian fondness of throwing around bombastic titles] gravedigger: *burial consultant, *burial engineer.

versumpern *v/i* [cp. *Sumper*] *colloq.* (*geistig stagnieren)* to stagnate mentally, to get bogged down in mental mediocrity; *wenn man hier auf dem Lande nichts liest oder zumindest ein Steckenpferd betreibt, versumpert man ganz* if you don't do any reading at all, or at least have a hobby, you're bound to vegetate (*AmE a.,* … to become a rural Babbitt).

verwienern *colloq.* **1.** *v/t* to viennafy. – **2.** *v/i* to become viennafied.

verwurstelt, often in the *dial.* form **verwurschtelt** *p.p., colloq.* said of a dress, carpet etc.: *([in Falten] verschoben, in Unordnung [gebracht]) BrE* rucked up, in a tangle *or* mess, *AmE* (all) tangled up, all wrinkled up, screwed up; *am Tag der Offenen Tür mussten die Schonteppiche schon bald neu gespannt werden, sie waren durch die vielen Füße ganz ~* on the day of Open House, the roll-out carpets were soon in need of being straightened out because of all the gruesome mess from the feet tracking over them.

verzwicken *v* [second el. akin to OE *twiccian,* ModE *to tweak* and *to twitch* 'to pinch and pull with a sudden jerk and twist'] **1.** *v/t hum.* to eat up (*verzehren*): to polish off, to demolish; *er hat den Teller voller Zwetschkenknödel in einem Satz verzwickt* he polished off the plateful of plum dumplings in no time at all. – **2.** *v/refl colloq.* said of a bus conductor etc. and his ticket punch: to mark a ticket (*or,* to punch a hole) in the wrong place.

Viecherl *n* -s/-(n) [dim. of *Vieh* 'animal'] *dial. emot. (Tierchen)* little animal: little creature, little bugger, *ScotE* beastie; *das arme ~ hat heut den ganzen Tag noch kein bisserl (*or *Schluckerl) Milch gehabt* the poor little thing has not had a spot of milk all day.

Vogerl *n* -s/-(n) [a dim. of *Vogel m* 'bird' + dim. *-erl*] *emot. & nurs., colloq.* **1.** also

The Votive Church in Vienna, near the Ring, has been a conspicuous landmark since 1879

Vögerl *n* -s/-(n) used to or by children, but also among adults, esp. women, in an easy-going or cheerful mood – any small bird: birdie, dickybird, *less often* cockyollybird ‖ the first quatrain of an old Viennese folk song:

Das Glück is a Vogerl,
gar liab, aber scheu;
es lasst si' schwer fanga,
doch furtg'flogn is glei'.

Man's luck 's like a birdie,
Right charming, though shy;
To snare it is mighty hard,
Soon off, too, 'twill fly.

2. *phr.* (1) *hum.* a semi-proverbial catch-phrase used to indicate that the speaker knows something but prefers to keep the identity of the informant a secret; often said in reply to the (not necessarily expressed) question, 'Who told you?': *ein (kleines) ~ hat es mir zugetragen, ich hab' ein ~ singen hören* a little bird told me, *AmE a.* a little ladybug has told me. – (2) a photographer's coaxing invitation, tickling a small child's fancy, to keep still and stare into the camera: *gleich kommt 's ~ raus!* watch the birdie! – **3.** also **Vogi** *n* -s/- a parent's, nursery-school teacher's, etc. *euphem.* for a small boy's penis (*Kinderpenis,* Ger.: *Schwänzi*) dickybird, peenie, *AmE a.* little bird, weenie, *UlsterE a.* peedie. – **~salat** *m* -(e)s/pl. rare: -e the tender leaves of the *Valerianella locusta* plant, rich in vitamins A and C, a favourite type of salad eaten in spring (*Feld-, Rapunzelsalat*): lamb's lettuce, corn salad, rampion.

Vorderösterreich *n* -s; earlier also, **Vorlande** *pl.* (now obsolescent) *hist.* two collective names for the medieval possessions of the Hapsburg dynasty in Swabia, Alsace (Sundgau), and Switzerland (e.g. the Aargau, Thungau, and Zürichgau), in particular the Breisgau area (with the capital Freiburg for its political and spiritual centre): Further Austria; cp. *Innerösterreich* ↑.

Vorwärtswuzler *m* -s/- *hist.* [< a malintentioned pun on the initials of *Volkswagen*] *contp.* "vile wriggler", so called because of the limitations of space and speed earlier associated with this 'little man's car'.

Votiv [vo'ti:f-] **…: ~bild** *n* -(e)s/-er *R.C. & folklore* a usu. crude peasant painting displayed, with dozens of its mates, in a church, monastery, or wayside chapel: votive picture; *jedes ~ wandte sich einst mit einer stummen Bitte an Gott oder einen Heiligen, mit dem gleichzeitigen feierlichen Gelöbnis, eine bestimmte Tat zu setzen oder Bedingungen zu erfüllen* each votive picture once addressed itself to God or to a saint as a mute appeal for help and, at the same time, as a solemn vow to perform some service or fulfil certain conditions. – **~kirche** *f* - *R.C.* [see overleaf] "Votive Church" of St Saviour's *[Zum göttlichen Heiland],* with twin stone fretwork spires erected to the memory of Emperor Francis Joseph's escape from assassination at the hands of a Hungarian radical in 1853.

Vulgoname *m* -n/-n *folklore* a name used instead of one's own; rather than using the family name, a person will often go by the name of the occupation with which his house has been associated for hundreds of years; if a baker once lived in the house, the current occupants may also go by the name of Baker.

W X

Wadschunken *m* -s/- [the second element is a variant of *Schinken* 'ham', / ɪ / and /ʊ/ both being centralized half-close vowels; for their symmetrical relationship, and therefore easy interchangeability, cp. such pairs as *kumm* and *kimm* (the dialect imperative of *kommen*), *winzig* and *(klein)wunzig,* as well as *woman* /wʊ-/ and *women* /wɪ-/] *cul. (Rindfleisch von den Beinen [unterhalb der Schulter und unterhalb der Hüfte])* shin of beef.

Wahlzuckerl *n* -s/-(n) *polit. colloq.* a specious vote-catching concession by the (outgoing) government (*Wahlgeschenk*): election bait *or* giveaway.

Wald *m* -(e)s/ Wälder forest ‖ *phr.* an impatient protest at someone's unrefined behaviour such as eructating in public or sneezing in a restaurant without covering one's mouth: *sind wir im ~?* are we in the Dark Ages (*or,* in the jungle)?

Waller *m* -s/- [like *Wels m,* related to *Wal m* 'whale'] 🐟 a large, bottom-dwelling freshwater fish, known to reach a length of 5 m and a weight of over 300 kg; it has whisker-like barbels round the mouth, and a very long anal fin (*Wels*): catfish, sheatfish, wels.

Walzer...: ~könig *m* -s ♪ *hist.* "Waltz King", an epithet given to Johann Strauss the Younger, 1825–1899, because of his very popular dance compositions. – **~stadt** *f* - ♪ "City of Waltzes", an epithet for Vienna, once the birthplace and home of many waltz composers.

Wampeler *m* -s/- [dim. < *Wampe f* 'protruding abdomen'; cp. E *womb* [wu:m], 'uterus', originally 'belly'] **1.** Tyrolean *dial.* fat-bellied person: fatty, tubby, *AmE* fatso. – **2.** *folklore* "Fighting Fatty", one of the chief actors in the *Wampelerreiten* scuffle who, wearing a red skirt over his trousers, chest well padded with hay (hence the name) under a white shirt of coarse linen, impersonates a winter demon. – **~reiten** *n* -s *folklore* at Axams, at four-year intervals, on the last Sunday before Lent: "Jumping the Fatties", the main feature of a carnival procession, in which onlookers try to ride, and throw to the ground from behind, a group of "fat" winter demons; those roly-polies completing the tour of the village without being rolled on the floor are treated at the riders' expense.

Waschel, often **Waschl** *m* -s/- [< word stem *Wasch-* 'wash' (for its original meaning, see the etymology offered under *Ohrwaschel* ↑) + agent-noun suffix *-el* (see under *Drischel* ↑)] *dial.* **1.** *cul.* a small ball of wire or rough plastic for cleaning cooking pots and pans (*Scheuerknäuel*): scourer. – **2.** usu. **Bade**~ or

At Axams, the Wampeler *winter demons are a living link with the superstitions of an age long past*

Ba̲dwaschl, often slightly *pej.* someone employed to clean the tubs of a public bath or do similar menial duties on the premises (*Badediener*): bath attendant. – **3.** *pej.* an untrained, inefficient, or stupid person (*unnötiger Mensch*): twit, clown, *AmE a.* sad sack.

wạschelnass or **wạschlnass** *adj dial.* said of a person – often the speaker or writer (and then wallowing a little in self-pity) – who was caught unawares in a cloudburst or in a steady "stair-rod" drizzle of the *Schnürlregen* ↑ type – drenched to the skin (*triefnass*): dripping *or* soaking wet, soaked to the bones.

Wa̲serl *n* -s/-n [through *dial.* monophthongization < *Waise f* 'orphan' + dim. *-erl*] *dial., pej.* **1.** an unstable or irresolute person (*wankelmütiger Mensch*): softy, *BrE a.* clueless clot. – **2.** someone who is too frightened to do something (*Feigling*): backward in going forward, scaredy-cat, *AmE a.* fraidy cat, pussy (foot[er]).

Wa̲tsche *f* -/-n, *dial.* **Wa̲tsch(e)n** *f* -/- *colloq. (Ohrfeige)* slap on the cheek (*or,* face): smack on the ears; *sie hat ihm eine gesunde ~ gegeben* she smacked him a good one ‖ as a more or less humorous warning: *du gehst am Rande einer ~ spazieren!* you are walking (*or,* playing) on the edge!, you're playing with fire!, *AmE* you're cruisin' for a bruisin'!; → *Gusto.* – **wa̲tschen** *v/t colloq. (ohrfeigen)* to slap on the ears: to smack s.o. 's ears.

Watschen…: ~baum *m* -(e)s/…bäume an imaginary tree bearing the figurative fruit of "ear-smacks" that topple down over on whosoever misbehaves: "ear-box tree"; …as a verbal caution not to overstep one's bounds: *du beutelst am ~!, der ~ wird gleich umfallen!* *you're shaking the "ear-box tree"!, *AmE* timber! the "ear box tree" is coming down! –. ≃**einfach** *adj colloq.* said of an examination, etc. very easy: as easy as falling off a log, *NZ & AustralE a.* piss easy. – **~gesicht** *n* -(e)s/-er low *colloq.* a bloated face, usu. that of a male, which provokes one to reach out and slap it: *BrE* Percival Pudding-face, *AmE* Fat-faced Freddy; *der hat ein ~, da juckt's einen in der Hand* he's got a face that just begs to be slapped (around); he's got a good face for a bus-ticket – just waiting to be punched. – **~kadi** *m* -s/-s *colloq.* small-claims court judge, before whom only petty squabbles are tried: small-time judge. – **~mann** *m* -(e)s/ …männer **1.** a test-your-strength machine in the Vienna Volksprater, which is disguised in a human form: big-faced dummy. – **2.** *colloq.* a person held up for public criticism and made to take the blame for others *(Prügelknabe)*: whipping boy.

Weiberwirtschaft *f* - slightly *contp.* or purely *hum.* – but always used from a male chauvinist's angle resenting, or pretending to resent, the preponderance of females, or their very physical presence, in a business firm, private household, etc.: feminocracy; *er hat eine ~ daheim* at home, he is surrounded by skirts.

Weichsel ['-ksl] *f* -/-n [< MHG *wīhsel* < OHG *wīhsela,* related to Gr *ixós* and L *viscum* 'birdlime' – the sticky resin exuded by the tree bearing that type of cherry having once been spread on to twigs to trap small birds)] ✿ a dark cherry of a sour kind used in cooking (*Sauerkirsche*): sour *or* morello cherry, 🕮 Prunus cerasus.

Wein…: ~beißer *m* -s/- **1.** *colloq. (Weinkenner [welcher den Wein genüsslich auskostet])* wine connoisseur, wine expert: one who knows his way around wines. – **2.** *cul. (mit weißer Glasur überzogenes Löffelbiskuit)* iced gingerbread finger. – **~zeiger** *m* -s/- *vinic.* in a wine-growing village, etc.: "new-wine indicator" **1.** a notice board in a public place, bearing the names of taverns where wine can be drunk. – **2.** = *Heurigenbuschen* ↑.

Wetterfleck *m* -(e)s/-e *tex.* a wide raincoat without arms: cape, poncho; *sich einen ~ umhängen* to put on a poncho.

Widum, Widem *n* -s/-e [< OHG *widimo* orig., in heathen times, 'the maintenance fund given over on marriage by the groom to the bride in the event that she become a widow'] *R.C.* in Western Austria, esp. in South Tyrol – the residence of a parson, as provided by the parish or church *(Pfarrhaus)*: parsonage.

Wiener: ~ Brille *f* - -/- -n Viennese glasses (whose legs and bridge are directly fixed to the lenses). – **~ Genesis** *f* - - *relig. arts* Vienna Genesis, a fragment (26 sheets) of a Greek manuscript dating from the sixth century, on purple parchment with silver letters; it is one of the few early Christian manuscripts preserved. – **~ Humor** *m* - -s *soc. & ling.;* if *hist.,* often referring to the period around 1900: Viennese humour, a philistine, yet also amiable outlook on life, well chronicled by writers like Vinzenz Chiavacci (1847–1916) and Eduard Pötzl (1851–1914), witnessed also today in the local new-wine tavernry *(Heurigenwesen)* where sentimental music is sung to the accompaniment of violin, guitar, and concertina. – ~ **Klassik** *f* - - ♪ Viennese Classicism, a unique concentration in Vienna around 1800 of musical genius and power, a time when the compositions by Haydn, Mozart, Beethoven, and Schubert there attained sublime heights of human and spiritual expression. – ~ **Kreis** *m* - -es *phil.* Vienna Circle, an important school of Neo-Positivism whose main concern lay in translating scientific terms and statements into formalistic-logistic language; statements about metaphysics, values and norms were considered absurd. – ~ **Sängerknaben** *m pl.* - - ♪ Vienna Boys' Choir, a famous group of boy singers founded in 1925 in Vienna, having its roots in the original boys' choir of the Vienna Court Chapel (built in 1498); Franz Schubert, among others, belonged to that early choir. – ~ **Werkstätte** *f* - *-n* Viennese Workshop *arts* a school of craftsmen headed by Josef Hoffmann and Kolo Moser, specializing in deliberately ordinary and simply geometric home décor, between 1903 and 1932.

Wintersenner *m* -s/pl. rare: - *folklore* = *Kasermandl* ↑.

Wonne *f* -[related to OE *wynn* 'joy'] bliss; *phr.* a cheerfully worded warning, or verbal pat of sympathetic comfort, that our earthly existence is not just filled with pleasure and enjoyment, but involves problems as well: *das Leben ist (halt) nicht immer ~ und Waschtrog* life isn't always a bed of roses (you know); *BrE a.* ah well, life isn't all beer and skittles.

Wulfenia *f* - [discovered by, and named after, Baron Franz X. von Wulfen, an Austrian botanist, mineralogist, and Alpine explorer (1728–1805) ✿ also known as *Kärntner Kuhtritt,* a herbaceous perennial plant of the figwort family, having shiny leaves and long hairy stems with clusters of purplish two-lobed flowers; the only natural European home of this Asiatic plant is on the Gartnerkofel in the Gailtal Alps, SW of Hermagor: Wulfenia (carinthiaca).

Wurstel ['wuəʃtl], **Wurschtl** *m* -s/- **1.** *theat. (Hanswurst)* in a circus, etc.: buffoon; in a Punch-and-Judy show: clown. – **2.** *contp.* of a subservient or foolishly doting person: *er springt wie ein ~ um sie herum* he dances around her like a puppet, he follows her around like a puppy dog; *glaubst du, ich bin dein ~?* what do you take me for, your own personal slave (*AmE* … your stooge)? – **3.** *colloq.,* in gentle annoyance or mild reproach: *du bist ein ~! BrE* you're a (big) silly!, you clumsy clot! *AmE* you silly bird (*or,* goof)!

Wurstel…: ~prater *m* -s *geog. & soc. hist. (Vergnügungspark des Wiener Praters)* Prater Amusement Park, Vienna Fun Fair, between the Ausstellungsstrasse and the Hauptallee, i.e. a noisy and frivolous assortment, under the patronizing shadow of the Great Ferris Wheel, of swings, merry-go-rounds, grottoes, dodgem cars and switchback railways. – **~theater** *n* -s/- *(Kasperl[e]theater)* Punch-and-Judy show.

Wụ̈rstel or **Wụ̈rstl,** *dial.* spelling **Wụ̈rschtl** *n* -s/- (*dial.* -n) [< *Wurst f* 'sausage' + dim. *-(e)l*] **1.** *comest.* a long reddish, seasoned and smoked sausage made of beef and pork, sold in pairs, cooked and usu. eaten as a small snack (*Würstchen*): frankfurter, *AmE a.* frank, wiener, weenie *or* wienie. – **2.** *contp.* a simple-minded or easily imposed-upon person (*unbedarfter Mensch*): goon, goop, nitwit, thicko, *BrE a.* clot, nit, *AmE a.* birdbrain, dumbski, jerk; *zuwegn was hast denn du die Streifhölzln in 'n Frigidaire 'gebm, du ~?* what did you put the matches in the fridge for, you goon (*or,* you silly sausage)? – **3.** low *colloq.* a lengthy piece of solid faeces discharged from the intestines of a human being or a quadruped (*Stück Kot*): turd; *als der Lieblingsmops des Modeschöpfers beim Empfang ein ~ auf den Teppich praktizierte, klaubte es dieser gleich auf und schob es sich in die Tasche* at the reception, when the couturier's beloved little pug deposited a small turd on the carpet, he instantly picked it up and put it in his pocket. – **4.** ⚘ *colloq.* (1) also **Vogel~** a downy, pendulous flowering spike (*Fruchtstand*) of trees such as willow and hazel: catkin, lamb's-tail. – (2) the dark-red pendulous fruit of the honey-locust (→ *Würstelbaum*), which is dried and eaten as a sweetmeat: sausage. – **5.** Viennese *sl., contp.* a horse: nag, longface, *AmE a.* bushtail, hayburner, oatgrinder; *„Ihre ~n sind falsch geparkt", murrte der Beamte den Fiaker an* "Your nags are parked the wrong way", the official grumbled at the cabman. – **6.** *colloq. phr.* (1) an exclamation of emphatic rejection: *da gibt's keine ~n!* not a hope contradicting me!, nothing doing!, no siree bob(tail)! – (2) a perplexed comment on somebody having escaped, or otherwise disappeared, without a trace: *der is' verschwundn wie 's ~ aus 'm Kraut* he vanished into thin, air, *AmE a.* he pulled (*or* did) a Houdini [huːˈdiːnɪ].

Wụ̈rstel...: ~baum *m* -(e)s/ ... bäume *or* Viennese *dial.* the honey-locust, or Gleditsia, a spiny tree the longish pods of which (giving the tree its popular name [→ *Würstel* 4 (2)]) contain a sweet pulp: sausage tree. – **~finger** *m* -s/usu. *pl. iron.* short and thick fingers: stubby little fingers, sausage fingers. – **~frau** *f* -/pl. rare: -en (**~mann** *m* -(e)s/ pl. rare: ... männer) *colloq.* a person operating a sausage stand: hot-dog woman (man). – **~stand** *m* -(e)s/ ... stände *colloq.* a stand (*or* booth), sometimes on wheels, serving sausages and mustard, as well as other snacks, off cardboard plates; since open far into the night, it is also designed to protect revellers from the next-morning "queasies" (*Würstchenbude*): hot-dog stand.

Wụrsti or, more *dial.,* **Wurschti** *n* -(s)/- [< *Wurst f* 'sausage' + dim. *-i*] *baby talk* a word for solid waste from a child's body: doo-doo.

Wụrstigkeits... *colloq.:* **~spritze** *f* -/-n *med. (Beruhigungsspritze)* sedative injection, administered before an operation, etc.: jab of indifference; *j-m eine ~ verpassen AmE sl.* to gork; *nachdem wir ihm eine ~ verpasst haben, wird er sich schon beruhigen* he'll quiet down after we gork him. – **~standpunkt** *n* -es couldn't-care-less attitude; *du mit deinem ~ wirst es nie zu was bringen!* with that slack attitude of yours, you'll never amount to anything!

Wụrzel…: ~sepp *m* -/-en *colloq.* an unkempt rustic *(ungepflegter, ungehobelter Naturbursch)*: wild man of the woods; *schau, da kommt (ja) der ~!* look, here comes Rip Van Winkle! – **~werk** *n* -s/- *cul.* (*Suppengrün*) roots of parsley, celery, and carrots, added for flavour. – **~zwerg** *m* -s/-e *contp.* of an importunate or spiteful person (of small stature): little stinker, loathsome drip (*or* twerp), rumpelstiltskin, *BrE a.* rotten fellow.

wụrzen *v/t colloq.* to charge too much money *(überhalten)*: to fleece; *er lässt sich leicht ~* he is an easy one to fleece. – **Wụrzen** *f* -/- *colloq.* **1.** one who is (easily) taken advantage of *(auszunützende Person, Opfer)*: sucker, easy make (*or* mark), *AmE a.* fall guy; *ich bin allweil die ~* I'm always taken for a sucker. – **2.** a generous person *(freigebiger Mensch)*: open-handed person. – **Wurzere̲i̲** *f* -/-en *colloq.* with reference to a restaurant, hotel, etc. charging exorbitant terms: daylight (*AmE a.* highway) robbery; *so geschmalzene Preise sind eine reine ~* such steep prices are a plain case of overcharging.

wu̲zeln *vt/refl colloq.* **1.** *v/t* said with reference to hand-rolled cigarettes, an absent-minded or deliberate rubbing of dirt from one's hands, etc.: *(drehen, wickeln)* to roll; *der Opa hat sich immer seine Zigaretten über der silbernen Tabatiere gewuzelt* Grandpa always rolled his own right on his silver cigarette case; *mich hat gestern die Sonne arg erwischt, dass ich heute auf der Stirn und den Armen nur ~ kann* the sun got the best of me yesterday, so that today all I can do is rub off the dead skin from my forehead and arms. – **2.** *v/refl* (1) *(sich kugeln)* to be in ecstasies of mirth, at an act of clownery, etc.: to roll up (*or,* double up, curl up) with laughter, to be in stitches; *ich habe mich gewuzelt vor Vergnügen* I laughed my socks off. – (2) *(sich durchdrängen)* to edge one's way, to wriggle, to squeeze, *AmE* to snake one's way (*durch die Menge* through the crowd).

Wu̲zerl, rarely **Wu̲tzerl** *n* -s/-(n) *colloq.* **1.** in rural areas, often *emot.* (wee) baby; *wo ist denn das ~?* where's the baby darling? – **2.** said of a roly-poly child or adult: chubby-face; *ein kleines ~* a little fatty, a chubby darling; *mein Mann ist ganz ein schönes ~* my husband's pretty well padded all around. – **3.** *(Hautröllchen)* small curl of skin, rubbed off when taking a bath, or after a sunburn; *die ~(n) sind mir nur so heruntergegangen* I just flaked (*or* peeled) off like a snake.

wu̲zerl…: ~dick, ~fett *adj colloq.* usu. said of a child – plump *(wohlgenährt)*: chubby, podgy, roly-poly; *heute bin ich zwar eine Hopfenstange, aber als Kind, sagt meine Mutter, war ich ~, das kannst du mir glauben!* I may look like a beanpole now, but believe you me (my mother tells me) as a kid I was a real roly-poly!

xụnd [ksʊnt] *adj* a *hum.* dialect spelling of *gesund* 'healthy', e.g. in a boisterous answer in the affirmative to a question about the speaker's health: *~ samma* (lit., < *sind wir*)*!* (I'm feeling) the top of the world!

Z

Zahnderl *n* -s/usu. pl.: -n [< *Zahn m* 'tooth' + dim. *-erl* (here, with an intrusive *-d-* for easier pronunciation) *baby-talk* used to or of, and then naturally also by, very young children (*Zähnchen, Beißerchen*): *BrE* toothy-peg, *AmE* poose, toose, toofy; *wie unser Kleiner die ersten ~n gekriegt hat, hat er immer gejammert und geraunzt* whenever our little one cut a tooth he was a miserable and whiny lot.

Zaunstecken, usu. *dial.* **Zaunsteckn** *m* -s/- ↓ *(Zaunpfahl)* fence or fencing post ‖ *phr.* used in *hum.* or *sarc.* circumlocutions to mark a fictitious point of time, (1) when facetiously responding to an enquiry about the time of day: *es ist drei Viertel auf den ~* it's half past the corner, it's half past kissing time (and time to kiss again), or (2) when expressing the idea of 'never': *wann d' ~ blüahn* (lit., 'when fence posts are in bloom') when two Fridays *etc.* (*or,* three Sundays *etc.*) come together, when the Yellow River runs clear, when the world grows honest, *BrE a.* on St Tib's Eve, when Dover and Calais meet, *AmE a.* when the cows give beer.

Here is a Schnadahüpfl, or 'chatter ditty', about a confirmed bachelor and reluctant lover perjuring himself even twice in his little song:

Wart, i' werd' di' scho' liabm,
wann die Zaunsteckn tean blüahn;
wann da Bach auffi rinnt,
nacha heirat' ma gschwind.

*I will love you right true
When the week has Fridays two;
When the brook runs uphill
We'll be wed with a will.

Zeherl, *dial.* **Zecherl** *n* -s/-n [< *Zehe f* 'toe' + dim. *-erl*] **1.** *nursery talk,* used esp. to or of, and then naturally also by, very young children – a young child's toe: toesie. – **2.** ✿ *& cul., colloq.* any of the small bulbs making up a compound bulb of garlic (*Knoblauchzehe* [*Knob-,* altered from OHG *klovo,* and E *clove* being related]): clove (of garlic); *ein warmer Toast; ein ~ Knofel drauf, händisch verrieben; ein Stückerl Butter dazu, zergehen lassen – einfach, und einfach köstlich!* a piece of hot toast; one clove of garlic grated on it by hand; with a small pat of butter to melt and soak in – a simple fare, and simply fabulous!

Zeller *m* -s/- ✿ and *cul., colloq.* a biennial herb (📖 Apium graveolens), cultivated mainly for its stems, which are blanched and used as a salad (*Sellerie m* or *f* [AusG: *f*]): celery.

Zelten *m* -s/- [? < Germ. *teld-* 'to provide with a flat cover'] *bak.* a very sustaining type of food (which needs to be well buttered), made mainly at Christmastime: flat fruit-cake, a mixture of almonds, dates, figs, raisins and other dried fruit, encased in a thin, firm, unleavened pastry.

Zentralfriedhof *m* -(e)s Central Cemetery, a huge burial ground on the outskirts of Vienna ‖ *phr.* in a mock comparison setting off the sober character of the Swiss against the Viennese joy of life: *was ist der Unterschied zwischen Zürich und dem Wiener ~? Zürich ist doppelt so groß, aber nur halb so lustig!* what is the difference between Zürich and the Vienna Central Cemetery? Zürich is twice as big, but only half as lively!

zerfrạnsen *v/refl colloq.* to strain oneself *(sich sehr anstrengen)*: to bend over backward(s), to wear oneself out; *er hat sich zerfranst, um eine Gemeindewohnung zu bekommen* he just about knocked himself out getting a municipal flat. – **zerfrạnst** *adj colloq.* of cloth, etc.: *(ausgefranst)* frayed, frazzled; *dein Hemd ist aber schon arg ~* your shirt is just about tattered to shreds.

Zịppverschluss *m* … schlusses /… schlüsse *tech. (Reissverschluss)* zipper, zip, zip-fastener, *weißt du, dass dein ~ halboffen ist?* are you aware that your zipper's only at half-mast?

Zịrbe or **Zịrbel** *f* -/-n [< MHG *zirben* < OHG *zerben* 'to turn' – reference is to the strikingly 'well-turned' shape of the very large and glossy brown cones of that tree] ⚘ an umbrella-shaped alpine conifer which thrives in parts of the Tyrol; its fine grain, when polished to a beautiful honey-brown gloss as well as its strong smell make it a favourite everywhere in the province for the panelling of walls and the making of furniture; and Tyrolean wood-carvers, too, use it almost exclusively for their famous figures (*Arve*): cembra(-pine), (Swiss) stone pine, umbrella pine, 🕮 Pinus cembra. – **Zịrbel …: ~kiefer** *f* -/-n ⚘ = *Zirbe (1).* – **~nuss** *f* -/ … nüsse ⚘ the edible seed of the cembra-pine: pine nut. – **~stube** *f* -/s-n *archit.* the prize possession of many a Tyrolean family home, hotel, or inn, its wall-to-wall panelling and much cosiness and ease: cembra-pine snuggery.

Zịs *m* -/-(se) low *colloq. (Polizist)* policeman: cop, copper; *braucht man einen ~, ist keiner da!* never a cop around when you need one! – **~posten** *m* -s/- *school sl.* **1.** *(Beobachtungsstand)* observation post, from which the fact of an approaching teacher etc. is relayed to the rest of the class: lookout post. – **2.** *(Aufpasser)* watcher, lookout; *wer ist (*or, *hat) heute ~?* who's keeping watch today?, who's on lookout today?

zịzerlweis *colloq.* [like E *tit, ziz-,* the stem syllable, originated as a baby word (*Lallwort*), denoting anything very small, be it any of various kinds of small songbirds, a small horse, a girl, etc. – dialectal *Zizerl n,* in our country, denoting the wren (*Zaunkönig*), which has very short wings and a short tail carried erect] **1.** *adj* piecemeal, fragmentary, done bit by bit (*stückweise*): bitty; *im Zuge der ~en Europäisierung unseres Landes ist es gelungen, das Format der österreichischen Bierflaschen um einen Kopf kürzer zu machen und damit dem Standard in der Europäischen Wirtschaftsgemeinschaft voll Genüge zu lei-*

sten in the course of the bitty Europeanization of this country the size of Austrian beer bottles was successfully chopped by the length of their old head, and thus full justice was done to the standards laid down by the European Economic Community. – **2.** *adv* by instalments (*nach und nach*): titbit fashion, little by little, itsy bitsy (*or,* itty bit ty) fashion; *alles, was mir über die Geschichte von Schwaz bekannt ist, habe ich mir ~(e) zusammengetragen* all I know about the history of Schwaz I have gleaned titbit fashion; *das Geld kommt ~(e) herein BrE* the money comes in dribs and drabs, *AmE* the money dribbles in; *die Brücke hat man mit einer elektrischen Motorwinde ~(e) über die Donau gezogen* the bridge structure was pulled bit by bit (*or,* inch by inch) across the Danube by means of an electric winch.

Zornbinkel *m* -/-(n) *colloq.* a hot-tempered person: hothead; *hast du je schon so einen ~ gesehen?* have you ever seen someone fly off the handle like that (*or,* someone lose their temper like that)?

zufleiß *adv colloq. (absichtlich, zum Trotz)* intentionally, deliberately, on purpose; *etw. ~ machen* or *tun* to do sth. on purpose, with a view to causing damage or annoyance to a person; *die Hälfte meiner Lehrer ist erkrankt, wie ~* half of my teaching body have fallen ill, as if to spite me (*or,* as if from spite).

Zügen… [pl., < (*Glocken-*)*Zug m* 'bell pull']: **~glocke** *f* -/pl. rare: -n; more often in its dim. forms, **~glöckchen** and **~glöcklein** *n* -s/pl. rare: – **1.** *eccl.* a small, high-pitched bell which is loudly rung as a signal for prayers after a death has occurred in the community (*Sterbe-, Totenglocke*): (little) passing *or* death bell. → **2.** usu. **~glöcklein** sing. only, *lit.* & ♪ the title of a poem by Johannes Gabriel Seidl, 1804–1875: *eines der schönsten, von Franz Schubert vertonten Lieder ist „Das Zügenglöcklein"* 'The Passing-Bell' is one of the most beautiful songs set to music by Franz Schubert.

Zummel *m* -s/- [< Cz *cumi* (now obsolescent)] *colloq.* = *Luller.*

zündeln *v/i colloq.* said of children adventurously and carelessly making inflammable material and live matchsticks meet *(mit dem Feuer spielen)*: to play with fire. – **Zündler** *m* -s/- *colloq.* **1.** a cheerfully insouciant child tampering with fire: juvenile fire flirt. – **2.** a person who deliberately starts a fire, or fires, in order to destroy property = *Brandleger* ↑.

Zunder *f* -/-n [< OHG *zuntra* '(pinewood) torch'] ✿ *dial.* = *Latsche.* – **~gams** *m* -s/- *zo., dial.* "dwarf-pine chamois" [ˈʃæmwɑ:], preferring the dwarf-pine region for its habitat *(Standort).*

Zungenspragler *m* -s/- [second el., < *sprageln* ↑] *ling.* a sentence hard to speak fast, mostly because of alliteration or a sequence of trickily similar sounds: tongue-twister, jaw-breaker, *AmE* jaw-cracker (like G *Fischers Fritze fischte frische Fische,* or E *she sells sea shells by the seashore*).

Note: Two typical Austrian dialect examples are *Zwirnknäulerl* 'little ball of thread' and *wann's Hendln war'n* [wa:n], *gogatzatns* [ˈgɒ:gətsətns]*!* 'if they were hens they would cackle!'

zusammen…: ~böhmakeln, ~bömakeln *v/t colloq.* to speak with a strong Czech (or other Slavic) accent; to speak faulty German, to speak unintelligibly (cp. *böhmakeln*); *er böhmakelt da etwas zusammen, ich versteh ihn nicht* he speaks such broken German (*or* pidgin-German) that I can't understand him. – **~essen** *v/t colloq.* **1.** *(den Teller leer essen, aufessen)* to eat one's meal without leaving any remains: to eat up, to put away a meal, to clean one's plate; *es war gar nicht schwer, diese Zwergenportionen zusammenzuessen* it was no problem at all to finish off these midget portions; *jetzt iss[t du] schön brav das Grießkoch zusammen* now eat your semolina (*AmE* tapioca) pudding like a good boy [girl]. – **2.** said by one aghast at the sight of a person eating a strange meal, one of unusual composition: *ja, was isst du denn da zusammen?* what on earth (*or,* the heck) are you eating there? – **~fahren** *colloq.* **1.** *v/t* to hit s.o. with a moving vehicle *(überfahren)*: to run over s.o., to run s.o. down; *der Raser hat die Fußgängergruppe zusammengefahren* the speed-demon just mowed down that group of pedestrians. – **2.** *v/i* to make a sudden uncontrolled movement, esp. of surprise *(erschrecken)*: to give a start, to jump out of one's skin. – **~führen** *v/t* [hyper-correct] = *zusammenfahren* 1. – **~hauen** *v/t colloq. (zerbrechen)* to shatter, to break. – **~kagatzen** *v/i hum.,* or *critical* – to sing, from nervousness or inexperience, with an uneven voice (in rehearsals interrupted by slight coughs, etc.): to hem (*or* hum) and haw in one's singing. – **~läuten** *v/t eccl.* to ring (the bells) for Mass ‖ *phr.* (1) as a *sarc.* comment: *einige junge Leute ziehen es vor, den Gottesdienst dort zu feiern, wo man mit den Gläsern zusammenläutet* some young people prefer to answer the call of clinking glasses rather than that of ringing church bells. – (2) said *sarc.* of a woman who became pregnant before marriage: *sie ist vor dem ≈ in der Kirche gewesen* she couldn't make it to the church quickly enough. – **~putzen** *v/t colloq.* – **1.** to scold severely *(abkanzeln)*: to give s.o. a dressing-down, to give s.o. a good telling-off, to call s.o. on the carpet. – **2.** = *zusammenessen* 1. – **~raufen** *v/refl colloq.* to argue out one's differences (with a view to coming to an understanding): to have it out; *wenn zwei Kinder hacheln, sollte man nicht unbedingt eingreifen, sondern ihnen eher Gelegenheit geben, sich zusammenzuraufen* one shouldn't always step in the middle of two children squabbling, but rather give them a chance to sort (*or* work) it out themselves. – **~räumen** *vt/i* **1.** with reference to a room, one's desk, etc.: *(saubermachen)* to clean up, to tidy (up); *wann beliebt denn der gnädige Herr endlich, seinen Schreibtisch zusammenzuräumen?* when would His Majesty stoop (so low as) to clean up his own desk? – **2.** *(auf-, einsammeln)* to pick up (and pack away) one's things; *räum dein Glumpert zusammen, gleich kommt die Bedienerin!* put away that mess, the cleaning lady's coming! – **~reden** *v/t colloq.* to talk nonsense *(Unsinn reden)*: *BrE* to blather, to blether, *ScotE & dial.* to haver, *AmE* to babble, to blabber, to yammer; *was redest du denn da zusammen? BrE* what are you blathering?, *AmE* what are you babbling about?; *du redest was zusammen, wenn der Tag lang ist!* you talk as much as the day is long!, *AmE* you talk like there's no tomorrow! – **~spendeln** *v/t (mit Stecknadeln zusammenheften)* to join with pins; *sie spendelte Vorder- und Rückseite des Kleides zusammen und schaute, ob es passte* she pinned the front and back pieces of the dress together and tried it on for size.

Zuzel, less often **Suzel** *m* -s/- [< It *ciuccio* 'dummy teat for a baby'] *dial.* **1.** a specially shaped object, now of plastic or rubber, that is put in a baby's mouth for it to suck (*Schnuller [für Säuglinge]*): comforter, *BrE a.* dummy (teat), *AmE a.* pacifier, *AmE baby-talk* passie.* – **2.** the rubber cap on a bottle from which a baby nurses ([*Gummi-*]*Sauger*): *BrE* teat, *AmE* nipple. – **3.** usu. *hum.* or *contp.* a cigarette (*Zigarette*): *BrE* ciggy, fag, *AmE* drag, root, smokestick. – **4.** either *hum.* or *contp.* a pipe (*Pfeife*): smokestack, stove.

* Back in the 1840s, Dr. W. R. Wilde, a distinguished Member of the Royal College of Surgeons in Ireland, when visiting hospitals in Vienna, was scandalized to notice a "singular" and "highly prejudicial" practice in the treatment of infants; and he angrily held forth about it in his book called *Austria: Its Literary, Scientific, and Medical Institutions* (Dublin, 1843), p. 230: "Each infant, no matter whether it suckles at the breast or is spoon-fed, is provided with a kind of artificial nipple called *Zuzel* or *Zulp,* and formed of a bit of linen, in which a piece of pap or bread and milk, about the size of the thumb, is bound up. This is not only given it to derive nourishment from, but whenever the child cries it is crammed into its mouth. Now, although a good nurse will change the food in this every twenty-four hours, yet I have been informed that many do not do so for a week together; in either case fermentation ensues, and this, added to the saliva of the infant with which it is saturated, the dirt of the thing itself which is constantly falling from the child – its becoming hot and cold twenty times a day – renders it one of the most unhealthy substances a child can possibly have access to, as its general sour smell plainly attests. It is not alone given to them when teething – for I have seen it in the mouths of numbers of children not a week old."

Zuzelfleck *m* -(e)s/-e [cp. *zuzeln* 1] *hum.* an amorous blotch left on the skin by biting or sucking (*Knutschfleck*): lovebite, *AmE & CanE a.* hickey, monkey bite; *wer hat dir denn den ~ (da) verpasst?* who gave you that lovebite?

zuzeln, less often **suzeln** *v dial.* **1.** *vt/i* to draw into the mouth by producing a partial vacuum with the lips and tongue (*lutschen*): to suck; *magst d' an meinem Steckerleis ~?* (d'you) want to try and suck (*or,* … to have a taste of) my lollipop? ‖ *fig.* said of an idea or a piece of startling news: *sich das nicht aus den Fingern gezuzelt haben* not to have sucked that out of his [*etc.*] fingers. – **2.** *v/i phon.* to pronounce certain sounds with the tongue against the upper teeth or gums, as *th* for *s* or *z* (*beim Sprechen mit der Zunge anstoßen: lispeln*) to (have a) lisp, to speak with a lisp.

Zuzler, less often **Suzler** *m* -s/- *dial.* **1.** a person who sucks (cp. *zuzeln* 1): sucker. – **2.** *phon.* a person who, when speaking, pronounces *s* sounds as *th* (cp. *zuzeln* 2): lisper. – **3.** = *Zuzel* 1. – **4.** a bottle for supplying liquid food to a young child or animal ([*Säuglings-*]*Flasche*): nursing-(*or* feeding-)bottle, feeder; *das Rehkitzerl werdn mir wohl kaum durchkriegn, es nimmt koa Milch aus'm ~ an* our chances are slim of getting the kid (*or* fawn) through – it won't take any milk from the feeder.

Zwętschke *f* -/-n [distantly related to E *damson* 'plum (of Damascus)'] plum: *gedörrte ~n (Backpflaumen)* prunes ‖ *phr.* said mostly with reference to immediate departure: *seine sieben ~n zusammensuchen, die sieben ~n einpacken* to gather up one's things (*or* belongings), to pack one's bag(s) (and leave, *or* go); the opening lines of a famous Viennese tavern song:

Erst wann's aus wird sein
mit aner Musi und mit'm Wein,
dann pack'n ma die siebm Zwetschkn ein,
ehnder net.

*Why look peaked and pine,
And dream of pushing daisies fine?
We'd rather sing and drink good wine
To the last.

Zwętschkene *m* -n *bev. colloq. (Zwetschkenbranntwein)* home-made plum brandy, slivovitz; *ein selbstgebrannter ~r gefällig?* how about trying my own slivovitz?

Zwętschken ...: ~branntwein *m* -(e)s/-e *bev.* = *Slibowitz.* – **~knödel** *m* & *n* -s/-(n) **1.** *cul.* plum dumpling, a damson dumpling in which fruit is wrapped in a fine paste of potato or wheat flour, dusted with breadcrumbs and served hot with a sprinkling of castor sugar. – **2.** *phr.* (1) a warning not to be overconfident in one's boast about physical strength: *dafür musst du noch viel mehr ~ essen!* if you want to do that you'd better eat a lot of spinach! (2) *interj.* as an impatient reply to an unnecessary question, equivalent to an "Of course, what else do you think?": salted peanuts. – **~kompott** *n* -(e)s/-e *cul.* stewed plums *pl.* – **~krampus** *m* - or -ses/-se **1.** *folklore & cul.* an ornamental figure made up of prunes, representing the Devil (the companion, on December 6, of St Nicholas) in Austrian childlore: "plum devil". – **2.** *contp.* a person, usu. male, of frail physique: weedy fellow, wimp, apology for a man. – **~mus** *n* -es/-e = *Powidl* 1. – **~pfeffer** *m* -s *cul. (steifes Zwetschkenmus)* prune cheese. – **~röster** *m* -s/- **1.** *cul.* sourish plums preserved in glass jars *pl.* (a dish lending itself as a savoury with various sweet dishes). – **2.** *phr.* in a humorously patronizing address to a younger, usu. subordinate person who is about to be given a warning to mend his ways: *mein lieber Freund und ~!* well now, then, my good friend. – **~rummel** *m* -s *mil. hist.* "Bustle about Plums", a contemporary Austrian nickname for the series of minor skirmishes, and vain military marches, that typified what is known as the War of the Bavarian Succession (July 1778 to March 1779) between Austria and Prussia-cum-Saxony; the caution and indecision shown by the generals concerned is also reflected in the epithets "little war" and "war about potatoes" (the latter coined in an angry outburst by King Frederick II). – **~schnaps** *m* -es/ ... schnäpse, **~wasser** *n* -s/ ... wässer *bev.* = *Slibovitz.*

Zwętschkerl *n* -s/-n [dim. of *Zwetschke f*] **1.** slightly *emot.* little plum; *das ist doch nur ein ~, gib mir doch was Anständiges* that is just a smidgin – give me something of real size. – **2.** *fig., hum.* or slightly *apprec.* thin and tiny person, usu. female: svelte thing, dainty little something, petite little thing.

Zwiebelrostbraten *m* -s/- *cul.* fried beef and onions in gravy.

Glimpses of Austria

A Medley of Impressions Had by Native Speakers of English over the past two Centuries

1

1779 Maria Theresa nourishes many narrow and illiberal prejudices. Neither exempt from, nor superior to the uncharitable notions, which bigotry necessarily inspires, she firmly believes every heretic excluded from the divine mercy; but, of all heretics, she conceives the English to be the most impenitent, hardened, and irreclaimable. I know that she enjoined her youngest son, the Archduke Maximilian, when she permitted him to visit France and the Low Countries, on no consideration whatever to pass over into England. Her apprehension of his being corrupted by the contagious society of London, and losing all his religious principles or impressions, was the motive of this curious prohibition. She exacted a similar promise from the Emperor himself, when he went to Paris two years ago. "The English", said she to him, "are almost all Deists, Infidels, and Free Thinkers. I tremble, lest an intercourse with such a nation should contaminate your manners, and shake your belief in every thing sacred among Catholics."

N. WILLIAM WRAXALL, *Memoirs of the Courts of Berlin, Dresden, Warsaw and Vienna, in the Years 1777, 1778, and 1779* (London: T. Cadell jun. and W. Davies, [2]1800), Vol. II, pp. 326f.

2

1780 Having left Vienna, we proceeded through the Duchies of Stiria, Carinthia, and Carniola, to Venice. Notwithstanding the mountainous nature of those countries, the roads were remarkably good. They were formed originally at a vast expence of labour to the inhabitants, but in such a durable manner, that it requires no great trouble to keep them in repair, to which all necessary attention seems to be paid. [...]

[Passing through] Gratz, the capital of Stiria, we [made a point of] visiting the shrine of St. Allan, a native of England, who formerly was a Dominican Monk of a convent in this town, and in high favour with the Virgin Mary, of which she gave him some proofs as strong as they were extraordinary. Among other marks of her regard, she used to comfort him with milk from her breasts. This, to be sure, is a mark of affection seldom bestowed upon favourites above a year old, and will, I dare say, surprise you a good deal. There is no great danger, however, that an example of this kind should spread among virgins. Of the fact, in the present instance, there can be no doubt; for it is recorded in an inscription underneath a portrait of the Saint, which is carefully preserved in the Dominican convent of this city.

JOHN MOORE, *A View of Society and Manners in Italy* (London: A. Strahan and T. Cadell, [6]1795), Vol. I, pp. 1f., 4f.

3

1793 To the Tyrolese Alps, you may hurry through the territory of Wirtemberg. […] Ulm and Augsbourg then conclude for you the circle of Suabia. Ulm, a free city, which will launch a traveller down the Danube for five livres, and, in five days, to Vienna: and Augsbourg, another free town, of larger population (33,000) and which will do better for him still! If referring to the Diet and the Confession of Augsbourg, he can profit from the Protestant Reformers. And rising at the ennobling perfections of Luther and Melancthon, their zeal for truth, their magnanimity and eloquence – the Tyrolese Alps, then bold, and captivating as they are, will yield to the more noble exaltations of his mind. […] Prejudice and perverseness, like the dark and foggy meteor are below you. And the spirit brightens at the look of light and life!

Rev. CHARLES ESTE, *A Journey in the Year 1793, through Flanders, Brabant, and Germany, to Switzerland* (London: J. Debrett, 1795), pp. 346f., 349.

4

1814 The chateau of Habspourg is situated upon an elevation, about a league from Brougg. In going to it, you would expect to find a vast castle, corresponding with the power of the ancient Counts de Habspourg, founders of the august House of Austria, but the building – erected at the commencement of the 11th century – is small and simple; and although now in ruins, you may judge what it has been.

[GEORGE WILSON BRIDGES,] *Alpine Sketches, Comprised in a Short Tour through Parts of Holland, Flanders, France, Savoy, Switzerland and Germany, during the Summer of 1814* (London: Longman, Rees, Orme, and Brown, 1814), pp. 289f.

5

1820 In Carinthia, one requisite to a comfortable meal [is] very difficult to obtain, namely, clean table-linen: we, indeed, were obliged to purchase table-cloths and napkins on our journey; so much were we disgusted by the dirty linen which was produced every where, except in the very large towns.

Women, in this country, seem to work harder than men; and at public-houses female servants not only cook the dinner, and wait at table, but even feed the horses. The peasantry have fine complexions, with a great appearance of health and strength, but their countenances seldom express good-humour, or quickness of apprehension; they dress neatly, and wear high shoes, like those of our English Farmers. The women are said to be depraved in their morals.

MARIANA STARKE, *Information and Directions for Travellers on the Continent* (London: John Murray, [5]1824), p. 306.

6

1826 We observed near Bregentz a singularly isolated rock rising abruptly, and almost perpendicular from the plain, the summit of which is crowned with a chapel, and the back ground waving in lofty gradations of pine. This feature in the evening sun had a pleasing effect. In times when the country was covered with forests, and pilgrimages the business of every day, these *visible* churches were extremely useful both to priest and pilgrim. They served as landmarks, and instructed the pious way-farer where he might at all times obtain prayers for his pence; and woe to him who wittingly passed by without depositing his offering!

On entering Bregentz there is a fine specimen of a covered bridge, built entirely of wood, and exhibiting a naval style of architecture which is both curious and instructive.

[At] the gate, sentinelled by Austrian troops, the formality of viewing the passport was again, for the third time, strictly observed. Suspecting all the world, and suspected by one another, these functionaries trust their fellows no farther than they see them.

WILLIAM BEATTIE, *Journal of a Residence in Germany, Written during a Professional Attendance on Their Royal Highnesses the Duke & Duchess of Clarence, Their Most Gracious Majesties, during Their Visits to the Courts of that Country in 1822, 1825 & 1826* (London: Longman, Rees, Orme, Brown & Green, 1831), pp. 236f.

7

1826 Passing through Rheinek, we [...] crossed to the Austrian side of the river. Though I have nothing personally to complain of, from having always gone to and fro through the lines of the Austrian *douaniers* under good escort, I have seen few frontiers better garnished with official dignitaries of every kind. The whole right shore of the Rhine, from Feldkirch on the boundary of the principality of Lichtenstein to the Rheinspitz, is one continued line of spies, patrols, chasseurs, and revenue officers, ever on the hunt after smugglers. There had just been an affray at this point between two companies of these adverse professions, in which a poor smuggler had lost his life. The booty must have been worth fighting for, as one of the soldiers told me his share had amounted to above a hundred dollars, or near twenty-five pounds. The penalty upon the smuggler is, eight times the value of the articles intercepted, or the galleys in case of non-payment.

CHARLES JOSEPH LATROBE, *The Alpenstock; or Sketches of Swiss Scenery and Manners, MDCCCXXV – MDCCCXXVI* (London: R. B. Seeley and W. Burnside, 1829), p. 360.

8

1828 We proceeded along the banks of the Lake of Klagenfurth to Velden. [...] The scenery, at first, is rather flat and uninteresting, but towards Velden it becomes more diversified and beautiful. Sir Humphry intended passing the night at Velden, but the old ruined chateau, which now serves as the post-house, was better adapted for the habitation of bats and owls than the accommodation of a sickly and susceptible traveller; and accordingly he ordered horses for Villach, in spite of the approaching night. Whilst they were being put to, we enjoyed a fine view of the lake through the arched windows of the earth-floored hall of the chateau.

J[OHN] J[AMES] TOBIN, *Journal of a Tour Made in the Years 1828–1829, through Styria, Carniola, and Italy, whilst accompanying the late Sir Humphry Davy* (London: W. S. Orr, 1832), pp. 134f.

9

1833 I could perceive nothing in the external appearance of the Tyrolean and the Austrian, that indicated the master and the slave; the Tyrolean peasant has an air of true nobility about him: he walks as if he knew the soil were his own; and as if he deserved, if he did not enjoy freedom. [...]

An Englishman (whatever policy may, for the time, direct the British Government) is looked upon everywhere abroad as the friend of liberal institutions – a feeling which is particularly cherished in the Tyrol, since they have not forgotten the pecuniary aid that reached them from this country; and an Englishman cannot travel far, or live many days in the Tyrol, without hearing expressions of the bitterest antipathy against the Austrian government and its head; and wishes breathed for a deliverance from it.

HENRY D[AVID] INGLIS, *The Tyrol; with a Glance at Bavaria* (London: Whittaker, Treacher, & Co., ^{3}1833), Vol. I, pp. 163f.

10

1834 A very readable account of Styrian society and customs. Here is an excerpt from the cordial written invitation to the author by Countess Jane Anne Purgstall – a native of Scotland, 'long renowned in the country of her adoption' (p. 29), now widowed and bedridden ([?] 1760–1835) – to come for a prolonged visit with his family: "The country is truly healthy; the soil rich and well cultivated, and the hills and distant mountains covered with forests. The people resemble their oxen – they are diligent and docile. [...] Styria is also a country little known, owing to the singular fancy or fashion of the English always to fly between Vienna and Italy, by the way of Tyrol. Kotzebue says, 'The English carry their prejudices, as they do their tea-kettles, all over the world with them.' This, in general, is merely an impertinence; but in what respects the Tyrol road, it holds true – our road is in many respects preferable. [...]."

Captain BASIL HALL, *Schloss Hainfeld; or A Winter in Lower Styria* (Edinburgh: Robert Cadell; London: Whittaker and Co., 1836), pp. 10f.

11

1838 At Vienna, an Englishman in a café was speaking to a friend about his partiality for tea, and observed, in the language of the country, "Ich liebe thee", or 'I am fond of tea'. One of the undress police, catching indistinctly the last three syllables, immediately accosted him, saying, "Sir, Liberté is a word not to be uttered in Austria!" ... The above anecdote is current at Vienna; but the authenticity of it rests on an on dit.

C. B. ELLIOTT, *Travels in the Three Great Empires of Austria, Russia, and Turkey* (London: Richard Bentley, 1838), I, pp. 41f.

12

1843 And then, as to dancing – Orpheus must have been a *Wiener.* [...] It is really quite intoxicating for a foreigner to look at so many things turning round on all sides of him –

men, women, and children – the infant and the aged, the merry and the melancholy – round and round they go, spinning away the thread of life, at least gaily, if not profitably. I do verily believe, that if but the first draw of Strauss' or Lanner's fiddle-bow was heard in any street or market-place in Vienna in any weather or season, or at any hour of the day or night, all living, breathing nature within earshot, would commence to turn: the coachman would leap from his carriage, the laundress would desert her basket – and all, peeresses and prelates, priests and professors, soldiers and shopkeepers, waiters and washerwomen, Turks, Jews, and gentiles, would simultaneously rush into one another's arms, and waltz themselves to a jelly. In fact, this dancing mania, like animal magnetism, or the laughing gas, is quite irresistible, at least during the carnival.

W. R. WILDE, *Austria: Its Literary, Scientific, and Medical Institutions* (Dublin: William Curry, 1843), pp. 79f.

13

1847 [A brief space after the lofty picturesqueness of Aggstein,] look! further on rises to view another ruin, – a mere mass of shattered masonry, with one donjon, "tall and drear", and a quantity of battlemented lines of wall, straggling like the hideous legs of a dead starved spider, down to the water's edge. And that ruin was once the castle of Dürrenstein. And the castle has a legend – nay, a history to tell of English romance, that will make our Walter-Scott-bound hearts beat thrillingly. There, among some of those masses of wall, starting from the thousand clefts of the rock that bristles itself with pinnacles and fissures like *chevaux de frise* of Nature's own making – there, on that rugged naked hill, so desolate, so bare, except where it is flanked by the dark pine woods – there was confined, for long, long months, by the vindictive treachery of Leopold of Austria, our Richard the Lion-heart. Was it there that the captive king listened to the minstrelsy of the faithful Blondel? Danube legend and tradition say so, and will not be fought out of their say. But, I fear me, history tells another tale; and yet I would it had been there, in that wild romantic scenery, so congenial to a tale so romantic, that it had been really acted on the stage of history.

JOHN PALGRAVE SIMPSON, *Letters from the Danube* (London: Richard Bentley, [2]1854), Vol. I, p. 62.

14

1848 On the morning of the 4th of October I left England, stopped a day and a night at Hamburg, reached Vienna early on the 9th, and after some difficulty and trouble found myself safely lodged at "The Arch-Duke Charles", one of the best hotels in the town, situated in the Kärnthner-Thor Street. We had already heard, while changing carriages at the Breslau station, that a disturbance had broken out at Vienna; that the rails on many parts of the line had been taken up; that the *Bahn-hof* had been burnt; and that the military were defeated and driven from the town. [...]

On returning home to our hotel, we were suddenly stopped by a sentry, who challenged us with "Halt! wer da?" accompanied by the disagreeable clang of his musket being lowered to the charging position. We dared not retreat for fear he would fire upon us;

neither dared we advance for the like reason; and as "freund" and "feind"* sound so very similar in German, we were obliged to hold our tongues. While hesitating in our minds what course to pursue, we were saved the trouble of a wrong decision by a guard of soldiers coming up in our rear, and taking us into custody. The officer of the party, being a civil sort of man, finding us to be foreigners, addressed us in French, and told us that he was going to build a small battery at the top of the Jägerzeil, where a couple of cannon would be planted to command the Ferdinand Bridge and the Rothen Thurm Thor. Catching at the chance of convincing him of our friendship for the cause in which he was employed, we immediately offered to assist his men in constructing the barricade. He smiled at this proof of our sincerity, and accepted our services.

* Anglicè, "enemy".

The Hon. HENRY J. COKE, *Vienna in 1848* (London: Richard Bentley, 1849), pp. 3f., 55f.

15

1855 [Throughout the province of Vorarlberg] every one you meet on the road salutes with a friendly *"Morgen"*, and everywhere you see signs of industry – the rattle of looms in the cottages, and women at the doors, making their spinning-wheels hum again, while keeping up a lively gossip. There is something screeching in the tones of their voice like what may be heard among the women of Caernarvonshire; and their dialect is a strange one, abounding in corruptions and contractions, puzzling even to a German. In some words of two syllables, the second is entirely dropped; now and then you may hear *"Atte"* and *"Omme"*, for father and mother: and the diminutives of baptismal names are some of them amusing; Johann Jacob, becomes *Hansjok,* and Maria Margaretha, *Marigret.* The Vorarlbergers, indeed, are noted for their plainness of speech, and away from the high-roads you will find them addressing the gentleman and the peasant with equal familiarity: nor do they scruple to speak their mind concerning their rulers.

WALTER WHITE, *On Foot through Tyrol in the Summer of 1855* (London: Chapman and Hall, 1856), p. 36.

16

1866 At the frontier station, giving access to Poland, I had a foretaste of the rigors of the Austrian police system. My passport had been duly *vised* by the United States consul general and the Austrian minister at Frankfort-on-the-Main. I delivered it up to the authorities at the dépôt with the easy confidence of a man who believes himself to be all right. There was a delay of an hour required by the vexatious formalities of the Custom-house. Having no baggage except a small knapsack, I got through this ordeal without much trouble. The officer, indeed, hesitated a moment when he came to a sketch-book in which I had drawn some caricatures of the Austrian soldiers at Frankfort. They were officers of all grades, elegantly dressed in white coats, compressed by some hydraulic process at the waist – perfect patterns of form for any lady – their hair beautifully sleek and parted all the way down behind, with the prettiest little cap imaginable on the top of the head. As it is, the Custom-house man did not appear to understand the attempted satire, he gravely closed the book and let me pass.

J. ROSS BROWNE, *An American Family in Germany* (New York: Harper & Brothers, 1866), pp. 114, 333f.

17

1873 Gastein, little known to the English, is frequented principally by Prussians, Russians, and Hungarians; less generally by the Austrians, though actually in the dominions of his Catholic Majesty. The polished, pleasure-seeking Austrians possess other places of resort, gayer, brisker, and less difficult of access. Pre-eminent amongst these stands Ischl, in the Salzkammergut, one of the most delightful and romantic spots on the face of the whole earth.

[CHARLES WILLIAM WOOD,] *A Month at Gastein: or, Footfalls in the Tyrol* (London: R. Bentley & Son [, 1873]), pp. 95f.

18

1874 The "Votivbild", or "Marterle", as it is termed by the peasantry, is a striking feature of the Tyrolese districts. Wherever a fatal accident occurs [...] the friends of the deceased set up a little picture on the spot, about a foot square, showing, in graphic manner, how the casualty happened; and generally there is appended a request to the passer-by to say an "Ave Maria", or "Vater Unser", on behalf of the departed. These paintings sometimes last fifty or sixty years, and their number soon accumulate by the wayside, for obviously during this period an accident may well happen in every village. The pictures are, of course, very crude, but they all possess that strange fascination which the description of anything horrible always excites. Now it is a man being drowned in a rapid stream; now, a waggoner being crushed by his horses; now, a woman found perished in the snow, &c. The ambition of the village artist to show every detail of the accident is very apparent, and the way in which the work is performed in different parts of the country affords much scope for study.

H. BADEN PRITCHARD, *Tramps in the Tyrol* (London: Tinsley Brothers, 1874), pp. 111–13.

19

1876 The game of 'Fingerhackeln', – interlocking of fingers, literally translated – affords one of the most amusing sights possible. The two competitors, seated opposite each other at a table, stretch their right arms across, and putting the middle finger into the shape of a hook, intwine it with that of their rival; they then commence pulling, the object being to pull the antagonist right across the table on to the floor on the other side. Practice with a well-developed biceps frequently enables a smaller and weaker man to 'pull' his heavier antagonist in this manner. The most impossible positions of the human body, yells of despair, or growling curses and much laughter, are the invariable features of this game.

W[ILLIAM] A[DOLPH] BAILLIE GROHMAN, *Tyrol, and the Tyrolese: The People and the Land in Their Social, Sporting, and Mountaineering Aspects* (London: Longmans, Green, and Co., 1876), p. 82.

20

1885 The first thing that struck me in Tirol was the primitiveness of the country. At Ranalt we found a little wooden inn where the sole attendant appeared to be the landlord himself, who never parted with his hat. In the evening he (his hat still on) played the zither, while I (in my slippers) and the guide (as lady, in stockinged feet) danced a mazurka.

There, as everywhere […], the traveller made up his own bill. The *Kellnerin* came round with a slate and an air of business and asked each, When he came? Whether he had dined? How many pieces of bread? What meats, and 'how many times'? [*Einmals, zweimals,* etc., refer to our 'portions'.] And so on. All statements were accepted at once. […] Such entire trust in the travellers' honesty was very pleasing.

WALTER LARDEN, *Recollections of an Old Mountaineer* (London: Edward Arnold, 1885), pp. 48f.

21

1905 The folk of the valleys [in the Venediger mountains] seem unusually devoted to such religious art as their means and taste can attain. Almost every house prides itself on having its painted Madonna, and in most gardens, and often by the wayside, are carved and painted Crucifixions in little tabernacles. Many are decorated with branches of green, bearing red berries, or with poppies, or other red flowers.

Sir WILLIAM MARTIN CONWAY, *The Alps from End to End* (London: Archibald Constable, 1905), p. 229.

22

1927 The Austrian Custom House at Scharnitz is only 15 miles from Walchensee. As soon as it is passed we are in Tyrol. To me it is always a pleasure to find myself back there. For I love that gracious country and I like its kindly people. Between it and its neighbour Switzerland it is a rivalry in loveliness. There is no mountain in Tyrol as lofty as some in Switzerland, no glaciers as extensive, no lakes as spacious. On the other hand, if in the latter some of the works on Nature are on a scale more sublime, in the former most of those of man are to me more congenial. The Tyrolese villages, especially, while to the full as picturesque, are in their general character decidedly more attractive. There is less conventionality, less laboured spick-and-spanness, more individuality of a curiously seductive sort. Well, to put it briefly: of Tyrol I can say that I love all of it.

FRANK C. RIMINGTON, *Motor Rambles in Central Europe: Some Descriptions and Some Reflections* (London: Methuen & Co., 1927), pp. 173f.

23

1928 Viennese restaurateurs should worship a Golden Calf. *Kalbsbraten, Schlussbraten, Nierenbraten, Kalbsbrust,* and, of course, the ineffable *Wiener Schnitzel,* with its unclothed version, *Natur Schnitzel,* are all furnished by that universal provider, the calf. […]

At a restaurant of the middle class one should always try to face soup for lunch, even in summer, if only because it is usually unprocurable at dinner. It is merely an excuse for the Austrian specialities which swim in it – wafer-strips of pancake, tiny liver dumplings, little baked nondescripts which the Viennese adore. Their names – *Knödel, Nockerl,* and so forth – puzzle the German from Germany as much as anyone else.

All the year round the restaurant aquaria accommodate a motley assembly of brook and lake trout, char, carp, pike, and that abundant but disappointing Central European substitute for lobster, the crayfish. 'Flour foods' – *Mehlspeisen* – is a most unpromising name for the delicious pastries and other sweets which for the Austrian are by far the most important part of the meal.

G[EORGE] E[RIC] R[OWE] GEDYE, *A Wayfarer in Austria* (London: Methuen & Co., [4]1931), pp. 18f.

24

1931 The people of Austria are of the same stock as the South Germans, but [...] centuries of separate existence and of contact with other races have given them a marked individuality. Every traveller in Germany must notice as he goes south the increased prevalence of that attractive quality with the untranslatable name, *Gemütlichkeit,* whose chief ingredients are good humour, kindliness, love of comfort and peace and goodwill. [...] The Austrian is, besides, lively and merry and quick to the right sort of laughter, so that there can hardly be a more delightful people in the world, and none with more friendliness and disinterested courtesy. And this charm of manner is the greater because it is so clearly instinctive in the men and women and children of every class in the land.

J[ACK] D[OUGLAS] NEWTH, *Austria* (London: A & C Black, 1931), pp. 48f.

25

1935 I know the whole of Europe very thoroughly, but in Austria [...] one finds a warmth of feeling and a real kindliness of heart which is not afraid to express itself. In all the bitterness of strife and competition since the Great War throughout the world, the Austrians have remained unspoilt, not here and there as individuals, but as a people.

The veriest stranger passes you and he says, 'Grüss Gott', which really means 'God be with you', a beautiful and appealing blessing which makes the stranger feel at home and happy. Naturally you answer in the same words and pass on, unless you care to stop and have a chat. For those who know you, the custom with men is to kiss your hand. 'Küss die Hand' they say, and suit the action to the word, bending down and seeming to brush the back of it with their lips. This is an act of homage and courtesy. In the West of Ireland the warmness of heart of the dear old people arouses the same impulse. I have also met with this form of greeting in Gloucestershire by an old farmer who has been my friend for many years, and it always touches me very much and takes me back in imagination to an age of chivalry and grace of manners.

AIMÉE WATT SMYTH, *Austria: 'The Land of Smiles' – and Tears* (London and Cheltenham: Ed. J. Burrow, 1935), pp. 30f.

26

1953 The role Austria is best suited to play in Europe is that of a cultural Switzerland. Like Switzerland, Austria is a country of great natural beauty, ideally fitted to be a tourist centre. Like Switzerland, her interests and characteristics mark her out for a neutral part in international affairs. She is not powerful enough to exert much diplomatic influence; her natural resources are not sufficiently extensive to arouse the greed of her neighbours, and European stability would be greatly strengthened by the extension of the traditionally neutral area from Switzerland to the Hungarian frontier. But, without under-estimating the unique contribution of Switzerland to modern civilization, it is true to say that Austria in addition has something special of her own to offer to the world, and particularly to those who visit her, largely owing to her imperial history and great musical heritage.

The word 'culture', that is used perhaps too readily in America and too reluctantly in England, is not an entirely satisfactory term. It has a pretentious flavour and is commonly used in a narrower sense than the German word, *'Kultur'*. Yet it is a word that cannot be avoided in attempting a general description of Austria. Anyone who has sensed the atmosphere of Vienna, seen the beauty of Salzburg's buildings and setting, and observed how baroque and Gothic architecture and the national dress of the people merge naturally into the Austrian landscape, knows something of the country's great civilized tradition. It is a tradition that the Austrians themselves tend to take for granted, but of which in a quiet and inoffensive way they are deeply proud. There could be no better proof of the strength of their pride and of their determination to maintain the tradition than the extent of the cultural revival in Austria since the War and the speed at which it has taken place.

RICHARD HISCOCKS, *The Rebirth of Austria* (London: Oxford University Press, 1953), p. 162.

27

1957 Austria lies on the crossroads of Europe and her people have been forced to live the life of the crossroads – back to back, their eyes turned watchfully on all points of the compass. They never knew and never will know that isolated security in which the English grew strong and unified behind the water barrier of the Channel. [...] Their territory both joined and divided the races and religions of the Continent. Through Austria's valleys, from north to south, came the ancient 'Amber Route' which linked the shores of the Baltic and the Mediterranean. Across the Austrian lands, from west to east, the Alps and the Danube have always run – Europe's greatest mountain range and her longest river. She was thus open at all times and on all sides to the Continent; and Europe's principal paths of trade and migration all passed through her.

This has encouraged a natural Austrian cosmopolitanism in culture, politics and military history. Her musicians and artists have come from the Germanic north, the Roman south and the Slav east. Her own genius came to lie not so much in any 'national' culture as in the fusion of the apparently irreconcilable cultures of other nations. Baroque architecture, the triumph of compromise, is among her greatest contributions to European art.

GORDON SHEPHERD, *The Austrian Odyssey* (London: Macmillan & Co., 1957), p. 33.

28

1958 Why is it that Austria is so popular? [...] The real answer is [...] because it and its people reflect a true love. Somehow or other, in some almost uniquely subtle way, the Austrian has managed to transmit to others the magic of this mental music that comes to him with the first snowfall – and which stays until the snows have melted. The real truth lies in the fact that it is the heady atmosphere – a combination of happy-go-lucky gaiety, charm, enthusiasm, and technical efficiency – that this love of the game has engendered, and which infects all who come in contact with it, that has done the trick. This it is, which no amount of propaganda could do, that has already caused so many countless thousands to fall in love with Austria. It will cause many more to do just the same in the future.

JAMES RIDDELL, *The Ski Runs of Austria* (London: Michael Joseph, 1958), p. 16.

29

1959 Coffee is one of the few vestiges of the Turks which the Viennese hold dear. On a small side street I saw the plaque commemorating the town's first coffeehouse, originated about 1683 by a Polish mercenary who found a sack left behind by the vanquished foe and decided to experiment. Worship of the bean has gone on steadily since those days, and in a peculiarly civilized manner.

The Austrian coffeehouse is a last refuge of leisure, a club for every man. Here one can retire, call for a newspaper, and vanish into the day's news without further fret. No one will bustle about, trying to sell you a full meal; no one will cough meaningfully as you spin out your cup of *espresso* the whole length of the *Times*. If you wish to chat, you may; if merely to contemplate the passing parade, that is all right, too. Some of the men ensconced behind their daily papers appear not even to have been dusted off for weeks.

BEVERLEY M. BOWIE and VOLKMAR WENTZEL, "Building a New Austria", *The National Geographic Magazine* (Washington), February 1959 (Vol. CXV, No. 2), p. 183.

30

1965 Gastronomically we found Austria one of the most 'English' of countries. They certainly expect one to have an enormous appetite, and I must admit that days out in the Tyrol, in the lake districts, and at Semmering sharpened my appetite! Meals are important in Austria, whether one is dining in a restaurant, or enjoying a snack in one of the many cafés in the old parts of towns like Innsbruck or Salzburg. It is never a question of snatching a meal in order to live; one eats to enjoy, and the owners of the humblest and most obscure cafés neglect no detail that adds to one's enjoyment. [Indeed,] one of the great charms of Austria is the leisurely way in which things happen, and on holidays I for one am ready to adjust my tempo to what already prevails.

Such brief and casual reminiscences of a gourmet, however, should be added to, and rounded out, by a remark of my wife's summing up our impressions very neatly: "I can't think of anything I didn't like in Austria!"

O. S. NOCK, *Railway Holiday in Austria* (Dawlish: David & Charles, 1965), pp. 152f.

Austrian Songs … now also sung in English

In die Berg bin i gern

A Carinthian Air

Und der Schnee geht bald weg,
mei! da werd's wieder schean,
und dann werd'i bald wieder
auf die Alm aufegehn.

With the snows soon to go,
What a riot to share!
I'll again then be climbing
Soon to my dairy up there.

Wo i geh, wo i steh,
denk i allwei' an di;
Werst wohl du, wenn i fortbin,
aa no denkn an mi.

You are aye in my thoughts
Wheresoever I be;
With me gone, you will, too,
I trust, still be thinking of me.

Tirol is lei oans

Words by Sebastian Rieger
Music by Vinzenz Goller

Mei Liab is Tirol,
is mei Weh und mei Wohl,
is mei Guat und mei Håb,
is mei Wieg und mei Gråb.

My love is Tyrol,
She's my heart and my soul;
All I have is what she gave,
She's my cradle, my grave.

Tirol is lei oans,
wie dös Landl is koans,
in der Näh, in der Fern
is koans auf der Erd'n.

There's none to compare
With Tyrol, o so fair!
In the world far or near
There's no country so dear.

Andreas-Hofer-Lied

Words by Julius Mosen, 1832
Music by Leopold Knebelsberger, 1844

Zu Man - tu - a in Ban - den der treu - e Ho - fer war, in
At Man - tu - a brave Hofer chained, his cour-age nev-er gone, to

Ma - tu - a zum To - de führt ihn der Fein - de Schar. Es
see him shot, his cause de-stroyed, the grue-some foe pressed on. His

blu - te - te der Brü - der Herz, ganz Deutsch-land, ach in Schmach und
fight - ing friends' hearts bled in vain, all Ger - ma - ny felt shame and

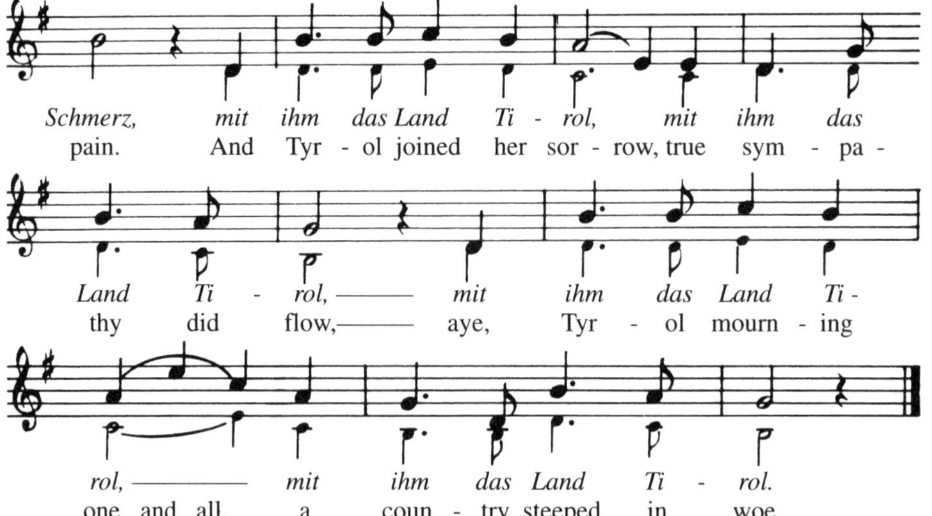

Die Hände auf dem Rücken der Sandwirt Hofer ging
mit ruhig festen Schritten, ihm schien der Tod gering,
der Tod, den er so manchesmal
vom Iselberg geschickt ins Tal,
im heil'gen Land Tirol.

On his last walk, hands tied behind, / Steps firm, serene his breath;
None guessed our Landlord Hofer here / Went forth to meet his death.
Such death he'd from Mount Isel sent / Quite oft to those invasion-bent.
O'er sainted Tyrol's soil, aye, shall Freedom ever fly,
A goal for which a Tyrol man is game to do and die.

Doch als aus Kerkergittern im festen Mantua
die treuen Waffenbrüder die Händ' er strecken sah,
da rief er laut: „Gott sei mit euch,
mit dem verrat'nen deutschen Reich
und mit dem Land Tirol!"

When moving past those iron teeth, / Fort Mantua's dreadful jaw,
His friends-in-arms stretched out their hands / In friendship and in awe.
Loud came his shout, "God bless you all, / With Germany, too, held in thrall.
And blessings be on Tyrol, to which we shall be true,
In mis'ry and in victory the land our love goes to!"

Dem Tambour will der Wirbel nicht unterm Schlegel vor,
als nun der Sandwirt Hofer schritt durch das finst're Tor.
Der Sandwirt, noch in Banden frei,
dort stand er fest auf der Bastei,
der Mann vom Land Tirol.

The drum-roll that the drum-boy beat / Groaned out a muffled sound,
With Landlord Hofer nearing now / The ever-gloomy ground.
Hands tied, but eyes undaunted, free, / The sturdiest on the bastion he.
A man in Tyrol born, aye, in Tyrol born and bred;
A native freedom fighter he, a life in freedom led.

Dort soll er niederknien. Er sprach: „Das tu ich nit!
Will sterben, wie ich stehe, will sterben, wie ich stritt,
so wie ich steh auf dieser Schanz.
Es leb' mein guter Kaiser Franz,
mit ihm das Land Tirol!"

When bidden that he now kneel down / He told them, "Surely not!
I'll die the way I stand, straight up, / I'll die the way I fought.
On this redoubt, for all to hear – / It's Emperor Francis I revere!
The same goes for my Tyrol, no need to question why:
In Tyrol born and bred was I, for Tyrol shall I die."

Und von der Hand die Binde nimmt ihm der Korporal,
und Sandwirt Hofer betet allhier zum letztenmal.
Dann ruft er: „Nun, so trefft mich recht.
Gebt Feuer! – Ach, wie schießt ihr schlecht!
Ade, mein Land Tirol!"

A corporal duly loosed the cords / From Landlord Hofer's hand;
A last prayer said on this vile earth – / Time always runs like sand.
Then to the soldiers, "Take your aim! / Away! … Your shooting's bad, for shame!
Now, fare thee well, my Tyrol, the land I loved to roam;
My Tyrol, fare thee well, good-bye – you were my home, sweet home!"

Därf ih 's Dirndl liabn?

Words by Peter Rosegger
(from his *Zither and Dulcimer)*

Bin ih vull Valonga
Zu da Muada gonga:
„Därf ih 's Dirndl liabn?"
„O du feiner Knob, es is no zfrua,
Noch funfzehn Jahrln erst, mei liaba Bua!"

Longing quite unwearied,
I then mother queried,
"May I love a lassie?"
"Time 's too early yet, my goodly lad;
Once you're past fifteen, love may be had."

Woar in grossn Nöthn,
Hon ih 'n Vodan betn:
„Därf ih 's Dirndl liabn?"
„Duners Schlangl!" schreit er in sein Zurn,
„Willst mein Steckn kostn, konst es thuan!"

All a-dither, rather,
I went up to father,
"May I love a lassie?"
"Blood and thunder!", he went purply red,
"Wanna taste my stick? Just go ahead!"

Wos is onzufonga?
Bin zan Herrgott gonga:
„Därf ih 's Dirndl liabn?"
„Ei jo freilih", sogt er und hot glocht,
„Wegn an Büaberl hon ih 's Dirndl gmocht!"

Help now sorely needed,
"O Lord God", I pleaded,
"May I love a lassie?"
"Why, of course", He laughed, in bounteous glee,
"It's for lad's own sake I made lass be."

Es wird scho glei dumpa

A charming Tyrolean and Bavarian lullaby,
from a child of the mountains to the one in the manger of Bethlehem

Vergiß iatzt, o Kinderl, dein Kummer, dei Load,
dass d' du da muaßt leidn im Stall auf da Hoad.
Es ziern ja die Engerl dei Lagerstatt aus,
möcht schener net sei drin im König sein Haus.
Hei, hei, hei, hei, schlaf süaß, herzliabs Kind.

Forget now, my sweet one, your sorrow and pain
That your only cradle's a crib on the plain.
Look! angels so tenderly make pretty your bed
A king might be eager to rest there his head.
Hush-a-bye, hush-a-bye, slumber sweetly, my baby boy.

Ja Kinderl, du bist halt im Kripperl so schen,
mi ziamt, i kann nimma da weg von dir gehn.
I wünsch dir von Herzen de süaßeste Ruah,
de Engerl vom Himmel, sie deckn di zua.
Hei, hei, hei, hei, schlaf süaß, herzliabs Kind.

Dear child in your manger, so lovely to view,
It seems I could never bear parting from you.
I wish you warm-heartedly sweet dreams, little dove,
While angels from Heaven enwrap you with love.
Hush-a-bye, hush-a-bye, slumber sweetly, my baby boy.

Schliaß zua deine Äugerl in Ruah und in Fried
und gib ma zum Abschied dein' Segn no grad mit!
Aft wird ja mein Schlaferl so sorgenlos sein,
aft kann i mi ruahli aufs Niadalegn frein.
Hei, hei, hei, hei, schlaf süaß, herzliabs Kind.

Now close your fair eyes, dear, and peacefully rest,
But let me, on leaving, by you first be blessed.
I'll sleep then so free from care, my worries all past,
And calmly look forward to resting at last.
Hush-a-bye, hush-a-bye, slumber sweetly, my baby boy.

Da streiten sich die Leut herum

The Song of the Plane

Words by Ferdinand Raimund
(from his musical fairy tale, *The Spendthrift*)
Music by Ferdinand Raimund and Conradin Kreutzer

Die Jugend will halt stets mit G'walt
in allem glücklich sein,
doch wird man nur ein bisserl alt,
da findt man sich schon drein.
Oft zankt mein Weib mit mir, o Graus,
das bringt mich nicht in Wut,
da klopf' ich mei nen Ho bel aus
und denk': du brummst mir gut!

The youth so happy and so bold
Is always after fun,
But let them get a little old,
With less they'll carry on.
My wife is sometimes raising hell!
T hat doesn't bother me:
I do my work, and do it well,
And let her angry be.

Zeigt sich der Tod einst, mit Verlaub,
und zupft mich: „Brüderl, kumm!",
da stell ich mich im Anfang taub
und schau' mich gar nicht um.
Doch sagt er: „Lieber Valentin,
mach keine Umständ, geh!",
da leg' ich meinen Hobel hin
und sag' der Welt ade.

If Death appears – please do forgive –
And whispers, "Brother, come!"
I wish I could still longer live,
And act like deaf and dumb.
But says he, "My dear Valentine,
Come now with me to dwell",
I put my plane into the shrine
And bid the world farewell!

Fein sein, beinander bleibn

A Salzburg Folk Song

Fein sein, bei - nan - der blei - bm, fein sein, bei - nan - der blei
Be a pal, and make friend-ships last, be a pal, and make friend-ships

-bm, mag's regn o - der win - dn, o - der a - ber-schnei - bm,
last! May rain or winds be rag - ing, Snow be fall-ing thick and fast:

Fein sein, bei - nan - der blei - bm, fein sein, bei - nan - der blei-bm!
Be a pal, and make friend-ships last, be a pal, and make friend-ships last!

|: Gscheit sein, nit einitapm, :
es steht oft der Fuchs
in der Zipflkapm
|: Gscheit sein, nit einitapm! :|

|: Frisch sein, nit ummamockn, :
und geht aa dei Häusl
und die Liab in Brockn.
|: Frisch sein, nit ummamockn! :|

|: Treu sein, nit aussigrasn, :
denn d' Liab is so zart
wia-r-a Soafnblasn.
|: Treu sein, nit aussigrasn! :|

Use your brains, there's traps everywhere!
And foxes lurk in hidings,
Such wily guises scare.
Use your brains …

Be alert, and don't mope about!
Well may your cabin crumble,
And affairs go up the spout.
Be alert …

Faith's a must, philanderings be curst!
For Love's a dainty bubble,
Aye, the parloust one to burst.
Faith's a must …

The Many Lives of the Austrian Chatter Ditty

The above are only three of some two dozen melodies to which a *Schnadahüpfl* is sung.

One of the encouragements to make merry on these occasions is an unassuming yet chatty type of verse that, just like those who sing it, loves company and never appears alone. A stanza has but four short lines of two beats each, and walks on anapaestic feet, though its cheerfully volatile nature makes its gait at times uneven and slightly unpredictable. at the outset, the stanza often trips along on iambs, as if in hesitation, and only then will it move with its regular stride to the end. Also, it freakishly misses an unaccented syllable or two (as the unwary singer may blush to discover), or adds one or two for good measure; and there are instances of its setting out on the wrong foot, turning anapaest into dactyl.* The skipping rhythms of the Austrian dialects are, to some axtent, responsible for such irregularities.

The rhyme scheme is rather erratic too; in fact, almost anything goes. Still, two couplets are of fairly common occurrence. In the following example, a broad Scots translation attempts to convey the spirit of the dialect (in all further illustrations, however, colloquial English has been chosen because it is more generally understood):

Is ma lusti und froh,
mog da Hergott oan scho.
aba wuisln und reahrn
mag er gar nit gern hörn.

Gin ya grin wi' guid cheer,
God 'Il think y'are a dear;
But He' Il sin change His min'
Gin ya whimper an' whine.

The most usual pattern is to have the second and fourth lines rhyme. The coupling of lines is structurally significant: the first one introduces the theme simply and innocently, and the second adds a comment, which, as a hallmark of quality, is wrapped in a witty turn of phrase or a pun.

Und wann i beim Tanzn
mei Deandl betracht,

When swinging my sweetheart
I gaze at the sight:

* Subscript dots are, therefore, used to indicate unexpected accents. They act as stepping stones through the following collection; instances can easily be detected by the eye.

dann lob i den Mann,
der die Oawat hat gmacht.

My thanks to the man
Who produced such delight.

Das Oansiedlalebm,
das geht mir nit ein,
i wollt' scho viel liaba
a Zwoasiedla sein.

A hermit's existence
I wouldn't pooh-pooh
Were each one permitted
A hermitees, too!

The verse form I am talking about is indigenous to the mountains and foothills of Austria, South Tyrol and Southern Germany; it is known under the dialect names of *Schnadahüpfl* [nɑ:dəhypfl; ˈʃnɔ:–] and *Gstanzl* [ˈkʃtantsl]. Linguistically, the latter is a hybrid formation, in which Italian *stanza* 'set group of rhymed lines' (the word has also been English since Shakespearean times) links arms with a typically Austrian prefix and a diminutive suffix. the name proclaims the bearer and candidly says what it is: a little piece of poetry. The term *Schnadahüpfl* is of completely Germanic origin, but nevertheless has long posed a doublebarrelled problem to the etymologist. There are two spellings of the second element, *-hüpfl* and *-hüpfel,* due of course to syllabic *-l*; this can be interpreted either as a diminutive or as an allomorph of denominative *-er,* thus referring to 'someone or something that hops or skips'. And that verbal hint is amply borne out by the facts. Ever since the genre has been known to exist, which is for around two centuries, it has been connected with the dance floor and with folks celebrating a harvest home, a wedding, or perhaps the feast of their patron saint; it is always an event in which the family, a wide circle of friends, or even the whole village are invited to share.

Und mi' freut grad a Gsangl,
recht frisch und vadraht,
und a Tanzl, dass 'n Staub
von der Stubm aufwaht.

Don't I like a fresh song
From the heart, without guise,
And a dance that's full of stompin'
The dust's bound to rise!

Ja mei Deandl is handsam,
zum Tanzn schö langsam,
Zum Busslge'm gschwind
und zum Halsn schö lind.

Well, my beauty is sprightly,
She 'Il dance slow and lightly;
She's fast with a kiss,
And to hug her is bliss.

William A. Baillie Grohman, a famous mountaineer of Anglo-Austrian descent, and no less famous as the author of *Tyrol and the Tyrolese* (London, 1876), was also a keen observer of the custom. The 'Schnaddahüpfler', as he idiosyncratically spells the word, is

> a short song, or rather series of rhymes, … sung by one of the dancers, standing in front of the slightly raised platform upon which the musicians are seated.

However, let us pursue our linguistic inquiry a little further. The first element of the compound is usually written as *Schnada-, Schnoda-, Schnader-* or, in an even more genteel manner, *Schnatter-*. Some scholars have linked the word with *Schnitter* 'mower' or 'harvestman', but since the spellings of the stem vowel invariably show an <a> or, when too obviously dark, an <o>, such attempts should be discouraged. In any case, it is much more plausible to etymologize on the strength of Standard German *schnattern* 'to chatter', which both does away with phonetic improbabilities and finds with phonetic improbabilities and finds confirmation in real life. For those little verses come, or at least once came, trippingly from the tongue of the young peasant dancer, as exuberant utterances of a *joie de vivre* which, as we know, may readily lead to boasts and challenges, chiefly intended for some rival's ear.

Hast an Juhschroa im Herzn,
nur außá damit!
Graunzt hat die Welt gnua,
aber gjuchazt no nit!

If yer heart feels like yodellin',
Come, on, let it out!
Cheer's what the world's needin',
Too many folks pout.

I bin vo obn awa,
a lustiga Bua,
hab a Truha voll Mentscha,
geht da Deckl net zua.

I've come from yonder mountains,
A jolly young pup;
With a chestful of wenches
So the lid must stay up.

Baillie Grohman proves as good a witness as any:

> It is marvellous with what rapidity the object of that affront or scoff will compose his reply, replete with imputations of like or worse kind, and in this manner two rival bards will continue for a considerable lenght of time to take turns in casting impromptu slander or scornful contempt at each other.

Oan und zwoa fürcht i net,
drei und vier aa no net,
fünf und sechs hab i ghaut –
Bua, da ham s' gschaut!

Taking on one or two,
Three or four's still too few,
Five and six, cinch to beat –
Boy, what a treat!

Geh, leich mir dei Gsicht
zum Jüngsten Gericht,
dass i 'n Teufl derschreck,
denn sunst bring i 'n net weg!

Hey, lend me, but quick,
Your mug for Old Nick:
Gotta scare 'im away
When 'e 's up Judgment Day.

So, the setting is clear. Those little ditties of defiance or derision were intended to fill up the intervals between the dances, which lasted some five or six minutes each; and the result was a lively to and fro of verbal skirmishes, held in check and balance by the intermittent whirls on the floor.

Jetzt hat oana gsunga,
bin eahm fei net neid;
z' Haus hammar a Goaß,
die grad ar aso schreit.

You' ve just heard one singing,
All hoarseness and cracks;
The ducks on the duck-pond
Give less ugly quacks.

I sing, wiar i will,
und i krah wiar a Hahn,

My singing's quite poor,
Not a patch on a lark's;

weil so fein wiar a Zeiserl	But I like to hold forth,
i' 's neama net kann.	Be it crowings or barks.

The art of stringing along repartee in song has become less widespread over the past two or three generations. However a dramatic form of presentation continues to be popular in rural gatherings, in whose presence are "sung out" amid more or less good-humoured banter the weaknesses, real or reputed, of some crabby wife or mother-in-law, doddery old schoolmaster or foolish young milkmaid too generous with her favours:

D'Schwiegamuatta und da Bandwurm	Mothers-in-law are like tapeworms,
san a Plag spat und fruah,	They're a pest night and day:
solang no da Kopf dran is,	As long as the head is on
gems an Teifl a Ruah.	There's the devil to pay!
Die Katzn im März	In March-time the cats
ja und d' Sennrin drom auf da Alm	And the dairymaids on the hills,
ham all dieselb Krankheit	All need but one ointment
und brauchnt oa Sal'm.	To cure common ills.

Inviting targets also readily offer themselves to vocal pranksters whose ironic or invidious eye happens to fall on members of certain local trades that, as a rule, enjoy some degree of affluence or other privilege. Brewers and tapsters, for instance, may hear themselves pilloried for "baptizing" their merchandise too generously; one ditty, in feigned innocence, congratulates a certain *Bräu* on having set up his place conveniently close to *wo da Bach fließt vorbei,* thus making the temptation to water down the beer even greater. This quip, if phrased in the plural, also hits out in another direction, turning from an individual butt to a collective one: besides the faked or real tensions between social groups, geographical rivalry has proved a frequent topic in the past for many a caustic rhyme bandied from one village or township to another. For example, the girls in one such community are mercilessly maligned by parish-pump acrimony as possessing lower limbs of peculiar, if conveniently utilitarian, shape – *mit oan Fuaß tean s' mahn / und mitn andern heign s' zsam* 'one leg does the mowing / the other makes hay'. Yet these victims, or rather, their male protectors in song, retaliate glibly and with like impudence on the flimsiest evidence or none, charging the maidens of the other village with gross unchastity. Alas, such lusty verbal battles were beginning to lose a great deal of their zest even before the last War: many contestants were obliged to travel outside their village for schooling and employment, a change in circumstances that did much to whittle away their local pride and integrity.

There is another type of ditty that deserves to be mentioned for it has survived the social and technological changes rather well. This is the more kindly, reflective or autobiographical *Schnadahüpfl,* based on the rustic singer's own native sentiments, which have inspired the unknown village poet of the eighteenth century and the modern versifier alike. Despite the distance of time separating them, both speak and sing according to the almost immutable environment they were born and bred in. These ingenious rhymings mirror the wide spectrum of country life without the slightest distortion. Here nothing is concealed, prettied up or glossed over. Every *Schnadahüpfl* makes it clear that our young or middle-aged peasant singer does not have his head in the clouds; on the contrary, he has both feet on the ground and never loses touch with reality. To him only his five senses make sense, and anything else is suspect. He sturdily takes things as they come, without dressing them up in fancy words or claiming to see what is not there. A balanced personality, he does not take life or himself too seriously, but is always ready with a joke:

Es gibt nix so Lustigs
wiar i und mei Bua:
er redt nix und deut' nix –
und i lus eahm zua.

Mei lad an' mesel'
Are a pair unco' gay:
He 's glum, keeping mum,
An' me listenin' all day.

De Pfeif is ma brocha,
De Hosn hat an Riß,
und der Geldbeitl is krank,
der hat 's laufade Gschiß.

My pipe 's long bin brokened,
My trousers are in bits;
And my moneybag, so woeful,
Is plagued by the shits.

Han Erdäpfl droschn,
han Haslnuß g'maht,
han 's Rüahrmili g'spunna:
han 's sauba vadraht.

Ah 've threshed me potaters,
Ah 've mown off me pears,
Ah 've churned whey to butter –
Right screwy affairs!

Beim Deandl bin i gwesn
und hab mi verspat,
wiari hoamzua bin ganga,
ham d' Maahder scho gmaaht.

'Twas late I left my lassie,
Night dawning to day;
And my path led through meadows
Past folks making hay.

Da hab i übern Kopf
halt mei Hemad schnell ghängt,
weil des Gsicht ham 's net gsehn
und 'n Arsch ham s' net kennt.

I hoisted up my shirt
O 'er my head for to pass:
So the face was well hidden,
And none knew the arse.

Wiari fensterln bin ganga,
war 's Fenster fei zua,
und i denk, 's schlaft mei Deandl
in himmlischer Ruah.

Once I stole to my lass,
But the window was closed,
And I stupidly thought
That she peacefully dozed.

Aba 's Deandl, jetzt woaß i 's,
des schlaft net alloan,
denn des kann ja koan dopplten
Schnaufer net toan.

But my lass wasn't sleeping
Alone, now I know:
For at one time how could she
Snore high and snore low.

In his view, even love is just as concrete and ordinary as a bite to eat. Since growth and decay confront him daily, he finds the end of life just as natural as its beginning. Sentimentality and romantic exaggeration run contrary to his outlook on life. Seldom can he give tongue to what moves him deeply; he is far more likely to put it into song.
And since the lad's sentiments are shared by those around him, everyone will soon join in the singing, each member of the group in turn intoning his or her *Gstanzl,* stopping only for the chorus to boom out its *Holla-da-riadio, hollada-ro, holla-da-riadio, was sagst denn da?* in lusty confirmation. It is again a pleasure for an Anglicist to quote from an English source, and a venerable one at that – Charles Boner's essay "On Schnadahüpfln", appended to his famous book about *Chamois Hunting in the Mountains of Bavaria and in the Tyrol* (London, ^{2}1860):

> … each [of the *Schnadahüpfln* sung] ought either to be an answer to that which preceded, or, from an allusion made to something in the foregoing one, to spring as it were from it, and in this way form a connection between the two. These verses are very frequently extempore; and there are some persons who for hours will continue thus singing against each other, till a succession of strophes have arisen, each one separate and complete in itself, yet, like beads on a string, forming part of a whole and having reference to the rest.

What we have just observed is the true, and indeed uninhibitedly self-revealing, type of chatter ditty, to which the whole verse form owes its name. It loves company, and when sung demands an equally strong reply in kind. The melody suited to it skips briskly up and down. the listener is impressed by a helterskelter jollity which blithely ignores the dictum (obviously laid down by the pedantic) that the thought should end with the line, and that breaking verse feet is as atrocious as breaking human ones.
However, it is not only the ebullient who bend the form of the *Schnadahüpfl* to their purposes, but also those that are more withdrawn may sometimes express themselves with thoughtful tenderness. For such a singer, however earthbound and tongue-tied in his everyday life, the anapaestic short-line serves as a fitting vehicle for flights of fancy. This may be unexpected for the casual onlooker but, given the atmosphere and setting, such wonders do occur, and may even result in miniature masterpieces of a country lad's lyrical mind. Whether it is the silence of the night that moves him, or thoughts of love in springtime, or the holiness of the season then upon him, it remains a fact that some mute, inglorious Sidney has found expression in the mood and rhythm of the Austrian soul:

Dei Herz und mei Herz *ham mitananda an Bund,* *und wann dei Herzl krank is,* *is meins a nit gsund.*	Your heart and mine, dear, Are like two twins tightly bound; And if your heart is stricken, Mine cannot be sound.
Wann i still geh, wann i stad geh, *so wunderts enk nit,* *denn i trag ja mei Deandl* *im Herzkammerl mit.*	Soft and still, you need not wonder, Is the fall of my feet: Cradled deep in my heart Lies aslumber my sweet.

Suggestions for Further Readings

BAREA, ILSA. *Vienna: Legend and Reality.* London: Secker and Warburg, 1967 (1966). [Both scholarly and rich in texture.]

BASCHIERA, KARL, and OTTO HIETSCH. *A Classroom Vocabulary.* Vienna: Österreichischer Bundesverlag, ²1971.

BAUMANN, EDZARD. *Crossroads of European Art: A Concise History of Art and Architecture in Austria.* Salzburg: Festungsverlag Salzburg, 1964.

BROOK-SHEPHERD, GORDON. *Anschluss: The Rape of Austria.* London: Macmillan, 1963.

–. *The Austrians: A Thousand-Year Odyssey.* New York: Carroll and Graf, 1998.

CREED, VIRGINIA. *All about Austria.* (The New Europe Guides.) New York: Duell, Sloan and Pearce, 1950.

DURSTMÜLLER, ANTON. *The Mountaineer's Terms: English-German for Tourists and Mountain Guides.* 2nd ed. Vienna: Franz Karner, n. d.

GEDYE, G[EORGE] E[RIC] R[OWE]. *A Wayfarer in Austria.* Continental Edition, revised. 2 vols. Vienna: ISB, 1947–48. (Original edition: London: Methuen, 1928).

–. *Introducing Austria.* London: Methuen, 1956 (1955).

GIBBON, MONK. *Austria.* London: B. T. Batsford, 1953.

HIETSCH, OTTO. *Der moderne Wortschatz des Englischen: Nach Sachgruppen ausgewählt und kommentiert.* Vienna: Österreichischer Bundesverlag, 1957.

–, ed. *Österreich und die angelsächsische Welt: Kulturbegegnungen und Vergleiche.* 2 vols. Vienna: Wilhelm Braumüller, 1961–62. [A collection of sixty-six essays.]

–. "Heimatkundliches Englisch", *Erziehung und Unterricht,* February 1955 (Vol. 105, No. 2), pp. 76–87.

–. "Englische Kulturvignetten: Marginalien zur geistigen Stellung Wiens im Spannungsfeld anglo-österreichischer Beziehungen", *Lebendige Stadt: Almanach 1960* (Vienna: Verlag für Jugend und Volk, 1960), pp. 44–59.

–. "Lied im Widerhall: Auch im Englischen ‚isch Singen Freud': For Joy We Sing", *Der Schlern: Monatszeitschrift für Südtiroler Landeskunde* (Bozen), December 1984 (Vol. 58, No. 12), pp. 699–709.

–, trans. & ed. *Austria – Land of Enchantment: The Land and Its History.* Regensburg, Salzburg, and Vienna: Schmid. ²1998. [Richly illustrated.]

HISCOCKS, RICHARD. *The Rebirth of Austria.* London: Oxford University Press, 1953. [Especially useful on economic and cultural data.]

JARKA, HORST. "The Language of Skiers", *American Speech,* October 1963 (Vol. XXXVIII, No. 3), pp. 202–08.

JOHNSTON, WILLIAM M. *The Austrian Mind: An Intellectual and Social History, 1848–1938.* Berkeley and Los Angeles: University of California Press, 1972.

LIPPMANN-PAWLOWSKI, MILA. *The Most Beautiful Alpine Flowers.* Trans. OSCAR KONSTANDT. Innsbruck: Pinguin, n. d.

MACCARTNEY, C[ARLILE] A[YLMER]. *The Habsburg Empire, 1790–1918.* London: Weidenfeld and Nicolson, 1971 (1969).

MARBOE, ERNST, comp. *The Book of Austria.* Vienna: Österreichische Staatsdruckerei, 1958 (1948).

MAYER-BROWNE, ELISABETH. *Austrian Cooking for You.* Vienna: Wilhelm Frick, ⁵1968.

MUSULIN, STELLA. *Austria: People and Landscape.* London: Faber and Faber. 1971.

NEWTH, JACK DOUGLAS. *Austria.* Illus. by EDWARD HARRISON COMPTON. London: Black, 1931.

PIRKHOFER, A[NTON] M. *England – Tyrol: Vom Bild Tirols im englischen Schrifttum – Ein 500-jähriger Spiegel der tirolisch-englischen Beziehungen.* Innsbruck: Wagner, 1950.

PORTER, DARWIN, and DANFORTH PRINCE. *Frommer's Austria: Complete Coverage of Vienna and the Alps.* New York: Macmillan, [8]1999.

RIDDELL, JAMES. *The Ski Runs of Austria.* London: Michael Joseph, 1958.

SCHEIBENPFLUG, LOTTE. *Specialities of Austrian Cooking.* Innsbruck: Pinguin, 1969.

TALLANTIRE, PHILIP A. *'Felix Austria': Hut-to-Hut Touring Guides.* 5 vols. Edinburgh: privately printed, 1964–72. [Copies obtainable from the Austrian Alpine Club, 124 Finchley Road, London NW3 5JA.]

–. *Edward Theodore Compton (1849–1921): Mountaineer and Mountain Painter.* Rietz: privately printed, 1996. [Contact the author at Holzleiten 9 a, A-6421 Rietz.]

WAGNER-WITTULA, RENATE. *Imperial Austrian Cuisine: The Best Recipes from the Austro-Hungarian Royal Kitchen.* Innsbruck: Löwenzahn, 1999.

WICKHAM, CHRISTOPHER. *Modern German Dialect Poetry as a Linguistic, Literary and Social Phenomenon: The Case of Bavarian and Austrian.* Ann Arbor: University of Michigan Press, 1982.

Acknowledgments of Illustrations Supplied

Stamps of the Austrian Postal Service, by Auguste Böcskör (87), Werner Pfeiler (27), Maria Schulz (30), Otto Stefferl (72, 73), and Adolf Tuma (135).

The Gallus Second-hand Bookshop, Innsbruck, kindly placed atrour disposal the engraving of the Vienna Capuchin Vault (129) as well as the following valuable books:
Heinrich Penn. *Die Geschichte der Stadt Wien und ihrer Vorstädte.* Brünn & Wien o.J. [um 1880] (26, 31, 35, 40, 64, 105, 107, 125, 147, 149, 181)
Alt- und Neu-Wien. Ein Heimatbuch für die Kinder der 3. Klasse (219)
Carl Brockhausen. *Österreich in Wort und Bild.* Berlin 1924 (59, 188)
Franz Brauner. *Mein Steirerland, mein Heimatland!* (23, 47, 159, 198)
Rudolf Holzer. *Wiener Volks-Humor* (184)
Steirisches Bilderbuch, Graz 1930 (116)

Various illustrations come both from our own Tyrolia archives (19, 21, 22, 25, 33, 44, 79, 89, 99, 103, 109, 158, 173, 200, 214), from these photographers and artists: Josef Aufschneiter (29), Hermann Blassnig (98), Andrea Frischauf/Wolfgang Zoller (58, 140, 175, 191, 203), Friedrich Haider (95, 187, 222), Heidi Leipelt (175), Klaus Markovits (112, 115, 199), Kurt Mimmler (65, 209), Gustav Sonnewend (82, 205), Wilhelm Stempfle (50), and „Aus dem Bildarchiv der Österreichischen Nationalbibliothek" (38, 57).

The author, of course, used practically all of the works (plus others besides) listed in the Bibliography; and Ingrid Hietsch, his competent helpmate, took a number of photographs, among them those on pp. 43, 49, 52, 69, 71, 85, 86, 114, 127, 131, 139, 144f., 151, 154, 210).